VOICES ROSE HIGHER.
PEOPLE JUMPED TO THEIR FEET.

More shouting, more roaring, more swearing ensued. So much tension developed that Becca could feel it. It impeded her breathing and got in the way of her ability to think. She needed to get *out* of the place, so she fumbled through the crowd and got to the door, and once outside, she took gulps of cold air.

Darkness had fallen, and the shadows around her spelled a warning of danger. Someone in Langley needed to heed it, Becca thought, before it was far too late.

OTHER BOOKS YOU MAY ENJOY

THE EDGE OF THE WATER

ELIZABETH GEORGE

THE EDGE OF THE WATER

speak

An Imprint of Penguin Group (USA)

SPEAK

Published by the Penguin Group
Penguin Group (USA) LLC
375 Hudson Street
New York, New York 10014

USA * Canada * UK * Ireland * Australia
New Zealand * India * South Africa * China

penguin.com
A Penguin Random House Company

First published in the United States of America by Viking,
an imprint of Penguin Group (USA), 2014
Published by Speak, an imprint of Penguin Group (USA) LLC, 2015

THE LIBRARY OF CONGRESS HAS CATALOGED THE VIKING EDITION AS FOLLOWS:
George, Elizabeth.
The edge of the water / by Elizabeth George.
p. cm.
Summary: Fifteen-year-old Jenn McDaniel's life on Whidbey Island becomes more complicated and her relationships with old and new friends take strange turns, partly due to the arrival of a woman researching a strange black seal.
ISBN 978-0-670-01297-8 (hardcover)
[1. Interpersonal relationships—Fiction. 2. Secrets—Fiction.
3. Abandoned children—Fiction. 4. Seals (Animals)—Fiction.
5. Psychic ability—Fiction. 6. Sexual orientation—Fiction.
7. Selkies—Fiction. 8. Whidbey Island (Wash.)—Fiction.] I. Title.
PZ7.G29315Eh 2014
[Fic]—dc23
2013014160

Speak ISBN 978-0-14-242674-6

Printed in the United States of America

1 3 5 7 9 10 8 6 4 2

For Gail Tsukiyama, beloved younger sister,
who said the word that gave me the story

I have done nothing but in care of thee,
Of thee my dear one, thee my daughter who
Art ignorant of what thou art . . .

—WILLIAM SHAKESPEARE,
THE TEMPEST

PART ONE

Deception Pass

Cilla's World

I was two years old when I came to my parents, but the only memories I have before the memories of them are like dreams. I'm carried. There's water nearby. I'm cold. Someone runs with me in his arms. My head is pressed so hard to his shoulder that it hurts every time he takes a step. And I know it's a *he*, by the way he's holding me. For holding doesn't come naturally to men.

It's nighttime and I remember lights. I remember voices. I remember shivering with fear and with wet. Then something warm is around me and my shivering stops and then I sleep.

After that, with another flash of a dream, I see myself in another place. A woman tells me she's Mommy now and she points to a man whose face looms over mine and he says that he's Daddy now. But they are not my parents and they never will be, just as the words they say are not my words and they never will be. That has been the source of my trouble.

I don't speak. I only walk and point and observe. I get along by doing what I am told. But I fear things that other children don't fear.

I fear water most of all, and this is a problem from the very start. For I live with the mommy and the daddy in a house that sits high above miles of water and from the windows of this place, water is all that I see. This makes me want to hide in the house, but a child can't do that when there is church to attend and school to enroll in as the child gets older.

I don't do those things. I try to do them, the mommy and the daddy try to make me do them, and other people try as well. But all of us fail.

This is why I end up far away, in a place where there is no water. There are people who poke me. They prod me. They talk over my head. They watch me on videos. They present me with pictures. They ask me questions. What I hear is "You have to *do* something with her, that's why we brought her" and the words mean nothing to me. But I recognize in the sound of the words a form of farewell.

So I remain in this no-water place, where I learn the rudiments that go for human life. I learn to clean and to feed myself. But that is the extent of what I learn. Give me a simple task and I can do it if I'm shown exactly what to do, and from this everyone begins to understand that there is nothing wrong with my memory. That, however, is all they understand. So they label me their mystery. It's a blessing, they say, that at least I can walk and feed and clean myself. That, they say, is cause for celebration.

So I'm finally returned to the mommy and the daddy. Someone declares, "You're eighteen years old now. Isn't that grand?" and although these words mean nothing to me, from them I understand things will be different. What's left, then, is a drive in the car on a January morning of bitter cold, a celebration picnic because I've come home.

We go to a park. We drive for what seems like a very long time to get to the place. We cross a high bridge and the mommy calls out, "Close your eyes, Cilla! There's water below!" I do what she says, and soon enough the bridge is behind us. We turn in among trees that soar into the sky and we follow a twisting road down and down and covered with the foliage of cedars shed in winter storms.

At the bottom of the road, there's a place for cars. There are picnic tables and the mommy says, "What a day for a picnic! Have a look at the beach while I set up, Cilla. I know how you like to look at the beach."

The daddy says, "Yep. Come on, Cill," and when he trudges toward a thick growth of shiny-leafed bushes beneath the trees, I follow him to a path that cuts through it. Here is a trail, part sand and part dirt, where we pass beneath cedars and firs and we brush by ferns and boulders and at last we come to the beach.

I do not fear beaches, only the water that edges them. Beaches themselves I love with their salty scents and the thick, crawling serpents of seaweed that slither across them. Here there is driftwood worn smooth by the water. Here there are great boulders to climb. Here an eagle flies high in the air and a seagull caws and a dead salmon lies in the cold harsh sun.

I stop at this fish. I bend to inspect it. I bend closer to smell it. It makes my eyes sting.

The seagull caws again and the eagle cries. It swoops and soars and I follow its flight with my gaze. North it flies, and it disappears high beyond the trees.

I watch for its return, but the bird is gone. So is, I see, the daddy who led me down through the trees and onto this beach. He'd stopped where the sand met the trail through the woods. He'd said, "Think I'll have me a cancer stick. Don't tell Herself, huh, Cill?" but I have walked on. He has perhaps returned to the car for the promised picnic, and now I am alone. I don't like the alone or the nearness of the water. I hurry back to the spot where the car is parked.

But it, too, is gone, just like the daddy. So is the mommy. In the place where the picnic was supposed to be, only two things stand on the lichenous table beneath the trees. One is a sandwich wrapped in plastic. The other is a small suitcase with wheels.

I approach these objects. I look around. I see, I observe, I point as always. But there is no one in this place to respond to me.

I am here, wherever this is, alone.

ONE

When people said "Money isn't everything," Jenn McDaniels knew two things about them. First, they'd never been poor. Second, they didn't have a clue what being poor was like. Jenn was poor, she'd been poor for all of her fifteen years, and she had a whole lot more than just a clue about the kinds of things you had to do when you didn't have money. You bought your clothes at thrift stores, you put together meals from food banks, and when something came along that meant you had even the tiniest chance of escaping bedsheets for curtains and a life of secondhand everything, you did what it took.

That was what she was up to on the afternoon that Annie Taylor drove into her life. Had the condition of the very nice silver Honda Accord not told Jenn that Annie Taylor didn't belong on Whidbey Island—for God's sake the car was actually clean!—the Florida plates would have done the job. As would have Annie Taylor's trendy clothes and her seriously fashionable spiky red hair. She got out of the Accord, put one hand on her hip, said to Jenn, "This is Possession Point, right?" and frowned at the obstacle course that Jenn had set up the length of the driveway.

This obstacle course was Jenn's tiniest chance to escape the bedsheet curtains and the secondhand everything. It was also her chance to escape Whidbey Island altogether. The course consisted of trash can lids, broken toilet seats, bait buckets, floats, and ripped-up life jackets, all of which stood in for the traffic cones that any other kid—like a kid with money—might have used for a practice session. Her intention had been one hour minimum of dribbling up and down this obstacle course. Tryouts for the All Island Girls' Soccer team were coming up in a few months, and Jenn was *going* to make the team. Center midfielder! A blazing babe with amazing speed! Her dexterity unquestioned! Her future assured! University scholarship, here I come. . . . Only at the moment, Annie Taylor's car was in the way. Or Jenn was in Annie's way, depending on how you looked at things.

Jenn said yeah, this was Possession Point, and she made no move to clear the way so that Annie could drive forward. Frankly, she saw no reason to. The redhead clearly didn't belong here, and if she wanted to look at the view—such as it was, which wasn't much—then she was going to have to take her butt down to the water on foot.

Jenn dribbled the soccer ball toward a broken toilet seat lid, dodging and feinting. She did a bit of clever whipping around to fool her opponents. She was ready to move the ball past a trash can lid when Annie Taylor called out, "Hey! Sorry? C'n you tell me . . . I'm looking for Bruce McDaniels."

Jenn halted and looked over her shoulder. Annie added, "D'you know him? He's supposed to live here. He's got a key for me. I'm Annie Taylor, by the way."

Jenn scooped up the ball with a sigh. She knew Bruce, all right. Bruce was her dad. The last time she'd seen him he'd been sampling five different kinds of home brew on the front porch, despite the early February cold, with the beers lined up on the railing so that he could "admire the head on each" before he chugged. He brewed his beer in a shed on the property that he always kept locked up like Fort Knox. When he wasn't brewing, he was selling the stuff under the table. When he wasn't doing that, he was selling bait to fishermen who were foolhardy enough to tie their boats up to his decrepit dock.

Annie Taylor's mentioning a key made Jenn first think that her dad was handing over his Fort-Knox-of-Brewing shed to a stranger. But then Annie added, "There's a trailer here, right? I'm moving into it. The man I'm renting from—Eddie Beddoe?—he said Bruce would be waiting for me with the key. So is he down there?" She gestured past the obstacle course. Jenn nodded yeah, but what she was thinking was that Annie had to be talking about a different trailer because no way could anyone live in the wreck that had stood abandoned not far from Jenn's house for all of her life.

Annie said, "Great. So if you don't mind . . . ? C'n I . . . ? Well, can I get this stuff out of the way?"

Jenn began to kick her obstacles to one side of the lane. Annie came to help, leaving her Honda running. She was tall—but since Jenn was only five two, pretty much everyone was tall—and she had lots of freckles. What she was wearing looked like something she'd purchased in Bellevue on her way to the island:

skinny jeans, boots, a turtleneck sweater, a parka, a scarf. She looked like an ad for the outdoor life in Washington State, except what she had on was way too put together to be something a real outdoorsman would wear. Jenn couldn't help wondering what the hell Annie Taylor was doing here aside from being on the run from the law.

Soccer ball under her arm, she trailed Annie's car to the vicinity of the trailer. Her reaction to the sight of it, Jenn decided, was going to be more interesting than dribbling.

"Oh!" was the expression on Annie Taylor's face when Jenn caught up to her. It wasn't the oh of "Oh how cool," though. It was more the oh of "Oh my God, what have I done?" She'd gotten out of her car and was standing transfixed, with all her attention on the only trailer in the vicinity. "This is . . . uh . . . it?" she said with a glance at Jenn.

"Pretty cool, huh?" Jenn replied sardonically. "If you're into living with black mold and mildew, you're in the right place."

"Possession Point," Annie said, pretty much to herself. And again then to Jenn, "This is . . . for real? I mean, this is it? You don't live here, too, do you?" Annie looked around but, of course, there wasn't much to see that would reassure anyone about this dismal place.

Jenn pointed out her house, a short distance away and closer to the water. The building was old but in marginally better condition than the trailer. It was gray clapboard, with a questionable roof, and just beyond it at the edge of the water, a bait shack tumbled in the direction of a dock. Both of these structures seemed to rise out of the heaps of driftwood, piles of old nets, and masses of everything from overturned aluminum boats to upended toilets.

As Annie Taylor took all this in, Jenn's father, Bruce, came out of the house and down the rickety front steps of the porch. He was calling out, "You Annie Taylor?" to which Annie replied with little enthusiasm, "You must be Mr. McDaniels."

"You are in the presence," he said.

"That's . . . uh . . . That's great," Annie replied although the hesitation in her words definitely indicated otherwise.

Jenn could hardly blame her. In her whole life, Annie Taylor had probably never seen anyone like Bruce McDaniels. He enjoyed being a character with a capital *C*, and he played up anything that made him eccentric. So he kept his gray hair Ben Franklin style down to his shoulders. He covered his soup-bowl-sized bald pate with a ski cap that read SKI SQUAW VALLEY although he'd never been on skis in his life. He was in terrible shape, skinny like a scarecrow everywhere except for his belly, which overhung his trousers and made him look pregnant most of the time.

He was digging in his pocket, saying, "Gotcher key right here," when the front door opened again, and Jenn's two little brothers came storming out.

"Who the hell's *she*?" Petey demanded.

"Dad, he ate a damn hot dog and they were 'posed to be for damn dinner!" Andy cried. "Jenny, tell 'im! You heard Mom say."

"Desist, rug rats," was Bruce McDaniels's happy reply. "This is

Annie Taylor, our new neighbor. And these, Annie, are the fruit of my loins: Jennifer, Petey, and Andy. Jenn's the one with the soccer ball, by the way." He chuckled as if he'd made a great joke although Jenn's pixie haircut and lack of curves had resulted in her being mistaken for a boy more than once.

Annie said politely that it was nice to meet them all, at which point Bruce ceremoniously handed over the key to the trailer. He told her he'd given the door's lock a good oiling that very morning and she'd find the place in tiptop shape with everything inside in working order.

Annie looked doubtful, but she murmured, "Wonderful, then," as she accepted the key from him. She settled her shoulders, unlocked the door, stuck her head inside, and said, "Oh gosh." She popped out as quickly as she'd popped in. She shot the McDaniels spectators a smile and began the process of unloading her car. She had boxes neatly taped and marked. She had a computer and a printer. She had a spectacular set of matching luggage. She started heaving everything just inside the door of the trailer.

No one in the McDaniels group made a move to help her, but who could blame them? For not one of them even began to believe that she would last one night in the place.

JENN AVOIDED ANNIE Taylor for the first twenty-four hours of her stay, mostly out of embarrassment. Three hours after Annie had emptied her car, Jenn's mom had come rumbling home in the Subaru Forester that did service as South Whidbey

Taxi Company. Bruce McDaniels had been continuing his extensive experiment in the quality control of his brews for those three hours, and when Jenn's mom got out of the Subaru and began trudging tiredly toward the house, he'd greeted her by belting out "Kuh-kuh-kuh Katie! My bee-you-tee-full Katie!" He ran to greet her, falling on his knees and singing at full pitch, and Jenn's mom had cried, "How could you! Again!" and promptly burst into tears. Jenn recovered from the excruciating humiliation of all this by hiding out in her bedroom and wishing her parents would both disappear, taking Andy and Petey with them.

From her window, she spied on Annie Taylor, who left the trailer periodically either to haul wood inside for the stove that heated the place or to walk on the driftwood-cluttered beach. When she did this latter thing, she carried a pair of binoculars with her. Perched upon the gnarled roots of a piece of driftwood, she used the binoculars to scan the surface of the water. Jenn figured at first she was looking for the resident orcas. Killer whales made use of Possession Sound at all times of the year, and seventy of them lived within fifty miles of Whidbey Island. To Jenn, they were the only sea creatures of interest.

The third time Annie walked the beach, she took a camera and tripod with her. Jenn decided she was probably a wildlife photographer, then, and she asked her father this at breakfast on the day after Annie's arrival. He was the only person up aside from Jenn. The day was freezing cold outside, and as usual it wasn't much warmer in the house. Everyone else in the family had apparently decided the best course was to wait out the cold beneath the covers, but it wasn't raining, and clear weather meant running practice, which was what Jenn intended to do. Still, there was the matter of Annie. . . .

"Hell if I know," was Bruce's answer to Jenn's question about the young woman and photography. "All I do is collect the rent and all I care about her is: is she quiet at night and will she keep from scaring the herring in the bait pool. You'll have to ask Eddie if you want to know more. Far's I'm concerned, ignorance is *b-l-i-s-s*." He'd been reading a week-old edition of the *South Whidbey Record* as he spoke. But he looked up then, took in Jenn's attire, and said, "Just where the hell you going?" when she told him she'd see him later.

"Sprints," she said. "Tryouts coming up. All Island Girls' Soccer. You know."

"For God's sake be careful if you're going on the road. There's ice out there and if you break a leg—"

"I won't break a leg," she told him.

Outside, she began to stretch, using the porch steps and the railing. Her breath was like a fog machine in the freezing air.

A bang sounded from the trailer on the far side of the property, and Annie Taylor stalked outside. She had on so many layers of clothing that Jenn was surprised she could move. She headed for the woodpile and grabbed up an armful.

"Stupid, idiot, frigging, asinine, useless, oh yeah right," came from Annie to Jenn across the yard. "Like this is supposed to . . . Oh *great*. Thank you very much."

Jenn watched as Annie piled up wood and staggered with it

back to the trailer. She gave a curious look to the woodpile. The Florida woman was sure going through it. Except . . . Jenn realized that there was no scent of woodsmoke in the morning air.

She went over to the trailer's door. She stuck her head inside and said, "Sure are going through the wood, huh?"

Annie glanced over at her from a squat woodstove in front of which she was kneeling. "Oh, I sure as hell wish," she said. "None of it's burning. I'm just trying to find a damn log that will."

"Weird," Jenn said. "It should burn fine."

"Well, *should burn* and *does burn* are two different things. If you see smoke coming out of this trailer, believe me, it's going to be from my ears."

"Want me to take a look?"

"Be my guest. If you can make this shit burn—pardon my French but I am so frustrated and I spent the whole damn night freezing my tits off—I owe you breakfast."

Jenn laughed. "Frozen tits, huh?" she said. "Ouch. Lemme look at the stove."

TWO

Jenn took one look around the inside of the trailer and said, "Gross. Why'd you rent this place?"

"I need the water around here." Next to the woodstove, Annie grabbed a log from among the two dozen others already scattered on the floor.

"Uh . . . this is an island?" Jenn said. "Last time I looked there was water everywhere."

"Sure. Right. But I need this water."

"It's the same all over."

"Wrong," Annie said. She pointed to the woodstove, its door hanging open like a toothless black mouth. "So, d'you know anything about these things?"

"I know you got to clean out the ashes," Jenn told her after giving it a quick look. "Nothing's going to burn inside the stove till you do that. What about the dampers? Are they even open? Bet no one checked the flue, and there's probably bird nests on top of the chimney."

Annie said, "Oh," but she made no move to address these problems. Instead she sank onto a filthy chrome-legged kitchen chair and looked dismally around the place.

To Jenn, the interior of the trailer suggested a serious health hazard. Aside from the chromed-legged chair that Annie was using, the furnishings consisted of another similar chair, a ripped-up banquette, a sloping table, and a mildewed couch that stood beneath a window so leaky that something looking suspiciously like moss appeared to be line dancing along its sill. The place was a death trap in various forms. Jenn wondered how long Annie planned to stay.

She scratched her head and said, "D'you want me to get this woodstove working?"

"Oh *would* you?" Annie said, brightening at once. "I'd get on my knees and kiss your ring. Except . . . I saw you stretching. Were you about to go running or something? I mean, I don't want you to—"

"No worries. This'll just take a sec."

Jenn went outside and grabbed one of the bait buckets she'd been using for her dribbling practice. She took this to the woodstove and began to shovel the ashes into it. She figured that Annie had decided the fireplace tools standing next to the stove were part of the overall décor. The amount of dust on them suggested that no one had touched them in years.

As she shoveled, she said, "No one's lived here in, like, for my whole life. You sure you want to stay? I mean, you could probably get real sick."

"It needs to be fixed up, that's for sure," Annie agreed. "I was sort of hoping that hot water, ammonia, baking soda, bleach, and white vinegar would take care of the problem."

"Either that or blow it up," Jenn said.

"Which," Annie added, "might not be exactly a bad idea."

They laughed together. Annie had a nice laugh. She had neat white teeth and a pretty smile. Jenn liked her and wondered how old she was. A lot older than herself, for sure, but Jenn wondered if they still might become friends. Friends were scarce on this part of the island.

She spied some newspapers sitting beneath a few of the logs, and she yanked these out and showed Annie how to build a proper fire: crumpled newspapers first, followed by a good amount of dry kindling, then logs on the top. She glanced at Annie to see if she was following, and Annie shot her a smile, although what Jenn had to admit was that a woman with Florida plates on her car probably hadn't built fires very often.

She got to her feet and brushed off her hands. When Annie offered her the matches, she said, "Chimney first," and she went outside, where she hoisted herself to the trailer's roof and picked her way through the debris she and her brothers had been hurling up there for years. She found the chimney just as she thought she might find it: with a large bird's nest perched on its top. She cleared this away and shouted down the chimney, "Let 'er rip, Annie." In a few moments, a satisfying belch of smoke shot into the air.

Back inside the trailer, she found Annie kneeling in front of the woodstove, warming her hands like someone praying to the fire god. Jenn fed more kindling into the blaze and explained how to bank the stove at night. Annie nodded vaguely and leaned back on her heels. She cocked her head at Jenn and said, "I was thinking. . . . You need a job or anything?"

Jenn *always* needed a job. Along with potential friends, jobs were also scarce in this part of the island. "Doing what? Keeping your fire going?"

"Ha. That, too." Annie waved vaguely around the trailer's interior. "Let's face it, Jenn. This place needs a ton of work. I can do some of it but I can't do it all because I've got to get on with some other things. D'you want to help out? Obviously, I'll pay."

The pay part sounded good. The having to be near the trailer part didn't. "I dunno," Jenn said. "Maybe. I mean, this place is such a dump and spending a bunch of time in here fixing it up . . . ? No offense, but it sort of creeps me out. How much're you shelling out to stay here, anyway?"

When Annie named the sum, Jenn gawped at her. "You're *so* way being cheated," she declared. "That's *totally* unfair. You need to track down Eddie Beddoe and get a better deal."

Annie's expression became chagrined as she glanced around the derelict place. "It's sort of my fault for being in such a rush, I guess."

"Being in a rush doesn't mean you deserve to be robbed."

"Sure. But I agreed on the price. If I tried to change it, he might tell me to go somewhere else."

"That's not a bad idea, if you ask me."

Annie shook her head. "It's like I said before: I need Possession Point and I need this water."

"Why?"

"Just . . . well, just because."

"Is there some big secret? Like we got Bigfoot swimming

in Possession Sound and you're here to take its picture or something?"

Annie said nothing at first, so for a moment Jenn thought she'd actually hit on the truth, as ludicrous as that truth sounded. She added, "Or maybe a prehistoric water thing? Like our own Loch Ness Monster?"

As things turned out, she wasn't too far off the point, for Annie caved and said, "Hell. I guess you'll find out eventually. Especially if you work for me."

"Find out what?"

"*Will* you work for me?"

"Okay. All right. But you have to pay me."

"I said I would. Deal?"

"Deal. Okay. Now, why're you here?"

Annie glanced back at the door, as if worried about listeners. "I'm here because of the seal," she said.

A RATHER LONG time later, Jenn would think that she should have called *whoa Nellie* when Annie Taylor brought up the seal. For there are seals and there are seals, but Jenn knew in an instant that there was only one seal that Annie was talking about. This seal was called Nera. She was coal black from her flippers to her eyeballs. And for some reason that no one would ever speak about no matter how they were questioned on the topic, she'd been showing up for ages in the Whidbey Island waters at the same time every year. She usually hung around a place called Sandy Point as well as the small village of Langley, cavorting in the water near the Langley marina and barking at tourists, townspeople, and fishermen, like a swimmer trying to get their attention. But—and this was the weirdest part of her behavior—she made the swim from Langley to Possession Point on the very same day, at the very same time, of the very same month each year. She remained in Possession Point's waters for exactly twenty-four hours, swimming restlessly back and forth, moaning and barking like an abandoned dog. After that, she returned to Langley, spent another month or two hanging in the water below Seawall Park before leaving for wherever she went until the next year rolled around and she did the same things all over again. Her comings and goings were magical and completely mysterious to the people on the south end of Whidbey Island. And the way Jenn figured it, the people on the south end of Whidbey Island were *not* going to be happy if they found out someone was here to mess with their magic and mystery.

So Jenn said, "A seal? What seal? What d'you want with a seal?" as if she didn't know exactly what seal Annie was talking about.

Annie said, "Come on. Don't tell me you don't know about her. Langley's got . . . Here, wait a sec. . . ." She went to one of her boxes and pulled out a manila folder from which torn-out magazine pages frothed. She opened this and fingered through them. She brought out an article with brightly colored pictures: a festival, children eating ice cream, yokels wearing bizarre seal costumes, balloons, booths, and a banner across the entry to a park screaming WELCOME BACK NERA!!! in huge red letters.

Jenn couldn't pretend not to know what this was: one of the village of Langley's festivals. The dumbnut city fathers had a festival for everything, all to lure tourists to the town's struggling bed-and-breakfasts, cafés, galleries, boutiques, and T-shirt shops. Nera was practically custom built for a town that welcomed whales, celebrated a "soup box" derby, used alpacas as camels in a pageant at Christmastime, and killed a citizen every year for Murder Mystery Weekend.

So Jenn had to say, "Oh. You must mean Nera."

"Uh, yeah. I must mean Nera. Is there another seal?"

"Well . . . no. I mean, not exactly."

"What d'you mean 'not exactly'?" Annie looked thoughtful before her eyes lit up. She cried, "Jesus, Jenn. Is there more than one? God, wouldn't *that* be a coup!"

Jenn frowned. Annie obviously had something cooking, not only to do with Nera but also with Possession Point. If it was Nera alone, she'd be parking her body in Langley: Nera's central hangout. But for her to come to Possession Point, to insist that she had to be here where the waters were somehow "necessary" to her . . . ? It didn't sound right to Jenn, so she said directly, "What d'you want her for?"

"Nera?"

"Yeah, Nera."

"Nothing, really." And when Jenn looked skeptical, Annie went on. "Okay, two things. One is the possibility of a genetic mutation. The other is the even better possibility of new species of seal."

"And you care about this, why?" Jenn asked.

"I'm a marine biologist," she said. "Or at least that's what I'll be officially if I ever finish my damn dissertation, and I *need* that seal to do it."

"To write it for you? I don't think she's up to the job."

"Very funny. I need her to prove my argument. Or to reveal something new to the world. Either way, I'm made."

Annie explained the rest in what Jenn would come to know as Annie Taylor fashion. She dipped into one subject, slid over another, painted gloss on a third. Jenn wasn't sure what this said about Annie, except that when she wanted something, she was a really fast talker in order to get it. So what she revealed in a rush was that Nera either had the rarest of rare conditions called melanism—"All-black, just the opposite of an all-white albino," Annie explained—or she had a genetic mutation or she was a new species of seal. "She looks vaguely like a Ross seal," Annie said, "but if that's the case she's seriously out of territory. So I figure she's either a new species or a mutant."

"Or the opposite of an albino," Jenn said.

"Yeah. But my money's on mutant. Which, for my purpose, is almost as good as being a new species."

"Why?"

"Because the frigging oil companies all over the world keep claiming that their spills aren't hurting the animal life. Nera's my chance to prove them wrong. I mean, look at the facts: Oil spilled here around twenty years ago and now we've got a freak seal at our fingertips, saying 'Look at me please and run a few tests.'"

Tests? That rang *all* the alarms. "No one's letting you get close to Nera," Jenn said. "Just so you know. And when was there ever an oil spill around here, anyway?"

"I already said. Twenty years ago. Something like that. It saturated Possession Point. You don't know about it? Well, maybe you wouldn't. How long have you lived here? How old are you anyway? You look . . . Are you twelve?"

"Hey! I'm fifteen, okay? And if there was an oil spill, I'd *know* about it."

"Why? It would've been cleaned up. This place's remote, sure as hell, but no one's going to let bilge oil sit on the beach for twenty years. And that's what it was. Bilge oil. The worst there is. It'd've been cleaned up within weeks, maybe two or three months. But in a couple of years there wouldn't even have been a sign of it. Except in the sea life."

"Like Nera."

"Like Nera. Who just happened to show up a year after the spill? Two years after it? What does that tell you? I know what it tells me. So I need to get a close look at her. I need some samples. One way or the other, she's proof of something. I just need to know what the 'something' is."

"Samples? No way. No one's letting you near that seal, Annie."

"Oh?" Annie gave an airy, dismissive wave. "Believe me, we'll see about that."

THREE

Asking her dad about an oil spill at Possession Point got Jenn nowhere. Asking her mom offered much the same result. Her dad was deep into his yearly preparations for Seattle BrewFest, so the only answer he gave to her questions was to grunt, "Hon, do I look like I got time for a discussion on ancient history right now?" as he wrestled with a huge glass jug of amber ale in his brewing shed. Her mom was deep into her daily reading of the Bible, so her reply had to do with God's speaking to mortal man through natural disasters. When Jenn tried to argue that an oil spill at Possession Point was hardly a *natural* disaster, Kate's response of "You just look at all the tornadoes hitting the Midwest this year, Jennifer, and ask yourself if God's displeasure isn't evident when houses get blown to bits and semis get tossed in the air" told Jenn that any conversation with her mom was going to be less flavored with facts and more flavored with her mom's interpretation of whatever part of the Old Testament she and her church friends were in the midst of studying. What Jenn knew from all this was that if she wanted to discover the truth about any long-ago oil spills, she was probably going to have to do it on her own.

School was the best place for this, since she had nothing at home to help her do any delving. So when lunch rolled around the next school day, she took off for the library's computers.

She was a dolt with technology. It would have helped to have a computer at home, but that was out of the question since food took priority over modern conveniences of a technological nature. She knew how to get onto the Internet, naturally. She knew about search engines as well. But as for the extreme fine-tuning she needed to find *exactly* what she was looking for . . . ? That required a defter hand than hers. She needed an assistant. Squat Cooper was her man.

She scored him just where she figured he'd be, at a library study carrel doing his homework. Why eat lunch when one could do math? He was scribbling away on some obscure problem, and as usual, he was totally oblivious to what was going on around him. He didn't look up when Jenn tapped him on the shoulder. He didn't look up when she said his name. She finally resorted to wetly licking the back of his neck and making *yum, yum, yum* sounds. He leapt to his feet and cried, "*What* the heck?" with his ruddy face going ruddier and his hand wiping at the sopping spots Jenn had left.

"I need your help, Studboy," she told him.

"Doing what? Passing germs?" He slapped at his neck. He was cute as a puppy and just as open and friendly. Jenn had known him since kindergarten.

"Ha. You loved it and you're dying for more." She wagged her tongue at him.

"Bleagh. In your dreams."

"*Exactly* where I want you nightly." She closed his math book, and when he started to protest, she said, "You're getting an A, you're always getting an A, you'll always *be* getting an A. I need your brain. Since it's attached to your body, you got to come with me."

He sighed but followed her. He said, "It was kindergarten, wasn't it?"

"What was?"

"When I let you share my milk that one time. We used the same straw. You jumped to conclusions about what that meant and you've been deluded ever since."

"Meaning?"

"Meaning I'm not yours for the asking."

"Yes, you are. You try to hide it and who can blame you since I'm so hot, but I've known everything about you since second grade. Quit trying to fight it. See this, my friend?" She held up her little finger.

"What about it?"

"You're wrapped."

He snorted but smiled. "So what d'you want?"

She sat him next to her at the computer. Just as she thought, Squat had things sorted out in a matter of mouse clicks that zipped them back through time to exactly what Annie Taylor had claimed. There *had* been an oil spill. It had happened at night, and it had washed up on and polluted all of Possession Point. The heaviest kind of oil there was, the bilge oil had left its traces upon everything it touched, and there were plenty of pictures to make this point. Seventeen years in the past, it had happened. Annie Taylor hadn't been too far off in her timeline.

"Yuck," was Squat's remark when they came upon the pictures of drenched seabirds, belly-up crabs, and filthy shores. "So why d'you want to know about this? You writing a paper or something?"

"Nah. There's a babester moved into that old trailer by my house? She was talking about it. Nera's probably a mutant seal because of it is what she says. *Or* she's a new species."

"A new species because of an oil spill? A mutant? Not hardly," Squat said. "Crabs with two heads? Shrimp shaped like porcupines? Fish with eyes on their tails? There's your mutants. A black seal, though? I don't think so. And even if she is a mutation, so what? I mean, she's healthy, right?"

"It's to do with her dissertation. I mean *Annie's* dissertation, not the seal's. Anyway, I didn't even know there *was* an oil spill and I got curious."

"Oh. Whatever. C'n I go back to calculus now?"

"Only if you can tear yourself away from my company."

He rolled his eyes. "I'll manage." He went back to his study carrel.

Jenn turned to the computer. She continued to read and she searched out more pictures. She found additional ones by following a few links. In a moment she was looking at a Possession

Point two years before the time of her birth. The house was there, the bait shack was fairly new, and the trailer that Annie Taylor was occupying was there as well, in good condition with a neatly planted garden in front of it. The picture was a before-the-spill shot. After-the-spill consisted of a tarlike goop clinging to driftwood, rocks, and the beach itself.

It was odd that no one ever talked about the spill, Jenn thought. But then, it had happened long ago and there were no remaining signs of it that she'd ever seen at Possession Point, so why *would* anyone talk about it? Still, it seemed to Jenn that Annie Taylor had her work cut out for her if she was going to make something of the spill and of Nera for her dissertation. As for Jenn, she had to agree with Squat. Nera might have been as black as a lump of coal, but that was the only thing different about her.

Of course, that difference was the key to her value to Whidbey Island in general and the village of Langley in particular. The citizens, shopkeepers, and souvenir hawkers weren't going to want someone messing with their Nera. The magical yearly return of a coal black seal was one thing. The magical yearly return of a mutant was another. When it came to Nera, Annie Taylor was going to have to mind her p's and q's, because no one was going to let her mess with that seal or that seal's reputation for being half magic and three-quarters homing pigeon.

Whispering conversation from near the door interrupted Jenn's flow of thoughts. She glanced in that direction and felt her mood sour immediately because South Whidbey High School's answer to Love Eternal was entering the library, hand in hand, heads together in earnest conversation. They were the island's own version of Bella and Edward without the blood and the fangs. Jenn could even have managed to put up with them had the boy not once been one of her good friends and had the girl not been . . . well, who she was.

Becca King was someone Jenn had loathed from the first instant they'd come into contact with each other on the ferry coming across from Mukilteo to the island last September. Derric Mathieson, on the other hand, was someone Jenn had been pals with since, as an eight-year-old, he'd been adopted out of an orphanage in Uganda by a family on the island. Why they were a couple was a mystery to Jenn. Derric was tall, athletic, and terrific-looking, from his gorgeously and deliberately shaved head to his perfect toes. Becca was . . . Well, okay, she'd lost the blubber she'd been carrying when she'd first landed on the island and Jenn had dubbed her SmartAss FatBroad. But the rest of her was exactly the same: hideously dyed dark brown hair, thick rimmed glasses out of another century, shapeless clothes, and so much makeup that, if the circus wasn't going to be her next stop, she needed to rethink her destination. Derric and Becca were living proof that opposites attracted. All they had in common was brain power, and *that* they had in mountains.

They sat at one of the library tables, across from each other but still conversing quietly. They seemed even more intensely focused on each other than usual, and when Derric's whispered "No, that's just the point. It does bother me. And it would bother any other guy, and it *would* bother you if the tables were turned.

Why don't you get that, Becca?" came across the room, it caught Jenn's attention in a way that only a hint of great gossip ever could. Was there—gasp!—trouble in paradise? She could only hope. If there were potholes in true love's road, she wanted to be the first to know about them.

Unfortunately, Becca's response didn't give her much to go on. She said quietly, "It doesn't *mean* anything and it never could. Why don't you get that?"

"How am I *supposed* to get it?" He shoved back from the table.

"Derric, you said we could talk about this." Becca reached for his arm and closed her hand over his chocolate skin. He was meant to cover her hand with his, Jenn figured, but he wasn't about to do that. He was totally pissed.

"Every talk we have ends in the exact same place," he said fiercely. "'It doesn't mean anything.'"

"Because it *doesn't*."

What doesn't? Jenn wanted to yell. What, what, what for crying out loud? But before she could get an answer to this or even imagine one, Derric had shaken Becca's hand from his arm and had stormed out of the library, the walking cast he wore no impediment to him. The door hit back against the wall so hard that even Squat looked up from his math.

For her part, Becca stared after him. Slowly she removed from her ear an earphone that she always wore, in class and out. She got away with this for reasons Jenn hadn't ever been able to figure out. It was like the creepoid put a spell on people. Whatever she wanted, she always, *always* ended up getting.

Jenn couldn't resist, so she didn't try. She rose from her position at the computer and sauntered over to the FatBroad's table. She was thinking, Bet he breaks up with her butt by the end of the week.

Becca turned her head slowly and looked at her, "As if that'll change anything in your life," she said.

Jenn stopped in her tracks and examined the other girl. "What's with you," she demanded.

"Nothing you'd ever understand," Becca told her.

FOUR

Becca King knew that Jenn McDaniels hated her because of Derric. There were probably other reasons—beyond her inclination to be generally snarky just for the heck of it—but Derric was the main one. He'd taken a terrible fall in Saratoga Woods not long after Becca's arrival on Whidbey Island, and his time in the hospital after that had offered Becca the chance to get to know him. From the first instant she'd seen him on the ferry coming from Mukilteo over to Whidbey Island, she'd felt drawn to the African boy. That he'd also felt drawn to her was still what it had been from the first: something of a miracle to Becca.

She hadn't thought of Jenn McDaniels and her place in Derric's life as she'd got to know him and maybe this had been a bad thing. But the truth was that with Derric she'd felt safe, treasured, understood, and accepted in a way that her appearance alone should have made impossible. Fat cow, dyed hair, thick glasses, eye makeup like an aging rock star on drugs . . . It was all part of who she had to be on this Washington island. None of it was part of who she really was.

Somehow Derric had managed to see that, to see the *her*

beneath the *her* she was forced to present to the world. When he'd recovered from his injuries and left the hospital, he'd sought her out. He'd made her life livable in this place where she'd been left by her mother in the early autumn.

Now in midwinter, they'd grown close. But Becca could only let him into her world just so far. It was for his own safety, but he didn't know that and to tell him . . . ? The worm can *that* would open was so full that both of them would be overcome by its contents, and that would sink their relationship. Which, of course, would please Jenn McDaniels from the top of her head to her running shoes.

Jenn's thoughts had become as plain as broadcasts over the school's PA system once Becca had removed the AUD box earphone from her ear. In the past four months, she'd grown a bit in her ability to pick up others' random thoughts when the AUD box wasn't blocking them with static, and these whispers—as she'd learned to call them—were helping her find her way in this place. In Jenn's case, the whispers had allowed Becca to know from the first that the girl was determined to be her enemy. They'd locked horns on the ferry that evening of Becca's arrival, and Becca's interest in Derric had only made things worse. When Derric returned that interest . . . Well, that was it. She and Jenn McDaniels were oil and water. As females, they were made of the same *stuff*, but there it ended.

Becca knew she probably shouldn't have given the other girl any indication that she'd read her thoughts, but at the moment she was just too miserable about Derric to care. He was being unreasonable, he didn't understand, he was making a demand she couldn't hope to fulfill, he couldn't see the truth, he didn't want to know why she couldn't tell him everything he wanted to know. . . . And all the rest, she thought wryly.

Jenn shot her a drop-dead-now look and stalked out of the library. On her way, she stopped to have a word with Squat Cooper, and for some reason she decided an exchange of spit with poor Squat was in order because she kissed him squarely on the mouth when he looked up. He didn't exactly push her to the floor, but he said, "Hey, wha' the heck?" when she was finished with him.

She said, "Later, Studboy. And I want some tongue next time," and she laughed when he went red to his hairline.

Becca knew what Jenn was up to: I got *my* man. She also knew it was a total lie. But that didn't matter at the moment because the moment was really about all the things that she couldn't tell Derric.

JENN HAD LEFT her computer on, still fixed to whatever Web site she'd been perusing when Becca and Derric had come into the library. Becca sat to use it, but out of curiosity she traced back through what Jenn had been studying first: an oil slick at Possession Point long ago. Whatever, Becca thought. Maybe Jenn was a budding environmentalist.

At any rate, Becca herself had a bigger issue than an oil slick from history, and his name was Jeff Corrie. He was the reason she was on Whidbey Island. She and her mother were on the run from him. There wasn't a day that Becca didn't expect her step-father to pop out of a bush as she got off the bus near her hiding place, and she'd been checking once a week to see if he was still walking around San Diego as a very free man. So far that had proved to be the case.

She did her usual search. It had to be time, she thought, for the disappearance of Jeff's partner Connor to be *noticed* by someone. No way was Jeff Corrie *not* involved in Connor's vanishing act.

The first part proved true. At long last, someone in Connor's family had begun making noises about the fact that Jeff Corrie's partner in a San Diego investment house appeared to be missing. Not returning phone calls, not answering e-mails, no updates to his Facebook page, mail left languishing in his mailbox, news-papers piled up, no one opening the door when the doorbell was rung . . . Becca found this information by surfing through the latest editions of San Diego's main newspaper. But *still* no one's eye had fastened on Jeff Corrie as a person of interest in this mat-ter. He claimed to be as much in the dark as everyone else about Connor's whereabouts.

Fat chance, thought Becca. She'd read Jeff's whispers just before she and her mom had fled, and every one of them said he'd had a hand in getting rid of Connor. Those same whispers also said that Jeff Corrie was more than willing to turn his atten-tion to Becca and her mother if they didn't play their cards right. So they played their cards all the way up to Washington, getting away from the man. Becca's mom, Laurel, was still playing them in Nelson, British Columbia, where she'd been heading once Becca herself was on the ferry to Whidbey Island.

Only . . . absolutely nothing had worked out as they'd planned, and now Becca was looking over her shoulder morning, noon, and night as she waited for Jeff Corrie to show his face yet another time on Whidbey Island. He'd tracked her here once because of a cell phone, because of Derric's fall, and because of the police. He'd gotten nowhere, and he'd left, but that didn't mean he'd given up. It wasn't his way.

But for now, he had issues of his own in San Diego, which was fine with Becca. Let him stay there and try to answer questions about where Connor was. He'd run out of lies eventually. He'd face arrest and trial and prison and then Becca and her mom would finally be safe. Until then, though, she was on Whidbey Island, waiting for Laurel to return from British Columbia. She'd come back when it was safe to do so. Becca told herself that with every day that passed.

These were only some of the facts that Derric Mathieson wanted to know about Becca and her life. She couldn't blame him, but she also couldn't tell him. This was partly to keep him safe. But it was also partly because his dad was the under sheriff of Island County.

AFTER SCHOOL BECCA was wretched. She'd had one more class with Derric before the end of the day and she'd said before it started, "Let's not fight, okay?" She'd slid her fingers into his hand so that they could walk together as they always did. But he'd not taken her fingers and his only comment in reply was, "Whatever, Becca," before he ducked into class. There, he kept his gaze fixed on the teacher, and he'd taken so many notes that Becca figured he was writing everything word for word.

At the end of class, he was gone before she had a chance to say anything else to him. When she left the room, she saw him at the end of the corridor. He'd been stopped by one of the school cheerleaders for a conversation that involved smiles and laughter, so Becca walked off. *Wretched* didn't do justice to how she felt.

She decided not to take the school bus home to her hideaway in the woods. It was up the highway on the route to the next town, but she knew she could get there on one of the public island buses later in the day and that would be fine. At the moment she just needed to be away from all things related to South Whidbey High School, and she knew where to go for the break she wanted.

It was a very long walk on a very cold day, but Becca figured she could survive it. She'd already survived three snowfalls and countless rain- and windstorms since she'd been in the woods. A walk from Maxwelton Road to Clyde Street wasn't going to kill her.

It took more than an hour of hills and forests and fields, and by the end of the trip in the icy cold, Becca was so chilled that her bones were aching, and she promised herself that she'd bring her bike to school the next time she decided she needed to see the woman who lived above the beach called Sandy Point. When she reached the gray house overlooking the water, she rang the bell with fingers that had long ago gone numb.

Diana Kinsale's pickup truck was in the driveway, but the bell in the house didn't rouse her dogs nor did Becca herself when she went to the far side of the place and inspected their kennel.

It was empty. But as Becca looked around, joyful barking floated up from the distant water, and soon enough Becca caught sight of Diana throwing tennis balls for her dogs to retrieve. She was far off down the beach toward the end of the point, but Becca knew her by her mannish clothes and by her gait. And by her dogs, for there were five of them, and one of them was an elegant and silent black poodle called Oscar. He wasn't chasing the balls. Diana would say that Oscar believed ball chasing lacked dignity.

Becca made her way down toward the beach. It fronted a community of cottages, most of them vacant for the winter, a few with curls of smoke rising like silver scarves into the icy air. She curved through a few dunes where sea grasses lay dormant in the February weather, and when she finally came out onto the beach itself, she saw Diana Kinsale hurling one of the tennis balls and all the dogs save Oscar hurtling after it.

On their way back to Diana, though, they caught sight of Becca. She knelt and held out her arms to them. They stormed her, all nuzzling cold noses and dog breath. She laughed and cried, "Stop! No treats! Ach! Get 'em *off* me!" even though she loved the welcome they gave her.

She heard footsteps, then, and she looked up to see that Diana Kinsale had joined them. She wore a baseball cap over her short gray hair, and from her ears gold studs flashed in the fading afternoon light. She had on a thick parka, gloves, and knee-high fisherman's boots. What she said was, "Ah, Becca. There you are. I *thought* the dogs were expecting someone."

FIVE

Becca wasn't surprised. Diana Kinsale, she had discovered, had a way of knowing things about both people and animals that kept her in the loop of what was going on around the island. She also, however, had no whispers that Becca could ever hear unless Diana *intended* her to hear them, and from the first this had made the older woman not only a curiosity but also someone Becca wanted to understand.

She said to her, "Was it Oscar?"

"Telling me he was expecting someone?" Diana removed her baseball cap and ruffled up her hair before replacing the cap on her head. "No. The others. They didn't have quite the enthusiasm for ball chasing that they usually do. And, of course, Oscar never chases balls, so he was inscrutable on the topic of expecting anyone."

The dogs milled around them, snuffling the sand and, alternately, the pockets of Becca's jacket. "I told them I didn't have treats," she said to Diana.

"Hope springs eternal," Diana replied. "How are you? You look . . . Something's on your mind. No trouble at Debbie's I hope?"

Becca kept her expression as neutral as she could in the face of being reminded of the lie she'd told her friend. Diana believed that Becca was still living at a place called the Cliff Motel where, when she'd first come to the island, she'd worked for its owner Debbie Grieder in exchange for room and board. But she'd fled the motel for the woods just before Thanksgiving and so far she'd kept Debbie Grieder in the dark by telling her she was living with Diana. It was a deceptive dance that she knew she couldn't keep up forever. But for now it was the best she could do.

She said, "Debbie's great," which wasn't a lie. "So are the grandkids," which was also the truth.

Diana eyed her and said, "So . . . ?"

A sharp *crack* split the air around them and all of the dogs—including Oscar—began to bark. Diana swung toward the sound. Becca did the same. What they saw was a man with a rifle standing atop one of the stone walls that were used to separate the cottages from the beach. He was aiming his rifle not in their direction but at the water. He shot again. The dogs made an uproar.

Diana muttered, "Damn fool man," and began to stride in his direction. She said, "Dogs! No bark! Stay!" and to Becca, "You wait here." Then she started shouting, "Eddie! Eddie Beddoe! Stop that right now!" But if he heard her, he didn't acknowledge it. Instead he shot into the water another time.

He was pausing to reload when he apparently heard Diana's approach. He swung toward her, rifle ready.

At that Becca forgot Diana's admonition to stay where she

was and took off down the beach in aid of her friend. Becca's movement prompted the dogs to set off, too. They loped past Diana and surrounded the man.

He'd jumped off the wall. He was hefty and tall, and he looked like someone that no one would want to tangle with. Despite the frigid weather, he wore only a T-shirt and blue jeans. He didn't even have on shoes, and he wasn't acting bothered by the cold. What he was bothered by was his mind, Becca thought. *Kill her . . . want . . . die now . . . die . . . die* seemed to break in the air around him like ice hit by a hammer.

She said Diana's name in warning. Diana motioned for her to stay where she was. She said, "Dogs, dogs, quiet now, dogs," and she approached the man. She said to him not unkindly, "Now you listen to me, Eddie. Put that rifle down before you hurt someone."

"I got something to hurt." He raised the rifle toward the water again.

"Don't be silly. Out there? What're you aiming at? A piece of driftwood? You need to get back home."

"She's out there," he said with a jerk of his head in the direction of the water. "She's back already, and this time I mean to—"

"No one's out there," Diana told him. "No one's back. And if you accidentally hit someone on the beach, there'll be hell to pay. You know that."

"I'm in hell already," was his reply. But he lowered the rifle at last, and Diana closed the distance between them. She took the gun, unloaded it, and pocketed the cartridges. She handed the rifle back empty and ventured closer to the man.

"Eddie," she said. "Eddie." She sounded sad but gentle. She raised her hand and rested it on his shoulder.

Becca watched, alert. She was ready to launch herself at the man if he made a false move, and she could tell by their raised hackles that the dogs were ready as well. But he made no further move toward anyone. He seemed strangely depleted, just at the touch of Diana's hand. His body gave a shudder. His spine seemed to relax. Whatever form of madness had possessed him was gone, if only for the moment.

Then he looked at Becca with eyes like gray skies and what came to her was *kill her when I can that's what* as if he'd spoken the words aloud.

She said, "Diana," in a shaky voice.

Diana said, "Hush now," and it came to Becca that, so gently spoken, the words were not directed at her.

THEY WAITED TILL Eddie Beddoe had departed before they too left the beach. It wasn't until his truck belched exhaust smoke all the way from Sandy Point to Wilkinson Road above it that Diana said, "All dogs come," to her animals and added with a smile at Becca, "All girls, too."

She didn't say anything about their encounter with the man as they walked back to her house above the water. Instead she talked of other things: mostly the bulbs she'd planted last autumn in anticipation of spring and what the winter was doing to her perennials. It wasn't until they were inside the house, having fed four of the dogs outside and Oscar inside in the mudroom, that Diana was willing to talk about what had happened on the beach below them. She put water on for her afternoon cup of tea, held out a mug to Becca with a questioning look on her face, and put three scoops of her favorite Assam into a pot to steep. Then she said to Becca, "I expect you wonder what that was about."

"I thought he was going to shoot you."

Diana indicated the nook in her brightly painted kitchen: yellow, red, orange, and green. She was not a woman afraid of bold color. She set a plate of Girl Scout cookies on the purple table, and she joined Becca there with the teapot and the mugs.

"He's trying to kill a seal," she said.

"Isn't that against the law?"

"It is, but he doesn't think about that. He thinks only about shooting what he can't bear to face."

"Which is what?"

"The same as most people. The consequences of his own actions. He lost his boat in the water. He blames a seal. It's as simple as that. Well, as simple as any form of madness can ever be. Truth is that he went out in one of those bad windstorms we get in the winter. He was no match for it and he'd also forgotten to put in the boat's transom plugs. He might have been drinking as well, but he'd never say that. In any case, the boat went down and he was lucky to make it to shore. It happened just out there"—she indicated the beach from which they'd walked—"and I think the truth is that he'd like to be thought of as a victim and not the instigator of his own misfortune.

Well, most people would prefer that, wouldn't they? It's human nature."

"A seal," Becca murmured. "Well, I guess that's better than blaming on another person."

Diana lifted her mug and gazed over it at Becca. She cocked her head one way and then another, as if to say "Maybe yes, maybe no."

"What?" Becca asked her.

Diana smiled. "Nothing."

"No way. There's something. I c'n tell. Come *on*."

Diana chuckled, running her hand through her choppy gray hair another time. "It's just that, if you ask me, there are seals and there are seals. Not a single one bears shooting at and some . . . well, some are creatures that a man like Eddie ought to avoid at all costs."

"Why?"

"Because they're far too important to die prematurely. Or to be wounded. Or even, Becca, to be brought to land."

BUT THAT WAS all Diana would say on the subject of the seal. When Becca pressed her, her reply was, "Really, my dear, there's nothing else." She added more tea to her mug and said, "You and I haven't seen each other in a while, so this is a welcome visit. But something tells me you've come for a reason."

Had she? Becca asked herself. There had been comfort in hanging around Diana Kinsale from the moment she'd met her on the night of her arrival on the island. So why did she need comfort now?

"I guess things are iffy with Derric," she admitted. Diana said nothing, merely watching her brightly for more information. There wasn't much that Becca could tell her that wouldn't accidentally spill the truth about her place of hiding, so she settled on saying, "Relationships are tough."

"Is Derric your first boyfriend? I mean your first real boyfriend, with all the trimmings."

"I guess. And he . . . he wants some things that I can't really give him." Becca grimaced as she realized how that sounded. "It's not sex. Well, I mean it's always sex, huh? But that's not what I'm talking about. We haven't done it. I'm just . . . I don't think I'm ready for that and that's what I told him and he's not pressuring me about it. He's not like that. I mean, he *is* but he isn't." She paused to think how she could put things. She decided on, "Sometimes we're a couple and sometimes we're not. I think right now . . . maybe we're not."

"That must be painful," Diana said. "I know how important he is to you."

Derric was more than important. He was close to everything. Becca loved him and she wanted him, yes. But there were times when she also felt that she *was* him and that he was her. It was as if they occasionally exchanged souls. So when times were rough, her soul went missing. Becca knew that, at heart, Derric felt the same way. What do you do when another person is also your soul? she wondered. When the soul gets angry with the body that houses it, what comes next?

"Sitting with the pain," Diana murmured. "Lord, I remember how that is."

"The worst," Becca said.

"Especially when the only way through it is . . . through it." Diana put her hand on Becca's arm across the purple table. For a moment she said nothing and yet despite her saying nothing, Becca felt enormously comforted by her touch.

Still Becca said, "Sometimes I wish stuff between people didn't have to be so tough. Sometimes I wish life didn't have to be so tough."

"I hear you on that," Diana replied.

Something in her tone made Becca look at her hard. There was always an undercurrent with Diana, a suggestion that things weren't as peaceful as they seemed to be. But Diana never said word one about what those things were, and since Becca couldn't hear her thoughts when Diana didn't want them to be heard, she had no clue what elements in Diana Kinsale's life might not be what she wanted. Becca knew that Diana was a longtime widow with no children, but that was it. Anything more, Diana never revealed.

Yet something from the first had told Becca that she and Diana shared numerous qualities of character. So still she came to see Diana when she was able, drawn to her in much the same way as she was drawn to Derric. She had a feeling they'd been fated to meet. She just didn't know why.

Diana released her arm with a pat. "I didn't see your bike outside. Did you come on foot?" When Becca nodded, Diana got to her feet. "Let me drive you back to the motel."

There was no way to get around this one. When Becca said that a ride into town wasn't necessary and that the exercise would do her good, Diana pointed out that it was dark outside, the day had been freezing cold and was getting colder, and Becca's declaration that she would rather walk or jog just wasn't going to cut it. So Becca ended up saying she'd be grateful for the lift into town, and all along she hoped Diana didn't intend to stop by the motel and have a friendly chat with Debbie Grieder, which would put her in a very bad spot.

As things turned out, she didn't have to worry. Diana plucked a list off the bulletin board in her mudroom on their way out and said she had to pick up a few things at the Star Store in Langley anyway. So it was all good, and in a few moments, they were trundling on their way in Diana's pickup, along the rolling route that was Sandy Point Road. They had no further conversation since the Dixie Chicks were singing at nearly full volume and Diana was singing along with them.

At the Cliff Motel, Diana stopped at the edge of the parking lot. She said, "Give my best to Debbie," and Becca promised that she would. She made a pretense of walking in the direction of her old room, but once Diana had turned the corner and headed into town, she ducked through a line of rhododendrons that formed a boundary between the motel's parking lot and a vacant lot next to it, and she quickly crossed this and hurried in the same direction that Diana herself had taken. She needed to get to the closest stop for the island bus. It was, unfortunately, not far from the Star Store.

The distance wasn't great. It took her along a street called Cascade that followed the top of the bluff on which the small village of Langley sat. Beneath this was an old marina with a bulwark protecting a few boats docked there from the roiling waters of Saratoga Passage. In the distance, the lights from the city of Everett blinked on the mainland. Closer at hand, the lights along Cascade Street cast pools of illumination on the first of the old island cottages that defined the little town.

Along this street, an unusual number of cars were parked. As Becca walked along them, she began to smile, for there was a car she recognized—a 1965 restored VW bug—and its presence meant that she might not have to wait for the bus for the long journey to her hiding place after all. For somewhere in town was the only person who knew exactly where she was staying, and Becca had a fairly good idea where she would find him.

SIX

The place was called South Whidbey Commons. It stood on Second Street, which broke to the west off Cascade and ultimately climbed a route to the woods outside of town. Unfortunately, South Whidbey Commons was also directly next door to Diana Kinsale's destination, the Star Store, but Becca had a feeling that if she ducked inside the place, she'd be able to locate Seth Darrow quickly enough.

Seth was a regular at South Whidbey Commons, an ancient cottage that had been transformed into a community gathering place. A front garden there offered tables and chairs, flower beds and planters, and some whimsical art pieces for the summertime customers who bought coffee, tea, and baked goods inside, while the rooms of the cottage itself provided a bookstore, an art gallery, and a game room featuring secondhand PCs. The gallery could be transformed into a meeting space, too, which members of the community sometimes used. And when Becca entered the place on this late afternoon, the gallery was crammed with arguing people.

She felt a little dizzy with the assault of noise. It combined not only whatever was going on in the gallery, but also the whispers of the dozens of people present in the rest of the building. The result for Becca was a bit like having a wall of bright colors directly shoved just inches from her eyeballs, only in this case the colors came in the form of words like *better work this year . . . more time for tourists . . . an ass for sure . . . into her pants she's so majorly hot . . . wouldn't know a doer . . . if her period's late like she's saying . . . be grateful for . . .* and a great deal more. As quickly as she could, she grabbed the earphone of the AUD box from her jacket pocket and fastened it into her ear for relief. That left her with what was being said aloud, and as she gazed around the place in a search for Seth Darrow, she couldn't help hearing it as most of it was shouted by one party or another in the gallery.

Inside the room, someone had set up a white board. There, a man with Coke-bottle glasses and thatchlike hair bursting from beneath a baseball cap was listing things. Seemingly unrelated items were being offered by the gathered crowd. He jotted "feeding from pier" alongside "boat tours," which in turn had an arrow pointing to "picture opportunities" as well as "beach possibilities." Along one edge ran "protection from orcas?" while at the bottom was "is early bad?" Not a single word made any sense to Becca, and she was about to turn away from the group when she saw among them Jenn McDaniels.

Jenn was sitting with a red-haired young woman who was taking notes in what looked like a state of high excitement. Becca looked beyond them and saw that the walls of the room held dozens of pictures of seals. She frowned at these, at the people, at the shouting, at the statements still being listed on the white board.

Seals and Langley appeared to have a very strange relationship, she thought. Some people apparently wanted to keep them at a safe distance from possible encounters with human beings while others wanted to feed them from the marina's pier. But everyone wanted to argue about them, especially about an unusual-looking black one whose picture was just being flashed on the white board in lieu of a screen. The writing already on the white board was making it tough to discern the details, though.

Thus someone shouted, "Erase all that crap, Thorndyke. We can't see what we're looking at."

Thorndyke was the man with the Coke-bottle glasses. He shouted back, "Now just hold on a minute," but a chorus of protests met his words.

That was when Jenn McDaniels caught sight of Becca. The girl's eyes narrowed and her upper lip rose. Her expression said she smelled something bad.

Right, Becca thought. It's you.

Jenn's middle finger lifted in an unmistakable message. Becca turned from the sight of her. She turned also from the chaos going on inside the room. Seth had to be here, she figured, if his car was here. He met his GED tutor in the far back room, and he practiced with his trio there too.

She edged along the spillover from the meeting, and she had good luck before she got ten feet. She saw Seth coming toward her from the back of the cottage, outfitted in his usual garb of flannel shirt, baggy black denims, thick-soled all-weather sandals, and fedora. He had on brightly colored homemade socks and he carried his guitar case. This told her that either practice was finished or the trio had given up in the face of the noise.

Seth winced and fingered one of his ear gauges as shouts of "No way!" "This means something and it's bad!" "Oh just sit the hell down!" came from the meeting room. Then he saw Becca and gave one of his Seth nods: a lifting of the chin and nothing else.

He reached her, said, "Man, I am out of here. What about you?" and he shouldered his way to the door, saying, "Later," to some people, and "Nah, it's cool," to someone who leaned toward him and spoke from one of the tables.

Becca followed him outside where the wind had risen and the growing evening seemed colder than ever. She said, "What's going on in there?"

He said, "Meeting of the seal spotters."

"The who?"

"Bunch of people from up and down the island who watch for a bizarro seal every year." He indicated the people inside the Commons by flicking his thumb in their direction. "Lemme tell you, Beck, the way they're acting, you'd think the freaking Apocalypse was going on. This seal shows up a few months early and it means everything from global warming to an announcement of the Second Coming of Jesus." He shoved his fedora back on his head, then, and gave her a look. "What're you doing here anyway?" And with a look around, "Shit, Beck, are you supposed to be floating around town like this?"

"He's still in San Diego," she said. "I checked the Internet. They're finally asking about his partner. 'Where's Connor and why hasn't he picked up his mail since last September?' Duh. If Jeff Corrie leaves town now, they're after him."

"You *think*," Seth said. "How're you getting home, then?" And when she looked at him hopefully, he laughed and said, "Right. Come on."

"Yes! That's why I love you," she said. "You c'n read my mind."

"As if," he told her.

SEVEN

Derric Mathieson was just coming out of the Langley Clinic when Becca King and Seth Darrow passed its parking lot. He was hobbling in his walking cast to his mom's old Forester, and as soon as he saw them, Derric wanted to punch someone's lights.

Two things stopped him from going after Darrow. First, his mom was right behind him locking up the clinic for the evening. Second and aside from his healing leg, what the hell good would it do? Yeah, he'd deck Darrow. And yeah, he'd feel a nanosecond of satisfaction at the sound of Darrow hitting the ground. But then he'd have his mom to contend with, and he'd also have gotten not one step closer to resolving *anything* with Becca.

The *mom* part of the deal would be bad. Rhonda Mathieson was the greatest person to have as a mom about 80 percent of the time. She was in his corner, on his side, at his back, and whatever else. She'd been that way since she'd first locked eyes on him in a Kampala orphanage when he was six years old. It had taken her and his dad two years to get everything together to adopt him, and in that time she'd never let him forget that she intended to be his mom, no matter what. She'd flown to Uganda for extended visits, she'd written to him practically every day, she'd phoned the orphanage at huge expense. She was major.

But the other 20 percent of Rhonda . . . ? That was the problem. He was African. She was not. He'd been abandoned by the death of his parents when he was five years old. She had not. She didn't get how it felt sometimes to be black on an island peopled almost exclusively by whites. She also didn't get the dead space inside of him. She sensed something, sure, but she didn't get it. To make up for not getting it, she *hovered.* Every tiny mood shift on his part was under her microscope. She held her breath if he frowned. She stood at his bedroom door and offered him ice cream, cookies, pizza, neck rubs, and trips over town to the mall if she thought he was blue. She just wanted so *much* for him to be happy, content, at peace, and all the rest. But he couldn't be. There were reasons for this, but the last thing he could do was to tell her what they were.

The Becca part of the deal was actually worse than his mom, though. She'd been a huge part of his thoughts for months, ever since he'd opened his eyes from a coma in early November, found her gazing at him earnestly, and felt her hand clutching at his. He'd known *before* that moment that there was something about this girl that he'd found compelling from the second he'd seen her on the ferry with her bicycle, her backpack, and her saddlebags. He also knew that they were the weirdest couple imaginable. But from the first that hadn't mattered. All that had mattered was getting close to her. He wanted her, sure.

Five seconds into kissing her the first time had been enough to tell him that. Even the sound of her voice on the phone had told him that. But more than sex was involved in his relationship with Becca. It was a connection he'd had with no one else.

That connection *meant* things. He wanted it to grow. The way he saw it, the growing came from truth and honesty. She knew the secrets of his soul, and he was cool with that. But they'd been together from mid-November and *still* he knew virtually nothing about her. He'd told himself that he'd *get* to know her. His mom and dad had said the same thing. "Everyone's different, sweetie. Don't *push* at her so much," was how his mom put it. "Play it cool, son," was his dad's advice.

But how the hell could he do that with Seth Darrow hanging around? He didn't know. He did *not* know.

"A guy can be my best friend, for God's sake," was what Becca said when he brought up Darrow.

"This isn't about being friends with some guy and you know it," was Derric's reply.

"Then what *is* it about? D'you think we're hooking up or something? Don't you trust *me*? Is that what this is?"

"It's that you don't trust me," Derric told her.

But that remark was the slippery slope. It led to what he wanted from her in order to balance the scales between them. She knew the darkest part of him, the secret he had kept from the world. He didn't know the darkest part of her. And since December he didn't even know where the hell she was living. No one knew that except one person. Darrow, of course.

When he saw them heading up Second Street, then, Derric knew that Seth Darrow would be taking her home. They'd be in his VW, laughing and talking, and when they got to wherever they were going, no doubt they'd laugh and talk some more. Derric gritted his teeth. When his mom said, "Isn't that Becca?" and drew in a breath to call out a hello, he said, "Come on," in what he knew was a surly voice. He felt her glance at him.

At least Rhonda waited till they got home before she started in. They lived due west of Langley, near Goss Lake, not directly on it among the fir trees that sheltered it but rather on a nearby road that took the lake's name. It was dark as pitch when they pulled into the driveway. The sheriff's car wasn't there, so Dave Mathieson was still at work. This was going to give Rhonda time to do a little delving, Derric thought. He steeled himself for the worst.

It wasn't long in coming. She said, "You didn't want to say hi to Becca."

Duh, he thought.

"Want to talk about that?"

He shook his head.

"You two on the outs?"

He gave a shrug.

"I know she means a lot to you."

Uh, yeah. She meant pretty much everything but what the hell did that matter? He said, "It's okay, Mom."

"Hey, I c'n see it's not okay. Did something happen between you?"

"Nope."

"Derric, come on. It helps to talk things out. I'm concerned. You haven't been yourself—"

My self is someone you don't even know, he thought. "I said it's *okay*. Everything's okay. Everything's just dandy."

"You haven't been yourself for weeks now, and I know it has something to do with Becca."

"Lay off, Mom."

"Laying off is the easier thing to do. I'm not into easy. Is this about sex?"

"Crap! What the hell—"

"Because it usually is, between kids your age."

"Mom . . ."

"And sex alters relationships big-time, Derric. It can't help altering things. Now I can see something's gone wrong for the two of you so . . . Have you been intimate with her?"

"What the hell do I have to tell you to get you—"

"You have condoms, don't you? You know you can always get them from me, yes?"

"Mom! Stop it. *Stop* it." He shoved open the car door and then leaped out, stumbling when the cast on his leg got hung up with an empty grocery bag. "Let it go, for God's sake," he snapped at her. "Just for one time in my life, *please* let it go."

"Derric, you're young. When these things happen, they feel wretched, but they always pass. You're going to see that—"

He slammed the door on her. He knew he'd pay for that move later, but at the moment he just needed to get away.

HE WENT TO his room. His leg was aching, as it sometimes did at the end of the day, and he looked down on it morosely, wondering when the stupid cast would finally come off. He'd been just two weeks away from getting his driver's license when he'd fallen down the bluff in the woods and the thought of the freedom that a driver's license would have provided him in a moment like this made him hate the world.

He threw his backpack on the floor and his body on the bed. He wrestled his cell phone from the pocket of his jeans and checked for voice mails and texts. None of the former. Two of the latter. He felt more eager than he wanted to feel. She didn't have a cell phone but she could have borrowed one to text him.

She hadn't. The first text was his mom, earlier in the day. *Pizza 2nite?* He hadn't seen it, and once she'd caught sight of Becca, she'd obviously forgotten she'd made the offer.

The second was from Court. He was puzzled by *Court* for a moment till he read the message. *Want 2 hang? Clyde 2morrow?* It had to be from Courtney Baker.

Derric looked at the message, his lips forming an O. The Clyde was the local cinema in Langley, and . . . What was Courtney doing? Inviting him out? Derric thought about that one. They had French class together, she'd asked him about homework in the hall just today, and while they were talking she'd smiled and touched her hair in that way girls did when they wanted to communicate something. Only . . . He hadn't known what she wanted to communicate. Amusement? Interest? What?

He wanted to text her back. *Yeah, babe, let's do it. We'll sit in the dark and watch a film. Or you watch the film and I'll watch you. I'll check out your boobs and figure out how to cop a feel. You're the cure for the sickness inside me.* Only this wasn't true, and he damn well knew it. He'd think about how to get a hand on her boobs and maybe that would distract him for a while. But it wouldn't solve a single thing.

Someone tapped on his door. He shoved the cell phone into his pocket. He said, "Yeah," and the door opened. Dave Mathieson stuck his head into the room.

He looked sheepish. Obviously, Rhonda had given him his instructions about talking to their son. He said, "Everything okay, Der?" and he rubbed his hands through his salt-and-pepper hair. He tilted his head in the direction of the kitchen from which dinner noises were emanating. "Your mom . . . You know how she gets."

"Yeah. I know."

"And . . . anything?"

"And . . . nothing. She thinks something's going on with me. Nothing is."

Dave eyed him with an expression that spoke of having two older children and having had the experience of seeing them through adolescence and into adulthood. They were the children of his first marriage, though. Derric was the only child of his second. "You're important to her. You know that, don't you? If she worries about you, it's because—"

"—she's a physician's assistant and she's seen a lot of things. I know it, Dad. But there's nothing going on. I just need . . . I don't know. I don't _know._"

Dave was silent for a moment in the doorway. He finally said, "Can you give me something to work with, son?"

"I absolutely can't," was Derric's reply.

EIGHT

They were heading onto the main island highway when the question struck Becca. "How d'they even know it's the same seal?" she asked Seth.

Seth said, "Huh?" and cranked the VW's heating higher.

"You said those people watch for a seal every year and this year it's early. How d'they know it's even the same seal?"

He gave her a look as he shifted to fourth gear and turned the windshield wipers on against a soft rain that had begun to fall. A few more degrees and it would be snow. Becca hoped that wouldn't happen. Seth said, "I always forget."

"What?"

"That you're not a local and you're not a tourist either. Local, you'd know. Tourist, you would've seen a postcard."

"Of what?"

"The seal. She's totally black. Nera's what she's called. Anyway, she's been showing up the same time every year for . . . I dunno how long. This year she's early so they're all freaking out."

"Because?"

"Because they got a festival for her and if she shows up early, she might leave early and then what happens to their festival where she's usually swimming around looking for handouts or whatever? I say put someone in a frigging seal costume and have him swim around Langley marina barking, but who's asking me?"

Becca thought about this in the light of everything that had passed that day. She said, "Seth, there was this guy . . . Eddie somebody? . . . I can't remember his last name. Diana Kinsale knew him and he was down at Sandy Point shooting a rifle at the water. Diana said he was shooting at a seal."

"Sounds like Eddie Beddoe," Seth said. "He's as bizarro as the rest of 'em. There's all sorts of people just totally whacked out about that seal, Beck. Ask me why and I do . . . not . . . know." He glanced at her then and said, "Something for you in the backseat. Star Store throwaways. I thought you might want 'em."

Seth worked in the Star Store early every morning. It was how Becca had come to meet him in the first place. Now, she squirmed around in her seat and saw the grocery bag. She said, "Seth! Hey. Thanks," as she grabbed for it. Food past its sell-by date comprised the bag's contents, along with a few items that she knew Seth had paid for on his own. She said to him, "I'll pay you back."

He gave her a wink. "No problemmo. You're my entertainment."

She made a face at him. He laughed and reached over and ruffled her hair. It reminded her of how much older he was: nineteen years old to her fifteen. But still her good friend, her best friend if it came down to it.

Some distance along the highway, Seth made the turn onto Newman Road. This cut northwest and ultimately looped into the commercial town of Freeland, but a good distance before that, he pulled to the side and stopped the car in a quarter-moon turnout. Some twenty yards farther along the road from this was a trail into the forest that Becca needed to hike. She grabbed her backpack and the bag of Star Store goodies and opened the door.

She said, "Thanks. I owe you big-time like always," but was surprised when he got out as well. He scored a flashlight from his glove compartment first. He said, "I'll collect someday. Come on."

"You don't have to—"

"No problemmo," he said again. "'Sides, I want to make sure you're not wrecking the place."

The place was a tree house in the woods, a structure that Seth himself had built. It sat in the interlocking branching of two great hemlocks, deep within a forest on a huge tract of land that Seth's grandfather owned and on which he, too, lived. But Ralph Darrow had no idea that Becca had been in residence on his property since November. Seth had helped her keep things this way.

They hiked for ten minutes to reach the clearing where the hemlocks stood. It was pitch-black out there, and Becca ended up grateful for Seth's companionship. She had her own flashlight, which she'd rustled from her backpack, but the wind had risen along with the rain, and the creaking branches of all the alders, firs, and cedars made her jumpy. It was comforting to have Seth hiking in front of her. It was even more comforting when he didn't pause as they reached the clearing, but instead grabbed an armload of firewood from its spot behind a fallen tree's massive root-ball. He carried this to the ladder of the tree house and heaved it upward and through the trapdoor.

From the first, it had been no ordinary tree house. It had been built to last, tightly constructed, with a sound roof that kept out the wind, the rain, and the snow, as well as double-paned windows that held in the heat. It contained a small woodstove to make the place warm, and here Becca had hidden night after night, week after week, with a lantern for light, a cot and sleeping bag as her bed, jugs of water to quench her thirst, and a Coleman stove to cook her meager meals. Her "bathroom" was a bucket squirreled away in the bushes, along with a shovel and a rake to bury whatever needed to be buried. It was a grim kind of life, complete with showers in the girls' locker room at school, but she was surviving.

It was also the life Derric wanted to know about. "Where the hell are you staying?" had become the demand he'd started making along with "Come on. What's with Seth Darrow? What the *hell* is going on?"

She couldn't blame him. She'd spent Thanksgiving at his family's house: Derric's chosen girlfriend. But when it came time to leave, she left they way she'd arrived, on her mountain bike, refusing all offers of transportation. When she did the same at Christmas, Derric started asking questions. He'd asked more questions when he'd seen her in town in Seth's VW. "We're just friends" didn't cut it for Derric. "There isn't a *problem*," she tried to tell him. But of course, this was a lie.

There *was* a problem, and it was his father. Since Dave

Mathieson was the under sheriff of Island County, it wasn't likely that he would let things go unnoticed if he learned that a minor was living alone in a forest tree house. Besides, in the autumn he'd been on the trail of a cell phone owned by someone called Laurel Armstrong. He'd given that up but the last thing Becca wanted him to know—aside from where she was living—was that Laurel Armstrong was her own mother, on the run with Becca from San Diego.

Her secrets from Derric were driving a wedge between them. The fact that he had a secret—which she alone knew—only made things worse. He wanted to make the ground level between them. You know my stuff, I know yours. But this was something she couldn't allow. She told herself it was for his own good, but sometimes she wondered if she was being honest.

Inside the tree house, Seth went for the little wood-burning stove. He'd taught Becca how to bank a fire, but all along she'd had trouble getting it right. This time was no different. He frowned at the cold and put his hand on the stove top. "Beck." He sighed.

"I know, I know."

She set about unpacking the Star Store bag. It contained cold cuts, a carton of milk, a dozen hard-boiled eggs, a loaf of bread, two sandwiches, three rolls of toilet paper. There was even a magazine, an old issue of *People* with The Sexiest Man Alive! on the cover. She set it to one side and took one of the eggs. As Seth rebuilt the fire, she peeled it, watching him. Funny how you couldn't tell about people, she thought. Seth seemed and looked like a parent's worst nightmare: He was a high school dropout with too-long hair, ever-enlarging ear gauges, and—she saw—a newly pierced eyebrow. He wasn't tattooed, but that was probably coming. That he was nicest person ever was something that didn't ride on the surface of her friend.

"How's the music going?" she asked him. He slammed the door of the woodstove once he had the fire lit.

"Two gigs coming up in Lynwood. Another in Shoreline." He grinned. "We're working our way toward Seattle. Any day now, baby."

"You write anything new?"

"Yep."

"Cool. C'n I hear?"

"S'pose. If I could play the woodstove, which I can't."

She rolled her eyes. "Very funny. You know what I mean. When're you guys rehearsing again?"

"Don't know. GED's coming up. I'm sort of concentrating on that. The music part—I mean the writing, composing, you know—that's just on the side right now."

"Got it." She extended one of the eggs to him.

"That's for you," he said.

"I'll pay you back."

"Someday," he said. "Either that or I'm gonna beat it out of you."

She knew he was kidding, but she also knew that she couldn't go on taking money from Seth in the form of the supplies he'd brought her for the last two and a half months. It wasn't fair, and the only way to end the unfairness was to find a job. She said, "Whatever. But I can't let you keep spending money on me."

"Like I said, it's cheap entertainment," he told her. "What's happening these days with Derric?"

She made a face. "Still the same. 'What're you doing with Darrow? Where're you living? What's going on?'"

"You should probably tell him. I can see why he's getting the wrong idea, Beck. It's a guy thing. You can't blame him."

"I'm not blaming him. I'm just asking him to trust that what I'm telling him is all I can tell him. It's like he thinks you and I are hooking up in secret. As if," she said.

"Uh . . . thanks."

"I didn't mean it like that. Anyway, he got ticked at me again today and then I saw him deliberately having one of those let's-get-chummy conversations with one of the cheerleaders later. And he *wanted* me to see them talking, I know it. He wants me to see he can have anyone he wants. And I know that, too. I'm not exactly stupid."

Seth rustled in the backpack he'd worn from the VW as he listened to this. "One of the cheerleaders?" he said. "Major bummer." He brought out a sack of cheddar popcorn and he used his teeth to rip it open. He said, "Want some, then? It's past its sell-by date, but nothing says 'screw the world's cheerleaders' better than popcorn."

NINE

J enn McDaniels decided that the amusement value of being Annie Taylor's guide to Langley was pretty much nil. She'd ended up inside South Whidbey Commons with Annie because she could have gone two ways in the late afternoon: accompany Annie to the meeting of the seal spotters that the young woman had read about online or wrestle her brothers into cleaning their room while her mom cooked dinner and recited dutifully memorized passages from the Old Testament. Between the two options, showing Annie Taylor the ropes in Langley had seemed more appealing. Now, though, Jenn wasn't sure she'd made the right choice.

It was hot as hell in the room. There were too many people in too little space coughing and hacking with winter colds. And she wanted a cigarette. Annie had promised pizza when the meeting was over, but the meeting had gone on forever so far and not a single thing had been resolved. Jenn couldn't see what the fuss was all about. The coal black seal had shown up early. And this was a dire event in the lives of the islanders . . . why? No one seemed to have an answer to this question. Least of all did

Annie Taylor, who had spent most of the meeting taking notes like someone about to be tested on the topic. When she wasn't scribbling onto a legal tablet, she was leaning into Jenn whispering, "Who's that guy talking?" and "What d'she say, Jenn?" and "How many seal spotters are we talking about?" and "Is there more than one organization watching for that seal?"

Jenn had no big answers. The identity of the main guy talking was the only question she could address. He was Ivar Thorndyke, and as far as Jenn knew, he was the person who'd established the whole dumb organization of people who watched for the black seal up and down the coast. They had binoculars, telescopes, and a telephone tree. They had an Internet site and documents of the seal's every movement. What they didn't have was a life, Jenn scoffed. God, she wanted a cigarette.

While she was sitting in the room enduring the general oddball nature of the seal spotting debate and wondering whether Annie Taylor would ever have enough of it, she caught sight of the SmartAss FatBroad, which made everything worse. Geez, she wished that creepoid would take a very long walk off a very short pier. It was bad enough having to see her ugly mug at school. Running into her in town was enough to make Jenn vomit. She flipped her one when Becca caught sight of her and she sputtered a laugh when the FatBroad's eyes took this in and widened with surprise. What? Jenn thought. You don't know I'd like to kick your fat butt all the way to wherever you came from? Hell, I thought I'd made that clear from Day Number One.

She saw Seth Darrow, then. Obviously, he was who the

FatBroad had come looking for. What they were up to was one for the books. What did she want with Seth? She had Derric and he wasn't enough?

They left together, Becca King and Seth Darrow. Jenn gave them time to disappear. Then she caught a glimpse of a Goth from school who followed them shortly upon their departure. Cool, she thought. If anyone in the place had a cigarette to bum, it was going to be Augusta Savage. She loved nothing better than corrupting people. Jenn squeezed out of the meeting to catch up to her.

As luck would have it, Augusta was lighting up under a nearby streetlamp. Two Goth boys were slouching her way from the direction of a little community park up on the corner of Second and Anthes streets. But they were still some distance away, so Jenn figured she could score a smoke before the guys got to Augusta and distracted her with their dubious wonderfulness. She was that kind of odd-o. Boys came first. As long as they had the appropriate equipment, they were fine with Augusta.

Jenn said hey to her and Augusta cast an indifferent look in her direction. They'd been to grade school together, but you wouldn't know it by how Augusta appeared now and how she acted. Then she'd been all blonde ringlets and Mary Jane shoes with tights that matched her myriad outfits. Now she sported a half-shaved head of black hair with ends so split they might have been snake tongues, and the rest of her was piercings, chains, and Doc Martens all the way. She pretended not to recognize Jenn. Whatever, Jenn thought. Just hand over a smoke.

She said, "Got a coupla extras?" to Augusta.

"Extras of what?" Augusta said, ennui itself making the supreme effort to speak aloud.

"Smokes," Jenn said impatiently.

"Oh. Smokes," Augusta said. "I thought you meant tits." She smiled her slow and knowing smile, her eyes fixed on Jenn's non-existent breasts. "When're you going to grow some?" she asked. "You even started your period yet?"

"You could've just said no to the cigarettes," Jenn advised her. "It'd save you all the effort, Augusta."

Augusta rolled her eyes and dug in a black hobo bag that hung from her shoulder. She took out a cigarette and broke it in half. "Best I can do," she told her.

The two Goth boys were upon them then, and Augusta drew one of them into an embrace by hooking her leg around his. She kissed the other guy in a way that made kissing *anyone* look completely repulsive. Jenn left her to it and headed for one of the outdoor tables in front of the Commons. There she lit up and took a very nice hit. It wasn't good for her, it slowed her down in soccer, and she had to quit if she wanted to make it athletically. But she'd been smoking since she was ten years old, and it was a habit now. She'd quit tomorrow. She closed her eyes and settled back to enjoy the guilty delight.

Someone snatched the cigarette from her fingers. Her eyes flew open as Squat Cooper stomped it to bits on a paving stone. She said, "Hey!" to which he replied, "Stunts your growth, gives you cancer, makes wrinkles, turns your teeth yellow, and creeps out your breath. Not to mention what it does to the now extremely remote possibility of anyone putting his tongue inside your mouth."

"I just bummed that from Augusta Savage," she told him.

"Who names their kid Augusta?"

"If my name was Fergus and everyone called me Squat, I don't think I'd be mentioning anyone else's name," Jenn pointed out.

"Piquant and amusing, my friend. What're you doing here, anyway?"

"What're *you* doing here?"

"First asked, first answered."

She sighed. Squat was . . . so completely Squat. She told him about the meeting going on.

Squat lowered himself into one of the chairs at her table, rested his elbows on his knees, shook his head, and said, "This's got to be the only place on the planet where they'd call a town meeting about a seal."

"It's not a town meeting. It's Ivar Thorndyke and the seal spotters."

Squat guffawed. "Even better. This is the only island on the planet where people join a club to *watch* for a seal." He pretended to hold binoculars to his eyes and he altered his voice to a high-pitched tone. "'Oh, Jeffrey, Jeffrey! Come and see! I think she's arrived! Shall we alert the media?'" Then he lowered the binoculars and his voice as well. "'No, Bunny-pie. That's a small submarine you're looking it. We're being invaded by the terrorists, but no worries. As long as they don't touch our Nera, all's well, my dear.'"

Jenn had to smile. He was right. Whidbey Island was a loony bin half the time. The other half it was so boring to live here that she thought she'd petrify before she managed to get herself permanently onto the mainland. "So what're you doing in town?" she asked him.

"Babysitting the twins."

His half-brother and half-sister, fruit of his father's second marriage to the executive assistant for whom he'd left Squat's mom. It had been one of those scandals-of-the-century kinds of departures for Mr. Cooper because Squat's older brother had walked in on Dad and the executive assistant. And she'd not been executively assisting him.

Jenn looked around. "So where are they?"

"At the Clyde. There's a Pixar movie showing. *Toy Story Twenty-Five: Finding Nemo under the Ratatouille.* I have no clue. I left them there with popcorn, M&M's, Junior Mints, and Milk Duds. If I play my cards right, someone'll abduct them for the candy. I can't hope they'd be abducted for themselves."

Jenn chuckled. "You're evil."

"Hey, the babes *all* want evil guys. Nice guys like me when I'm the normal me? No one's interested. Except you, of course. That kindergarten milk-sharing thing we've got going."

"Or something," she told him.

"When you figure it out, let me know what it is." He got to his feet.

"Where to now? Want to check out the meeting?"

"That seal," he said with a shake of his head. "I think I'll go peep into windows instead."

He sauntered off, hands in the pockets of his jeans. There wasn't much to do to kill time in town, aside from reading the public announcements on the bulletin boards in the coffeehouses, the post office, and the vestibule of the Star Store. But she figured that didn't bother Squat Cooper. He'd probably just work a few calculus problems in his head.

There was nothing for it but to return to the Commons. Inside, Ivar Thorndyke had set up his computer. He was showing everyone the most recent picture of the seal that had been taken. He was telling everyone that she hadn't been close to shore yet, but this picture had been taken up north from the beach at Joseph Whidbey State Park and she swam near enough for people to tell it was Nera.

Ivar's concern was Nera's health, he said. Showing up early might mean she was sick. They'd had a pod of bottlenose dolphins in the sound that one year, did everyone remember? They were out of territory and all of them died and no one knew why. "Now, we don't want that happening to Nera," he declared.

That'd definitely ruin the seal festival, Jenn thought, unless they wanted to do the taxidermy thing on the seal and carry her through the village like some saint in a big glass coffin. Jenn worked her way over to Annie Taylor, who was squinting at the picture of Nera as if trying to see the seal more clearly. She said, "Any idea of her age?"

Several heads swiveled in Annie's direction. She was a stranger, and it was odd for a stranger to turn up at one of the seal spotters' meetings. Jenn thought about introducing Annie to the people but she didn't have to, for Annie introduced herself.

She told them she was a marine biologist, and if there was something she could do to help . . . ?

Ivar's face lit up at that one. He picked two brochures from a nearby table and passed them over to her. "You might be the answer we need," he told her. "Let's talk after the meeting and see 'f that's the case."

The meeting ended with commitments made on the part of the seal spotters. Now that Nera was in the area and a photo proved it, there had to be regular watchers along her route, which followed the west side of the island. They needed daily reports at specific times. They needed to know where the seal was sighted, what time she was sighted, what she appeared to be doing, how long she lingered wherever she showed up. Anything unusual needed to be reported, Ivar told them. Use the Web site.

What*ever*, Jenn thought. She was starving to death. Village Pizza was over on First Street, and she was ready for a large one with sausage, olives, and mushrooms. But when the meeting broke up, Annie approached Ivar.

She got all over the topic of Nera's early arrival, telling Ivar that if the seal was sick, there was only one way to help her. She'd need medication, and a wildlife specialist had to be brought in to deal with this. An evaluation of her health could be made and while they had her in captivity, it would be an excellent opportunity to take a sample of her DNA.

Ivar Thorndyke reared up at that one. Jenn had been drifting away but his roar of "No one's touching that seal!" not only got her attention but also rendered Annie mute for ten seconds. Finally, she managed a "No one would take her from the island.

I'm talking about an enclosure where she'd be safe until her health—"

"No way," Ivar said. "I won't have *anyone* trying to catch that seal."

"Geez, it's not like you own her," Jenn muttered.

Annie said, "Catching her isn't what would happen. Look, there has to be a reason she's here early. I hate to say it, but there also has to be a reason that she looks the way she looks."

"What the hell's that supposed to mean?" Ivar demanded, like a man whose child has been insulted. "She looks the way she's always looked." He gestured at the white board where the picture of Nera out in the water had been displayed. "You can't tell from a picture that she looks any different. *And* have you ever seen her before?"

"I'm not referring to how she looked last year versus this year. I'm talking about how she looks in the first place: black, every inch of her. There has to be a reason. The seal could be a victim of—"

"That seal's a victim of nothing," Ivar declared. "And she's not about to become a victim by getting herself caught and tested for anything."

"Well, gosh," Annie said. "She's not exactly your property, Mr. Thorndyke. And from this meeting you've just had, it seems to me that people would like to keep her alive."

"You stay away from the seal," Ivar snapped.

Annie's face asked the questions that were on Jenn's mind. "Why?" was one of them. "What's that seal to you?" was the other.

PART TWO

Saratoga Woods

Cilla's World

Days and nights have passed. What I did at first was the only thing I knew, which was to follow the turns of the climbing road to depart the place where the mommy and the daddy had left me. I looked for them. I looked for the silver gray of their car. But when I reached the top of the climbing road, there was no one around. So I began to walk.

I walk to the south. For me there is only light and dark. In light, I wander along the roadways that I come to, turning right or left as the feeling suggests. I walk along the top of bluffs. I walk next to fields. I walk deep into forests. This is what I do in the light. In the dark I sleep. I try to find a safe place to lie hidden from sight, and I try to stay warm.

Cars whiz by me when I walk on the roadside. In the rain or the snow, they slow and someone within them rolls a window down and calls out, "Hey! You need a ride?" But I have no words, and I do not answer. Need, I think. What is need?

I feel hollow with hunger and this hunger has taken me to the backs of isolated houses, where cans hold garbage. In the one town I've come to, it has taken me to containers behind buildings where the scent of food tells me meals are being cooked and served. But after that town, there have been no others, so I have just walked.

The nights are long. The days are cold and brief. Frost powders the fence posts when I come upon them. It forms a skin on the leaves of bushes and on the fronds of spear ferns in the forest. It hardens the ground.

I move merely from one object to the next. I seek nothing in the distance beyond what I can reach. I have always lived this way in the world and I understand that it's how I must live now.

I'm caught in a tide that's sweeping me somewhere. I let it take me.

TEN

Of all things, it was a project for their Western Civilization class that more or less brought a complete end to Becca and Derric. When she thought about it later, Becca couldn't believe something so totally meaningless in the scheme of her life would have had the power to kick them to the curb.

Step one had been their teacher Mr. Keith making the assignment: You'll be doing it in pairs, it'll be oral and written, and I *don't* want to see or hear a damn thing off the Internet, all right? It's due in six weeks. I'll be checking, and you can trust me on that.

Step two had been pairing off: Naturally, everyone wanted Squat Cooper for a partner because no one anywhere matched him in brain power. Jenn McDaniels yelled "Kindergarten and milk!" for some bizarre reason, to which Squat replied, "Told you. Scored," and indicated they'd be coupled for the work.

Step three had been everyone else scrambling to find someone worthy to work with. During that step, Becca should have asked Derric and would have asked Derric and *wanted* to ask Derric, but she heard *him* asking EmilyJoy Hall to partner up, and that was that.

Step four was ending up with Tod Schuman as a partner, because within thirty seconds, he was the only person left. That fact, along with his nickname Extra Underpants Schuman, should have told her *something* was off about him, but even if it had, she didn't have a choice. She had to have a partner; the only partner was Tod.

"Library at lunch," he told her as they left the class. "Easy A. We got it made 's long as *your* part's rad. My part? A-plus. No big deal."

But his whispers weren't as confident as his words and they revealed a plan that didn't soothe Becca's worries. *Keith . . . stupid dickhead . . . internet because how would he ever . . .* pretty much made him an open book. So did *get her to do that part 'cause no way . . .* that accompanied his phony smile.

She met him in the library as requested. There was no librarian, just a volunteer mom from the PTA who sat on a stool behind the checkout station and watched them suspiciously when they dropped onto chairs at one of the tables. She said to them, "No make-out sessions, you two."

Tod said, "As if," and gagged himself to illustrate his point in case the PTA mom didn't get it. His additional thought of *Rather kiss . . . cow pattie for a butt* made Becca want either to slug him or to ask why he assumed *he* was such a prize. But she ignored the whisper and took out her notebook. Maybe, she figured, they could divide the work up so she'd never have to see him until the day of their presentation to the class.

Unfortunately, Tod had a Big Plan. He was blazin' on it, as he put it. The assignment was to create alternatives to conquest that could have easily resulted in ancient cultures being preserved instead of destroyed by their European conquerors. Students could choose among existing European countries as the conquerors, but the primitive culture and its preserved traditions were to be their own creations.

No one would think of using Switzerland as the European conqueror, Tod announced happily, like a man expecting Very Big Applause for his Incredible Moment of Complete Genius. So they'd start with the Swiss people, get it? The Swiss guys would build a whole bunch of ships and sail off in 1500 or whatever to conquer the world. They'd come to a tribe in Polynesia, he said, or maybe Patagonia or even Antarctica, which would be so *excellent*—

"I don't think so," Becca said.

Tod stared at her. "Like . . . why the hell not?" *Dumbshit skank.*

Her eyes narrowed and she clenched her jaw for a moment to control her temper. "Because Switzerland is landlocked," she explained. "They don't even have a port, so why would they be building ships? Are they supposed to've carted them over the Alps or something?"

Tod threw himself back in his chair, his face transformed to an expression of disgust. "Why d'you happen to think you're so hot?" he asked her. "Because lemme tell you, you ain't."

"Huh? What's that have to do with anything?"

"You got a better idea? Let's hear it, smart hole." *As if.*

"I'm only saying . . . Look, we want a decent grade, right? Well, we're not going to get one if we start out with something that's completely impossible in the first place."

"Who says it's impossible?" he demanded. *Stupid . . . thinks she's so hot and . . . all the time uglier than a flattened toad* constituted what he really wanted to say.

Becca found her earphone finally and smashed it into her ear. Otherwise, she figured she'd be smashing something else. "I'm only saying it probably needs to be realistic, Tod. There're lots of countries with seaports and all we need to do is find one."

"Switzerland has lakes, dummy."

"And this is important why?"

"*Duh?* 'Cause they have *boats* on lakes?"

"So what're those boats gonna do? Sail out on the lake to the other side so one part of Switzerland can conquer another? Come *on*. I want us to get a good grade."

"Like I'm not gonna get us a good grade? Listen, cow pattie—"

"Hey!"

"Yeah, that's what they eat. Hay. Har har har." He shoved his chair back. "You come up with a better idea, you let me know. Meantime, I'm outa here. One of us has work to do on our project and you better start being glad I was willing to partner up with you."

She stared at him. She opened her mouth to speak, but there was nothing she could come up with to say other than to point out to him nastily that a boy who can't even spell his own first name isn't exactly prize material. He said, "Yeah, right," like someone with every answer on the test. Then he swung away from her and out of the library.

THINGS GOT WORSE at once. Derric Mathieson and
EmilyJoy Hall walked in. EmilyJoy was chatting enthusiastically.
Derric was listening with a half-smile on his face. This half-smile
went to no-smile when he saw Becca.

Becca refused to turn her head away. He was angry with her?
He didn't want to talk about why he was angry? He wanted to
make her squirm? He wanted to make her jealous? Fine, she
decided. Go ahead and try. She gazed at him until *he* was the
one to drop his eyes. He and EmilyJoy sat three tables away, close
enough to be seen in an earnest conversation that Derric kept up
with the other girl. They chatted and laughed and opened notebooks. They each began to make some sort of list that, in two
minutes, they compared.

"No way!" she heard him say. "I can't believe that!"

"Great minds thinking alike," EmilyJoy enthused.

"We are on the same wavelength for sure," he told her.

This was all Becca could stand. She went over to their table.
EmilyJoy looked up, her bright face a smile. Becca said hi to her
and then spoke to Derric, "C'n I talk to you for a minute?"

"We're sort of working here, Becca," EmilyJoy said.

"This is important," Becca told her. "It won't take long."

Derric said to her, "What?"

Becca said, "Private," and she walked to the stacks, only hoping he'd follow.

He did. She eased the earphone from her ear. She almost
never did this with Derric, generally giving him the privacy of
his thoughts. But things had gotten to a point where she *didn't*

understand him and she *needed* to know him, and she had to get to understanding and knowledge before it was too late.

No way . . . wish she . . . trust is what but no way does she . . . came from him, the same sort of broken thoughts she picked up from others. She muttered to herself in sheer frustration. *When*, she asked herself, and *how* would she get to the point of the whispers becoming clear enough to do her some good?

When Derric joined her in the stacks, he crossed his arms. He stood near enough that she caught the scent of him, that nearly nonexistent fragrance of cooking fruit that rose, she knew, not from his body but from the memories he tried to keep at bay. *Doesn't get it . . . equal is what . . . can't happen . . . face it . . .* were on his mind.

She said, "We could've been working together on this. We could've been getting a good grade."

"I'm going to get a good grade," he told her.

"You know what I mean."

"Nope. I don't."

She'd never seen his eyes so flat. *Never understand . . . never want to either* told her what he felt was more than anger. Hurt, jealousy, bitterness, sorrow? What was going on with him?

She said, "I don't want to fight with you."

"We're not fighting," he said evenly. "We were, at one point. But we're not now."

"What are we, then? Why're you *doing* this?"

"I'm not doing a thing. Neither are you. That's sort of the point."

He looked away from her, back to the table where EmilyJoy was quietly writing in her notebook.

"What's *that* supposed to mean?"

"Whatever you want it to, Becca."

Her throat was tight because his words were as final as the *over* that comprised the only whisper she could hear. She said past lips that were suddenly dry, "But we're special. The you-and-me of us. We're special."

He turned his gaze back to her, and she read it in his eyes before he said a word. "We were," he said. "We had something good, but it's gone. I don't know if that's how it is for you, but that's how it is for me."

"*Why?*" she asked, and she could hear the desperation in her voice.

"We went as far as we could," he said.

"This is about *sex*?" she asked incredulously.

He cocked his head, his expression altering. It hovered between surprise and disgust as *completely and totally out of it* floated in the air between them. He muttered a curse and said, "Don't play me, Becca. You know exactly what this is about."

"You're ending things, aren't you?" she demanded. "Because I won't tell you where I'm staying. It's like . . . It's like you're threatening me. No, you're not *threatening*. You're actually *doing*. I wouldn't tell you. I'm still not telling. So you're walking away. Like where I'm staying is even *important*. I thought who I *am* is what's important, not the information you want and can't get from me."

He shook his head. "Information, Becca, is the symbol, okay? It's the . . . it's the symptom. The disease, though? It's something else."

She felt the bite of tears, but she *refused* to let him see her cry. She said, "What*ever*," and she pushed past him.

There was nothing left but to get away. *Why can't you* followed on the air behind her, but like all the other whispers, it was incomplete, just like her.

ELEVEN

In very short order, Becca got to see the Derric Transformation, and she had to ask herself how well she'd ever really known him. She'd thought he was different from the typical high school boy. Africa, she'd thought, had *made* him different. She'd thought he'd been molded by losing both of his parents by the time he was five years old, by having lived in a cardboard box in an alley in Kampala, Uganda, till he was picked up by a children's charity. She'd thought all of this made him see the world differently. But that didn't turn out to be the case.

Courtney Baker was every girl's nightmare. She was also the living embodiment of what—and whom—every boy wanted: blonde hair, blue eyes, satin skin that didn't need makeup, great body, pretty hands with nice oval fingernails, excellent legs. She was one of those girls who were friendly to everyone, a Homecoming Queen in waiting, Becca thought sardonically. But the worst thing about her was that not a single one of her characteristics seemed phony. That alone allowed Becca to know absolutely what the future held the first time she saw Derric and Courtney talking together after school.

Other kids might have thought, No way does Mathieson have a chance with her! because Courtney was in eleventh grade and Derric was not. But their ages matched, and even if they hadn't, it was pretty clear that what mattered to them both was some sort of connection they felt. They talked eagerly. They laughed together. Courtney gave Derric a little shove on the arm at some remark he made. He beamed at her and grabbed up her backpack to carry. He jerked his head in a "let's go" movement, and when they moved off, they walked in sync, Courtney altering her pace to match his.

South Whidbey High School being South Whidbey High School—which was to say that everyone knew everyone along with everyone's business—what went out was the Word. The Word, or perhaps better said the *Words*, were "hooked up," and they applied to Derric and Courtney. Someone had seen them together at the Clyde, someone else had seen them at Village Pizza. They'd taken an electric boat out onto Goss Lake despite the cold, and when the motor went dead, they'd had to wait for rescue but they'd laughed their heads off at how dumb they'd been. They'd been in South Whidbey Commons, hunched over the table and drinking whatever. They'd been over town to Alderwood Mall. Becca had no clue how they managed to spend so much time together, considering that they were both also "A" students, but somehow they were managing it.

So, okay, she and Derric were over. It hurt as badly as anything ever would. But Becca found that the strange part for her was what hurt worse than being ignored by Derric and seeing him with Courtney. What hurt worse was seeing him change. It was like he'd given up part of himself. He removed the small Ugandan flag from the inside of his locker door, he took down a picture he had of the street band he'd played in while at the Kampala orphanage, he didn't attend a concert of Zimbabwean musicians at the local art center that at one time he would not have missed, and worst of all, he stopped shaving his head. That smooth dark scalp of his had been his cultural trademark, the way he told the world who he truly was. But once he began dating Courtney Baker, he let his hair start to grow. And this saddened Becca more than anything else.

He was putting Africa behind him. While this might have been understandable under some circumstances for a boy who'd been adopted into an American family, for Derric to do it meant something more than moving on. It also meant leaving someone behind.

That person wasn't Becca King. That person was Derric's sister Rejoice, abandoned by him in the Kampala orphanage when he was adopted by the Mathiesons, with no one the wiser—aside from Becca—that Rejoice had been his sister at all. This was the secret that Becca held, the one thing that she knew about Derric that he wished no one on earth to be privy to. It was the secret that had unbalanced their relationship and had caused it to falter. She knew his secret; he did not know hers.

But hers, she thought, had nothing to do with who she was at the heart of her. While Derric's secret did. And to see him reject Africa in favor of *whatever* it was . . . She couldn't stand watching it. Intuitively, she knew it was wrong. Intuitively, she also knew she had to stop him.

BECCA HADN'T BEEN to Saratoga Woods in ages. When she'd lived in Langley at the Cliff Motel with Debbie Grieder and her grandkids, it had been simple enough to get there. Even after she'd become expert at using her bike's twenty-seven gears, it wasn't exactly an easy ride to the place, considering that the route was continuously hilly, generally windy, and universally narrow. But it was a direct one, and the woods were only a few miles from the center of town.

Now that she was living some distance from the village, though, she had to rely on the free island bus to take her to the woods. No matter how she went at it, this meant two bus rides and a long wait in the bitter cold, but she was determined that nothing was going to put her off from what she had to do.

She went out to the woods on a gray winter day in late February, when the water of Saratoga Passage exactly matched the dismal color of the sky. She had to hike a bit once the bus dropped her off, so she made her way along the rutted roadside where the ground was frozen and the puddles wore silver skins of ice. Soon enough she reached the woods, looming darkly across a meadow where dead grasses lay beaten down by the weather and openings among the thick fir trees indicated trailheads leading into the shadowy forest.

She made her way to the far southwest side of the meadow.

There a path climbed steeply into the trees. The ground was slippery, and she took care. If she fell on this trail, it wouldn't be anything like the day when Derric had fallen here in the autumn. Then she'd come upon him as she'd chased Seth's dog. Today there was no one around to find her if she tumbled down the bluff.

High on the trail, she reached the spot where Derric had taken his fall and broken his leg so badly. She gave it a glance only. She wasn't here on a pilgrimage to the spot where he'd entered into a prolonged coma. She was here on another mission, and her destination was immediately opposite, up a narrow ill-defined sketch of a path that Derric himself had made through the trees.

It was a trail that no one would even notice, easily overlooked if you didn't know that it was there. It led up a hillside to where some fallen branches and the trunk of an old-growth hemlock formed a low teepee. This looked insubstantial but it was actually sturdy, having been built over time by storm and wind. Becca took a breath, grabbed onto an alder's trunk, and began to climb upward.

When she reached the teepee, she crawled inside. She worked her way to its farthest reaches. There, carefully wrapped in several old plastic shopping bags and even more carefully tucked away, she found the package where she'd first discovered it. It had been in this spot for ages. Impeded by the cast on his leg, Derric hadn't touched it since October.

Well, Becca thought as she removed it, he would touch it now. Touching it, he would see the difference between the Derric

Mathieson he actually was and the Derric Mathieson he was trying to be. This wasn't about Courtney Baker, Becca assured herself. This was about Derric being true to himself. If nothing else, he needed to do that.

Becca put the package into her backpack. Quickly she got herself down from the teepee and out of the forest. Daylight was fading as she began her walk back into Langley. It was several miles, but the day was growing late and she couldn't risk waiting for a bus to come along.

SHE REACHED LANGLEY sooner than she thought she would, for as she trudged along the road, an elderly woman with a purple streak through her hair pulled over and offered her a lift into town. Chilled to the bone, she was happy to hop inside and be assaulted by two mini-dachshunds, ABBA's greatest hits, and a heater running full blast. Five minutes later, she was in front of the Langley Clinic where, she knew, Derric generally waited for his mom to finish her workday.

He was alone in the waiting room. His head was bent over an open notebook, and he was referring to a text and then writing something. He looked up as the door opened. His eyes locked with Becca's for a second before he looked away and continued writing.

Becca didn't pause to take a reading from his whispers. She'd removed the AUD box earphone on her way out to the woods, and she'd not returned it to her ear, but she didn't wait to gauge what his reception of her might be. She figured she could easily lose her nerve if she did that. Instead she strode across the room and sat right next to him.

He started to move. She put her hand on his arm. He said, "Hey, what're you . . ." but that was all because at that point, she opened her backpack and in one second she had the package out and he knew as well as he knew his own name what was inside of it.

Then she heard it tumbling from him: *No way . . . she'll . . . couldn't . . . now there's going to be . . . damn damn damn . . . this is what . . . oh great . . . when it comes to trust . . .* came at her, and she could have finished the broken thoughts easily because she knew they referred to what she held in her lap. Inside the package were dozens of letters, all of them written by Derric to Rejoice. She'd been five years old when he'd left her behind. Less than three when she'd been orphaned, she hadn't even known that he was her brother.

Derric said in a whisper so fierce that it felt like a slap, "What're you *doing* with those? What the *hell* do you think . . . No way do you even have the right—"

"This is who you are," she said to him. "It's who you're running from. And that gives me the right."

"You don't know what you're talking about. What d'you expect's about to happen? I fall on my knees and declare my love and beg forgiveness and—"

"This isn't about us," she hissed. "There isn't an us and you've made sure I know it. Okay. I get it. End of story. We're over. But *this* . . . what I'm holding right here? This is about you and this is about your sister."

"Shut up! Shut *up!*"

"I won't shut up. You've hidden Rejoice for the last eight years and now you're hiding yourself. D'you think I can't see that?"

"I said shut up!"

"You've taken down flags, you've taken down pictures, you're growing your hair and everyone thinks Oh look, he's becoming *American* while all the time what's really going on is—"

"Get out of here!" He grabbed the letters from her.

"You can't keep hiding—"

"What the *hell*?" He shoved the package into his backpack. His expression was as hard as Becca had ever seen. He whispered fiercely, "You think you c'n talk to me about hiding anything from anyone? That's really messed up. That's frigging *unbelievable* is what it is. I'm not the person hiding anything but a bunch of letters. While you—"

"That's what you think? This is just a bunch of letters? Please. Don't even try to go there. You're hiding your own sister. You're pretending Rejoice doesn't exist, so you're hiding the truth. You think if you turn yourself into some one hundred percent *American* dude with a cute blonde girlfriend and—"

"*That's* what this is about! I'm with Courtney and you—"

"Oh please. Give me more credit than that. This is about you. It's about Kampala. It's about who you left behind and what you can't face anyone knowing."

"Shut up, shut up, get away from me, shut up!"

Becca knew that the ferocity of his tone came from the fact that he was terrified someone might overhear them. His horror was the same as most people's fear: that admitting to something dark about themselves might lead to being scorned by others. But what he didn't see was that where he was *heading* with this new Derric of his led to scorn, while where he had *been* before his transformation led only to the truth about what it had meant to be alone and afraid and only five years old on the streets of Kampala.

"Okay," she said. "I'm shutting up. You can do whatever you want. You're a free agent. Have at it. Whatever. But maybe with all the *doing* you're engaged in, you'll eventually decide to *do* the right thing."

"Which is what, according to the Book of Becca?" he demanded.

"Which is tell the truth."

He threw the backpack to the floor. He did the same with his notebook and the text he'd been reading. "You are *really* an amazing hypocrite," he told her. "Try thinking about *that* with all the other thinking you've been doing."

Becca started to reply, but that was the precise moment when someone called her name. She turned to see Derric's mom, Rhonda, with a chart in her hand, smiling at her from the hall-way where the examining rooms were.

"We've missed seeing you!" she cried happily. "Where on earth have you been hiding?"

Derric looked at Becca and raised an eyebrow. His expression said, So here's your chance. Gonna tell the *truth*? I don't think so.

Of course, he was right.

TWELVE

Derric wasn't surprised when Becca got out of the Langley Clinic as fast as she could. The last thing she wanted to talk to *him* about was where she was hiding out, so there was no way she was going to have a conversation with his mom about it. He almost wanted to laugh at how fast she beat her retreat when Rhonda asked her question. Course, his mom hadn't meant *hiding* as in really hiding. But the fact that she didn't know how close she was to the truth of what was up with Becca was part of what made her question so funny.

He had to come up with an explanation for Becca's showing up at the clinic, though. There was no way Rhonda was going to let that dog doze. Since she had one last patient to see, he had time to cook something up. So when she let loose with her typical grilling, he was ready for her.

Becca had stopped by to ask him a question about a project they were working on in their Western Civ class, he explained to his mom. She'd been given Extra Underpants Schuman for a partner.

"Oh dear," was Rhonda's reply. She knew Tod Schuman.

Everyone knew him. Everyone also knew why he had the nickname. "That's not going to be easy for her. You didn't want to. . . ?"

"We were assigned," he lied.

When they arrived home, he went straight to his bedroom. His dad wasn't back from work yet, and his mom went directly to the kitchen to start dinner. He had a few minutes, then, when he was off her radar. He intended to use that time to find a place to hide the letters to his sister.

His preference would have been in the basement, squirreled away among his childhood stuff. But the route to the basement was through the kitchen, and he couldn't risk his mom asking why he was heading down there. Besides, she'd also make a big deal about him trying to go down the old wooden stairs with a cast on his leg. It would be "Let me do that for you, sweetie. I don't want you to fall. What d'you want down there? I'll get it in a flash," and that was the last thing he needed.

In his room, though, there weren't a lot of options. Closet? Possibly. Drawers? No way. His mom was always putting clean clothes in the dresser. Under the bed? Maybe not because of the vacuum. In the ancient beanbag chair? Well . . . It was so old it had been repaired three times, and the last repair involved about four feet of duct tape. Beneath this patch, the chair had split along its seams, and his mom was after him to throw the thing out.

But he liked to lounge there with his headphones on and his music cranked. It was his *space*, he told his mother. It was ugly but comfortable and he *liked* it, he told her. So, to respect him, she never touched it.

In short, it was perfect for hiding the letters. He peeled back the duct tape. Then he quickly removed the letters from his backpack. They were stored in an old Star Wars lunch box that Derric had found in the basement years ago. It had belonged to Dave Mathieson's older son and had languished forever up on a shelf along with Little League mitts, baseball bats, cleats, and dusty athletic trophies. He'd scored it in order to protect the letters from the elements so that he could hide them in the woods. Once he had them in the beanbag chair, though, the question was what to do with the lunch box.

He was considering this when his cell phone alerted him to a text. The text was from Courtney: *Pick u up7? xxx* What the hell . . . ? he wondered. Did they have a date and he'd forgotten? That would be radically uncool. Becca showing up with his letters to Rejoice had thrown him, sure. But he didn't think he'd been thrown enough to forget a date with Courtney.

He sorted through his mind for what was up before he replied since he didn't want to come off like a dolt. School night so it couldn't be a date as in a date. Were they supposed to be studying together? Could be, for sure. What else was there? Basketball game? Not right now. Club meeting? They weren't in any club together. But the idea of clubs jogged his memory. It wasn't a club, it was Courtney's Bible study group. She'd been after him from their first date to give her prayer group and her Bible study group a try. She did Bible study once a week, and three times now she'd asked him to join her. He'd given her an excuse each time, avoiding the moment when he was going to have to tell her directly that he wasn't a Bible kind of person. For she was a Bible kind of person, and Bible-reading, prayer-circling, and church-going were the only subjects on which they didn't see eye to eye.

He texted her back. *2 much 2 do. Math sucks. Nx time? Xxxxxxx*

It took nearly ten minutes for her to reply. Her *oK* spoke volumes. She wasn't happy.

He texted her again. *Sorry. Miss u big time, babe.*

Another wait, but only two minutes this time. *M2. Cuz after the meeting . . . ;).*

He knew what that meant: After Bible study they'd stop somewhere. They'd park in one of the thousand and one places on the south end of the island where you could hide in the darkness with no one the wiser that you were even there. No matter the cold outside of the car, they'd warm each other soon enough.

She was tempting him. Just thinking about doing anything with Courtney got him going. But the Bible part of it . . . ? Could he really sit there and talk about the Bible while all along knowing that afterward he and Courtney were going to get it on with each other? He *supposed* he could. But if that was the case, why didn't he jump at the opportunity she was giving him? He wanted to, didn't he? He wanted to be in the dark with her, right? She let him do some things, but not others. He touched here but not there. He kissed this but not that. Her legs were smooth and her stomach was tight and her breasts were soft and *why* the hell didn't he just do what anyone else in his position would do? Read the Bible, go to the prayer circle, get on his knees and pretend to ask Jesus-God-Buddha-Whoever for world peace or whatever it was that the prayer circle prayed for because then Courtney would maybe in the darkness in the back of her car . . . She *would*, wouldn't she? Or would she?

Derric groaned. He dropped down onto his bed and he shoved the Star Wars lunch box beneath it. Courtney Baker had him turned every which way and she kept him turned every which way until the only thing he could think of was the hot pressure building between his legs.

He sputtered out a weak laugh at himself. At *least* Courtney managed to keep him from thinking about Becca King. He owed her that. She was one hell of a diversion.

He rolled onto his side and reached for his cell phone. *Naked* he texted her.

!!! was her reply.

??? was his next text.

In a moment she sent a picture instead of words. A total nipple shot. She was out of her mind. He unzipped, lowered his jeans and jockeys, took a picture . . . but then he didn't send it. Instead, he texted, *luv u crazy got 2 go*. Then he deleted the shot he'd taken and he spent a few minutes staring at the one she'd sent.

It was like she was more than one person. She was the Courtney everyone saw in school: the Bible study Courtney, the prayer-circle Courtney, the friendly bubbly Courtney with a smile on her face and a happy greeting for everyone she knew.

But she was also the Courtney who knew of an overgrown driveway on Surface Road that led into the woods to an abandoned
house and who parked her car there and turned to him and said,
"You are the hottest guy at school," and when he kissed her, she
kissed him back. And when he touched her, she touched him
back. And she slid her hands across his bare chest and teased the
flesh at the top of his jeans.

She'd said to him at the very first before they'd done anything,
"Are you and Becca King over? I'm asking 'cause no way do I
invade some other girl's turf, but *if* you're over, I'd like a chance."

Stupidly, he'd said, "A chance for what?"

She'd smiled and said, "A chance with *you.*"

He'd opened his mouth to reply, but nothing had come out.
Courtney Baker? A chance? Him? All he could manage was
"Why?"

"Because you're special and you totally don't know it. I'd sort
of like to kiss you, if that's okay."

Had it been okay? He didn't remember. She wasn't like anyone
he'd ever known.

So, dude, why not *go* tonight? he asked himself. Spend an hour
reading the Old Testament or whatever, and then . . . then . . .
What the hell was he avoiding? When the hell had he become
so lame?

That was the question of the hour, he thought sourly. He had a
feeling the answer was that insufferable know-it-all called Becca
King.

THIRTEEN

It didn't take long for Becca to figure out that handing over those letters to Derric had been a very dumb idea. If she'd thought she was going to remind him of his roots in Uganda—of who he really was, she'd told herself—she'd been wildly wrong. She did accomplish something, though. Where before he'd been coolly polite to her, now she didn't exist for him.

The fact that she was condemned to working with Extra Underpants Schuman on a critical project in her Western Civ class made everything worse. She could at *least* have had an A to look forward to in her life. But with Extra Underpants hanging around her neck like a dead German shepherd, there was no possibility of anything other than a C. And *that*, only if she was lucky. And *that*, only if she could talk him into being something more than a certified idiot.

When he showed her his completed part of their report, her spirits tanked. She eased the AUD box earphone from her ear in the hope she might pick up from his whispers some reason why he was such a dope. *She'd better because no one . . . only way . . . talk her into it because if I . . .* only told her that he expected her to buy the garbage he was putting together. It was all from Wikipedia and Askme.com, she saw: a jumble of information that he'd scored about a tribe in the Amazon, First Nations in Canada, and the Maoris in New Zealand. He'd applied it every which way to their assignment. When she read it, she wanted to put her fist through his head.

She said, "We're supposed to be creating our *own* primitive culture, Tod. I guess we can start with this and throw some ideas back and forth, but—"

Tod grabbed the papers. "Hey, I worked my butt off on that," he declared. *Don't make me . . . if I . . . you'll be way sorry, toadbutt . . .*

As if, she thought. But what she said was, "It looks like cut and paste from the Net. You're not even putting it into your own words."

"So?"

"So Mr. Keith *said*—"

"Keith's a buttwipe." *Find out why as soon as . . .*

"—he's going to be checking the Internet. So if we use this . . . Look, it's not that hard. We c'n do it together if you want instead of dividing the work up. I mean, I c'n help with the primitive culture and you c'n help with the European one."

"You took the easier part of the assignment anyway," he sneered. "If I'd'a known you'd do that, I would've chose another partner."

Chosen, she thought. He couldn't even speak correct English. She said, "So we'll trade, then."

"No way! I already worked on this." *The other part . . . not fair . . . this is the only way . . . stupid . . . the rest of them already . . .* He snatched up the papers. "All *right*, I'll fix the stupid thing," he hissed. "Geez. I *knew* I should have picked someone else."

"It has to be original," she reminded him.

"Just shut your fat mouth," was his reply.

So things weren't good. And when she next saw his paperwork, things weren't better. It *looked* different but ninety minutes on the Internet at South Whidbey Commons were enough to prove that all he'd done was retype the original, mix it up a bit, and add adjectives and adverbs liberally.

She sighed, gave it up, and Googled *Jeff Corrie.* He'd lawyered up, she saw. Connor's vacant condo had finally been searched, dusted for fingerprints, examined for signs of violence, the whole nine yards. So had Jeff's house. So had his car. The police thought Jeff had information, but Jeff wasn't talking. He also wasn't leaving San Diego. She was still safe.

Under other circumstances that would have made her feel marginally better. But with Derric's anger hanging over her head and Extra Underpants Schuman's incompetence driving her nuts, it didn't do a lot to lift her spirits to know her stepfather wasn't coming after her, at least for now.

She left South Whidbey Commons and trudged in the direction of the bus stop. She hadn't made it there when a pickup truck pulled over to the curb, a window lowered, and Diana Kinsale leaned over the passenger seat. She gave Becca one of her long, knowing looks. She said, "Get in, my dear," and she spoke with such compassion that Becca did as she asked without question.

"Blue?" Diana said to her. For once, she was driving alone, without the dogs who were her regular companions.

"Bummed." Becca found she didn't want to go into it, though. Diana was a friend, but to unspool the story of Derric's letters, of Courtney Baker, of Extra Underpants Schuman . . . The very thought of doing that made her just want to take a nap instead.

Diana said, "I bet what you need is a pick-me-up."

"I sure as heck need something."

She thought Diana meant a latte from one of the several coffeehouses in town. But instead of pulling into a parking space, Diana drove them out of the village and onto the highway.

THEY ENDED UP on the other side of the island, northwest of Langley, on a patch of farmland that overlooked a huge scythe-shaped body of water called Useless Bay. There, Diana drove under an old wooden arch spanning a gravel driveway. HEART'S DESIRE had been carved into this arch so long ago that lichen filled in most of the letters.

The lane they were on curved around a long, enormous unpainted chicken coop and ended between a huge red barn and a yellow farmhouse with a porch wrapping all the way around it. The house stood on a rise of land in the middle of a lawn. It overlooked the bay and, in the distance, a sprinkling of cottages along the shore.

The pick-me-up was inside the house, and she was called

Sharla Mann. She operated a single-chair beauty salon in her mudroom, a stick-thin woman with two round spots of bright pink blusher on her cheeks and worn-down Uggs, fleece pants, and two hooded sweatshirts on her body. She looked like someone without an ounce of joy inside her, Becca thought, and the only whispers she could catch from Sharla were *know what he wants but I,* which didn't tell her a thing about the woman.

Sharla had been in the process of sweeping the floor of hair clippings. She took one look at Becca and said, "Girl, who the hell did that to your hair? People've gone to prison for less. Sit down and lemme take a look at you."

Becca knew instantly, then, what Diana's pick-me-up was destined to be. But the problem was her hair was *supposed* to stay ugly. The rest of her was supposed to stay ugly as well, from her phony glasses with their out-of-fashion frames to her overly made-up face to her ill-fitting clothes to her dirty tennis shoes with their broken laces. For her altered appearance was crucial to her mom's plan for their escape from Jeff Corrie, and it had saved her once. It was intended to save her again.

Diana put a hand on her shoulder. She gazed directly into Becca's eyes. "It will be a good thing, you'll see," she said. "All things pass."

There was that lifting she always felt at Diana's touch. It compelled Becca to say, "Okay."

"Can you take Becca back to her original color?" Diana asked Sharla. "It's grown out a bit. Can you match it?"

"I c'n come close," Sharla told her. "But only if she swears not to mess with it again. You ready to swear, Miss Becca?"

"I guess," Becca said. But what she wondered was how she was ever going to pay for what Sharla Mann was about to do.

IN THE WORLD of fantasy, Becca would have emerged from Sharla's ministrations like the ugly duckling grown up into the swan. That didn't happen. But Sharla did work enough magic on her that her former hair color of blonde-streaked light brown was back in place and the cut of her hair made it cup her head and allowed it to fall airily around her face.

"Now that's a haircut," Sharla said as she stepped back from it. "A trim every six weeks will keep it nice."

Becca had no idea how to pay for this haircut, not to mention the dye job. The thought of coming up with the money to keep the style in shape every six weeks . . . No way. Before she could bring this up, though, Sharla turned to Diana and said, "You next, lady. You want the regular?"

"Shorter I think," Diana said. She ran her hands through her hair, which was short and choppy and salt-and-pepper colored, and it came to Becca that this look was intentional whereas she'd always thought Diana chopped it off herself.

"You sure?" Sharla was saying to her as Diana climbed in the chair. "But not too short, huh?"

Sharla and Diana exchanged a look in the mirror and it seemed to Becca that they were saying something to each other that she didn't understand. Diana's reply was, "We'll go supershort later."

"That's what I like to hear," Sharla said.

Diana glanced at Becca and said she ought to have a look around Heart's Desire because the views were wonderful. Becca said okay, but felt reluctant. Something was going on beneath the placid surface of Diana's exterior. She wanted to know what it was, but she had a feeling that now wasn't the time she was going to learn it.

She went outside.

DUSK HAD FALLEN. She saw that while she'd been inside the house, someone else had arrived at Heart's Desire, for a large, white open-bed truck was parked next to the enormous chicken coop and lights from within the building cast a glow on the ground from a partially opened door.

On the truck's door, Becca saw that THORNDYKE LAWN, MAINTENANCE, AND HONEY-DO were painted to form a medallion. When she looked past purpose-built storage cabinets to the bed of the vehicle, she saw a jumble of all sorts of equipment.

A man's voice said, "Who might you be?"

She turned to see that a tall older guy was watching her as he polished very thick and very unfashionable glasses on the tail of his flannel shirt. Becca recognized him. She'd seen him conducting the seal meeting inside South Whidbey Commons on the night she'd scored a ride home from Seth. Like then, he wore a baseball cap over lots of hair that sprouted from beneath it like straw from a scarecrow.

"What's 'honey-do' mean?" she asked him.

He looked from her to the door of his truck. "'Honey do this, honey do that.' I'm the honey that gets called to do it. It's my business. Ivar Thorndyke: lawn man, garden man, handyman." He put his glasses back on. "That's my answer. What's yours?"

"To what?"

"To who the hell you are and what the hell you're doing peering into my truck."

"Sharla cut my hair. She colored it, too." Which, of course, brought to her mind the subject of money. She said impulsively to Ivar, "D'you need an assistant? I'm good at all kinds of stuff and I need a job."

Ivar put his baseball cap back on and examined her. She caught *pretty little thing . . . could be . . . wrong to be here now* coming from him, none of which Becca could interpret very well. He said, "Assistant, huh? What kinda work you do?"

"Anything," she said. "And I'm excellent at learning stuff."

"You're a little young to be working, aren't you?"

"I'm fifteen."

"No way."

"Yes way."

"And at what point am I gonna learn your name?"

She strode to him and held out her hand. "Becca King," she said. "I could take care of your tools and clean them and oil them and put them away. I could work with you when you're doing the handyman stuff. Like you tell me what you need and I hand it to you. I could work for you weekends. After school, too.

I don't live far from here and I could ride my bike over."

Just like . . . reminds me . . . when Steph wanted that damn horse . . .

Ivar said, "Not a bad idea if I needed someone, which I don't. Winter's sparse around here when it comes to work. Too bad you didn't come by last summer because I was overrun then. Autumn, too. But now? Thin pickings." He grabbed up an armload of tools and headed into the chicken coop.

Becca wasn't about to be defeated so easily. She grabbed up some tools and followed him. There were no chickens living in the coop, but she figured there must have been hundreds at one time because the place was like a vault. It had been altered at some point to a combination of shop, storage unit, and collection center for a billion rusty farm implements, with an off-season hothouse at the far end where grow lights shone down on a few dozen spindly plants.

Ivar dumped his tools on a workbench and strode to this hothouse area. There he squatted and examined his plants. Becca joined them. She saw at once they were pot plants, and she did the math quickly. He had forty. Whoa, she thought. Forty was more than he could smoke, and that meant only one thing.

Ivar glanced at her and seemed to read her expression because he said, "Think you've dropped into a drug den, I bet."

"Not really."

"Work on the poker face, girl. What'd you say your name is?"

"Becca King."

"Well, Becca King, you got to work on looking like you're

thinking something other than you're thinking. I'm not a drug dealer. Least not in the normal sense. This is . . . let's call it a sideline. It's medical marijuana. I use it and so do some other folks. They buy it from me for a real good price, which saves them a trip over town to find it."

"Oh," she said. There didn't seem to be a reason to doubt him. His whispers were saying nothing different from his words.

He went on with a smile. "Course, I could be lying my head off, couldn't I? There could be a meth lab over there in the barn. Matter of fact, expanding the ol' business might not be a bad idea. You know anything about meth? Now I could definitely use an assistant if I get into that."

"You're making fun," she said.

"You sure of that?"

"Yeah. Pretty much. I sort of think you joke a lot."

"Do you now, Becca King."

"I do."

He shot her a smile. *Serious like her . . . Steph would've . . . but then she always did, didn't she . . .* made Becca wonder who Steph was and why Ivar thought about her instead of Sharla. But she didn't say anything other than, "I could learn to take care of them," with a nod at his plants.

"They don't need taking care of," he told her. "There's a reason it's called weed and I expect you c'n figure it out."

"You mean weeds don't need taken care of."

"Smart," he said, tapping his index finger to his baseball cap. "I like that in an attractive woman."

Diana came into the chicken coop as Ivar was saying this last bit. She said, "I thought I'd find you in here. What're you two up to?"

"Miss Becca King here is looking for work. She's rejected pot growing out of hand."

"I'm glad to hear that."

"I thought I could maybe be his assistant," Becca said. "When he does his handyman stuff."

Diana looked around the chicken coop and frowned. She said, "This place is chaos, Ivar. Maybe she can organize it for you. Someone needs to. How do you find anything?"

"Hunt, peck, throw, grunt, and curse," he said.

"That doesn't seem very time effective."

"You got a point."

"I could organize this place," Becca told him earnestly. "I could do it easy as anything. I wouldn't throw anything away, either. Not without asking you, I mean."

Ivar Thorndyke cast a fond look in her direction. He shook his head, but in a way that told Becca he was giving in. He said, "Now that's something I might be able to use you for, Becca King."

"When?" she asked. "Soon? Now?"

Diana said to him, "She's got a haircut she needs to keep up with."

"And other things," Becca added. She thought of what money could do for her situation. She might even have enough to get out of the tree house and rent a real room somewhere.

Ivar waved them off, a gesture of defeat that really meant acceptance of their plans. "So you won't throw away a thing, right?" he said to her.

"Absolutely swear. Not without asking you. When d'you want me to start?"

PART THREE

Langley Marina

FOURTEEN

Jenn wanted to do an hour of wind sprints and forty-five minutes of dribbling practice. The tryouts for the All Island Girls Soccer team were coming up faster and faster, and she didn't really need anything more to distract her. So when Squat Cooper asked her if she had time to go over their Western Civ report so that he could show her what he'd come up with, she wanted to say no way. But she knew how lucky she was to have Squat for a partner, so she said yes instead, which ended up involving a trip to his house at the edge of the sand on Useless Bay.

The place was a palace. Squat's mom had scored it as part of a divorce settlement from his dad. When Mr. Cooper had done the evil deed with his executive assistant, the fool had decided to do it right in the marital bed. That had cost him the massive stone house, a pile of money each month, and a new Range Rover every five years.

She and Squat took their stuff upstairs. Somewhere a television was blasting, but where they sat the sound was muted. This was a study area at the far end of the house. It had two computer stations, bookshelves, two desks, a leather sofa, coffee table, and a flat-screen TV. It also had a bar with a glass-fronted minifridge. To Jenn, it was like a superdeluxe hotel. To Squat, it was business as usual.

He got out his iPad. He was handling the alternatives to conquest on the part of the European explorers who supposedly had stumbled upon the primitive culture that Jenn was inventing. His idea was to create visual aids to go along with their presentation. He wasn't a 4.0 student for nothing.

"I pretty much got the alternatives to conquest figured out," he told her.

"Give me the details, Studboy," she replied.

He shot her a look. "You gotta control your craving for me if we're gonna get this done. I know how desperate you are for my bod, but we got work to do."

"My knuckles are white," she said. "Continue."

He brought the first of his work onto the screen, saying, "First thing I figure is we got to decide what *makes* the Europeans want an alternative to killing, capturing, pillaging, raping, enslaving, and whatever-ing, know what I mean? The rest of the class's going to just list alternatives. But if we delve into the European culture and find something that makes them *want* to be different, we got Mr. Keith's attention."

Squat had her attention, too. Damn, he was so *totally* smart. Jenn scooted over next to him and put a friendly arm around his shoulders. "Lemme see," she said and she began to read.

It was vintage Squat. It was good beyond good. Jenn read it, squeezed his shoulders, and spontaneously kissed him on the cheek. Then she turned his head to her and planted one on his mouth for good measure. "Freaking gen-i-us," she announced. "Instant A and our name in lights. I want tongue, Studboy. Let's celebrate."

Squat started to say something but someone else spoke instead.

"Crap, you must be desperate, bro." Squat's older brother Dylan had come into the room. His jeans were so baggy that he had to hold them up as he attempted to saunter in the direction of the sofa. Over the pants, he had a sweatshirt on that looked filthy. Jenn suspected the last person to wear it had been Sasquatch. On his feet were unlaced tennis shoes. On his face was a smirk. "Tryin' to do it with a lesbo, huh?" Dylan asked nonchalantly as he dropped onto the sofa.

"Hey! Jenn's not—"

"A lot you know." Dylan was sitting next to Squat, but he leaned forward and gave Jenn a look. "Lemme touch your tit," he told her. When her lip curled in response, his reaction was, "See, bro? She don't want nothing from me, she ain't going to want nothing from you."

"I think you might have an overinflated idea of your desirability," was Squat's reply.

Jenn guffawed. Dylan's face flamed. "You," he said to his brother, "better watch yourself."

"And you better go play with yourself. That's about all you're going to get."

"While you're getting *her*? Ohhh, I'm so jealous."

Dylan rose and slouched from the room. He managed a massive fart in the doorway just in case they might forget he'd been with them.

"Sorry," Squat said when he was gone. "The scum also rises. He may evolve from name-calling some year, but I wouldn't hold your breath."

"Whatever," she said. "With you for a brother, being a creep's the only thing he's got."

Squat thought about this one. "Should I say thanks to that?" he asked her.

"No need to say thanks to the truth. Perfect gentleman, A student, Boy Scout, all-around good guy? Everyone knows it. Hey. How 'bout getting naked?"

He went beet red.

IT WAS JUST about dinnertime when Jenn got back to Possession Point, courtesy of Mrs. Cooper's Range Rover, which she was reluctant to drive the length of the cratered lane that led up to the McDaniels house. It was dark as pitch, but dim lights shone in the distance from the bait shack, so Mrs. Cooper said, "D'you mind . . . ?" with a look that told Jenn she didn't wish to risk her vehicle's suspension. Jenn didn't bother to tell her that a Range Rover was equal to whatever the lane might wish to dish out. Instead, she said, "No problem. Thanks." And with a "Later, Studboy," to Squat, she was out of the car.

Annie Taylor came out of the trailer as Jenn headed by. At

first Jenn thought the young woman had been waiting for her, especially since she said, "Hey, Jenn, come over when you can, okay?" But then Annie went to the woodpile and stocked up on logs. Jenn said sure, as soon as she saw what was laid out for dinner. Since the island taxi wasn't in its usual spot, Jenn knew she was expected to rustle up something for the boys and her dad in her mother's absence.

Beef and vegetable soup, seriously light on the beef. Her mom had already made it and it just needed reheating. Fine. She could do it once she went to see why Annie wanted to see her. More cleaning of the trailer, probably. They'd been working on it when they each had free time. It was now livable, but Jenn still thought Annie was being ripped off when it came to rent.

As it turned out, though, when she went back over to Annie's, what she discovered was that Annie had plans, and these plans had nothing to do with the trailer. They did, however, have everything to do with Nera. Annie's mind was one track when it came to that seal. And the track's destination had to be called Getting Her Hands on Nera. Nothing else would do.

Annie was sitting at her laptop, and when Jenn came in, she said, "Great. There you are," and she accessed some Web site. She also said, "Have a cookie. Peanut butter."

"You baked cookies?"

"Hardly. I can almost boil water. I got 'em in Langley." She gestured aimlessly in the direction of the kitchen, such as it was. On the counter a white bag was half crumpled open. Inside were the cookies. Bakery cookies. Food of the gods.

Jenn took one, savored her first bite, and went to join Annie, who said, "What d'you weigh?"

"Why?"

"I need the info. It's for this site."

"What is it?"

"Just tell me." And when Jenn told her, she asked her height, whether she wore contacts, whether she could swim. When she'd logged everything into the site she was on, she said, "I've found exactly what we need."

"For what?"

"For getting close to Nera."

"What's the *deal* with that seal? And what's getting close to her going to prove? And how're we supposed to get close to her?"

"Scuba," Annie said. "We're going to dive together."

"In the middle of the frigging winter? We'll freeze to death."

"Not in dry suits we won't," Annie said airily. "I'm already certified. Well, you more or less have to be in my line of work. And listen, Jenn, this is something you can do later to make money. You said you need money, right?"

"Uh . . . How do I make money with that? Give underwater tours?"

"You live on an island. There're boats everywhere. People need their hulls scraped and their whatevers dealt with." Annie waved a hand airily. "You know what I mean. They lose anchors and crab pots and God knows what else. There's got to be a ton of business."

Not to mention a ton of equipment to buy, Jenn thought, which she couldn't afford and didn't want to buy anyway. She'd made a bit from Annie for helping out with the trailer's livability problem, but those bucks were meant to pay for membership on the All Island Girls Soccer team *if* she made the team. Which reminded her that now it was too dark outside to do windsprints or to dribble. She *had* to get her butt in gear.

Annie patted the banquette where she was sitting. She said, "Park it, Beauty," and Jenn smiled in spite of herself and joined the young woman. "Here's how it'll work," Annie said happily. "Far as I'm concerned, learning to dive'll be part of your job, so I'll spring for the lessons and we can rent whatever you need."

"Like rent it where?"

"Like rent it here."

Annie directed her to look at the Web site, which was for a new island business. It was a chandlery and dive shop and it was operated by someone called Chad Pederson who'd been hired by the harbor commission. The harbor commission, Annie told her, wanted someone run the shop and to offer scuba, kayaking, and snorkeling lessons. Chad Pederson was the someone.

"It's at a place called Drake's Landing," Annie told her. "You know where that is?"

"In Langley Marina," Jenn replied, looking at the picture of delighted snorkelers, happy kayakers, and thrilled-to-their-fins scuba divers. "Why don't you just ask him to dive with you?"

"Who?"

"That guy. The lesson guy. Chad Pederson."

"Because I want you," Annie said. "We're working together, aren't we?"

Jenn was oddly pleased with the question. "Yeah," she said. "Sure."

Annie linked her arm with Jenn's then, and she pulled her closer to gaze at the laptop's screen together. "So one for all and all for one, I say. Let's get to know that seal."

HOW TO FIND her was the real question, but Annie was on top of that as well. Thanks to the seal spotters, every movement Nera made was photographed, documented, telephone-treed about, and otherwise recorded for posterity. The group had a Web site that traced the animal's movements. The last sighting had been that very afternoon. She was swimming around Point Partridge Lighthouse.

"That's near Coupeville," Jenn said and added "midway on the island," when she realized Coupeville didn't mean anything to someone who'd come to Whidbey from Florida. "She's heading south, just like Ivar said at the meeting."

"Perfect," Annie said. "So we'll get you certified by this Chad Pederson guy, and by the time she's here, we're on her like leprosy."

Jenn's eyes widened. "Hey, I dunno if this is—"

"I was joking!" Annie gave her arm a squeeze. "God, I wouldn't hurt that seal."

"Then what *would* you do?" Jenn asked her seriously. "'Cause . . ." She shook her head. There was something about this plan that smelled funny. She said, "I don't know, Annie."

Annie hopped to her feet. She went to one of the many boxes she had stacked around the room and she brought out something that looked like a small, bright X-Acto knife. She said, "I'll take a scraping from her. That's all, Jenn. The scraping will get me to her DNA. No way on earth is she going to get hurt."

"How're you getting close enough for a scraping?"

"Your dad's bait pool," Annie said. "I'll have bait for her—I'll buy it from your dad—and we'll contain her. Just for maybe thirty minutes or so. Probably less. I'll offer her bait and build her trust and when she comes close, that's all I'll need. Jenn, she won't even feel it. And *if* she feels it, it won't feel different than scraping a rock, which she has to have done in the past. She's a seal. She swims around rocks all the time. So are you in? Come on. I *want* you with me on this."

The light from behind her shone on Annie's hair. The light from in front of her shone on her skin. She had a smile that said "Best friends, Jenn?" as clear as anything. Jenn was still reluctant, but she told herself it was because of scuba and not because of Annie. Okay, she told Annie. She was with her on this.

FIFTEEN

Jenn set aside time the following day for wind sprints, but as things turned out, Annie had other plans for them both. It was time to arrange the whole diving enterprise, she announced. So they set out for Drake's Landing.

This was at the bottom of Wharf Street in the village of Langley, across from the weather-worn wrecks of Langley's old piers, dangerous and long unused. There was a sheltered marina in this location, where boats were docked along barnacle-encrusted slips. Drake's Landing was tucked into the base of a bluff at the far side of the marina's parking lot. A sign in front of it creaked from a newly painted post in the frigid wind. It read DRAKES' LANDING CHANDLERY and across the new front window of the building a GRAND OPENING banner flopped unevenly.

The place was dark inside. Jenn remarked on this and was secretly grateful. She didn't like the idea of learning to scuba dive in the middle of winter anyway. Beyond that, she *had* to get to her soccer workouts if she was going to have a chance at all during the tryouts for the All Island team. So if the chandlery was closed, it was fine by her, as long as they could get home before dark.

"Damn," Annie murmured, gazing at the clearly uninhabited building. "He said he'd be here."

"Who?"

"Chad. Him. The guy. I told him I'd bring you by this afternoon and he said—"

Someone knocked on the driver's window and Annie and Jenn turned. They drew in breath simultaneously. If this was Chad, Jenn thought, oh hot mama. He looked like a sculpture. He was chiseled from chin to lips to nose to forehead. His eyes were a friendly brown and his skin was lightly flushed from the wind.

"Annie?" he called out through the closed window. When she nodded, he said, "Sorry. I was on the boat. Come on in," and he hustled up to the chandlery's door, which he unlocked.

"Wow," Annie said in a hushed voice as they followed him. "What a looker. Well, I've got a partner back home, so he's all yours, Jenn."

Jenn snorted. "As if."

Annie stopped her with a hand on her arm. She frowned. "Hey. You're a beauty. Don't forget it," she said.

Inside the chandlery, Chad was emerging from his parka, knitted cap, and gloves like someone out of a film. He had short brown hair and the well-defined shoulders and chest of a swimmer. He was slim at the hips and he walked *with* his hips. When he smiled, he flashed a mouth full of perfect white teeth. No doubt he knew he was the Complete Package, Jenn thought. What the hell was he doing in Langley?

"So," he said, placing himself behind the counter and getting a record book of some sort from a shelf. "You ready to go underwater?" he asked Jenn.

"How cold is it, exactly?"

He waved off Jenn's concern. "Don't worry about that part. We're starting out in a pool. We won't do 'real' water till your final lesson in the marina and then the check-out dive in the passage. And for those dives, you'll be wearing a dry suit, so the cold won't bother you." He shot her a grin. "At least not much." And then to Annie, "You done much cold water diving?"

She shook her head. "None of that in Florida."

"Well, I'll be there to rescue you both from hypothermia. Come on back here, let me show you the stuff we're going to be using. We c'n get Jenn fitted up with what she needs."

He took them into a supply room where scuba equipment was neatly arranged along one wall. The harbor commission had put some serious money into the place, Jenn thought as she looked around. While Chad and Annie chatted about the need for a dry suit for Annie to use in the open water, Jenn wandered among the wet suits and dry suits, the tanks, the weight belts, and all the other items she was going to have to learn about. Seeing it all, she realized that she lacked enthusiasm for the whole enterprise. She'd never liked enclosed spaces, and there was something about having to breathe from a tank and look through a mask that made her feel scuba wasn't a route that would earn her a dime, no matter what Annie said. But she'd said she'd go for it, so she'd go for it. She didn't think she was going to enjoy it much, though.

Chad suggested they take a look at his boat once he'd fitted Jenn with what she was going to need. That way, she'd see how easy it was going to be to get from the boat into the water, which might make the open-water dive look less threatening to her at the moment.

"I'm not threatened," Jenn said defensively.

"Sure you're not," Chad said with good cheer. "Let's take a look at the boat anyway."

She scowled as he headed out of the chandlery. He was treating her like a kid. What was *he*, anyway, nineteen years old? Maybe twenty, but no older than that.

Annie raised her eyebrows and jerked her head toward Chad's departing back. She murmured, "Nice butt, too," and Jenn had to smile. She followed Annie out of the door.

CHAD'S BOAT WAS a thirty-footer, an ancient thing that he and his dad had renovated from bow to stern. Below, every inch had been made useful with a berth, a head, a galley, and a table. Above this a small cabin protected the boat's occupants from weather while they were on the water. Chad said he'd take them out in advance of the checkout dive if they wanted to do that. They'd see then that it was a sturdy craft, he told them, so they'd have nothing to worry about. It was also big enough to live on, he told them, which was what he was doing in Langley's harbor. Now . . . did they want to return to the chandlery and fill out the rest of the paperwork? They did.

Afterward, with all of the details taken care of, Chad shook hands with Annie, said it was great to meet her, told her where and when the first lesson would take place, and walked with them to the chandlery door. When Jenn offered her hand as well, he put his arm around her shoulders instead. He said, "Okay, dive buddy. We'll fast-track you to certification so you'll be all ready. See you soon." Then he ruffled her hair, which made her want to punch his lights.

When they left, Jenn said, "I don't like being treated like a five-year-old."

"Don't blame you," Annie told her. "Give him time."

"For what?"

Annie shot her a look. "Guess, why don't you? I'm too old for him, so the door's wide open. You'll be in the pool, he'll be in the pool." Annie clasped her hands beneath her chin and batted her eyelashes. "'I was scared at first but I'm not scared now. Oh Chad, Chad, you're *such* a good teacher.'"

Jenn guffawed. "Right," she said.

"You think he wouldn't go for that?" Annie asked. "Stick with me. I'll teach you about men."

Jenn said, "Talking about men . . ." and she pointed at the dock. Ivar Thorndyke was coming along it, carrying a bucket that Jenn well recognized from the times she'd loaded it with bait from her dad. Ivar caught sight of them as he strode to his truck. He set the bucket in the bed and came across to them where they stood at the end of the walk that led to the chandlery's front door.

He said to Annie, "Renting a boat for a look-see around the passage?"

"Jenn's going to be my underwater assistant," was what Annie told him. "We're getting ready for dive lessons."

Ivar eyed them both. Jenn could tell his suspicions had just had a match lit under them. "What're you diving for?" he asked sharply.

Annie didn't answer at first, like someone wanting someone else to have a chance to evaluate his tone of voice. After a moment, she said evenly, "You seem sort of concerned, Mr. Thorndyke. C'n you tell me why?"

Jenn gave her a look. Ivar was a good customer of her dad's bait business, and she didn't much like getting into a tangle with him. So she said, "It's about that oil spill down at Possession Point, Ivar. Annie's studying it for her dissertation," because it seemed the best way to end their conversation and, more than anything, to keep it from veering in the direction of Nera.

She heard Annie hiss in a breath. Jenn gave her a glance and saw her face was stony. For his part, Ivar looked, if anything, more suspicious. Jenn was forced to wonder if she'd just blown it.

Ivar said, "How c'n you study an oil spill that happened . . . what? . . . seventeen, eighteen, years ago?"

"She's studying its effects," Jenn told Ivar.

"It was bilge oil," Annie added. "You're a boater, right? So you know what that means."

"A ship's engine oil," Ivar said. "What about it?"

"What about it?" Annie asked, eying him like someone surprised at another's lack of outrage. "For starters, when it spills from a ship, it either sinks to the bottom or it clumps into tar balls that wash onto the beach. If it stays on the bottom, it leaches into what's there: soil, sand, pebbles, whatever."

"And you think the oil's still out there? *That* what this's about?"

His tone told Jenn he was leading Annie to something, and she knew she'd been stupid to mention that oil spill at all. Ivar wasn't an idiot. He would connect all the dots: Annie Taylor's presence in town, her dissertation, her interest in Nera at the seal spotters' meeting.

Annie said pleasantly, "What I think is that the oil caused mutations in animal and plant life. My theory is—"

"You hold on right there." Clearly, Jenn thought, Ivar wasn't about to let the word *mutations* flutter past him. "This's about our seal. Bilge oil and leaching into the seabed and animal mutations and this is about our seal."

Annie stood her ground. "I think it's *the* seal, Mr. Thorndyke," she said. "It's not *our* seal or *your* seal or anyone's seal. The animal's wild. Wild animals can't be owned."

"They're not supposed to be messed with either."

"I have no intention of 'messing' with anything," Annie snapped.

"Yeah? Well, you watch your step 'cause I'll be doing the same."

With that, Ivar Thorndyke strode back to where he'd left his truck. Jenn watched him go and she became aware that next to her Annie was breathing hard. She glanced at Annie to see her face was pink with some kind of emotion she was trying to hold in. She glanced back at Ivar to see him climbing into his truck and slamming the door, hard.

It came to her that something was going on . . . beyond what was going on. It also came to her that she might want to find out what that something was.

Cilla's World

The road has been long and although time has passed in the form of light and darkness, I have no idea how many days have come and gone. The rain and the snow have fallen on me, and the wind has blown so fiercely that its force has cracked the limbs from trees. I have been afraid only of this wind, so when it has come, I have kept far away from the forests. Instead I have wandered the country lanes that weave and wind throughout the landscape.

There have been few cars, for I am very far now from the road that I first walked upon. I have followed a route that has climbed many hills, sunk into valleys, and taken me deep into forests. I have not felt lost, but I have felt called. I have felt required to keep walking.

Sometimes I have remained hidden for a day, sometimes for two, once for three. But always I have risen at last and begun to move on, dragging along the wheeled suitcase that the mommy and the daddy left behind them.

I must present a curious sight, for I hobble. I've lost a shoe somewhere in the mud along the route I've taken, and I have not sought another to replace it. I examine my foot when I stop. I have cut myself. I have bled. The bleeding has stopped and started again. And stopped and started. The foot feels afire but I cannot remain in one place and wait for it to heal. Moving is the only answer I have to the question of why I am alone in this place.

SIXTEEN

Becca was surprised when she found out that Ivar Thorndyke and Sharla Mann were housemates only. She'd figured they were live-in lovers, just as every one of her five stepfathers had been before her mom had married each of them. But it turned out that Sharla did the cooking and the cleaning in exchange for an upstairs bedroom and the use of the downstairs mudroom as her beauty salon. That was it. For his part, Ivar looked at Sharla with puppy eyes but didn't seem willing to do anything to change the way things were.

Becca picked up whispers from both of them, especially on the two occasions when Sharla asked her to stay for dinner at the end of her workday in Ivar's chicken coop. Ivar's whispers tended to be along the lines of *when . . . if she ever . . . what if I asked . . . no way after what happened to her,* which was pretty interesting, while Sharla's were of the *been there, done that, and have the certificate for it* variety, suggesting she'd had a husband in her life once and didn't wish to repeat the experience.

This made Becca curious about them both, so she did a little digging around in her spare time. What she uncovered from dropping by the office of the *South Whidbey Record* and going through old copies "for a school report" was a connection between Sharla and the man Eddie Beddoe, who'd been shooting his rifle into the water at Sandy Point. They'd been married. When Eddie Beddoe's boat had gone down in Saratoga Passage, his "wife of ten years, Sharla Mann" hadn't wished to discuss with the paper Eddie Beddoe's claim that a dangerous seal had had a hand—or a flipper, Becca told herself sardonically—in the accident. A reporter had tried to get her to make a comment of some sort, but Sharla hadn't gone for it. "You'll have to talk to my husband," was her only comment.

Becca considered all of this, and particularly she considered Eddie Beddoe and the air of danger that seemed to seep from him. She remembered how his whispers had been about "killing her," and she felt a stab of fear for Sharla. But they hadn't been married in years from what she could discover from the paper, so perhaps the *her* that Eddie felt like killing every now and then was indeed the seal.

More and more it seemed to Becca that Nera loomed large in everyone's legend. In Ivar's case, according to Sharla, the seal had broken his arm years ago. This turned out to be the reason he was determined to keep everyone at a distance from her. So when, less than a week after Becca had begun working for Ivar, he came into the chicken coop in a rush of whispers claiming *going to hurt . . . dangerous game they're playing . . . nothing to them and why would she be because . . .* Becca concluded in short order that it was the seal Nera he was thinking about.

He said to her, "Got a job for you. It's a real one, too, not just messing around in here trying to make sense of my mess."

Job with its implication of long-term steady work plus an income made Becca's ears prick up. She set down the rusty pitchfork she was holding and got ready to hear whatever Ivar intended her to do.

It turned out to be scuba diving, and he explained it all quickly. A scientist new to the island was having a kid learn to dive so she'd have a partner in going into the water and getting after Nera. They weren't saying as much, but Ivar *knew* that was what they were up to. He needed Becca to learn to dive, too. "I need you to be my eyes and ears on this, Becks," he told her. "I can't dive no more and I can't see a thing without my glasses anyways. But you can do both."

"I don't know how to dive." She could tell he was anxious; she picked up *no for an answer* and *when they're underwater* and *then she can watch*; and she wanted to help him because she liked him. But diving? She couldn't manage that one. She told him all this, but he brushed it aside.

"There's a young fella giving lessons to this kid who's gonna dive with the scientist. He'll give lessons to you. I'll be paying for it, so you got no worries on that score. It's deadly important, Becks. It's life and *death* important."

"But how d'you know they're going after Nera?"

"They more or less said it straight out down at the marina in Langley. And let me tell you, that can't happen. Becks, the law says people got to stay one hundred yards away from marine mammals and that's the law for a reason, which is *everyone's* safety, both the people and the animals. Now this woman intends to get up close to Nera along with this kid and believe me there'll be hell to pay."

"Sharla told me Nera broke your arm," Becca said, more to herself than to Ivar.

Ivar grew red in the face at the mention of Sharla. "And so she did," he said.

"But why does the scientist want to get close to her?"

"God knows. All I get's cagey answers when I ask. Like 'No one means to hurt that seal, Mr. Thorndyke.' And 'Seals do not attack human beings.' Well, it's *not* a seal, is it? It's Nera we're talking about, and she's been different from the first. She broke my arm like you say, and Eddie says she sank his boat and people say it's all hogwash, but I'm not taking chances. No how. No way. So will you help me, Becks?" It would be another part of her job, he told her. In fact, he'd already spoken to the diving instructor. The other kid's lessons had just begun, and Becca could join them easy as anything. Would she do it? She could be saving a life.

"I guess so," Becca said, and she was surprised at Ivar's reaction to his.

He hugged her fiercely and kissed the top of her head. "That's my lady," he said huskily.

AT LEAST IT would be something extra to do. And it would get her out of the tree house. That was the way Becca thought about the diving. It wasn't as if her days were crammed with activities, after all. Aside from working for Ivar at Heart's Desire and keeping low on the radar of Langley life in case Jeff Corrie put in another appearance, her days consisted of going to school, doing her homework in the village library, trying to mold her Western Civ project into something Mr. Keith would find acceptable in spite of Tod Schuman's stubborn refusal to use anything other than the Internet, and returning to her tree house to eat and sleep and begin the exact same list of activities on the following day. The only diversion from this relentless pleasure was getting to witness Derric and Courtney Baker do the boyfriend/girlfriend bit at school.

What made life worse was that something called Carnation Day was coming. This was, she discovered, an annual fund-raiser put on by the seniors to help pay for their all-night party on graduation day. For one dollar, you could purchase a carnation to send to another student, along with a message. The more dollars you spent, the more carnations you sent. It was, Becca thought morosely, a perfect opportunity for Derric and Courtney to wear complete *mantles* of the flowers as declaration of their feelings for each other. As for herself . . . She figured she was going to be one of the girls who tried surreptitiously to send themselves a flower or two so as to avoid the humiliation of having nothing to carry around on the Big Day.

The only bright spot Becca saw in her life was that her hair didn't look disgusting any longer. On the other hand, the new style and color hadn't done a thing to alter her world, since the only person who'd even noticed the change was Jenn McDaniels. And her comment had burst Becca's small balloon of pleasure soon enough. She'd given the hair a look, said, "Nice try, Fattie. Think that's going to make a difference?" in her typical Jenn McDaniels way.

So Becca was ready for something different to enter her life. At the moment the something different appeared to be scuba. So be it, she thought.

SEVENTEEN

Jenn wasn't used to naked women. She didn't like showing off her body, since she *had* no body to speak of, and she always felt weird when other girls stripped after soccer games, casually walking nude to the showers. So when Annie Taylor pulled off her clothes in the locker room of South Whidbey Fitness Center, Jenn felt a little awkward. She felt even more so when Annie stood there fully naked and chatted for a minute, not the least self-conscious about putting her nipples and pubes on full display. It was five in the morning, so at least Jenn was the only other person in the locker room. But still, she wasn't sure where to look. She knew where she *wanted* to look—everyone made comparisons when they had the chance, right?— but that felt odd when it came to Annie.

Annie was talking about the scuba lessons. Not to worry, she said, Jenn would pick up diving quickly. And what she didn't get straight off the bat, Annie would help her with in additional sessions. She finally got around to dressing herself in a bathing suit, which prompted Jenn to ask if Annie was going to be part of the lesson, too. It turned out, though, that Annie intended to use their time at the fitness center to swim laps. This made sense, although Jenn had to wonder how well Annie would be able to swim laps in a butt floss bikini.

Chad's jaw dropped at the sight of Annie when they walked from the locker room to the indoor pool. He snapped it back into place fast enough, though. He said, "Uh . . . okay . . . great," when Annie told him she herself would exercise during Jenn's scuba lesson. Then, while she walked to the far side of the pool, Chad never moved his eyes off her butt cheeks.

"Too old for you, bro," was what Jenn said to Chad since Annie herself had already mentioned the fact. But if Annie was too old for Chad, it was pretty clear that her butt cheeks weren't.

Chad said, "Good thing I like 'em older, Aquagirl."

"My name is Jenn."

"You're Aquagirl to me."

Annie lowered herself into the water. Once she began to swim, Chad managed to tear his eyes off her. Jenn said sourly, "For God's sake, she's thirty-three years old. She's got someone in Florida. What're *you*, nineteen?"

He glanced at her. "And what are *you*? Jealous?"

"As if," she said. "Are we having a lesson or not? 'Cause believe me, I could be home in bed if all you're going to do is drool after her. Not, by the way, that you stand a chance."

"But you do?" he asked.

"What's *that* s'posed to mean?"

He shook his head and seemed to shake off whatever was on his mind as well. He said, "Forget it. Let's get down to work. Into the water. Give me six laps."

"Huh? What is this? Boot camp or something?"

"Just do it," he said.

"I'm here to learn to *dive*."

"And if you drop your gear, you sure as hell need to be able to swim distance. So give me six laps any way you can. Dog paddle, breast stroke, crawl, whatever."

Jenn cooperated although to her it sounded like something between a waste of time and a drill sergeant's punishment. Still, she did the first two laps and she had no trouble. By the third lap, though, she knew that cigarette smoking was well on its way to doing her in. She barely finished at all. She ended up clinging to the edge of the pool panting like a Texas dog in the summer sun. Chad then told her to float on her back for ten minutes. "And no using your arms and legs," he instructed.

"I just frigging showed you that I can swim. Why the hell do I need to float?"

"Just *do* it, Aquagirl. D'you always argue?"

"My name is *Jenn*," she repeated.

And he said again, "You're Aquagirl to me. Now get out there and float."

Jenn muttered a few choice words that she hoped he heard, but she did as he asked. It was tougher than it sounded, floating without using her arms or her legs, but once she got the idea, she managed it. Then Chad told her to join him at a table he'd set up. There he began to recite what seemed like a billion facts. These had to do with air pressure, oxygen, buoyancy, blah, blah, blah. What*ever*. Jenn listened and nodded and tried to take it all in, but she was distracted by Chad's distraction.

He kept looking at Annie, who moved sleekly through the water like some obscure goddess of the sea. When she finally lifted herself from the pool, Chad even stumbled over a few of his words as she padded over to see how they were doing.

Jenn glanced her way. Great nipple shot, she thought sourly as Annie grabbed up a towel and used it on her hair. The rest of her body she left wet and dripping, with her nipples poking out against her bathing suit top like greetings that someone was meant to acknowledge.

"How's it going?" Annie asked, directing her smile at Jenn.

"We're just talking about air pressure," Chad replied.

"What're you learning?" again to Jenn.

"I'm explaining why it's important that she clear her ears."

"Know how to do that?" Annie asked Jenn. "Pinch your nose closed and blow. Like this."

Her demonstration wasn't done on herself but rather on Jenn. She pressed her nostrils closed and said that Jenn's head would feel like a balloon about to explode if she couldn't clear her ears underwater. Chad, she ignored entirely. To Jenn she said, "You're going to be great. No worries, Jenn."

Then she sat at the edge of the pool, her legs in the water to watch the rest of the lesson. She rested her arms on her thighs. She showed a lot of cleavage.

Somehow poor Chad got himself focused in spite of the cleavage and in spite of Annie's ignoring his general wonderfulness. He told Jenn that their next project was getting used to having the equipment on while in the water, and he helped her into hers and then donned his own. They were going to sit on the bottom in the shallow end, he said. They were just going to see what it was like to breathe through the regulator, okay?

Underwater, Jenn found life wasn't half bad. She sat Indian style, facing Chad, and they breathed in unison. Chad nodded at her and closed his eyes. She did the same and discovered that she actually didn't mind the strange new sensations. She began drifting in her thoughts. She considered what she might be able to do if she got good at diving. She was thinking of how she could make some money, just as Annie said, when suddenly her masked was ripped from her face.

She shot to the surface. She lost her regulator and took in a mouthful of pool water. She coughed and sputtered and when she could talk, she yelled, "What the hell! You pulled off my mask!"

Having surfaced next to her, Chad nodded placidly. "Yep."

"What the hell'd you do that for?"

"To see what you'd do. What you did was panic."

"What d'you *expect*, Bozo? How'd you like it if I did it to you?"

"Calm down," he said. "You panic, you drown. You panic, you shoot to the top like you just did. You panic, you don't decompress. In three feet of water? No problem. In fifty? You get the bends."

"That wasn't fair."

"Stuff happens underwater, Aqua—"

"My name is Jenn!" she shrieked.

IT TOOK FOUR tries before Chad was satisfied that Jenn could lose her face mask underwater without panicking and that she could also lose her regulator, get it back into her mouth, and remember to blow *out* to clear it instead of desperately inhaling and getting a mouthful of water. They went on from that to learning how to enter the water with fins on. The entire lesson lasted more than three hours. By the end of it, Jenn was exhausted.

Annie had long since showered and returned to the pool. She said to Chad, "How'd she do?"

"Aside from her tendency to panic, which'll probably kill her, she did okay," he said.

Annie followed Jenn back to the locker room. She said, "Have a shower. It'll make you feel better. You did fine, by the way, no matter what he said. For your first lesson? You did great." She stood there, arms crossed. Jenn waited for her to take herself back to the pool or out to the car or whatever, but Annie leaned against one of the lockers as if waiting for Jenn to strip. Jenn knew it was nothing, just a we're-all-girls-here sort of thing. Still she wanted to say "D'you mind?" at the same time as she also didn't want to say "D'you mind?" Well, they were friends, weren't they? She decided they were. She peeled off her bathing suit. "Nice bod," Annie said.

"If you like boards," Jenn retorted.

"Don't put yourself down." Annie gave her a playful slap on the butt as Jenn passed by, on her way to the shower. Then she left her alone, saying she would help Chad load gear into his pickup outside.

That was what she was just finishing doing when Jenn rejoined her. Daylight had finally arrived, always late in the Pacific Northwest at this time of year, and at one side of the parking lot, a dented white van with a Bondo-repaired door was idling, sending out a plume of white exhaust. There was someone leaning into the driver's window, Jenn saw. Crap, it was that scumbag Dylan Cooper.

He was someone she wanted to avoid on the general principle of his being so disgusting, but the white van was not far from Annie's car, and Annie was waving a good-bye to Chad and coming her way with a cheerful callout of, "Let's get a latte and a pastry, Beauty."

Dylan looked around from whatever he was doing at the van. He caught sight of Jenn, got a glimpse of Annie, said something to the van's driver, and slouched Jenn's way. He said, "This the place you lesbos hook up?"

She said, "What're you doing here? Scoring or selling? Never mind. I already know."

"She's hot, lesbo." He cocked his thumb at Annie. "Wouldn't've thought she'd want to do it with you." He waggled his tongue suggestively at her. "Good for you?" he asked, and she wanted to slug him.

"You're so pathetic," she told him. "You're like a freaking piano that only plays one key."

"Har har. Saying you aren't one? Maybe I should ask her." He gave a shout to Annie, "Hey! What was it like? Is she a moaner?"

"Drop *dead*," Jenn snarled at him and she swung around to face Annie.

But Annie had already gotten into her Honda and fired it up. Thankfully, she hadn't heard a word.

"JUST A BUTTHEAD from school," was how Jenn explained Dylan Cooper to Annie when she asked about him. "I know his brother. End of story."

"What was he shouting? Was he talking to me? Because—"

"We should stop at Bayview Corner," Jenn announced firmly. "They've got coffee there, and we c'n get a bagel or a muffin or something. And Eddie Beddoe works across the street. Have you talked to him about the trailer rent yet?"

Annie looked as if she was about to say something more about Dylan Cooper, but instead she shrugged and after a moment said, "Good idea about Eddie. Coffee first, though."

After they'd had their coffee and bagels, they walked across Marsh Road where Eddie Beddoe had long ago converted one of the defunct island gas stations into a car mechanics shop. The place was a pit of grime, and Eddie Beddoe was the last person on earth that Jenn would trust an engine to, but he made a decent living at the place and they found him adjusting the idle on a Toyota Land Cruiser.

He looked up from the engine when Jenn said his name. He said, "Jenn McDaniels. How's that dad of yours? Any new brews? I got some rent due at the start of the month and you tell him I don't want it paid to me in beer."

"Here's who's paying that rent," Jenn announced. "This's Annie Taylor and you're overcharging her."

Eddie adjusted his baseball cap as if he needed to do this to get a better look at Annie. He said, "Far 's I know, rent's whatever the market will bear."

"Yeah? Well, a look at the *Record*'s going to show you what the market is. Annie's looked and she's here to tell you—"

"She don't speak?" Eddie asked. "Now that's awful strange, Jenn, 'cause I recall talking to her least one time by phone. That'd be right when we agreed on the rent. What're you doing around here anyway on a Saturday morning?"

"Just having a diving lesson, Mr. Beddoe," Annie said. "I've looked at rents on the island and I know you're cheating me."

"Diving lesson? Who's taking a diving lesson? Why's anyone taking a diving lesson?"

Like it's any of your business? was what Jenn wanted to say. But she stopped herself because he'd ceased his working on the Land Cruiser engine and he was wiping his hands on a rag with a lot of industry. His brow was furrowed.

Annie was the one to respond. She said, "Jenn's taking lessons, Mr. Beddoe. She'll be diving with me."

"What sort of diving?"

"Marine studies, okay?"

"On what?"

"Look," Jenn cut in, "we're here about the rent. You're trying to get us onto another topic and don't think we don't see that because we do."

Annie put a hand on her arm to stop her. "There was an oil spill," she said. "A long time ago. I'm making a case for—"

"A lawsuit?" Eddie scoffed. "That'll be the day."

"—genetic mutations in sea life. It's for my dissertation. And frankly, Mr. Beddoe, it would help me a lot if you and I could renegotiate the rent before it comes due."

"We made an agreement."

"Come on," Jenn said, "you're taking her and you know it."

Eddie yawned. He removed his baseball cap and scratched his head.

Worm, Jenn thought. Slug. Banana slug. She said, "Okay. Forget it. Looks like that Possession Shores cabin's your only option, Annie. It's not as close as Possession Point, but it's not bad. Close enough, don't you think?"

Annie's lips curved. "It'll be fine. Good thing the owners—"

"You're not pulling one over on me," Eddie told them. "But I think we c'n come to an agreement anyways."

"What kind of agreement?" Jenn asked shrewdly.

"A diving agreement."

"What about it?" Annie asked.

Eddie pointed vaguely in the direction of Saratoga Passage to the east and miles away. "Find my boat," he said. "Get me proof that you found it and your stay in that trailer is *f-r-e-e* for as long as you want. Don't find it, and the rent stays what it is."

"How's she supposed to find that damn boat?" Jenn demanded.

"Not a clue," Eddie replied. "I was her, though, I'd get someone to help, someone with a boat has all the bells and whistles. That's what *I'd* do. It's up to her."

"With all of Saratoga Passage to look at?" Jenn said dismissively. "No way, Eddie."

"That boat went down off Sandy Point," he said. "I'd start there. But she can do what she wants."

EIGHTEEN

Dating Courtney Baker was heady stuff for Derric. She was smart and committed to more things than anyone Derric had ever known. But what he liked most about her was that there was a private side to her. She had her demons just like everyone else, and since Derric had his own demons, it was a relief to be with her.

She told him things: what it was like to be Courtney beyond what it seemed like to be Courtney. Sometimes, for example, she completely hated her sister. She knew that she was *supposed* to love her but she didn't and she thought she never would. Sometimes she hated her parents, too. She tried to stay true to the childhood principles she'd grown up with, but often she blew it. She wanted to live a bigger life and a fuller life than Whidbey Island afforded her. But she wanted the protected life of the island as well, and she didn't really know what this meant. Plus, she wanted Derric. Big Time All the Time, was how she put it. But she'd always thought that she'd be saving herself for one man only and what did it mean, she asked, if instead she did with Derric what she wanted to do? More, what did it mean that she really, truly, and actually *wanted* to do it? God, they were only sixteen years old! Shouldn't they have more on their minds than getting into each other's pants?

Derric tried to tell himself that he *did* have more on his mind, and most of the time this was true. He got reminded of it every time Courtney opened the old Star Wars lunch box he'd given to her. He'd gotten rid of it from his parents' house by filling it with candy, a scented candle, two jazz CDs, and an I-love-you note for Valentine's Day, but that idea had sprung to his head when his mom found the lunch box beneath his bed and asked what he wanted "this old thing for." He'd had to come up with some- thing fast, and Courtney was it. Now, however, Courtney carried it around like a vintage purse and she'd even started a fad among some of the girls at school, who were doing the same thing. But when Derric saw that stupid lunch box, what he thought of was what had been hidden within it. This led him almost daily to thinking of his sister. Thinking of his sister led to thinking of Becca. But he and Becca were *through* and that was how he wanted it.

He'd changed his Facebook page to reflect this at the begin- ning of March. Becca had never liked her picture on it anyway— she was weird like that about a lot of things—so he was happy enough to remove the three Christmas shots of them and replace them with pictures that he and Courtney took of themselves and of each other. On Facebook, they were at Double Bluff Beach building amazing driftwood structures with her family. They were sitting in the stands at a basketball game. They were at a party in Clinton and in line for a movie at the Clyde Theater. They were arm in arm, they were getting it on with a serious lip lock, they were posing in their finery on the way to a dance. Not all their shots made it onto Facebook, naturally, since some were way racy and didn't belong there. Only the ones fit for public viewing were posted. The others . . . ? Those pictures showed how hot things had really become between them.

Both of them knew it was only a matter of time. Derric had taken to being prepared. He carried condoms with him 24/7, and he waited for Courtney to give him the word. So far the word had been no. Sometimes it had been *Derric, we can't.* Once it had been *I think it's just that I'm scared for some reason.* But it always came down to the same ending for him: badly sore in all the wrong places and struggling to get his jeans back on.

What made it worse was that his mom absolutely knew what was going on. Every time he got back from a date with Courtney, she was waiting for him. She didn't ask where they'd been, and she didn't ask what they'd been doing. What she did do was say, "Talk to him, Dave," to his father.

"Rhonda, he knows what he's doing," was his father's reply.

Well, he did and he didn't know what he was doing. Sure, it had been drummed into his head from the time he'd started looking at girls that *whatever* happened, he had to use a condom. What hadn't been addressed was the pull and the push that went along with being with Courtney and wondering when and if and how and where. Everyone thought they were doing it, anyway. Guys at school said, "So . . . ?" and leered, waiting to hear what it was like with her naked. Girls at school smiled knowingly when they walked by. They said, "Hi, *Derri*c. Hey, *Court*ney," and the tone they used was as good as asking, "Where're you two actually *do*ing it? *His* house? *Her* house? The back of her *car*?"

"We might as well," was what Derric said to her.

What Courtney said was, "I feel like a hypocrite."

One of her problems was her prayer group at school. She was the group's leader. She'd started the group as part of her church's outreach program. They met once a week in one of the classrooms, and there they prayed for whatever needed praying for. When he'd been in the hospital in the autumn, they'd prayed for him. Before they'd prayed for him, they'd been praying for the family of a South Whidbey High graduate killed by gunfire one night in West Seattle. When they didn't have something or someone *specific* to pray for, they prayed for each other and for the strength to uphold the Pledge.

Courtney hadn't told him about the Pledge at first. She waited until what they wanted was each other naked and flesh to flesh, and then she explained how she'd thought he wouldn't want to go out with her if she'd been completely honest with him. When he asked what she meant, she cast her gaze downward and explained that her prayer group had promised chastity. That was the Pledge. Nothing until marriage, she told him. At least, not the *real* thing.

He'd said no problem because he'd *thought* no problem. But that was before the night she'd lifted her sweater and unhooked her bra and said, "I don't *care*." Which was shortly before she said,

"We can't." Which was a week before she said she was scared.

So he was turned around. He was inside out. And when she said to him, "Maybe we *both* should pray," he went along with the idea because the truth was, by March something *had* to give.

He'd never been to a prayer group. He went to church with his parents on some Sundays, but the truth was that they missed the service about as often as they went to the service. Other than knowing his mom's church had been what had taken her to Uganda in the first place, he had no religious instruction. Spiritual life meant nothing to him. But if going to a prayer group would help him know what to do about Courtney, not to mention *with* Courtney, then he was willing to give it a try.

The prayer group met in a classroom at lunch with their brown bags and their Bibles. Derric had neither, so he felt immediately out of place. But he knew the kids and they knew him, and when someone offered him half a sandwich and someone else offered him a Bible, he figured things would be all right.

At first, they ate their sandwiches and read their Bibles and were completely silent. It was only after they'd finished their lunches that they bowed their heads and got ready to pray. They were sitting in a circle of desks, and each of them reached for the hand of the person sitting next to them. One by one, they began to speak.

Derric felt a moment of horror. He'd thought prayer group was all about praying in a general sort of way, but these were deeply personal prayers. He had an immediate bad feeling about where the situation was going to head.

It headed there when Courtney's turn to speak arrived. "Lord Jesus," she said quietly, her eyes closed and her head lowered, "you know that Derric and I want to have intercourse. You know that we've done everything short of the real thing and I feel . . . I feel bad about that. I've wanted to and I *haven't* wanted to and I promise myself when I'm with him that I *won't* put my hands on his—"

Derric leaped to his feet. He did it so fast that the kids sitting on either side of him jumped half a foot. Everyone's head lifted and he looked at each of them and he felt more naked than he'd ever felt when he'd actually been naked. He knew he had to get out of the room.

HE HEARD HER call his name. What made it worse was that Becca King—of all people—was passing by the classroom. She was being trailed by Extra Underpants Schuman who was sneering, "Hey, you *said* you wanted to be in charge, cow pattie," to which Becca was saying, "D'you *always* live in a separate reality or *what*, Tod?" as angrily as Derric had ever heard her talk. She saw him and turned the color of ketchup. Derric saw her and wanted to run. Meantime, Courtney was out of the room, crying, "I thought you understood what the group is about! Prayer is honest. If it's not honest, it isn't prayer." And what he wanted to do most of all was to sink into the floor and disappear.

Becca gulped, looked from Derric to Courtney, and rushed off. Tod went after her, declaring, "No *way* are you getting out of this." Courtney's blue eyes filled with tears. Derric said, "Screw it. I need to just *think*."

TO MAKE MATTERS worse, that night his dad decided it was time to have the Talk that Rhonda had been insisting upon. Derric was in his bedroom, attempting to work on the Western Civ project he was doing with EmilyJoy Hall, when Dave Mathieson walked in. When he cleared his throat in that I'm-the-Dad way of his, Derric knew what was about to happen.

Dave sat on his bed. Derric turned from his desk. Dave was frowning down at his shoes. He finally said, "Girls, son," to which Derric replied, "I know where this is going."

"Yeah? Where?"

"Mom's worried about me and Courtney. But nothing's going on."

Dave Mathieson looked doubtful, and who could blame him? Derric knew his dad's story: He'd been first married at nineteen for the only reason a boy of nineteen marries. "Dumbest thing I ever did," was how Dave usually put it. And then he always added, "No *second* dumbest," in case Derric misunderstood.

Derric continued. The best idea, he figured, was to tell his dad about the Pledge and the prayer group. Dave Mathieson listened, same way he always did, sitting on the edge of Derric's bed with his gaze unwavering from Derric's face, but this didn't mean he was impressed with the information, and he more or less made this clear when Derric was finished talking about it.

He said, "Pledges don't mean much when things heat up, son. Things might start with pledging six ways to Sunday, but they don't end up there."

"This time they do," Derric assured him. "She really means it." And to prove his point, he told his dad about exactly what had happened in the prayer group that day.

His dad said, "How'd you feel about that?"

"The prayer group or her saying what she said?"

"Both."

"Lame. I mean, I'm not the prayer group type anyway. But I guess . . . well, at least she's trying."

"Trying to what?"

"You know. Not to. You *know*. And I don't think I want to anyway. But I'm not sure why."

"This have to do with Becca King?"

Derric shook his head. "It was different with her. I mean, it wasn't so . . . Things weren't going so fast like they are with Courtney. I don't know, Dad. Maybe they weren't going at all."

Dave nodded. He said, "Hard to know what's real and what isn't sometimes."

"That's the truth," Derric admitted. Except, of course, Courtney *felt* so real, every sensuous inch of her.

Dave had shifted his gaze from Derric to the beanbag chair for some reason. Derric tensed as he watched this, knowing what was inside. But Dave made no mention of the beanbag and when he finally looked up, he said, "I want you to take care, no matter what. I'm not just talking about condoms here. You got that?

I'm talking about seeing beyond the moment. That's the toughest thing to master." He rose from the bed, slapping his thighs as he did so. Then he picked up the beanbag, and Derric froze.

"God," Dave Mathieson said, "this thing's been around forever. Don't you want a new one? Or maybe a recliner or something else more comfortable?"

Derric's lip felt a bit stiff as he replied. "Nah, I like old stuff. I like stuff with history."

"Well," Dave said, "that certainly applies to this old thing."

He tossed the beanbag back onto the floor. It landed with the repair of duct tape on top. To Derric that repair looked like an enormous *X*. And *X*, of course, always marked the spot.

PART FOUR

Mutiny Bay

NINETEEN

Becca didn't even allow herself to think about Derric and Courtney Baker. She told herself that there was no point. She could see that they were totally at odds with each other when they darted out of the prayer circle's classroom, but she had bigger things on her mind than the extremely remote possibility that Derric had suddenly decided to return to being Derric again.

Besides, she had Tod Schuman to worry about. Moreover, she had his whispers to worry about. They'd been telling her that he was intent on offing his part of the responsibility for their Western Civ project onto her. *Make her do it . . . got to do it . . . no way in front of the class . . . stupid stuff she thinks is important . . .* were illustrating his Big Plan, and she wasn't about to let that happen. "You better get your head around the fact that no way am I doing this alone," she told him. His reply of, "Then *you* better get your head around the fact that you don't know everything there is to know about how to make a report, man," didn't reassure her of anything other than his complete obstinacy.

On top of that, it turned out that Ivar Thorndyke wanted her to start her scuba lessons ASAP. To facilitate this, he had dragged her away from her job in his chicken coop and bundled her into his truck soon after she'd said she'd be his diving spy. He wanted her to meet Chad Pederson, who would be her instructor, he said. Chad wanted to bring her up to speed before she joined the class with his other dive student.

But when they arrived in Langley, the marine chandlery door had a BE BACK LATER sign posted on it. Ivar swore when he saw this and said, "Damn fool *said* he'd be here to meet us." He looked around the marina in the biting wind and Becca did the same, trying to catch sight of anyone dumb enough to be out here in the drizzly cold.

Ivar squinted out into the passage and seemed to see something. He went to his truck and got out a pair of binoculars. He said, "What the . . . ?" when he focused the binoculars on a distant boat sailing in the direction of Sandy Point.

He handed the binoculars over to Becca and said, "Tell me what you see in that boat, Becks. My eyes aren't like they used to be," and she found the boat in question out on the water. Two people were in it, a man and a woman. They were going fast as far as she could tell. The water was rough, but they didn't seem to be letting that stop them.

Becca couldn't tell much about either of the people although she told Ivar that she could see that the woman had red hair and that the boat was from Port Angeles. But that was all Ivar seemed to need because *no way in hell are they going to* preceded his announcement of, "Come on. Let's go!" He made it fiercely and he didn't mean "let's go home" because he grabbed his keys and a heavy jacket out of the truck and he headed at a trot for the dock.

Becca followed him. They went up on one of the wharfs and then rattled down the metal gangway and along a dock. There Ivar leaped into a fishing boat. He said, "You handle the lines. Do what I tell you," and before Becca could assess the whys of what they were doing, they were on the boat, Ivar had his keys in the ignition, and they were chugging out of the marina, pulling on life jackets as they went.

She strained to pick up Ivar's whispers. Because of the noise of the boat's engine, though, all she could manage was *they mean . . . know it, know it . . . she finds out and Nera will be . . .* so she knew this had to do with the seal.

She shouted over the noise, "Whose boat is that, Ivar?"

He said, "Pederson's. He's got that damn scientist with him. You said red hair, yes? Well, that's the scientist. Annie Taylor. And if they're out on the water when he said he'd meet us in the harbor, there's only one reason. They're after Nera."

"How'd they even know where she is?"

"Internet site. Anyone an' his brother c'n find out where she is if she's been seen in the last twenty-four hours."

In open water, Ivar increased the speed of his boat. They barreled out into the passage. It was rough out there, and bitterly cold, and the water was a rolling, roiling seascape. Their speed made the boat crash into the waves, so Becca held on for her life and kept the other boat in sight. But what she thought was, *What is it about this seal?* The answer to that question *had* to be important, she figured, for all these people to act so crazy about the animal.

Up ahead of them Chad's boat was fast. So was Ivar's, but he didn't attempt to overtake it. Becca wondered about this till they finally came to their destination after nearly an hour. This was a bay on the west side of Whidbey Island, where the shoreline made an undulating curve and houses hugged the edge of a bluff overlooking a sandy beach below.

Here, Chad Pederson cut his engine, and his boat bobbed in the gentler waves. In its stern the red-haired woman stood with a camera focused on the water. Chad joined her with a pair of binoculars. They might have been tracing a route from the bay to the beach and up the bluff to the houses, except for the fact that swimming rapidly toward them was the smooth, entirely black shape of a seal.

Ivar muttered, "Oh no you damn don't," and he gunned the engine of his boat. He brought it up between the seal and Chad's craft. He seemed determined to put an end to whatever was going on.

"Back your boat off one hundred yards," he yelled at them. "You know the law."

Chad Pederson yelled back, "What're you talking about? I'm not approaching her. She's approaching me. Or at least she was till you put your boat in the way."

"You don't back off, you're getting reported," Ivar told him. "You got that? Back *off.*"

Annie Taylor said, "We're taking her picture, Ivar. That's *all.*"

Where it'll start came from Ivar. *Close enough almost and then* seemed to come from Annie or Chad.

Ivar said, "What you're doing is getting too close. What you're doing is bothering her. What you're doing is endangering her and endangering yourselves. You want a picture of her, you take it from the beach or from the ferry like everyone else."

Damn stupid old man . . . chance of a lifetime . . . no one stands in my way . . . if anyone knows, then everyone will . . . this could mean she'll . . . when someone's desperate . . . grateful and then what comes next will be . . . hurt for sure . . .

Becca fumbled for the AUD box earphone. Better the static, she figured, than trying to work out what everyone was thinking about everything that was going on.

In the other boat, Annie Taylor suddenly put her hand on Chad Pederson's arm. She said, "Chad, look," and they all followed her gaze. The seal had actually come between the two boats, putting herself so close that any one of them could have touched her.

Annie began firing off pictures. At first no one said a word.

Becca was astonished by the seal's strange beauty, every part of her black. Her sleek skin, her eyes, her nose, her whiskers . . . The only thing about her that wasn't black was her teeth, and these became visible when she barked a greeting.

That prompted Ivar, who said, "Back *away*. Your boat'll crush her," to Chad.

At the same moment, Annie said, "Wait a minute! She's got a transmitter on!"

While Annie angled for a better position to take a picture from Chad's boat, the seal turned to face her, which allowed Becca and Ivar to see what Annie meant. To Becca it looked like an old garage door opener fastened to the black seal's skin. She squinted at it and heard Annie saying, "It looks glued to her neck. Glued, Chad, *glued*!" as if this was the most important detail in the world. She took more pictures, saying, "Mother of God, I do *not* believe this!" while Ivar kept saying, "Get away. Get away!"

It came to Becca that Ivar was no longer speaking to Chad or Annie. Rather, he was talking to the seal. It seemed, too, that he got through to her in some obscure fashion because Nera finally dove beneath the water, disappearing from view. She resurfaced some two hundred yards away. She was heading at that point back out into the passage.

Annie Taylor looked from the seal to Ivar. She said, "You know something about that transmitter, don't you? You know why she has it on. And you know why she hasn't lost it, don't you?"

Ivar's reply was "I don't know nothing."

But Becca could tell that he was lying.

TWENTY

Afew days before her next scuba lesson, Jenn finally had time
to work on her dribbling. Annie wasn't there, Jenn's mom
had taken her brothers into Langley to look for shoes at the thrift
store, and Jenn's dad was inside the bait shack, doing some work
that involved a lot of banging and even more swearing. With
time on her hands, she set up her soccer obstacles and got to
work. She was thirty minutes into it when Annie arrived.

Annie didn't stop the Honda to have a chat. She just waited
for Jenn to kick the obstacles to one side, and she gunned the
car's engine a couple of times. She looked seriously distracted, so
when Jenn had made way for her, she decided to follow the car
and see what was up.

She found Annie inside the trailer, stoking the fire. Next to
the woodstove, she'd placed her laptop on a chair, and her digital
camera was attached to it, uploading pictures. When the door
closed behind Jenn, Annie looked up. She said, "Jenn. Hi," in an
absentminded way. She went back to the laptop and the camera.

Clearly, something was going on, and it was only a moment
before Jenn saw what it was. Somehow and somewhere, Annie

had taken pictures of Nera. They were so close that she could have been in the water with the seal.

"Wow. Where'd you find her?" Jenn asked. "How'd you find her?"

"Mutiny Bay," Annie said, rapidly scrolling through the shots. "Seal spotters Web site. Bless those loondogs."

"You got totally close to her."

"She swam right up to Chad's boat," Annie said.

"Oh," Jenn said.

"What?" Annie looked up at her sharply. She read something on Jenn that Jenn didn't want there because she said, "Hey, girl. I told you. I've got a partner at home. The Chad-boy is yours for the taking. I mean, if you want him."

"Big thanks," Jenn said. "I'm not desperate for him yet, but I'll let you know."

Annie chuckled. She put her hand out and grabbed Jenn by the waist. She pulled her over, said, "Check this out," and leaned her head companionably against Jenn's arm. She said, "I'm thinking she's not a Ross seal out of her territory at all. D'you know what that means?" She looked up at Jenn.

Her face was close, uplifted, and luminous with the light shining on it from above. Jenn found herself thinking it would be nice to kiss her. Then she found herself wondering what the *hell* she was thinking and she moved away quickly, covering her movement by pulling a second chair over so that she could sit and look at the picture on the screen. She felt Annie's gaze on her, and heat climbed up her neck. She said in answer to Annie's question, "Seems to me that a seal's a seal."

"Not if it can't be identified," Annie said. "Like I said before, she could be a species of seal not yet documented, but I've decided that's not likely. I mean, I can't exactly see some seal swimming around Puget Sound every year and going unnoticed as a new species, can you? So 'f you ask me, this seal's a mutant and if *that's* the case, we're onto something big. We're not the first ones to see her, though. My guess is she's been some place other than Puget Sound."

"Well sure. But we already know that. She's only here once a year."

"Yeah. But what I mean is . . . Look at this picture. She's got a transmitter on, and she sure as hell didn't put it there herself. Plus, it's an old one. Check it out. Ivar and his little buddy were there giving us grief, so I couldn't get the best possible shot, but you can more or less see it."

"How d'you know it's old?" For her part, Jenn couldn't tell it was a transmitter at all. She could see *something* on the back of the seal's neck, but it could have been anything. Still, she got Annie's point. No matter what it was, the fact that the seal was wearing it at all suggested that someone had put it there and, perhaps, that same someone was tracking her. But who was that person? she wondered. And why was the seal important to him?

"These kinds of transmitters," Annie said, pointing to what could be seen of the gizmo on the seal, "they aren't used any longer. They fell off, so something better had to be created, something that the seal couldn't shed." Annie flicked through more of the pictures. It seemed she was looking for the perfect shot.

It wasn't there, though, because she said, "Damn, damn, damn. I need one clear picture of that thing—just one clear picture—and we're in business."

"I thought you wanted her DNA."

"I want that, too, but this is something else. This is something that could be even better." She clicked off the pictures and turned to Jenn. She said, "I need you big-time, Beauty. We've got to get you certified to dive. We need to get our hands on that seal."

THE NEXT DIVING lesson rolled round in two days, and Annie made sure that Jenn was ready for it. They drove into the parking lot of South Whidbey Fitness fifteen minutes early, and Annie hopped out with a bright, "Good deal, he's already here," in reference to Chad Pederson's truck. Jenn followed her with less enthusiasm in the early morning darkness. She hadn't slept well, she still hadn't got a whole soccer practice in, and this entire Nera business was starting to feel like something that could seriously derail her life. So she trudged after Annie toward the fitness center. The only sign of life in the place was a bicycle chained to a rack by the door, along with a few lights burning inside the building.

In the locker room, Annie stripped as before, sliding her shapely legs into the butt floss bottom of her bikini. Jenn was sour enough in mood to say, "How'd you swim in that thing anyway?" and Annie turned to her, cupping her breasts and jiggling them playfully as she replied. "Honestly? I'd rather go nude in the pool. I like the sensation. But Chad might freak out. What about you?"

Jenn quickly looked away from Annie. "What *about* me?"

"Nude or dressed? I walk around my place in Florida butt naked most of the time."

"Bet the neighbors like that."

"Well, my partner does."

"Lucky him," Jenn said.

"Her," Annie said. And when Jenn glanced her way, Annie added, "Sorry. I probably should've said. Does that freak you out?"

Jenn shrugged, although her heart started break-dancing and she could tell her face had gone traffic-light red. "Why should it?" she asked. "This isn't, like, nineteen-fifty or something."

"Sometimes people are weird about sex, that's all," Annie told her. "Her name's Beth, by the way. She's a pediatrician. We've been together since—"

"I'm ready," Jenn said. She didn't really need to hear about Annie, about Beth, about *whatever*. It gave her the creeps. She was here to dive.

Annie said, "Sure." She slipped into the rest of her suit and padded out to the pool where Chad was setting up his gear. He gave her the once-over as he'd done before, and Jenn smiled inwardly with "If he only knew . . ." on her mind. Then, a second later, she was gut-punched when she saw who was about to dive into one of the swimming lanes set up in the pool.

It was SmartAss FatBroad Becca King. She made a neat dive, and she began to swim like someone with a lifetime of lessons behind her. Of course, Jenn thought, what else would she do?

Jenn wondered why the hell the FatBroad was at South Whidbey Fitness at five in the morning. Soon enough she learned the truth of the matter.

She'd put on a wet suit and a weight belt and was heaving her way into a tank when Becca King dripped her way over to them. She said to Chad, "Hope it was okay I warmed up," and Chad said, "Better than okay. You two know each other?" and without waiting for an answer, "This is Becca King. She's joining the class."

"*What?*" Jenn said. "Wait a minute. Are we starting over?"

"Nope. Becca's had a couple of private lessons. She's all caught up. Fact is, she's actually a little ahead."

Oh *right*, Jenn thought. That would be just like her. Anything to make everyone else look bad. She glared at Becca who was watching her solemnly. "I'm sorta slow to catch on," the other girl said, but Jenn believed that the way she believed in fairies.

Chad got them into the water after a review that seemed to last for hours. Each piece of equipment, its function, put it on, take it off, put it on again. Depth, air pressure, the bends, nitrogen narcosis, and on and on. He ended with, "When you have a problem, it's going to happen in the water so it has to be solved in the water. That's what we're working on today."

Turned out that "working on" solving problems in the water meant working—and diving—with a buddy. Jenn had a very bad feeling about where this was heading, and she wasn't surprised when Chad said that she and Becca would be diving buddies. "Into the pool, you two," he told them. "Becca, use the ladder and put your fins on in the water. Jenn, you're jumping in equipped."

"Hey! Why do I have to—"

"She already passed this part. She's ahead of you, remember? Now get going. Just do what I do. Take a giant stride. Point is not to lose your mask."

As Becca went down the ladder, Jenn watched Chad who, of course, made the whole thing look simple. Jenn followed him, trying to mimic his movements. She hit the water, lost her mask, got water up her nose, and nearly smacked her head on the side of the pool because of her fins. She shot to the surface, coughing and snorting. Becca had swum for her mask and was holding it out to her.

Jenn snatched it. "I can *do* this, okay?" and she threw in a couple of satisfactory thoughts about the FatBroad's sexual extracurricular activities.

Becca looked at her directly, an unnerving look that made Jenn want to rip her nose off. She said, "What? *What?*" and then she lowered her voice to add, "What are you *doing* here anyway? What d'you think? Expecting *Derric* to show up or something?"

"I'm helping out a friend," Becca said.

"You mean you *have* a friend?" was Jenn's retort.

Becca flinched, which satisfied Jenn. Stay out of my life, bitch, was what she thought.

Becca said, "Takes one to know one, don't you think?" and before Jenn could ask what the hell she was talking about, Becca said to Chad, "Okay, Teach, what's next?"

TWENTY-ONE

Becca steeled herself for the arrival of Carnation Day at South Whidbey High School. She knew it was just the sort of event that generally turned out to be a feelings smasher, something akin to not receiving a Valentine in your elementary school classroom, only worse. But she discovered soon enough that several years ago the PTA had developed a solution to the Carnationless-in-Langley problem. Every kid who was destined *not* to have a flower ended up with one from the PTA.

The flowers were distributed just before lunch, giving everyone time to read the messages attached to the carnations' stems. As a result, the cheerleaders were walking around the commons with so many flowers that they looked like Olympic ice skaters post performance. So were the kids deemed popular. So were the athletes, as you would expect. Cries of Wow! Cool! Chill! No way! were everywhere as these kids dumped armfuls of flowers onto the tables and sat to read their messages. But along with those cries and the chatter and the laughter came the whispers, which Becca recognized as hot and intense. They filled the air with a non-noise noise that was generated by the kids who'd received only one flower and the other kids who *saw* them with only one flower.

He is . . . she's hurtin' . . . try dropping fifty pounds, cow . . . what a loser . . . hate this hate this hate this . . . stupid idiot anyway . . . always this way . . . he didn't . . . she did . . . why doesn't anyone . . . made a lot of claims about how people were feeling. To Becca, the whole thing seemed like an idea guaranteed to cement bad feelings everywhere.

She'd prepared herself for the single carnation way in advance of the day. Although she'd thought about sending herself two flowers so she wouldn't look like such a loser, she'd decided she'd rather spend the money on something a little more important, like food. So she was surprised when she received three flowers.

She wasn't sure how they'd managed it, but Diana Kinsale, Seth Darrow, and Debbie Grieder had all sent her carnations, with messages that were funny and fond. She smiled particularly over Seth's—"You & Me, Sweatie, in it Togehter"—and especially at the Seth-like misspellings. She thought of what a real *friend* Seth was. If he'd still been a student at South Whidbey High School, she would have sent him six flowers, she decided.

So she was feeling far less horrible than she'd expected to feel because, of course, the one thing she knew was that she'd get no flowers from Derric. And she was relatively okay with this until Courtney Baker staggered into the room.

She had what looked like one hundred carnations in her arms. It was probably going to take her the entire lunch hour just to read the messages, Becca figured. She glanced around for Derric and assumed he'd be similarly burdened. But he wasn't in sight.

A cheerleader heaped with carnations joined Courtney, giving the eye to her haul of flowers. Becca heard her say, "Wow. Guess I don't need to ask how things're going with *you* two, do I?" to which Courtney leaned over and said something to the cheerleader, who responded with, "Courtney! You didn't! No way!"

Becca heard nothing more between the girls, for someone ran into the back of her chair with enough force to knock her into the table. A snarky voice said, "Oh, excuse me, fattie," and Becca didn't even need to raise her head to know Jenn McDaniels was passing behind her. Jenn added, "Wow. You have three friends?" in reference to Becca's three carnations. Becca swiveled in her seat and saw Jenn had one. In spite of herself, she said, "Talking about friends, Jenn . . ." and nothing more.

Jenn threw her carnation into Becca's lap. "Yeah right," she snapped. "Talking about friends," and she stalked off with *smart-ass . . . fat broad . . . so freaking ugly* following her, along with a few other words that always made whispers from Jenn McDaniels unmistakable in their origin.

Becca sighed, but at the same time she realized that Jenn's whispers didn't hurt her feelings as they had at first. She thought about this and wondered if it meant she was closer to what her grandmother had always told her about the real purpose behind hearing whispers: *The point is to use them to get inside someone's skin and walk around for a bit in order to understand them better* had been her instructions. While Becca hadn't understood at the time what her grandmother meant, she was getting the feeling that she might be closer to understanding that meaning now.

She opened the message on Jenn's flower, ready to see something like "Your Friendly PTA" printed upon the unfurled slip of paper. What she saw instead was, "From your personal Studboy." So she'd been wrong about Jenn McDaniels, she thought.

SHE WENT INTO town after school, taking the island bus, which dropped her close to the Cliff Motel. It looked empty and sad at this time of year, and the absence of Debbie Grieder's SUV told Becca she would have to wait to thank her older friend for her kindness and the message "DG and her munchkins think U R the best." She went on to South Whidbey Commons. Seth, she figured, was probably there.

So were a lot of other people, as things turned out. She walked in and immediately saw Seth sitting at a table in the corner reading a book that turned out to be *Siddhartha*. He was moving his lips and squinting at the page, but what Becca wondered was how he could read at all. The noise level in the place was excruciating. She tried to drown it with static from the AUD box, but even that didn't do much good. A crowd had gathered in the gallery room, but there were way too many people, and they spilled out into the coffee room as well.

She worked her way through them and joined Seth. He looked up from his book, his face brightening when he saw her.

She said, "Hey."

He said, "Back atcha."

"You sent me a flower. That was totally nice."

"You know me. Nice is my middle name. When it isn't Dumbnuts."

"It's never Dumbnuts."

"Oh con-trair," he countered. "It's Dumbnuts once a week, at least. Twice if my luck's bad. Anyways, I'm a say-it-with-flowers dude and you're a getting-a-flower babe. That being the case, I sent you a flower." He set his book down on the table, spine up. He removed his black fedora and messed with his ponytail. "But this doesn't mean we're hooked up, okay?" he said. "I don't want you to get the wrong idea. Just didn't want you to face the one-carnation curse."

"I got three," she told him.

"Damn. I shoulda saved my buck."

She said, "And Jenn McDaniels threw hers at me."

"Ooooh. She got just one? That's nasty. But not surprising."

"It wasn't from the PTA," Becca told him. "It was from Studboy. That's what it said."

"Then she probably sent it to herself," Seth told her. "Cuz that's one bull ain't no cowpoke gonna want to ride."

Becca frowned. "You don't mean . . ."

"I do mean. That plus all her personal crap . . . ? Keep about fifty yards between yourself and that one."

Becca began to respond, but angry shouting interrupted her. It came from the gallery and the ongoing meeting. A man was yelling, "Why don't you people get a life, for God's sake? You act like that animal's here to save this dump of a town." At this, outraged retorts came from all directions.

Seth said, "Weirdness prevails as usual," and Becca turned in her chair to see what was happening.

Becca recognized a man on his feet. Eddie Beddoe, she thought, the guy with the rifle on the beach at Sandy Point. Someone was yelling at him, "Shut up and sit down!" while someone else shouted, "When was the last time you did anything positive for Langley, Eddie?" Then another voice said, "Let's get ourselves calmed down, folks," and this was a voice that Becca knew. Ivar Thorndyke was in the meeting. She turned back to Seth and asked, "What's going on?"

"Seal spotters called an emergency meeting."

"The black seal again?"

"Oh yeah. If the seal spotters have a confab, there's only ever one reason."

Becca thought about this and about being on the boat when Ivar confronted Annie Taylor and Chad Pederson. She said, "Seth, d'you know much about that seal?"

"All's I know is she's a seal and she's black," he said. "She shows up once a year and gets a big hallelujah from the town."

Becca looked back at the meeting, where it seemed as if a little pushing and shoving was going on. She said to Seth, "I think it's more than that."

"How so?"

"She's wearing a transmitter."

"Who?"

"The seal."

"Like what? She's a *mechanical* seal?" He laughed. "Not hardly, Beck. She's always looked pretty real to me. Or d'you mean she's communicating with someone? Hey, maybe she's an alien life-form. Get too close and she'll put babies down your throat and they'll blast out of your stomach when they get their teeth."

"Very funny," Becca said. "But I'm telling you, I was there when Annie Taylor saw her and *when* she saw that there was a transmitter on her. . . . It was a huge thing, Seth. There's something going on."

She eased her way to the edge of the meeting, to the point where she could see into the gallery. Ivar was at the front of the crowd, which spread out before him like a human fan. Eddie Beddoe had elbowed his way forward, and he was in the act of confronting Ivar. The size of the room—which was small—made him look massive. The veins in his temples were so filled with blood that they looked like worms crawling across his skin.

He was saying, "You listen to me, all of you. That blasted seal don't belong here. You know that, Thorndyke, better 'n anyone. And the sooner the rest of you idiots get that into your thick skulls, the better off all of us're going to be."

More shouts ensued. Becca scanned the crowd. She was surprised to see that Jenn McDaniels was there, sitting next to Annie Taylor. On Annie's other side sat Chad Pederson, and he and Annie were in the middle of some kind of intense conversation. For her part, Jenn was slouched in her seat, watching Ivar and Eddie suspiciously.

Eddie Beddoe was going on, developing a real head of steam on the topic of the coal black seal. "That animal's been nothing but trouble since the day she showed up. She's already way too easy around people. She's at the point of attacking some kid on the beach. And *then* where's the lot of you going to be? She's probably already carrying a disease 'cause why else would she be so close to shore."

Voices rose higher. People jumped to their feet. Ivar did what he could to settle them down. It look to Becca like pandemonium, but it was a pandemonium that Eddie was clearly enjoying.

He went on with, "Fish and Wildlife need to be told. They need to get her out of here before she passes on whatever the hell she's got and our fishing and crabbing is ruined. You understand?"

At that, Annie Taylor jumped up. She shouted, "Listen to me! That seal is perfectly healthy. I've seen her up close. So has Chad"—here she put her hand on the young man's shoulder—"and so has Mr. Thorndyke for that matter."

Voices rose in horror at this information.

"You got close?"

"What the hell's going on?"

"You some kind of hypocrite, Thorndyke?"

"Yeah, you ask him that!" Eddie Beddoe crowed. "You ask him what he wants with that seal!"

More shouting, more roaring, more swearing ensued. So much tension developed that Becca could feel it. It impeded her breathing and got in the way of her ability to think. She needed to get *out* of the place, so she fumbled through the crowd and got to the door, and once outside, she took gulps of cold air.

Darkness had fallen, and the shadows around her spelled a warning of danger. Someone in Langley needed to heed it, Becca thought, before it was far too late.

PART FIVE

Goss Lake

TWENTY-TWO

Derric had known he'd blown it when the carnations were distributed. Courtney had sent him thirty-seven. He had sent her two.

He wanted to use The Guy excuse, that explanation for every romantic misstep any man might make. It was, "Hey, I'm a guy," and it was intended to convey that, as a male of the species, he would *never* really know the right thing to do in a situation involving the heart.

Problem was . . . he *had* known what the right thing to do was. He was her boyfriend and the whole world knew it. So why hadn't he made a big deal with the flowers?

Someone sure had. Or a lot of someones. Because when he saw her coming out of the commons at the end of lunch, Courtney was carrying what looked like two hundred flowers. She was also looking sad and confused. No doubt, he thought. "Love from Derric" on two measly flowers didn't go far to match the thirty-seven separate messages that she'd sent to him.

He knew what she would think: His failure in the flower department was directly related to their argument after he'd left the prayer circle. Well, it was and wasn't at the same time. Something was going *on* with him. He just didn't know what it was.

It didn't help matters that Becca King had been standing there when he burst out of that stupid classroom. She'd seen something bad was happening between him and Courtney and, for reasons he didn't want to consider, that made everything so much worse. The only saving grace about it all was that Becca had rushed off. She hadn't heard him and Courtney go at it, so at least he'd prevented her from feeling smug.

It had been a wrecked few minutes, though. The worst part of them was that nothing he said could make Courtney see she'd totally betrayed him with her supposed "prayer" about them.

She'd cried out, "Derric! Where're you going? What's wrong?"

He'd hissed back at her, "What's *wrong*? That's our private business. That's what's wrong. What're you doing talking about us like that in the middle of a bunch of kids?"

She said, "It's not like everyone doesn't know we're hooking up."

He wanted to kick a hole in the wall. "So what? Dude, I do *not* believe you."

Her blue eyes rounded. "And anyway I was talking to the Lord, not to them. And please don't call me 'dude,' okay?"

"Fine. Whatever. Sorry. *Courtney.* Well, you were doing your talking to the Lord in front of fifteen eavesdroppers. *And* you should have frigging told me you were going to start talking about our stuff."

"But you know that I pray. I pray all the time about a lot of things. And I've told you I pray about us. D'you think it's actually *easy* for me when we've got our clothes off and—"

"Okay, okay!" He looked around furtively. This was insane. The *last* thing he wanted was a public announcement in one of the high school halls on the topic of how far they'd gone with each other. "So am I right in thinking that you've been 'praying' about us in that stupid prayer circle ever since we started dating?"

"It's not a stupid prayer circle." Her voice was quiet and dignified, but her eyes were stricken.

"It's a group of high school kids, Court. They're hearing something that's none of their business. You're telling them exactly . . . I don't even want to *know* how much you've already told them while you've been 'praying.'"

"Don't say it like that. You make it sound like it's some big joke that I pray at school."

"Well, isn't it?"

"No, it isn't. Not a single person in the prayer circle's going to say a word about you and me. That's not who they are. They don't spread gossip."

"You got to be kidding. You're not that lame."

"Gossip has no place in the work of Jesus," she said.

What he said was, "I got to get out of here," and he left her standing in the hall alone. He walked off shaking his head. Either she was crazy or he was wrong. But one way or the other, things felt *bad*.

Yet this wasn't the reason he hadn't flooded her with flowers.

It was a good excuse, sure. It just wasn't the reason. The reason was what was going on inside him. It was the pull of wanting her so badly his whole body felt sore. It was the push of knowing that something very essential was missing when he was with her in a way that didn't involve making out.

So *what*? he thought. What did that matter? They were good together. They were practically on fire together. When they saw each other, they eased ever closer to the edge, and if he had to fall as he wanted to fall, then he definitely wanted to fall with her.

Didn't he? That was the question. His gonads were yelling, "Yeah, yeah, yeah, bro!" His heart wasn't that far behind. His brain was saying, "Come on be reasonable. You're only human and there's lots of protection available these days." But his soul was saying, "Hey, Der . . . Maybe not."

And he didn't know *why* his soul was saying that. Only . . . he did know why. Only . . . he wished that he didn't because life would have been so much easier for him that way.

What made everything so much more difficult was that Courtney turned out to be right about the kids who were in the prayer circle. Not a single one of them said a word. No one winked at him. No one leered. No one said, "Whoa, *mama*, are you guys hot or what?" There wasn't—*anywhere*—the slightest indication that Courtney Baker was praying for the strength to keep Derric Mathieson from taking from her what she wanted to give to the man she married. So she'd been right and he'd been wrong and even *that* was something he didn't understand.

He wanted to talk about the entire situation. He wanted to

look at it every way he could. But he found that the only person he wanted to talk to about what he was going through was Becca King, and no way could he talk to her.

TWO DAYS LATER he finally got the cast off his leg. Two days after that, Courtney suggested that they take a drive after school to a coffee place buried deep in the woods to the west of Langley. Mukilteo Coffee was a roasting establishment that sent clouds of an odd burnt-toast scent into the air, and since it wasn't easy to get to without a car, it generally didn't host a group of kids inside its woodland café.

"We c'n celebrate your leg," she offered. "I bet you're relieved to get rid of that cast."

He said okay, and when they arrived at the place surrounded by forest, they found that they had the coffeehouse all to themselves. They ordered their drinks and took them to one of the wide windows looking out at the trees. Courtney was the one who started them talking.

She said, "Actually, I sort of wanted to talk to you. I mean about a lot more than being glad about your leg."

"Okay," he said carefully. He waited for more.

"It's that . . . well, I got carried away. It just seemed like the right thing to do at the time. I mean, I thought you'd feel good about it. But . . . well, obviously, you didn't."

Derric stirred his hot chocolate. He hadn't particularly wanted it, but he felt bad about taking up space in the café without buying something, so he'd gone for it. He should've had something to eat instead. His stomach was rumbling. He would've liked to settle it. But her words relieved him with their suggestion that she was finally seeing the light when it came to talking about their private business in front of a group of kids.

He said, "Thanks for understanding, Court. See, it's not that I don't pray. And it's not that I don't want you to pray. But when you told them what we—"

"Oh gosh, oh wait." She sat up straighter in her chair. "Did you think I meant the prayer circle?"

"Didn't you?"

"No. I still think . . ." She looked down at her coffee, at the plate next to it. She'd ordered a scone and she took a piece of it. He did as well, but to him it tasted like extra-dry sawdust with a sprinkling of sugar. She said, "Well, that doesn't matter. I was talking about the flowers."

Oh, he thought. He hadn't avoided having to make The Guy excuse after all. He said, "I'm sorry about that, Court."

"Sorry?"

"You know. I only sent you two. What can I say? I'm a guy. Sometimes we don't think—"

"It's not that," she interrupted. "Well, it is in a way. But it's more that I sent you thirty-seven. I went totally overboard, like I was out of control or something. I sort of knew it was nuts to send that many flowers, but I did it anyway. I thought . . . It seemed to me that you'd be all joyous, I guess . . . I mean to get all those flowers and notes from me."

"But I was," he said, a little bit too quickly.

She cocked her head at him. "No, you weren't."

He bristled a little. "And you know this . . . how?"

"Because you didn't have them with you. When I saw you in the commons? What did you do with them? Did you throw them away? Or give them to someone? Did you read the messages? I mean, it doesn't matter only . . . I mean, I *shouldn't* have sent you thirty-seven. You must've felt like a . . . Oh I don't know. But when they got delivered, you must've wanted to crawl under your desk."

"No way," he said. "It was cool. Really."

"I don't think so," she said. "So what did you do with them, anyway?"

Trapped, he thought. He looked out of the window. The forest trees, he saw, wore the tight red buds of spring's unfurled leaves at the moment. In time they would be a wall of green. A guy could hide behind that wall, he decided. Hiding didn't seem like such a bad idea. He said, "My locker."

She said, "You put thirty-seven flowers into your locker? Did you read the notes?"

"Sure I read them!"

"Then why didn't you mention them to me? Why didn't you . . . say anything, really?"

That, Derric thought, was the question of the hour. It got right down to that soul thing that was bothering him. He only wished he had a decent answer, but he couldn't come up with one so he said, "I don't know. It didn't seem . . . I wasn't sure . . ."

"About what? Me? Us? Derric, what's going on?"

"Hey, you know how I feel about you."

"I thought I did. And I thought that you were proud that you and I are couple."

"I *am* proud." But even he could hear the defensiveness in his voice. *Why* did he feel under some kind of attack when all she was doing was asking some reasonable questions? He said, "Look, I'm sorry I didn't carry the flowers around. I guess I could have. Or I could've carried some of them. I don't know why I didn't. I just didn't."

Courtney said quietly, "People usually know why they're doing things. Or not doing things."

He felt bristly again. "Maybe you do," he said irritably.

"Maybe you do, too, underneath it all. Come on, Derric. You want to tell me what's wrong?"

"Nothing's wrong!"

"Yeah, something is. At some level you know. Maybe you don't want to admit it to yourself, but you do know. I hope you figure it out." She sipped her coffee, then, and joined him in looking out of the window.

He wondered what they would talk about next. Then he wondered why he was wondering. Then he found himself looking at the sweater she was wearing, at its V-neck, and at the soft skin that descended to the heady sweet spot between her breasts. *Then* he wanted to kick his own butt. Talk to her, he told himself, say something, be someone.

He said, "Sometimes I just don't know the things I think I

should know. Sometimes I feel like I'm caught between being a kid and being an adult. It's like I'm in the middle of a web that I didn't make, so I'm trapped somehow. That's where I am now. D'you know what I mean?"

She kept her gaze on the window as he spoke, but when he'd finished, she turned to him. "Trapped," she repeated. "I guess that doesn't feel so good, does it?"

That was all she said, but he knew from her tone that she'd mistaken his meaning. At least that was what he told himself. Later that evening when he was alone and she texted him *love you so much want this to be urs* and sent him a picture she shouldn't have sent anyone, he wasn't so sure.

TWENTY-THREE

Becca thought about a lot of things after the meeting of the seal spotters that she'd witnessed in South Whidbey Commons. Mostly, though, what she thought about was Eddie Beddoe. Danger had seemed to roll off the man along with all the anger he displayed, and it didn't take much for her to remember the day she'd run into him at Sandy Point. His whispers had spoken of *kill her that's what.* She'd thought at the time he meant Diana Kinsale. But Diana had told her he meant the seal. The seal was responsible for his life's hardships, he thought. The problem was, that didn't make sense.

Making sense didn't matter much, though. She'd felt the atmosphere that Eddie Beddoe created, and she figured his intentions toward Langley, its townspeople, and the seal they loved were very bad.

She hardly knew anything about the man, though. He'd lost a boat in a storm. He blamed a seal for that. At one time he'd been married to Sharla Mann. End of story. But after the seal spotters' meeting, Becca wanted to know more. She just wasn't sure how to discover it.

"Hey, Ivar, where's that guy Eddie from?" didn't get her far the next time she was at work in the chicken coop at Heart's Desire.

"Lived in Possession Point for years," was the extent to which Ivar illuminated her as he examined his pot plants and adjusted the grow lights over them. "Now he's over in Glendale. Why d'you want to know?"

"Because he wants to kill Nera" didn't seem like a smart way to go, all things considered. So she said, jiggling the truth a bit, "Sharla said one time she was married to him."

Ivar nodded. "Oh yeah. They were married." *Head examined* was his thought.

Becca didn't know if Ivar's whisper meant Eddie or Sharla. She waited for more, hoping to learn something, but all she got was *oil and water*, which made her think of the old saying that oil and water don't ever mix.

But later, alone in her tree house with the wind kicking up a March storm outside, she thought of oil in a different way. She remembered the information about the oil spill that Jenn McDaniels had left on the computer in the library when Becca had sat down to see what was going on with Jeff Corrie. The spill, she recalled, had polluted Possession Point. Was that what Ivar had been talking about?

At her next scuba lesson, she decided to brave the lioness's fangs and ask Jenn McDaniels about it. She hung around in the locker room after her shower, trying to make it seem less obvious that she was stalling for time by spending extra minutes on her hair. When the coast was clear and Jenn was alone by the lockers, Becca sauntered in, pretending to be gathering her things. She said casually to Jenn, "Hey, Jenn, d'you know anything about that oil spill in Possession Point?"

She might have said "D'you know there're six aliens standing in the locker room doorway?" because Jenn's reaction was about in line with having heard that instead of a simpler question. She turned slowly and examined Becca with so many swear words pounding from her head that Becca dug the AUD box from her backpack and slid it onto the waistband of her jeans, following this with making a very big procedure about screwing the earphone into place.

"What d'you *really* want around here?" was Jenn's demand. "I mean, aside from Derric Mathieson who, by the way, is totally inside Courtney Baker's pants in case you didn't know."

Becca took a few steadying breaths. She said to Jenn, "Thanks for the info, but he and I are way done, so he's free to climb into anyone's pants. He can wear them, even. So, what about the oil spill? D'you know anything? I know you live down there."

Jenn's eyes narrowed. "And you know this, how?"

Becca faltered under her gaze. "I don't even remember. Derric must've said. I dunno. Why? Does that make a difference or something?"

Jenn slammed the door of her locker. She was wearing only a towel, which she dropped to the floor. Becca, embarrassed, looked away. Jenn hooted. Then she began to talk.

Yeah, there was an oil spill. Yeah, it was in Possession Point.

It was bilge oil and it was bad and it wrecked a lot of sea life and a lot of the shore.

So far so good, Becca thought. She asked, then, about Eddie Beddoe. He lived there, right? At the time of the oil spill?

Jenn shrugged. "He has a trailer down there. He might've lived in it then. Hell if I know. And why d'*you* care?"

Becca fiddled around with her backpack long enough to make sure Jenn had put on some clothes. Then she looked up and said, "It's just that . . . I heard him going on at that meeting? The one in South Whidbey Commons? He was going on about the seal? I asked Ivar Thorndyke about it and he said Eddie came from Possession Point. So I just wondered. . . ."

"What were *you* doing there?" Jenn's eyes were narrow and her face was a scowl.

"Huh? Where?"

"*God.* Where else, Fattie? South Whidbey Commons. What were *you* doing there?"

"Like, I wasn't supposed to be there or something?" Becca asked.

"Like, I like my life better when you're nowhere near it and I was at the meeting. Why didn't I see you?"

"I was talking to Seth."

"Ohhhh. Seth. The new boyfriend Seth."

Becca sighed and tried to summon up patience. Jenn McDaniels had to be the most impossible girl on the planet. She said, "Look. I'm just asking. You don't have to tell me anything, okay?"

"Good because I'm not going to."

"I guess that means you don't know," Becca said.

"Hey, I know lots. I know a hell of a lot more than you. There was an oil spill and he probably lived there then and if you want to know for sure, why the hell don't you ask him? Or are you too scared? Yeah that's it, I bet. He scares you, doesn't he?"

"I get the feeling he scares everyone," Becca told her. She gave up on Jenn and left the locker room.

BILGE OIL *WAS* bad, as Jenn had declared, and it didn't take much effort for Becca to discover this. In the case of Whidbey Island, the bilge oil had been put into a ship in the wrong way, somehow. The result of this was pipes cracking in that vessel and oil leaking from it as it moved from the Port of Everett into the shipping lanes of Puget Sound. The leak happened at night, and no one knew about it until the morning when the tide had brought the sludge of it to shore and deposited it all over Possession Point.

She got some of her facts from the biology teacher at the high school. She put together others by ducking into a white cottage on Second Street in Langley, where the historical society had set up a museum about the village and where other information was stored, including information in the memories of the volunteers who ran the place. There, Becca learned that the stuff that had polluted Possession Point had been toxic to whatever it came into contact with. People wore hazmat suits just to go near it, and all sorts of individuals from the island had been hired to help clean up the mess.

Toxic meant deadly. Becca knew that. Wildlife died when it was covered by the oil. She wondered, though, what happened to people when they came into contact with the oil, too. Did it get onto their skin, into their systems, into their blood, into their brains? Did it eat at their minds? Was that at the bottom of what was going on with Eddie Beddoe? Why else, she wondered, would he see a seal as something he needed to kill? It's not like he was a fisherman being robbed of his catch or something.

She wanted badly to talk to someone who could answer her questions, but the only person she could think of was Sharla. And Sharla barely talked about anything at all.

She said, "Oil spill?" and her whispers said *too close past remembering happened and gone*, which wasn't helpful to Becca. She went on with, "I lived there, sure. My husband, he helped with the cleanup. Everyone did."

"It was bad, huh?" Becca said. They were doing the dishes on one of the nights that Sharla had invited Becca to stay for dinner after her work in Ivar's chicken coop. "I saw pictures at the historical society. People had on hazmat suits."

"Oh, sure," Sharla said. But *Not Eddie . . . oil like a second skin on the man* suggested something else, and Becca felt the hair on her arms stir.

"What about you?" Becca asked. "Did you have to wear at hazmat suit?"

Not Eddie not Eddie the sight and the smell eight days and then no no I won't.

What did she mean? Becca asked herself. *What* couldn't she bear to think about?

Ivar either couldn't or wouldn't help her. The subject of Eddie Beddoe was a sore one for him. All he would say was "F'r all I know, Becks, Eddie Beddoe was crazier'n a rabid raccoon long before there was any oil on the beach. And a helluva long time after, too."

That was it until one day in the chicken coop, and at that point Becca had pretty much given up trying to sort out what was amiss with Eddie Beddoe. She was hard at work with more of the chicken coop's contents, still doing her part to make sense of the place. Under a pile of what smelled like ancient blankets that had been used for horses, she came upon an old brass-bound trunk. It had no lock, so she pulled it into the center of the building where the light was better. It was covered with grime despite the blankets, and as it had no lock and she was curious, she opened it.

Right on the top was a pile of pictures, some in frames and some not. She took them out and slowly looked through them. Eddie Beddoe, she saw, and Sharla Mann. They were wedding pictures from a long time ago, but there was no mistaking Eddie Beddoe. He was as big as a member of the Bunyan clan and Sharla on his arm looked young and pretty. It was sad, Becca thought, how everything changed. She wondered if more than an oil spill had changed things.

So she looked. She knew it wasn't entirely right to be going through Sharla Mann's old belongings, but she did it anyway because Sharla's whispers—such as they were—told her there was more to know. And having such knowledge *could* be important, she told herself. It could help her keep Eddie Beddoe from doing whatever he intended to do to harm people.

Halfway through old clothes, tablecloths, and towels, she found it. Three small pairs of OshKosh overalls, three small T-shirts, three pairs of socks, one pair of shoes. They were sized for a toddler. But Sharla, she recalled, had never had a child.

BECCA THOUGHT ABOUT this as she rode her bike back to her hiding place in the woods. She stowed the bike deep within the trees and began the hike to the clearing where the tree house waited. As she walked, she reviewed what she knew: about the oil spill, about Eddie Beddoe, about Sharla Mann and those small child's clothes. She thought about Ivar Thorndyke, too. She wondered if he was one of the people who wasn't revealing everything he knew.

All of this was on her mind when the clearing came into view ahead of her in the evening shadows. A figure was moving slowly across it. She quickly ducked out of sight behind the huge trunk of an old-growth hemlock. Her heart slamming in her throat, she waited. Carefully, she peered around the tree to see what was going on.

She knew the old man who was gazing at the ground. It was

Seth's grandfather, Ralph Darrow. She'd never met him but she'd seen him with Seth: once through the window where she'd stood outside in the darkness and watched Grandpa and Grandson play chess in front of the huge stone fireplace in Ralph Darrow's living room and once alone and working in his garden. But she'd never seen him out this far into the woods, and she knew his presence meant trouble.

He was studying the area beneath the tree house. She knew what was there. Her footprints were all over the place. So were Seth's. As she watched, he went to the bottom of the tree house stairs and looked up at the trap door in the balcony floor which, Becca thanked God, she'd closed when she left. She also thanked God that there was nothing visible on the balcony to betray her. That wasn't the same for the galvanized bucket and the shovel and the rake hidden behind a tree not thirty feet from where Ralph Darrow stood. There was also a low pile of logs that Seth had filched from Ralph for her use in the woodstove, but they were hidden as well, so if he didn't look, he wouldn't see.

He put his hand on the tree house stairs, and Becca held her breath. If he climbed, if he went inside, she was totally finished. And there'd be hell for Seth to pay.

She could only imagine how things would play out then. Ralph Darrow would discover her. He would say, "Who the heck are you?" first. Second he would ask, "Do your parents know where you are?" and then, if she answered that question with any degree of truth, his next one would be, "What're you doing on the island, then?" And that would take them eventually to her mother, to San Diego, and to everything else.

In the clearing, Ralph Darrow put his foot on the bottom of the tree house stairs. He hesitated. Becca concentrated to catch his whispers. The only one she heard was *blasted boy . . . up to now.* Then he changed his mind about climbing up to see what the blasted boy had been up to. Instead, he turned away and headed in the direction of the main trail. It would take him away from Becca and back to his house.

For the moment, she was safe.

THE MOMENT DIDN'T last long. Becca waited for five minutes, shivering in the cold, after Ralph Darrow left the clearing. She listened hard for his return, but the only sound she heard was the *rat-a-tatt*ing of a pileated woodpecker on a dead alder nearby. She finally gathered up her courage and made a dash for the clearing, its two hemlocks, and the tree house. She scrambled up the stairs and across the balcony. She zipped inside the place and there she huddled, relatively safe. Or so she thought.

Not fifteen minutes later, she heard it. Someone was coming up the stairs. The movements were stealthy, but she was listening hard. She knew what had happened. He'd gone for a weapon.

Of *course*, she thought. He didn't know who was inside the tree house, aside from the fact that someone was trespassing on his property. It could be a criminal on the run, a dope dealer, a smuggler, a terrorist, anyone. For all he knew, the person inside the tree house was armed. Naturally, he'd arm himself as well.

The trap door made a small squeak when it opened. Becca stifled a cry as furtive footsteps came toward the door. She saw the knob of it turn, and it began to open. She wondered if she had time to get by him, time to run for the stairs, time to flee altogether. She gathered her wits and her courage to make a run for it, drawing in a deep breath and—

It was Seth. He had an armload of wood. She hadn't lit the lantern and the place was dark, so he didn't see her. He jumped and yelped when she said, "Don't light a fire."

"You scared the holy crap out of me!"

"Your grandpa was here," she told him.

"Here? Where? Inside the tree house?"

"Below. He saw my footprints everywhere. Yours too. He looked up the ladder but he didn't climb up."

"Cool. That means—"

"That means he's gone to call the cops or he's gone for a gun."

"He doesn't own a gun. Well, maybe he does, but I've never seen it." He went to the stove and dropped the wood onto the floor. He began to mess around with the fire.

"Don't!" she said.

"Chill," he told her. "It's okay. I'll talk to him."

"Talk? About *what*? Seth, you can't."

"Got to. If he's seen our footprints, he knows something's up. He's going to ask me what. I need to tell him."

"But he'll make me leave. He'll want to know . . . Seth, you can't tell him anything!"

"He's cool, Becca. It won't be a problem. I should've said something a while back."

"Seth, no! He'll ask . . . I can't tell . . . Please. Never mind. I have to leave."

She began grabbing her belongings, shoving them into the duffel bag that Seth had provided her months ago. He said, "Hey. What're you doing?"

"What's it look like? I'm packing up to go."

He headed for the door at this. He said, "No way. Where're you going to go to? For God's sake, let me try to handle this before you go tearing out of here, okay? Have a little faith."

"Where are *you* going?" she demanded.

"To *tell* him something. He knows I'm using the tree house, so I'll let him—"

"Are you *loaded* or something?"

"Hey—"

"Really, I mean it. Because you have to be if you think your grandfather's going to go for some girl on the run hiding out in his tree house."

"Cripes, you must think I'm an idiot. I'm not telling him that."

"*What*, then?"

"We're hanging out here, you and me. It's the place we come to . . . you know."

"What? To have sex? You're going to tell him we're having sex up here? Oh that's just great. He's going to love that. Especially when you tell him I'm only fifteen."

"He's not going to ask how old you are. And I'm not going to tell him we're having sex. Just that—"

"What? We're smoking dope? He's going to *know* I'm hiding out here."

"Don't be so paranoid. It'll work out." And to prove this to her, he left the tree house with the words, "I'll be right back."

BECCA'S DREAD OF the outcome increased while Seth was gone. At first, she thought about following him through the woods to Ralph Darrow's house. She'd tell a version of the truth to the old man, she decided. And then she'd throw herself on his mercy. But what version of the truth would work? The one in which her mom dropped her off at the ferry dock and then just disappeared? The one in which she read her stepfather's mind and ran with her mom from San Diego? The one in which she'd been hiding out on Ralph Darrow's property because she was afraid for her life? What could she tell him that wouldn't require one explanation on top of another explanation leading to the Big Explanation: I sort of read minds and it got me into trouble.

No. It seemed to her that, like it or not, she had to depend on Seth. She had to believe that he could cook up a story that Ralph Darrow would believe. And he needed to believe it as long as it took for her to find another place to live. For now that he knew there was someone using the tree house on his property—no matter what Seth told him the reason was—he'd be wary, aware, on guard, whatever. It stood to reason, too, that he'd be back to check on the place from time to time.

She peered out the window into the darkness. She willed Seth back. She double-willed him to tell his grandfather something that Ralph Darrow would accept. He needed to believe that no one was living in the tree house, that Seth and someone were using it only as the occasional hangout, a place to meet, to talk, to play music, to write music, to *whatever*, and then to depart. Anything else wasn't going to work.

Come on, she thought. Come on. Come *on*.

An hour passed. Then another. During the first one, Becca packed her belongings. During the second, she grabbed her flashlight, left the tree house, and descended the ladder. She knew the route to Ralph Darrow's house. It seemed to her that her only choice was to trace it.

It carved through the forest where the undergrowth was thick, even at this time of year. So one could leap behind a huge growth of salal just off the path if concealment was necessary. In the height of summer, with the brambles grown in and the stinging nettles flourishing, that would be impossible.

As she got closer to the clearing that held Ralph Darrow's house and his spectacular garden of rhododendrons, Becca began to smell the woodsmoke. A few more minutes brought her to the edge of the forest, where she paused and peered around to see what was what. No one was outside, but lights were on in the house. Smoke issued from the large, stone chimney. Seth, she decided, would still be inside.

She crept forward. She'd never been in Ralph Darrow's house, but she'd peered through the windows, which was what she did now. The fireplace, she knew, was in the living room. That would be where Seth was . . . if he was still within.

They were playing chess. *Chess,* of all things! There she'd been—out in the woods with what felt like her whole life in the balance—while Seth and his grandfather had been playing chess!

She fumed. She wanted to bang on the window. Had Seth actually managed to *forget* what he'd set out to do? Could she not even depend on him, her friend, her *only* friend . . . ? She wanted to stomp her feet and vent and yell.

He felt something because he looked up. His eyes met hers. He gave a nearly imperceptible shake of his head. He glanced at his grandfather, then back at her. She got the message and beat a retreat.

Not to the tree house, though. She couldn't return there without knowing the worst. She went as far as the path back into the forest and there she waited. She did not wait long.

"Now *that* was a dumb move," Seth said when he joined her ten minutes later.

"What the *hell* were you doing?" she demanded. "You said you were going to talk to him. Did you actually *forget* or something? I'm out there wondering and waiting and worrying, and you're playing *chess*? What's wrong with you?"

"Chill," he told her. He cast a look at the house before he set off into the woods. He said over his shoulder, "I told you it would be cool and it was. It is. But what'd you expect me to do? Was I s'posed to burst into his house and just happen to tell him a story about the tree house thirty minutes after *he* just happened to be out there scouting around it?" He huffed along the trail. Becca was hard-pressed to keep up with him. His whispers told her how badly she'd offended him with her questions and her accusations. *Thinks I'm . . . idiot would have . . . I am NOT dumb . . .* pretty much said it all.

They didn't speak again till they were in the clearing, where Becca apologized to him. She said miserably, "Sorry. I'm *sorry*. I didn't mean . . . I don't know what I'm saying sometimes."

"That's pretty clear," was his reply.

"And I don't think you're dumb. I'm just . . . I'm scared and mixed-up and sometimes what I think's going on isn't what's going on at all."

"Got that right," he said.

She shuffled her feet. She waited. She wasn't sure of anything.

Then he said, "You're one of my tutors for the GED. Applied Math. You've got a boyfriend who's got a big jealousy problem so we meet out here. We tried the library. We tried South Whidbey Commons. We even tried a conference room at City Hall. But the dude kept finding us and interrupting so we decided to hide out here."

"That's what you told him?"

"Pretty good, I thought. I mean, it's more or less true. All except the tutoring me part of it. He checks out the story, he gets a thumbs-up. I've met my tutor all these places. Only thing missing is her jealous boyfriend, but *you've* got that."

"Well, I did." She looked from the tree house back in the direction they'd come. "Did he believe you?"

"Sure he believed me. And the reason he believed me is that I didn't jump onto his porch and make some completely stupid announcement out of the blue. I had to wait for him to bring the topic up. When you're playing with the truth, that's your only choice."

Playing with the truth didn't sound so good, though.

"I hope this doesn't backfire on you," Becca said.

"It won't. I got everything handled," Seth told her.

TWENTY-FOUR

If Courtney was like two people—a public Courtney available to her friends and a very private Courtney who texted him pictures—Derric couldn't fault her. For he, too, was quickly becoming two people. He was the Derric who kept telling his mom to lay *off* the subject when she wanted to talk about what she always referred to as "the raging hormones of the adolescent male" because he and Courtney weren't *doing* anything and they didn't intend to *do* anything, all right, Mom? But he was also the Derric whose thinking appeared to be limited to one subject only these days and whose dreams left him damp and embarrassed and standing too long in the shower in the morning.

When he finally made the decision to go to Courtney's Bible study group, it was for only one reason. She'd told him it was held in the daylight basement of her church. That meant that she would need to drive them there. Driving them there meant driving them home at the end of the meeting. That meant being alone. Being alone with Courtney was what he wanted. They needed to talk. She *kept* texting. She *kept* sending him pictures. He was turned every which way, and, worse in his own mind, he'd started sending pictures to her. He *knew* it was dumb but he couldn't seem to stop. Something had to give. In some direction. Forward or backward. *Something.* So he'd say, "C'n we talk?" after the meeting and he'd suggest a spot on Goss Lake that was a swimming property where no one lived. No one would be there in the month of March, but there they could lay a blanket out on ground that the owners had groomed for picnics. There they could talk in the darkness and decide once and for all how things were going to be. *Nothing* was going to happen between them after a Bible study, he told himself.

Courtney's face transformed when he asked her if she'd take him to the Bible group. His mother's face, when he told her where he was going and with whom, transformed as well. But where Courtney's altered to delight, Rhonda's altered to deep suspicion. She said, "Ten o'clock," and when he protested, she added, "School night, Derric. Don't give me grief."

He said fine and he found himself soon enough in a group of eleven kids along with a youth pastor from Courtney's church. They sat in a circle of mismatched chairs and two sofas, Derric and Courtney having scored one of the sofas. She sat pressed to his side, wearing skinny jeans and a modest belted tunic, for which he was grateful. Otherwise, he'd not have been able to concentrate on anything, although, truth to tell, it was tough enough anyway because the Bible story Pastor Ken had chosen for discussion was called Susanna and the Elders. It was all about sex, although in the beginning it was just about some lady who wanted to take a bath in her garden. But two old guys spied on her from behind a tree, felt some serious lust at the sight of her naked body, and decided they wanted to do the deed with her.

Pastor Ken stopped the story at that point and said, "Now let's take a look at how this can be a metaphor in our own lives, okay? Let's take it beyond Susanna's nakedness to search for what her nakedness really means."

Kids offered suggestions, alternatives to nakedness, a richer and greater meaning from the Bible than the simple words suggested. Someone said virtue, someone else said honesty. Love for God was offered. So was devotion to the Ten Commandments. Derric tried to listen, but he didn't participate. He kept his eyes fastened on whoever was speaking, but his awareness was only Courtney. Everything else was driven from his mind.

They took a break midway through the meeting: punch, cookies, and cupcakes. Then they talked more and then they prayed their special prayers. More than one of them prayed for chastity. Courtney did, too, but he was prepared this time, and when she'd finished asking for strength, he said fervently, "Me, too, Lord. Please. Me, too." A couple of girls laughed at this, and a boy said, "I hear you, bro," and Pastor Ken said, "We all need strength for a variety of things. Me, I need patience to deal with my kids. Eight and ten. Girls. Both going on twenty. Jesus Lord, please give me the strength to be a good dad to them." And after that the meeting broke up. A few minutes later, and he and Courtney were on the road.

At first he thought maybe they *didn't* need to talk. They'd turned a corner, he thought. They'd turned over a new leaf. But then Courtney said, "If you want, we could go some place for a while. There's still forty-five minutes. Want to?" and without a thought of no in his brain at all, he said, "Goss Lake? Close to home and I know a place . . ." She flashed him a smile and off they went.

The swimming property was a forested lot that tumbled down an unbuildable hillside to the lake. It had been sold to someone years in the past as a picnic spot, a swimming spot, a place to launch a sailboat from a purpose-built dock. A trail led down to it from a narrow dirt lane. They fished in the trunk of Courtney's car, found three blankets and a flashlight, and set off through the trees.

It was a perfect night. The moon was a Cheshire cat's smile through the bare tree branches and the stars were bright. It was cold, but in the draping shelter of some hemlocks near the water, they laid out their blanket and wrapped themselves in the others.

Courtney shivered. "Colder than I thought," she said.

"Probably not the best idea." He scooted over and put his arm around her. She snuggled into him and sighed.

From beneath the sheltering branches of the trees, they could see the lake, still in the darkness, nothing breaking its surface and no wind blowing. An owl hooted somewhere in the trees and in the distance a coyote barked. Courtney shivered again. She moved closer to him. She murmured, "I know an even better way to stay warm." She put her hand on his leg and ran it up his thigh. She said, "Derric, if it's okay with you . . . I mean, I've got something I'd sort of like to say."

"Sure," he told her. "Fact is, I was sort of thinking the same thing. That we should talk. But the Bible thing . . . I don't know. It made me feel like maybe we don't need to after all."

"Why?"

"The chastity thing. I can't do it, Court, if we keep texting and sending pictures like we've been. I mean, don't get me wrong. I like to look at them. I mean, I really like to look at them. But it seems . . . I mean, I don't see how we can talk about one thing and then do another. Which, it seems to me, is what we've been doing."

He felt her turn her head to look at him. So he turned his. She kissed him. And then she put her hands on him. And then she eased him to the ground.

"That's exactly what I wanted to talk about," she said.

Only, at that point they didn't talk at all.

AFTERWARD, HE DIDN'T feel the way he thought he would feel. Inside where he'd always figured he'd be all lit up, where he'd feel connected, where he'd know who he was, he was completely numb.

He was also an hour late. He knew his mom would be waiting for him, and he failed completely in his effort to slide into the house and into his room without her knowledge. He'd just got to his bedroom doorway when he heard her coming in his direction from the living room. It was pitch-dark in the hall, and she flipped on the lights. She took one look at him. She knew.

No lectures, he thought. For once in your life, please, Mom, no lectures. I used a condom, all right? Just like you taught me. That's what you want to know, but don't ask me now.

She looked at his face, mostly his eyes. Then she said the most unexpected thing. She said it quietly, totally without judgment. "It wasn't like you thought it would be."

He shook his head numbly, his throat getting tight and his vision clouding with tears like a six-year-old. It wasn't like he thought it would be. It was wonderful and horrible all at once. It should have been a beginning. It felt like an end.

"I'm very sorry about that, sweetie." She approached him, and he wanted to shrink away. "Want to talk about it?"

He shook his head.

"Maybe tomorrow," she said. "You try to sleep now."

She passed him, then, and went to climb the stairs. He stood there alone in the quiet darkness till he heard the soft closing of her bedroom's door.

HE DIDN'T SLEEP. It seemed to him that everything in his life had gone very wrong. In the hours that passed as he stared at his ceiling, he tried to come up with the first moment when he'd made the move that had set him on the path to where he found himself now, but he couldn't even think straight enough to go back three weeks to whatever he had been doing then, let alone a month or two.

Courtney texted four times during the night.

Godgodgod!

And *So hot babe.*

And *Cant B leve.*

And finally *No regret.*

His answers came from him by rote.

!!!

U 2.

The best.

Not 1.

Then he just wanted her to go away. He wanted to *think* when he *couldn't* think anyway, and having her there texting and texting him only made what he was going through worse.

He got up at his regular time, staggering to the shower. He stood beneath the water and felt it hit his head and sink into his hair, which he grasped as hard as he could and which he washed and scrubbed as hard as he could, as if washing and scrubbing could rid his skull of it as well as of the thoughts inside his head.

In the kitchen, his mom was scribbling into a notebook on the counter, and his dad was eating his usual bowl of instant oatmeal. When Dave Mathieson said to him, "How's things cooking, sport?" Derric glanced at his mom and he understood that she hadn't betrayed him. He said, "Okay," and when Dave said, "You came in late. Don't let that happen on a school night again, okay?" he said, "I won't. Sorry. I should've phoned or something. I got caught up with Courtney after her Bible group's discussion."

Dave chuckled. "Now that's something you don't hear every day." He scooped up the rest of his oatmeal, carried the bowl to the sink, and ran water into it. Then he was gone, after kissing Rhonda and giving Derric a one-armed hug. Then Derric and his mom were alone together.

And still she didn't press him. It was only when he'd finished his own breakfast of cereal, orange juice, and toast that she turned from the counter where she'd been writing and said to him, "Seems like you discovered something about yourself last night."

"I think maybe I did."

"That's not necessarily a bad thing, you know."

"It doesn't feel good."

"Got you," she said. "But that's the thing about growing. Going through what you have to go through to grow . . . It pretty much doesn't feel good while you're going through it."

"This isn't the you're-growing-up-now lecture, is it?" he asked her.

"What d'you mean?"

"You know. 'My little boy is growing up.'"

She smiled although she looked a little sad. She said, "Honestly? I didn't even think of it like that. I was thinking more of inner growing, if you know what I mean. Heart growing. Soul growing. Whatever you want to call it. That's the tough stuff. But you'll get through it."

"Problem is, I don't even know what 'it' is."

"Yeah. That's part of the growing," she told him.

HE THOUGHT IT was strange. After her endless lectures about taking precautions and STDs and unwanted pregnancies and all the ways in which two kids could mess up their lives while they were still only adolescents, it came down to her knowing that he was trying to deal with consequences. He was trying to understand them first. Then maybe he could move on to doing something about how he felt about them.

It was completely backward, though. It seemed to him that of the two of them, Courtney should've been the one to feel tugged by conscience, tugged by desire, at war with herself without knowing why. She, after all, was the person who'd been pledging chastity. But she didn't seem to feel anything but happiness and *I luv U U U!* became her regular message, sent once an hour by text or mouthed in the hallway between classes at school.

He didn't understand her but that wasn't so much a problem as was the fact that he didn't understand himself. He needed to work this out, though. He needed the time to attend to . . . whatever the heck it was inside him that was eating at him.

So three of her *I luv U U U* messages he didn't answer one day. He wasn't surprised, then, to find her waiting for him after jazz band rehearsal.

She was sitting on the floor in the corridor, slim legs stretched out in front of her, her back to the wall, a textbook open on her lap. She got to her feet when he came out of the band room. She looked the same as always, good.

She said, "Don't have your cell phone today? I texted you a bunch of times," and she sounded a little nervous.

He said, "No. I got them. The messages. Sorry. I just figured . . ." He shrugged. "Hey, you know how I feel."

The other band members were leaving the room and some of them glanced over and some said hi to Courtney. A couple of the guys laughed at something. Someone said, "Oh yeah. Big-time," and Courtney looked from them to him, her eyes darkening to violet as she made an interpretation of this that she shouldn't have made at all.

When they were alone, she said in a low voice, "You told them, didn't you?"

He said, "What? No way!"

"Then how do they know?"

"Those guys? Court, I got no idea what they're talking about."

"You didn't text back."

"Because I already said. A thousand times I said."

"It's over, isn't it?" She turned then and she walked away from him, and there was nothing for it but to follow, which was what he did.

He said, "Hey, nothing's over," but her reply told him that her mind had gone to another place. She said, "I shouldn't have. I knew, I *knew*, but I did it anyway," and to his horror she began to cry. He looked around the corridor and knew that, of all places, they couldn't have this conversation here where anyone might walk by and then every soul in the school would know.

He took her arm. She jerked away. He took it again. "Come on," he murmured.

They walked to the line of big double doors that served as entrance to the school, and they went outside. It was very cold, and rain had begun to fall.

"It's like they always said." She fumbled in her Star Wars purse. She dropped her textbook. He picked it up. She brought out a package of tissues but then she didn't use them. She used her arm instead to wipe her eyes, the tissues in her hand ignored. "Boys want what they want and when they get it from you . . . It's like they said."

He swore soundly and he didn't regret it. "That's *not* how it is," he said.

"I love you. That's why I did it. I *love* you. I thought and I prayed and I thought. I read the Bible. And I prayed some more. I asked my heart and I asked my soul. My soul told me it was a kind of giving. D'you get that? I wanted to *give* to you. But all you wanted was . . . well, I guess we know, don't we?"

"You're not giving me a chance," he said. "That's not fair."

"A chance to what?"

"To explain how I feel." He walked away from the school, but he took her with him, into the parking lot where she had her car. He said, "Come on. Let's get out of the rain."

She said, "Why?"

"Because we need to talk."

She cooperated with this. She unlocked her car. They got inside. She said, "The flowers should've told me and they did and I didn't listen because I didn't want to know."

"That didn't *mean* anything," he said. "The flowers were flowers. That's it. They didn't mean . . ." He sighed and rubbed his head. He said, "Court, I didn't want it to happen. Not like it happened."

"Oh thanks," she said bitterly.

"Please, please listen. I don't even want to *have* this conversation now because I'm all twisted up inside and I don't know why or what it means."

"Good thing I do. It means you got what you wanted and you're ready to move on."

"It *doesn't* mean that. It means I need time."

"For what?"

"To figure out how I feel."

"I thought you *knew* how you feel. You acted like it."

"That was . . . before. Look, after we did it . . . It's just that I didn't expect . . . I mean, come on. We were reading the Bible and talking about those guys in the bushes and what they wanted from the bathtub lady and I can't remember her *name* even because I'm so messed up about you. But what I'm trying to say is it doesn't make sense to me. That's what I want to tell you, Court. I can't pretend to be praying and reading the Bible and making pledges to be pure and holy while all the time . . . Come on, Courtney. You know what I mean. I know you do."

"You're saying I'm a hypocrite," she whispered. She'd gone so pale, he thought she might faint. "You got what you wanted and now you're saying it's over between us because I'm a hypocrite."

He said in protest, "You're not being fair. And that's not what I'm saying at *all*." But he understood suddenly and with perfect clarity that part of what she was saying was true. Only it wasn't the hypocrite part. Or if it was, it really had nothing to do with her at all.

She seemed to read his dawning knowledge on his face. She turned her own away. She said, "Just go, okay?"

"Court, come on . . ."

"Go, okay? I need to get home."

TWENTY-FIVE

From all the texting that was going on and all the whispering that accompanied it, Jenn figured out fast enough that Gossip Central was passing along a message of vital importance to the life of the South Whidbey student body. It turned out to be the big breakup of Derric Mathieson and Courtney Baker. Since she and Derric had once been friends, Jenn might have cared about this or even spoken to Derric about it, but he'd dumped her friendship for SmartAss FatBroad's months ago, so she gave him ten seconds inside her head and then waved bye-bye to his heartbreak, or whatever it was. She had other things on her mind.

One of them was Annie Taylor. She'd been gone from her trailer two nights in a row, not all night but till really late. The sound of her car door closing when she'd arrived home had awakened Jenn. The clock said two-thirty when Jenn padded to the window to see Annie just going to her trailer's door, and while Jenn knew it was none of her business, it felt like her business when Annie wasn't there because it *felt* like Nera was the reason why. The last meeting of the seal spotters had been only too insane. Once it ended, Annie had doubled and tripled her intentions toward the seal. She had to contain her, she had to have pictures, she had to score a bit of her DNA. She talked non-stop about it and how she was going to do it and why it had to be done *N-O-W.* People were totally *crazy* because of that seal, Jenn thought. There had to be a reason beyond the obvious ones: To Langley she was a moneymaker and to Annie she was her ticket to finishing a PhD. Jenn could accept these as reasons for part of the craziness, but she sure as heck couldn't accept them as reasons for all of it.

It seemed to her that *everything* started and finished with the coal black seal, so that was what she did, too. After gagging down a PBJ on stale bread with inadequate J and way too much PB, she headed for the school library, where she accessed a computer. As luck would have it, the only other people in the place were SmartAss FatBroad Becca King and Extra Underpants Schuman, who were whispering fiercely in a corner. Jenn smiled to herself when she saw them at it because she knew that whatever they were up to, it had to do with the Western Civ project that was looming ahead of them. That would be the same Western Civ project that promised her an A and promised FatBroad something much less than an A. Extra Underpants Schuman would sink their ship. It was, after all, what he did best.

Jenn went for the computers under the watchful eye of the PTA volunteer mom. She said to Jenn, "Watch yourself because I'll be watching you," which Jenn took to meant that the computers were for serious users and not for kids wanting to surf the Net. Whatever, she thought. She said, "Science project on seals," and the volunteer mom said, "Make sure of that please."

Suck on a few rotten eggs, Jenn thought. But she smiled and nodded and got down to work.

Nera was a big deal to everyone. That was a given. But the why of her being a big deal was different, and Jenn figured that detail was worth exploring. She didn't know why she was so big a deal to Langley other than the money she brought it. She also didn't know why she was so big a deal to Eddie Beddoe aside from Eddie being a general nutcase. But she did know that the fire lit under Annie at this point had to do with the transmitter she claimed Nera was wearing, so she figured that was a good place to start. "She should have shed it," had been Annie's words.

It didn't take Jenn long to understand what this meant and why the presence of the transmitter was unusual. It took her a while of shifting among websites and following links, but she was able to work out a singular fact, one that she hadn't known ever, despite living in proximity to sea mammals all of her life: Seals molted. They shed their skin every year. They came up with new skin to replace it, and bits of the old skin were a good source of DNA for scientists who wanted to study them.

So far so good, Jenn thought. It came to her when she read that last point that Annie's excitement could well have to do with just scoring a piece of Nera's old skin and getting her DNA from that. Except that Annie had been lit up over the transmitter that Nera was wearing, so before she drew any conclusions from the shedding of skin, Jenn decided she should search out transmitters.

She was interrupted by, "Come on, Tod. Stop acting like this, okay?" which came from across the library. She glanced over and saw that Extra Underpants Schuman was on his feet, slamming things into his backpack as the FatBroad tried to stop him.

"I told you six times and I'm done telling you," was Extra Underpants's reply. "And if you ever stopped listening to that *stupid* music for three minutes, maybe you'd actually start hearing me, cow pattie." He leaned forward and ripped the FatBroad's earphone out of her ear. Jenn stifled a smile and thought, Go for it, dude, because she could never figure out why Fattie didn't get busted daily for the iPod she used.

"It's *not* music," the FatBroad said, "and will you please sit down so we can work this out?" She grabbed a couple of his books.

He grabbed them back. "Nothing *to* work out. I'm outa here."

He was as good as his word. The volunteer parent said, "You two quiet down or I'm afraid I'll have to—" and Extra Underpants interrupted with, "Ohhh, I'm so scared," as he banged his way out.

The FatBroad looked at Jenn and then away. If you only knew, was what Jenn thought. Fattie turned back. She said, "What?" to Jenn in that nasty kind of way that meant What are you looking at. Jenn said, "What *what*? I'm working here. You got a problem with that?" What a loser, she thought.

The FatBroad put her arms on the table and her head on her arms. Things looking bad? Jenn thought. Ohhhh, *so* sorry.

She saw Fattie fumble for the earphone and smash it back into her ear. Maybe, Jenn thought, she'd rupture her eardrum and not be able to have another scuba lesson.

She went back to transmitters and did more surfing. She found a decent picture of Nera and she located the transmitter on her back. She compared the transmitter that Nera was wearing to the transmitters she found as part of her search. When she read the accompanying material, she understood why Annie was curious.

Nera should have shed the transmitter when she shed her skin. The kind of transmitter she wore was old and it predated a new design that *couldn't* be shed at all. The new design was sleek and small, looking nothing like the older one. That, Jenn decided, would have been how Annie knew the moment she saw it that something was wrong.

The something wrong, or at least the something different, had to do with Nera. She didn't shed her skin.

Very interesting was Jenn's conclusion. She only wished she knew what any of it meant. One thing she figured was that Annie Taylor wasn't being entirely honest with her. If she'd found the black seal once on her own simply by following the seal spotters' sightings, it stood to reason she could find her again. And *if* she was doing this finding at night so that no one could stop her, it didn't look good.

JENN HAD A lot on her mind when she was heading out to the bus at the end of the day. Because of this, she didn't see Squat sitting on a planter near the line of double doors to the school. She walked right by him, clued in to his presence only when he grabbed her by the back of the neck.

She yelped and swung around, saying, "Hey! Get your filthy hands—" and stopping herself when she saw who it was. "The Squatman," she said.

"I thought I was Studboy."

"That's only when you take off your clothes and display your manly pecs," she told him. She enjoyed his blush. "Happening?" she asked, looking around to get a clue as to why he was there. "Waiting for that loser brother of yours?"

"Who else?" he said. "He's late, like always." He looked as if he wanted to say more. Jenn cast a look at her bus and waited for him to go on. He didn't.

She said, "*Any*way," and tilted her head in the direction of the bus. "Got to . . ." She began to head toward it. He followed her. She thought that was a little bit odd. She said to him, "Something going on, Studboy?"

He said, "That."

"What?"

"The 'Studboy' thing." When she stopped walking and looked at him with a frown, he said, "You never said. I know this is lame, but maybe . . . I figured you didn't get it, so I asked. They checked and said no, you got it all right."

She said, "Got what? Who checked what? Why? Uh . . . Squat, the hell're you talking about?"

He shuffled his feet, *totally* out of character for him. He said, brushing his rusty hair off his face, "That flower."

She stared. Flower? He wanted to talk about a *flower*? Then she remembered. He'd sent her a carnation, which she'd thrown at Fattie in the commons on Carnation Day. Damn, she'd never thanked him for it. It cost him a buck and he could way afford it, but still. . . .

She said, "Shoot. I forgot. Studboy, thanks. Very cool of you. Want some tongue?"

He looked straight at her. "Well . . . Yeah, I wouldn't mind. What about you?"

His words caught Jenn completely off guard. When she was able to reply, she said the only thing she could, carrying on with the joke, "Can't exactly take my clothes off here. It'd start a stampede of guys wanting my bod." He said nothing in response to this, which prompted her to say, "Hey, you all right, Squat?"

He said, "Yeah. Sure. But . . . Did you like it?"

"What?"

"That I sent you . . . You know. Come on, Jenn, you know what I mean."

"The flower? Oh hey, who wouldn't like it? Flowers are cool. I never got one before."

"I would've sent more but I didn't want you to . . . you know . . . think I was, like, a stalker or something."

She hooted at this. He looked offended. She said hastily, "I'd never think you were a stalker, Squat."

"Good," he said. "'Cause . . ." He looked around, possibly checking for eavesdroppers, but who the hell knew. "Well, I wouldn't want to you think . . . I mean I just wanted you to know. . . ."

"Hey, we've been engaged since kindergarten, remember? You don't need to remind me of anything," she told him.

He smiled that sweet Squat smile of his, the nicest boy in the whole ninth grade. Jenn thought about what a *friend* he was. She wished she'd sent him a carnation, too. She was about to tell him this when the family Range Rover roared to a stop next to the sidewalk where they were standing. Its passenger window lowered and Dylan leaned over and bellowed out of the window.

"Will you *quit* hanging around that dyke? Man, there's a name for idyats like you."

Squat swung around, and Jenn saw his fist clench. She said, "Save it, Squat."

"I'm gonna *make* him stop."

"No need," she said. "He doesn't bother me."

"He bothers *me*," Squat said.

TWENTY-SIX

Jenn tried to pick up a few details from Annie Taylor about seals, skin shedding, and transmitters, but it seemed to her that Annie was being cagey with what she was willing to reveal. So Jenn watched her comings and goings from Possession Point more closely to try to get *something* out of what the marine biologist was up to, and she also tried to overhear the murmured conversation Annie had with Chad Pederson at the last scuba lesson in the fitness center's pool. She picked up a few indications that they were doing some kind of search for Eddie Beddoe's boat, but she got nowhere further than that. And getting nowhere further irritated the living heck out of her.

She *almost* asked the SmartAss FatBroad to help her with the Nera project, but she just couldn't bring herself to do it. Fattie was proving as irritatingly competent at scuba as she was at everything else, and the fact that Jenn *still* tended to panic when Chad engineered something to go wrong underwater put the FatBroad on a whole different plane of skill than she was. She hated that. Indeed, she could hardly wait for their presentations in Western Civ to roll around so that she would finally have the infinite pleasure of seeing the FatBroad fall on her face.

For Jenn, though, it was A+ all the way. Indeed her final rehearsal with Squat not only ensured this, but also gave her the route she was looking for to find the answers she wanted on the subject of Nera, and she couldn't believe she hadn't thought of Squat earlier.

She and he were meeting, as before, in the boys' hangout upstairs at Squat's house. There, with the dismal weather of late March doing its usual thing of battering the windows and the roof with torrents of rain, they had huddled for an hour shoulder to shoulder on a sofa with Squat's laptop on the coffee table in front of them. He'd scored Cokes for them both along with a bag of Cheetos. They'd finished scarfing these and otherwise going over their material when Jenn brought up Nera and the transmitter she wore.

Despite how he felt about the lunacy of the seal spotters in general and their emergency meetings in particular, Squat was no intellectual slouch. So he was intrigued the moment Jenn told him about the transmitter that Nera should have shed. No shedding of transmitter, no shedding of skin, was how Jenn put it. What did the Squatman think about that?

He was quiet for a moment as he thought it all over. Then he went for the laptop and began to type. Project one was the transmitter, according to him. Who put it on her in the first place and why? Then project two was the shedding of skin. What kind of seal was she, really, and maybe she was a kind of seal that didn't molt.

"Like a mutant or something?" was Jenn's question. Mutation had, after all, been one of Annie Taylor's points from the first.

"Maybe." He paused in what he was doing and peered at her. "But why's all this such a deal to you?"

Because it's a deal to Annie Taylor, was what came into Jenn's mind. She didn't say this, though, because she wasn't yet certain of what she meant. She said, "The whole seal spotters thing . . . Ivar Thorndyke . . . That whacked-out Eddie Beddoe . . . I dunno. It just got me interested."

They did a little searching round the Internet, but to Jenn's disappointment, Squat's conclusion was exactly the same as Annie's. There were plenty of pictures of Nera but no clear and close pictures of the transmitter she wore. They needed that—a decent picture, Squat said—if they were to work out why she was wearing it.

Jenn groused, "I got no clue how we're going to come up with the picture. It's not like she's gonna swim by and pose while I happen to be standing on the dock with a camera."

He said, "I c'n do some searching and some talking to people, if you want. I bet bucks there's someone at U-Dub who c'n explain the transmitter thing, like why she's got it on in the first place." He paused and looked ceilingward, roughing up his thatch of ginger-colored hair as he thought. "And far as the shedding goes," he said slowly, "you know, there's people at the Seattle Aquarium. I bet they'll talk to us. We c'n say it's for school."

She felt her face light up as she said, "You'd do that for me?"

He said with a shrug, "Sure. Why not?"

She threw her arms around him. "Studboy, you are the very best," she declared. "I think I have to kiss you for this one."

"With tongues?" he asked her.

"With tongues," she said.

He went for it, and she found that, while it was more or less pleasant to have a kiss from Squat last longer than their previous quick kisses had lasted, she didn't care a whole lot for the open mouth part of it. So she broke off first. She gave him a hug and said, "Squatboy, Squatboy, you're the best," in a friendly way, for lack of anything else to say. But then he started another kiss. And then, with a shock, she felt him go for her breast.

"Hey!" She jumped to her feet.

He said, "What?" and he sounded startled.

"What d'you mean 'what?'" she demanded.

"Didn't you like it?"

"Squat! What the *hell* . . . ?"

"*What* the hell?" He was blushing furiously, but for the first time, Jenn wasn't sure what his blushing meant. It couldn't be the shyness she always associated with him. Going for a boob wasn't *exactly* shy.

She said, "I mean . . . hell . . . damn it . . . Squat, come on . . . I mean, you can't just . . ." She blew out a breath, walked to the window where the rain was beating, walked back to the sofa and looked down at him. Hand on her hip, she said, "What's going on with you?"

"Nothing. Geez, Jenn. You acted like . . ." He fiddled with the laptop, bringing up the Internet.

"Like what?" she asked him.

"Forget it," he said. "I just thought you wanted it."

"*It?* What? Your hand on my boob? Your tongue in my mouth? What?"

"Yuck. Stop being gross. And I said forget it."

"We're friends and I won't. What's going on?"

"Nothing. Obviously. Nothing's going on." And that was all that Squat would say.

THE PRESENTATIONS IN their Western Civ class began the next day. The loathsome Mr. Keith placed a large cardboard box on his desk to collect the written part of their reports, and once class began he produced a grab bag from which he drew the first slip of paper identifying the student-partners who were to present the oral part to the rest of the class.

There was the usual stirring, whispering, tittering, and murmuring, to which Mr. Keith said, also as usual, "Settle down, people. You knew this day was coming. Everyone is supposed to be prepared." He made a big ceremony about unfolding the paper on which the unlucky first presenters' names were written. He looked up and announced, "King and Schuman," and Jenn did what she could to stifle a smirk. This, she thought, was going to be entertaining. She wondered how far things would get before Extra Underpants illustrated once again why he was called Extra Underpants.

In front of her, she saw the FatBroad get to her feet. She eased her earphone out of her ear as someone from the back of the room murmured, "Go for it, Extra Undies. Show us what you've got."

Fattie glanced down at her partner, who not only had not gotten to his feet but was also clinging to his desk, as if finger peeling were going to be the only route to get him out of it. He looked up at SmartAss, and his face broadcasted terror. Jenn heard Fattie say, "Let's do this, okay?" in an encouraging voice spoken to someone who looked like a deer three seconds before the semi hits it.

Tod Schuman's whisper filtered back to Jenn. "I didn't do it," he said.

"What?" The FatBroad's face was a picture. Clearly, she didn't have Clue One what Extra Underpants Schuman was trying to tell her.

"My part of the oral," he said. "I mean, I did it but I didn't. I can't. I never . . . I'm going to . . . You gotta . . ."

"Mr. Schuman!" Mr. Keith's voice boomed from the back of the classroom. "Are we prepared? Because if we're not—"

"No, no, he's ready," Fattie said. "We're ready." And then in a low voice to Tod, "Come *on*."

"You don't *get* it." His voice was a frantic whisper.

"Pssss, psss, psss, *pissssssss*," someone tried to clue her in.

At this, Tod Schuman put his head on his desk. And the FatBroad seemed to figure it all out. The air went out of her. The spirit went out of her. Her shoulders sank. Tra la la, Jenn thought.

"Mr. Schuman," Mr. Keith said. Tod did nothing. Mr. Keith

roared, "Mr. Schuman! Either get to the front of the room with Ms. King, or take your F."

Tod Schuman didn't move an inch.

"Are you aware that this is a joint grade for you and Ms. King?" Mr. Keith demanded.

Tod Schuman nodded. The FatBroad cast a glance at Mr. Keith, the plea on her face so easy to read that even Jenn squirmed in her seat. But Mr. Keith's face was completely implacable, so Fattie dragged her butt to the front of the room. There, two music stands had been set up as lecterns, and she took her place at one of them. At the other music stand, no one stood. Certainly not Extra Underpants Schuman, whose lifelong disgrace would have been on full frontal display had he left his seat and stood before his classmates.

IT WAS PRETTY excruciating, even for Jenn, who completely couldn't stand Becca King. She almost even felt sorry for her, but she got over it quickly because her name and Squat's name got drawn from Mr. Keith's bag of tricks next. They sailed through their presentation smartly, as every person in the class had known they would, with visuals and a PowerPoint presentation that practically left Mr. Keith weeping for joy. The contrast between Presentation Number One and Presentation Number Two was thus immutably set down in the annals of Western Civ, and the only thing that would have put the icing on the FatBroad's cake of despair, Jenn figured, would have been Derric Mathieson and EmilyJoy Hall being called upon next. But that didn't happen.

Three other sets of partners presented, and while neither of them came close to what Squat and Jenn had done, both of them managed to make Becca's miserable job of covering for Tod Schuman look like the performance of a whining worm.

When the bell rang, everyone vacated the premises pronto. Jenn was about to do the same when she saw the SmartAss approach Tod Schuman. She was fingering her earphone nervously, and it was pretty clear she wanted to say something. This, Jenn thought, was too good to miss. She accidentally on purpose dropped her notebook, which cooperatively sprang open and dumped papers on the floor. She took her time about gathering them up.

Fattie said to Extra Underpants, "I'm sorry. I didn't know. I blew it," the *pss, pss, pisssing* having apparently done the trick. "I just wish. . . ." She sighed and her spine seemed to shrink. Yeah, Jenn thought, *bet* you wish he'd told you about his problem. As if that would happen in a million years. How would it have run? "I pee my pants when I get scared, and my mom won't let me wear Depends." Yeah, right.

He raised his head. "You wrecked everything," he snarled at her. "You total loser. If you hadn't argued with every single thing I wanted to do for this project . . . If you hadn't acted like you're the smartest person on earth . . . If you'd listened to me for exactly one second instead of preaching and telling me that everything I was coming up with was lousy . . ."

"That's not fair," the SmartAss whispered. "That's not what happened."

"Like hell," he said.

TWENTY-SEVEN

Derric told himself that what goes around, comes around, and that after dumping his letters to his sister upon him, Becca King deserved to face *some* sort of consequences. But he still felt bad about what had happened to her in their Western Civ class because he'd known, along with everyone else, why Tod Schuman would never stand in front of the class and give a report.

When he saw Becca at her locker after school, glumly pulling out books and stowing them into her backpack, Derric went up to her. He hadn't spoken more than a dozen words to her in weeks, so he wasn't surprised to see her give a little start when he said her name. She removed from her ear the earphone she wore to block out secondary noises and to help with her hearing. He figured this meant she didn't much want to talk to him, but that was okay, since he didn't expect their conversation to be very long.

He said, "Hey. I'm sorry about what happened with Schuman."

She said, "Oh. Well. I should've figured it out."

He wondered what she meant, since it wasn't as if she could

have expected Tod Schuman to confide in her about his pants-wetting problem. So he said, "It's not like you had any way of knowing. The rest of us . . . ? We've been with him since grade school, so we would've expected what happened to happen."

"I get that," she said. "But the thing is, people always give you clues about themselves, don't they? I mean, if you pay attention, the truth is always there right from the start. How they'll react to things, what they're really like underneath, that sort of thing."

He shot her a look. Was she talking about him? About him and Courtney and sex with Courtney? She might as well have been.

She blinked at him. The color on her cheeks deepened, the way it does when someone suddenly realizes there's more than one interpretation to what they've said. She quickly went on with, "Sometimes I don't like to wait to see how things're going to work out. I want to *make* them work out the way I want. That's what was going on with Tod. He was pushing to get his way. So I pushed back."

It came to him that this was exactly what had happened with his letters to Rejoice, too. Becca had decided that throwing those letters in his face at the clinic was going to change something, was going to make him do something because *she'd* decided it was time for him to do it. Not because he was ready, not because he wanted to, but because of herself. He felt his heart hardening a little at the thought when she said suddenly, "You know, I'm sorry about that day in the clinic, Derric. About what I did with those letters? I'm really sorry. It was way wrong of me. I was pushing you. Just like with Tod. I get that now."

"Yeah," he said. "Whatever. I guess." But he found he couldn't look at her then because the anger of that moment came back to him. So he said, "Anyway, I just wanted to tell you. Sorry about Tod."

She said, "Thanks. And good luck with yours, okay? Good luck."

He thought, My what?

She clarified quickly. "Your presentation in Western Civ," she said.

IT WASN'T A satisfactory conversation, but he didn't have a lot of time to dwell on it. Soon enough he was back at home, standing in the driveway with his mom and wondering why the heck she wanted to tie a blindfold around his eyes. She said she had a surprise for him. It was a cheer-you-up, she told him, and he knew she meant that, after what had happened with Courtney, he needed something to make things a little better in his world. He didn't exactly think a mom surprise was going to do that, but he played along.

She led him into the house and he could tell they were heading toward his bedroom. She stood him in the doorway and whipped off the blindfold. "Ta dah!" she cried. "How d'you like it, sweetie?"

He stared at what lay before him. Since he'd left for school that morning, she'd completely redecorated his room. He had no clue how she'd managed it other than bringing in a whole team, but in the hours he'd been gone, she'd had the room painted, had new carpet installed, had new window coverings hung, and had new furniture put in place of the old. It was amazing. It was sensational. It was masculine and right in every way. Except one.

"What happened to the beanbag chair?" he asked her quickly.

She said, "Beanbag chair? That's all you have to say?"

"Where's the beanbag, Mom?"

"Don't you like your room?"

"Did you throw it away?" He heard his voice growing louder and he tried and failed to bring it back under control. "Mom, did you throw it away? Where's the rest of the stuff? What did you do with it?"

"Good Cheer came for all the furniture. They sent a truck this morning."

"Where?" His voice became quite hoarse.

"What d'you mean? Here."

"You *know* what I mean!" he cried. "Where did they take it? I want that chair!"

Derric saw his mother's face alter. No wonder. He was out in left field. She said, "Derric, that beanbag chair was old when Dave Junior was your age. He had it because it belonged to his mother. She nursed him in it, for heaven's sake. It was covered with duct tape and bleeding beans or whatever they are, and anyway, you can't possibly think that—"

"Where does Good Cheer take furniture?" he demanded.

"Sweetie, I don't know."

"Well, you need to find out. *Now.*"

"You're not being reasonable," Rhonda Mathieson said. If she was sounding miffed, who could really blame her? "I've got to put dinner on. Plus that chair was a piece of junk. I don't know if they even kept it for resale because the way they looked at it. . . . You could tell they were doing me a favor just carting it off the property. Derric, don't you like your room?"

"I want it back," he answered stubbornly. "I want that beanbag chair back."

His mother was silent. In this silence he saw that she was trying to sort out the feelings beneath his words. She said, "D'you want to tell me what this is about?"

Derric searched for something that wasn't the truth but at least could stand in place of the truth. He said, "It had history, Mom. I gave it more history. That means something to me because in Kampala . . . You *know* how it was. . . . Just my clothes, that's it."

At this, Rhonda's hand climbed to her throat. She said, "Oh, Derric, I should have asked you first. I didn't think. Just that the room redone might cheer you up after . . . well, after Courtney and everything. I'm so sorry, sweetie. Let me phone them right now."

He'd lied to her and he felt wretched about that. But there was no real help for the matter. He didn't see an alternative to lying. For if that beanbag was gone, so was his only link to his sister.

IT DIDN'T TAKE long to find out the worst. The beanbag chair was history. They'd given it one look at the Good Cheer intake center and they'd tossed it into the nearest Dumpster. At three-fifteen, the Dumpster had been picked up, its contents hurled into a garbage truck. From there, who knew where it had ended up aside from beneath five or six tons of trash and rubble at a dump site somewhere.

Over dinner, his mother apologized endlessly. His insides felt hollow, though, and Derric couldn't take in the apology. He couldn't tell her exactly what she'd done, either. With his letters to his sister gone, his experience of growing up in this foreign culture of America was gone as well, and so was Rejoice. She seemed lost forever.

It was clear that his mom knew he was upset. She just didn't know how much and she didn't know why. She couldn't tell that within him now there was so much anger that he wanted to take one of his father's rifles, walk up and down Goss Lake Road, and shoot out the windows of all their neighbors' houses, just to feel that he was *doing* something. But he was condemned to being the grateful orphan who'd been rescued from Africa, so he did nothing but excuse himself from the dinner table as soon as he could and shut himself in his bedroom where he could try to think.

At nine o'clock, he found the thin volume that was the Whidbey Island telephone directory. He flipped it open and began to search. It was the only thing he could think of to do. And he *had* to do something or he would blow.

He made two calls. The first directed him to the second: Seth Darrow's father giving him the cell phone number of his son.

Derric dialed that number, and when Seth answered the call with "Talk to me," he asked for Becca.

"I figured you know where she is," he said. "I need to talk to her." Derric tried not to sound bitter about Seth being the one to know where Becca was at all times while he was kept in the dark. "It's for your *protection*, it's for your own good," she'd told him. Right, Becca, just like everything else.

Seth muffled the phone. A moment later, Becca's voice came over the line. She said, "Derric?" and she sounded confused, a little surprised. What*ever*, he thought.

"Just wanted you to know how it all worked out," he told her.

A pause as she dwelt on this, then, "Oh no. Did something happen to EmilyJoy Hall?"

God, she *actually* thought he was calling about his Western Civ presentation! Was she stupid, or something? Did she really think that was important to him?

He said, "I'm talking about the pushing thing, Becca, how you like to push once you decide you know what's best for people."

She said in a lower voice, "What happened?"

"The letters are gone. That's what happened. They were hidden—"

"Back in the woods?"

"No, not back in the woods. They were here in my room and now they're gone and I figured you might like to be in the picture."

"Oh my God. Someone *found* them?"

"That'd be way too easy. No, they got carted off to Good Cheer inside of a crappy beanbag chair that my mom decided to replace."

"We can get them back," she said quickly. "Seth and I can go—"

Her mentioning of Seth made him want to throw the new lamp on his new bedside table at the new mirror on the newly painted wall. He said, "Forget it. Okay. For*get* it. The chair got carted away and then tossed with the trash and wherever the hell it is now, I do *not* know. But it's with the rest of the trash from all of Whidbey Island, so it looks like you've made everyone's day. Not only Tod's but mine. Congratulations, Becca."

She let the Tod remark pass and instead said, "So we'll look—"

We. It was always *we.* He said, "Forget it, Becca. I said forget it and I meant forget it. I just wanted you to know how great things work out when you stick your nose where it doesn't belong. Enjoy whatever you and Darrow are up to. You deserve to have some fun after today."

And then he ended the call. He heard her cry out his name before he cut her off, and he expected to feel better, but he did not. What he felt was utter desolation, cut adrift from everyone and everything he valued.

TWENTY-EIGHT

The first dive in relatively open water was the next day, and Becca got herself to the marina in Langley on her bike. She wasn't feeling up to the dive. She certainly had no enthusiasm for it. The whole Derric situation sat on her shoulders like a concrete cape. She wondered how much worse her life could get.

When she saw Jenn McDaniels, she had her answer. Jenn's smirking "Hey, Beck-*kuh*" told her that the other girl was still deeply enjoying the mess that had been her presentation with Tod Schuman.

What*ever*, Becca thought with resignation. Jenn McDaniels wouldn't be satisfied until Becca King was out of her life. Doubtless, she'd try to drown her right there in Langley Marina if only she could.

Jenn was suited up already. Chad Pederson was checking the tanks. Annie Taylor was up on the wharf using binoculars to search the surface of the water.

"Anything?" Chad called up to her as Becca joined Jenn by the pile of equipment.

"Nope," was Annie's reply.

To Becca's question of what she was looking for, Chad told her that someone had rung the bell. She knew what this meant. There was a signal bell in a small bluff-top park on First Street in the village. It was rung when someone sighted a gray whale out in the passage.

Jenn groused, "That's all we need. Diving and having a whale show up."

Becca thought it sounded sort of cool, but wisely she kept this thought to herself.

The air among them was filled with whispers. For once it was easy to attach them to the thinkers. Jenn's had gone from *FatBroad not so SmartAss now* to *get it over with* to *get back* to *soccer or I'm finished* while Chad's dealt with the nice shape of Annie's butt and *like doggies but I guess*, which didn't exactly make a lot of sense. Meantime, Annie might have been looking for a whale but what she was thinking about was Nera. *The break I need* suggested that she was going to be relentless till she got what she wanted, whatever that was.

Because of the weather and the water temperature, they were using dry suits for the dive. When they were suited up, they moved toward the water in a line of three, with Chad in the middle, saying to them, "We're only going down ten feet the first time. We'll stay near the dock. Take it slow and see how it feels."

The water was clear, like glass, beyond the marina's protective bulkhead, and near the marina the bottom was sand and mud and stone. Within ten yards of shore, they were able to sink beneath the surface and put on their fins. While they were doing this, the first fish appeared. Seeing them, Becca smiled around her regulator. She enjoyed the sensation of the water around her. Being underwater was the only place where she had something other than the AUD box to prevent her hearing the whispers of others.

Chad led them along the pilings of the pier, where sea stars clung and barnacles formed lumpy masses. He began to go deeper until they were perhaps ten feet from the surface. It was, to Becca, a magical world.

Things changed quickly, though. A whip of water churned past them, like a strong current that none of them had been expecting. Becca turned to register two things at once: a coal black seal and its lightning fast approach. The animal was heading straight for Jenn.

In a flash, Jenn thrashed her way to the surface. Just as quickly, Chad Pederson followed. Becca turned this way and that to see where the seal had gone, but there was nothing till the water pulsed once again and the seal was there. She swam around Becca. Once, twice, a third time. Then she shot into the open water of Saratoga Passage. But before she did this, she looked directly into Becca's face. What felt like an electrical shock passed through Becca. It seemed to travel from the seal to her.

Becca surfaced. The scene above was modified chaos. Chad was yelling at Jenn, Jenn was yelling at Chad, Annie Taylor was yelling at them both from up on the wharf.

"—crazy? It was just a seal!" from Chad.

"All right! All right! I freaked out! She came out of nowhere," from Jenn.

"Jenn, was that Nera? Is Nera *here*?" from Annie.

"Hey, *thanks*, Annie," Jenn scoffed. "I'm just *fine*. Really."

Their whispers bombarded the air as well as their words. *All she cares about . . . got to get my hands on . . . that's the way . . . I'm out of here . . . five minutes is all . . . never should have started . . .* It was like at a tennis match, Becca thought, with three players firing balls at each other simultaneously.

Chad was arguing, "Look, you can't *do* that, okay? And no way am I certifying you if you can't show me you won't panic at the first sign of life underwater."

"Like I care?" Jenn cried and headed for shore. "Like you care? Like anyone cares?"

Annie said, "Come on, Jenn. Don't be like this."

"This whole thing is stupid. You're stupid. He's stupid. The seal is stupid."

No way no way constituted her whispers. She added to them, "You want a dive partner, Annie? Take the FatBroad with you."

"What? Who're you talking about?" Chad said.

"Me," Becca said. "She's talking about me."

They were silent at that. They made their way to the shore. Jenn took off for the restrooms and the showers. Becca stayed where she was. She was slow about struggling to remove her tank and the rest of her equipment. She wasn't in a hurry to join Jenn in the restroom, so instead she went to a spigot and washed off her fins, her hood, and her gloves. Because of this, she was near enough to pick up on the conversation Annie Taylor had with Chad Pederson when the marine biologist came down off the wharf.

"I need to get close enough for a better picture," Annie said. "That transmitter? It's going to tell me a lot. And I *need* a sample. Skin's okay but blood's a lot better."

Becca realized, hearing this, that she was listening to a discussion that had been ongoing between them. *Transmitter* told her that Annie was talking about the seal. *Skin* and *blood* made her sit up and take notice.

"You'll get close enough," Chad was replying. "No worries about that. We'll use inflatables and the net."

"I don't want to hurt her. I'd be strung up by the seal spotters. Not to mention the Langleyites, or whatever they call themselves."

"She won't be hurt. Just contained. And how long will it take? Ten minutes? Fifteen?"

"It all depends how hungry she is. And if she likes the bait."

"Oh, she'll like it," he said.

BECCA WENT STRAIGHT to Heart's Desire. It wasn't a workday for her, but that didn't matter. She had to put Ivar into the picture of Annie Taylor and Chad Pederson's plan for the seal.

At first Ivar didn't believe she'd even seen Nera. His first response was, "She popped up off Glendale yesterday. Figure she'll be near Clinton now. Hanging by the ferry. That where you saw her?" He was in the kitchen of the farmhouse, where he'd reduced the neat countertops, the stove, and the sink to a form of rubble in pursuit of making a Bundt cake, which was sitting on top of one burner. He was wielding a spray bottle of Simple Green, dousing everything in sight with puddles of the cleaner and smearing a towel through it. Becca winced and took the stuff and the towel from him.

She said, "Langley Marina. It was the first open-water dive. She was there."

Ivar said, "No way. That'd be some other seal, Becks. If it was Nera, one of the seal spotters down at Sandy Point would've put it on the Web."

"It was a black seal, Ivar," Becca told him, and when she went on to include the information about Annie Taylor and Chad Pederson and their plans, Ivar's eyes widened behind his thick glasses. When she was finished talking, he headed out of the kitchen and made for the stairs.

BECCA FOLLOWED. SHE'D never been beyond the farmhouse kitchen. Now she found herself in an old-fashioned living room where a double-wide doorway led to an entryway and the unused front door. The stairs were in the entryway.

Becca wasn't sure about heading up the stairs, but she could hear Ivar thrashing around. He was muttering to himself as well, so she decided to go for it.

There were three bedrooms above, along with a bathroom where a doorway opened onto old tiles and a claw-footed tub.

Ivar's room overlooked Useless Bay, and since there was a fine telescope at the window, Becca thought at first he'd gone to his room to search for the seal. But it turned out his search was at a computer on the opposite side of the room, and when she approached, she saw that he was on the seal spotters' Web site and his whispers spoke of *can't really be . . . should have seen . . . has to be mistaken*, which Becca knew for certain she was not.

Ivar read the screen, shoving his glasses higher on the bridge of his nose. He cast a look at her and said, "You sure of this, Becks?"

"Course," she said. "And Chad must've seen her, too, Ivar, 'cause like I said, he and Annie were talking about how to contain her. That has to be Nera, right? I mean, they wouldn't be talking about another seal, I don't think."

"That seal come close to you?"

Becca shook her head. "She spooked Jenn, though."

"Jenn's okay?"

"Sure. Yeah."

"What about you?"

"Me? I'm okay. Well, obviously."

"I mean did she spook you."

Spooked wasn't exactly the word, but Becca wasn't sure how to explain to Ivar what had happened when Nera came close to her. So she said, "She looked at me, is all."

How it started from Ivar's whispers told Becca there were things about Nera that Ivar knew that he wasn't saying.

Probably to anyone. He said sharply, "What d'you mean?"

Becca went at it carefully. There was knowledge here, inside Ivar's head, and she wanted to glean it. She said, "I mean, she looked at me . . . sort of the way a person does. You know how it is? They pass you on a street and they don't know who you are but they want to acknowledge you? That's how it was. Does that make sense? Sounds sort of dumb, I guess."

"No, it don't, Becks," Ivar said, but what he thought was *What should I . . . time comes when someone's responsibility is . . . why now why now is what I would . . .* which was interrupted by his words. "Thing's moving along."

"What things?" Becca asked. He'd turned back to the computer and was reading what the seal spotters had posted. She had to repeat her question and to say his name before he replied.

"That scientist, Becks. She's not going to stop till she gets what she wants. That being the case, we got to stop her ourselves."

THE *WHY* OF it was what Ivar didn't explain. At least not adequately, Becca thought. She understood why using nets and inflatables and bait to trap the seal was an idea leading right to trouble. What she didn't understand was the equal weight Ivar seemed to give to the thought of Annie Taylor's getting a close picture of the transmitter Nera was wearing, along with a sample of her DNA.

His explanation was not to explain. He said, "Some things're not meant to be understood. That seal's one of them," and that was the end of it. He went on to ramble a bit about nature: penguins marching into the heart of Antarctica to lay their eggs and baby elephants dying of sorrow. But all the time he was talking, his head was also whispering *believe . . . believe . . . got to make her believe*, which made Becca press him more than she might have done otherwise.

She said, "But it's not bad to try to figure things out, is it? Like figuring out why Nera comes back here every year. How c'n that be bad?"

"Where it leads is bad," Ivar insisted. "*How* it leads there is bad." He rapped his fingers on his desk and seemed to be struggling with a decision of some kind because what went with the fingers rapping on the desk was *it's time* and *go ahead*, suggesting more was coming.

Becca waited. *What to tell . . . how . . . if she knew everything . . . trust is always the key and this is beyond* gave her a lot of patience in the wait.

Ivar finally said, "Sometimes people think they can tame and understand nature, Becks. I was one of those people once. Just like Annie Taylor now. That was me. A long time ago."

"A scientist?" she asked.

He laughed. "I talk like a scientist? No, I was someone who wanted to know things that weren't none of my business. I wanted to know that seal instead of just accepting that seal. Nera's private but I didn't know that. I got too close, and she broke my arm trying to get away 'cause I grabbed her."

"Oh my gosh," Becca said. "*That's* how it happened? So if Annie Taylor gets near her—"

"That seal's going to defend herself and someone's going to get hurt."

"Like that guy . . . Like Eddie Beddoe keeps saying."

The air seemed to crack. She'd only said his name, but everything in the room became instantly different. Each object was supercharged with emotion and the emotion came from Ivar although he tried to hide it. *Now it comes . . . so close to what I should have . . .* indicated there was history here. Ivar made this clear when he said to Becca, "Well, Eddie Beddoe's a bad spot for me." *Married to her and he won't . . .* told Becca the source of the trouble.

"Sharla, huh?"

"He lost her and now she's here in my house and in his mind one and one equals two. I don't disabuse him of that notion and I probably should. Him and me? We squared off more 'n once about Sharla. Years ago, this was. He'd hurt her bad." He seemed to read something on Becca's face because he went on quickly with, "Heart hurt, Becks. He didn't hit her or nothing. All's I know is she took off for a while—off island somewheres—when they lived down in Possession Point. When she came back, she didn't want nothing to do with him. He came around here once and I drove him off with a shovel. I won't have no one bothering Sharla."

The way he said her name . . . Becca knew there was also heart hurt right in Ivar Thorndyke's bedroom. But the topic of Sharla brought to mind what Becca had found inside the trunk in Ivar's chicken coop: those tiny OshKosh overalls. So she said carefully, "Sharla seems really sad, don't you think?"

"Oh she's sad all right," Ivar agreed.

"'Bout Eddie maybe?"

"I do not know."

"They have any kids, her and Eddie?" Becca asked because those overalls and what they meant certainly could point to a very big reason for someone's sorrow.

But Ivar said, "Sharla and Eddie? Nope."

So Becca asked, "Sharla and someone else?" And when Ivar looked at her sharply, she went on quickly with, "I was just thinking of reasons she might be sad. Like she had a kid and something happened to it. Like it . . . I don't know . . . like it drowned or something?"

"No kids," Ivar said. "And the only one who *almost* drowned was Eddie."

"When he lost the boat, right?"

"That'd be about it. When Nera"—he made quotes in the air when he said the seal's name with a scoff—"sank his boat and he swam to shore. Course it would've helped if he'd known how to handle that boat in the first place, but that's Eddie for you. Always in a hurry to have more than he has and in an equal hurry to be someone he isn't. And when he fails—which he always does—he starts the blaming. Surprises me that he went for Nera instead of Sharla. But Sharla wasn't with him on the boat that night, so 'less she got out there and fiddled with it somehow, Eddie couldn't exactly point the finger at her."

Becca heard this detail and could see its importance in the overall Eddie-and-Sharla story. But the most peculiar part of it was still those little OshKosh overalls. Someone wasn't telling the truth.

TWENTY-NINE

Becca made good time into Langley. She was proud of how expert she'd become upon her bike. The added benefit to having a mode of transportation was that she had no spare weight upon her any longer. She knew that when she picked up Jenn McDaniels's whisper of *FatBroad* or when Jenn referred to her as *Fattie*, it simply was no longer the case. In fact, the only part of her that remained as it had been when she'd first arrived on the island was the amount of makeup she continued to wear and the phony thick-framed glasses that she put on daily. Other than that, she was totally different. The many pounds she'd lost, along with the glasses and the makeup and the hideous clothes, went some distance to assuring her that Jeff Corrie would probably not know who she was if he showed up on the island another time and looked right at her.

She passed through the village. Her destination was Diana Kinsale's house. She arrived there to see Diana in the dog run. Her five dogs were bounding around the front lawn. Diana herself was shoveling poop into a bucket.

It was a fine day, the only truly nice day they'd had in all of

March, which, Becca was discovering, was about three months long in the Pacific Northwest. It was endless rain, and when it wasn't rain, it was gray skies or fog or bursts of wind. Everything was becoming green and lush. But there were times when green and lush did not make up for sunlight.

Diana's dogs barked joyously when they saw Becca coast into the driveway. They bounded over and surrounded her. Oscar, the poodle, remained at a distance as usual, the sloppy enthusiasm of his pals far beneath his dignity. But he submitted himself to Becca's caress of his thatch of soft head hair. He padded after her as she went to the kennel.

"Need help?" she asked Diana Kinsale.

Diana paused, leaning against her shovel. "Some things," she said, "are far beyond friendship, and asking a friend to help shovel dog poop is one of them."

Becca warmed to Diana's use of *friend*. She looked at the wood shavings that covered the ground inside the waist-high chain-link fence. She said, "Five dogs make a lot of poop."

"Next time, believe me, I plan to have only field mice as pets." Diana went back to shoveling the poop. She said, "What brings you out this way?"

Becca began with the seal, with Annie Taylor, with diving. She segued from diving to Ivar and from Ivar to Sharla. Diana had lived on the island for thirty years. If Ivar had been lying about Sharla, Diana was probably going to know it.

"Children?" Diana said to her at the end of her story. "No. She's never had children as far as I know. I suppose she *could* have had a child as a teenager. But she would have lived up in Oak Harbor then, and if she did have a baby, she must have given it up for adoption. If that's what happened, though, she's never told me. Why, Becca? What's going on?"

"She seems sad, is all," Becca said.

Diana raised an eyebrow at her. Becca understood what that raised eyebrow meant. Diana knew there was more to the story.

So Becca told her about the OshKosh overalls: three pairs along with some little T-shirts and shoes. Diana's response was a sensible, "Are you sure the trunk was Sharla's? If it was in the chicken coop, it seems more likely that it'd be Ivar's. Or that he shares it with Sharla. And Ivar has a daughter. Steph. She lives in Virginia."

"Nope," Becca said. "It was all Sharla's stuff inside the trunk. Pictures and clothes and things."

"That's interesting, then, isn't it?"

"And what I was wondering is . . . well, have you *felt* anything when you've been with her," which was as close as Becca was going to venture to talking about Diana's own talent for touch and what happened when she put her hand upon another person.

"I've felt a lot of sadness," Diana said. "What you've seen in her yourself. But I've always had the idea that Sharla has much to be sad about."

"'Cause she was married to Eddie Beddoe?"

"That started things, yes. But I suspect a lot of other things added to it."

WHAT THOSE THINGS were, though . . . ? It was a case of Diana saying all she would say on the subject. That she knew more was a fact beyond doubt to Becca. That her belief was that Becca King was intended to discover things on her own was also beyond doubt, however. Becca was considering this and what she was meant to do about it when she reached the Cliff Motel as she pedaled into Langley. There, however, further considerations were driven from her mind as she rounded the corner from Camano Street and caught a glimpse of the empty lot next to the motel's parking area.

Derric and Josh were having some Big Brother/Little Brother time there. They were building some kind of hideaway in the farthest corner, using reclaimed materials along with a lot of hammering and the sound of rap blasting from somewhere.

Here was something else she'd been avoiding, Becca thought. She didn't think she had the courage to face Derric at the moment, but she knew she owed him some information. He would hate her even more at the end of it, but since things were finished between them, she didn't see how they could get any more finished.

So she left her bike at the edge of the lot and crossed the newly greened grass that was coming up. Josh saw her first and yelled, "Hey, Becca! Lookit this place! It's gonna be cool."

She waved at him gamely. Derric, who was pounding a nail into a board, gave her a glance but nothing else. She nearly turned on her heel and beat a retreat when she caught the coldness in his eyes. But she forced herself forward and after dutifully admiring the structure whose many beauties Josh pointed out to her, she said to the little boy, "D'you mind if I talk to Derric for a second?"

Josh looked from her to his Big Brother. He said, "But not for long, huh? 'Cause we have work to do."

Becca said, "Not for long."

Josh said, "'Kay, then," and returned to his pounding.

Derric didn't look exactly thrilled to have to talk to her, and Becca couldn't blame him. She'd messed up badly by producing the hidden letters to his sister. Hers was the primary action that had concluded with the letters being lost, and she could understand why forgiveness for that move wasn't going to be in the cards.

She eased the AUD box earphone from her ear and said to him, "I checked with Good Cheer."

Oh yeah big frigging deal wish I'd never flitted through his mind as his face settled into an expression that told her he knew pretty much what was coming.

She said, "Stuff in the trash goes up to Coupeville. But the same day it goes up there, trucks take it off island to another site."

He said, "Like this is some big discovery, Becca? I already knew that. My mom found it out." *Stupid lame all the trouble she causes . . . if I'd never . . . she'd never been . . . go away go away or I swear what I'll do is . . .*

"Please just listen," Becca broke into his thoughts. "Seth and I . . . We went up to Coupeville right after we talked to you. I mean, the next day because obviously we couldn't go that night 'cause they wouldn't've been open."

"So?"

"So they told us where everything went, to a site in Burlington. We went there, too. But in Burlington they said trash and junk and stuff ends up there from all over the island, from Camano Island, from the towns nearby, too. And even that's not the final place for it. See it goes to eastern Washington—"

Shut up shut up shut up shut up because you've made things too late do you get that Becca?

Full and complete, the whisper was so clear and so patently Derric and so comprehensible for the first time in her life that Becca gave a little gasp. Derric said, "What's wrong?" *Now she's being a frigging drama queen and let me tell you it ain't going to work.*

She clutched her stomach against a sudden pain. It was as if the words were like little beings that entered her body and took up residence there. But they were hungry beings and they ate at her and surely, she thought, this isn't how the whispers were supposed to be.

She said, "We went to Burlington like I said and we told them we had to look for the chair. Seth made a big deal of it, so they let us even though they said it wouldn't be there. But there was so much junk . . . I mean, how could they know for sure it wasn't there?"

Because they're not frigging dumb like you.

"Please," she murmured. "Can't you try to be fair?"

"Huh? Hey, when were you ever fair with me?"

"I'm sorry. I'm *sorry.* What I'm trying to say is we could've gone to eastern Washington and I wanted to go and Seth would've taken me but there'd be tons of garbage and trash and by the time we got there the bulldozers would have covered it all anyway."

Derric glanced at her, then. He'd been looking away, over at the town's performing arts center where the marquee was advertising an upcoming performance of the community's rendition of *Cyrano de Bergerac*. That put Becca in mind of the film *Roxanne*, which put her in mind of the town of Nelson in British Columbia, where it had been filmed, which put her in mind of her mom, who'd been in that town since the previous September and why why why had she not yet returned to take Becca her daughter away from this place to a new life somewhere, where they would be safe? She blinked hard against tears and she said, "I'm sorry," although at that point she didn't know whom she was apologizing to: Derric, herself, her mother, all of the above? And what did it matter when she was sorry for everything but especially for the moment she'd heard her stepfather's whispers and read danger in them for both herself and her mom. What if, she thought, she had screwed up that as badly as she'd screwed up Derric and his letters to his sister? Wouldn't *that* be icing on the moldy cake?

Derric said, "Yeah." It wasn't agreement. It was finality. He turned back and started to head across the vacant lot to Josh once again. She watched him walk off, his head lowered and his fists in his pockets, and she wondered if she could possibly ever feel any worse than she felt at the moment. She didn't think so.

PART SIX

Sandy Point

Cilla's World

I always turn toward the scent of salt water. Finally, I reach a junction where the call is urgent to follow a road that dips to the right and begins a steep descent. At once the brine on the air is sharp. I come to a curve and then another, a hairpin turn and then another. The trees are tall on both sides of this road, and the road itself is slick from rain.

Then where the road becomes even and straight, a gravel lane makes a break in the trees. In the distance a faint light glows. I head toward this.

At last spread out before me is water, rich with the salty scent of the sea. Across an expanse of it, lights speckle a distant shore, like thousands of stars tossed into the sky. It's too huge a shore to be an island like the one I've traveled on, and from it a brightly lit ferry sails.

Closer to me, more lights shine. They come from a trailer with rust climbing its sides like dying vines. They come from an old gray house. From both of the buildings, smoke curls from chimneys. The scent of it nearly obscures the brine of the water nearby.

I go to this water's edge. My feet sink into the sand and I move close, until the water laps near my toes. At that, I jump back. I look. I watch. But there is nothing to see. Until . . .

A fin breaks the water's surface. Then another. And then a third. Each is huge, each like a black sail on a boat, and I know that they mean danger to me. The words come from nowhere I can identify. They are orcas and killers. Around them I know I am not safe.

I back away slowly. I wish to hide but what my gaze falls upon instead of a hiding place is the diamond pattern of a chain-link fence and within it a glittering pool of water.

Inside this fence, I find that the surface of the water boils with the movement of fish. They shine silver in the night and I long to touch them and feel their slick bodies run through my fingers. But this would mean thrusting my hand into the water and that is something I cannot do.

I look around me. A long pole with a net on the end hangs from the fence not far from me. I grab this and lower it into the water. When I raise it, it teems with fish. In the moonlight, they are bright and alive, and their bodies whip furiously, as if they seek a path beyond the net that I hold them in.

I know then: what they want and what I am meant to do. I understand why I have been brought to this place.

I carry the net to the edge of the water beyond the fence and I fling its contents high into the air. The fish fly like coins tossed into a fountain. But they are living coins, and when they hit the water, they do not sink. Instead they circle. Once, twice, and then they are free.

THIRTY

Jenn was using the track at school to do wind sprints after hours. It made getting home more difficult because she had to use the island bus instead of the school bus and that meant a hike all the way from Bailey's Corner down to Possession Point, usually in the wind and the rain. But the school track was 150 percent better than trying to do her wind sprints either on the unpaved lane onto her family's property or along the road up from or down to Possession Point. Besides, it seemed that every time she tried to do anything remotely related to getting ready for the soccer tryouts, Annie Taylor showed up with a request for Jenn's assistance.

Squat found her on the track a few afternoons after their presentation for their Western Civ class. He sat on the bottom of the single set of bleachers. She saw him, but she didn't stop. They hadn't talked much after he'd gone for her boob that day at his house, and she knew they had one of two choices about the situation. They could pretend it had never happened or they could talk about it. As far as Jenn was concerned, pretending it had never happened seemed the best.

So she ignored him till it became only too obvious that he was going to sit there till the cows came home. Finally when it started to rain, she realized she didn't have much choice. She was going to have to get out of the weather eventually. She trudged over to the bleachers and plopped down next to him.

"'Bout time," he groused. He put up the hood of his jacket.

"I got tryouts coming," was her excuse. "I'm way behind where I oughta be. Stuff keeps getting in my way."

"Thanks," he said.

"I didn't mean *you*." But she felt impatient with him anyway.

"Good, 'cause I got what you need."

"'Bout what?"

"Sheesh, Jenn. What's *with* you anyway? D'you just more or less use me when I'm convenient or what?"

Here they were, exactly where she didn't want to be. She said, "You're mad because of the boob shot, huh?"

"No, I'm not mad because of the boob shot. It's your boob. You can let whoever you want to touch it. Animal, vegetable, mineral. Like I care?"

"Like you don't?"

He brushed his hair off his face with the heel of his hand. "Okay. So I do. So I thought you did, too."

"I *do* care," she said. But the problem was, she wasn't sure how. Or why. Or even *if,* really. It felt like lying but it wasn't lying. Yet the truth wasn't clear to her. "Anyway . . ." She hoped they could move on to something else.

He took the opening. "That transmitter," he said.

"The one on Nera?"

"Like, there's another?" He didn't wait for her to reply. "There's a lady over at U-Dub I talked to. I called about ten people and ended up with her 'cause she teaches ocean stuff and don't ask me what 'cause I can't even remember. I told her I had a project for school and I asked her about the whole transmitter thing. She said a seal would have one on if someone was tracking it. Like for migration or feeding or breeding."

"Well, we figured that," Jenn said.

"Yeah. But she *also* said that no matter what anyone told you it *couldn't* be an old transmitter because the way old ones were made, they didn't stay on. They *never* stayed on, so someone invented a new kind of transmitter. She says the one Annie saw has to be just banged up or something. But it's not old, no how, no way."

"Annie says it is. Annie says—"

"*So*," Squat cut in impatiently, "I called the aquarium like I said I would."

She linked her arm through his. "You *are* the best."

"I talked to a lady who's in charge of taking care of the sea mammals—otters and seals and stuff—and *she* said if we got a seal with an old transmitter still on her, we got 'one interesting animal there,' she said."

Jenn didn't see how this was useful. They already knew they had an "interesting animal there." Practically everyone on the island thought Nera was interesting. But that didn't turn out to be the important part of what Squat had discovered, as it happened. The important part was what he'd learned about the transmitters themselves.

They were numbered, each and every one of them, according to the woman at Seattle's aquarium. If you were able to get the number off the transmitter, Squat told her, you would also be able to discover who'd placed it on the seal in the first place and why and when and where. *That* was key information to have because *if* the transmitter was an old one and *if* Nera had truly never shed it along with her skin, then someone somewhere knew a lot more about the seal than he was saying and that was the person they needed to find. But they had to start with the transmitter's number.

"Great." Jenn sighed. "How're we s'posed to do that?"

"Don't know unless you learn how to ride her to get a close look."

"Oh yeah. That's a real possibility, Squat."

"Like you think I meant it?" he inquired. He thought for a moment before he sighed and said, "Well, you're diving now, right?"

"More or less. Last time I freaked out and got the Big Bad Lecture from Chad, the instructor. He lets me into the water again, believe me, it'll be a miracle. Plus, I don't know if I even *want* to go in the water again."

"You have to, way I see it," Squat said. "You're going to have to get close to her. Or someone is. At least close enough to see the numbers on the transmitter."

Jenn cursed. She thought of Nera coming straight at her.

She thought of what could happen if the seal got too close.

"Well?" Squat said.

"I just wish there was another way. I sort of want to forget the whole thing."

"Why? I mean, what's the big deal getting close to her? She's just a seal."

But that was the part that bothered Jenn. For one of the many things she was beginning to think was that *just a seal* didn't apply to Nera.

Into her silence, Squat said, "On the other hand, I guess we could keep looking for pictures of her."

"There's pictures of her all over town," Jenn groused. "Did you ever see *one* with a clear shot of that transmitter? I sure as hell haven't."

"Then . . . ?" he said. And when she didn't answer, "Why d'you care about this dumb seal anyway?"

"Because Annie does" was the real reply. But Jenn didn't want to say it because saying it would lead to another *Why*, and to that one she truly didn't know the answer.

JENN SWORE TO herself that there had to be another way short of another diving experience to get a glimpse of Nera's transmitter, but aside from finding a close-up picture of it through some miraculous means, she didn't know what that way could be. She did a few more Internet searches with Squat helping her, but to no avail. It was going to be a dive or nothing. That meant making up with Annie.

After her failed dive in the marina, she hadn't even let Annie drive her home. She'd been so furious at Annie's excitement when Nera had shown up and spooked her that she hadn't even wanted to *talk* to the marine biologist, let alone ride in the same car with her. Three times since then, Annie had called out a hello and had asked her to come over to the trailer. Jenn had pretended not to hear till Annie finally said, "Whatever," and left her alone.

But now . . . she told herself that even if she *did* the dive, she couldn't be sure she'd see the seal close up again. On the other hand, she also told herself, if she *didn't* do the dive she wouldn't see the seal at all.

She had her chance with Annie when she got home from school one afternoon a couple of days later. She was about to go up the steps to the porch when she saw her dad and the marine biologist down by the bait pools. They were inside the chain-link enclosure, and her dad was squatting next to the water, pointing here and there, then talking over his shoulder to Annie. For her part Annie was shaking her head and looking serious. Bruce McDaniels gestured and looked gravely ticked off. He seemed like a man accusing someone of something. Jenn went to join them.

Jenn heard Annie say, "It could've been a raccoon, couldn't it?"

"Raccoons don't climb up chain-link fences," Bruce McDaniels responded. "And far as I know, they sure as hell don't dig under 'em if what's under 'em is a bed of concrete."

"A cat then?"

"With a fishing pole maybe?" Bruce scoffed. "I'd say a heron but the enclosure makes it too much of a risk. So that leaves . . . let's call it human intervention."

Jenn went through the gate. The pool they were standing by had crystal water but the herring within it made it turbulent, like a liquid about to boil. She said, "Hey. What's up?"

Her father shot her a smile of hello, but it didn't reach his eyes. He said, "We're down on bait. Someone's been stealing it. A lot of it."

Jenn didn't look at Annie as she said helpfully, "For food, you mean?"

"Hell if I know. Could be, if someone's using it for fishing, but they're taking enough to set themselves up in business."

Jenn looked at the water again. She didn't see how her father could tell any fish were missing, since they were only flashes of silver to her. But it was his business to know his business. If he said that fish had gone missing, then that was what had happened, and losing bait was something they could ill afford. She didn't want to think that Annie Taylor had had a hand in this. But Annie Taylor was, in truth, the only person whose intentions suggested a need for bait by the bucketful at the moment.

"But that seems like a lot of trouble," Annie said. "Someone coming all the way down here to Possession Point, someone sneaking onto your property, someone using . . . what? A big net to scoop up your herring? Wouldn't it be easier to go out and catch them in the Sound?"

"If you want to pony up the money for gas and the time to track the fish and the time to cast the nets and haul them in and haul them back. That seem easier to you than showing up here and stealing them?" He looked around as if for answers: out in Possession Sound first and then closer on the property. He nodded at the ground next to the chain-link fence where the net he used to scoop up bait for customers lay discarded. It didn't belong there. He said, "You leave that there, Jenn?"

"Why would I do that?"

"Andy or Petey?"

"They can't get in the gate, Dad. They could climb the fence but they know you'll give them a good one if they try it."

He looked at Annie Taylor then. "And you?" he said. "Unless you have a need for herring, I rest my case."

Jenn shot her a look. Annie had a need for herring and both of them knew it.

Annie said, "Fact is, I do need herring. That's what I came over to tell you. I need some bigger bait, too, if you can arrange it."

"Why? What're you catching?"

"A seal. And I'm not catching it. I'm just containing it for a few minutes."

Bruce shook his head darkly. "It's that damn black seal again, isn't it? You trap that seal and there'll be hell all over. That animal hasn't done a lick of good to anyone in all the years she's been hanging around, but the way people act you'd think she was the Virgin Mary making a yearly appearance."

"She's helped Langley," Jenn pointed out. "I mean, they've got the festival and the tourists coming to see her and all that."

"Langley," Bruce McDaniels said, "would make a festival out of a killer squid if they could just get their hands on one. Anything to bring in ten tourists and sell them a T-shirt, Jenn."

"Actually, I just need to contain her for a couple of minutes to get a skin sample," Annie said. "It's just to look at her DNA. The fact that she's black suggests—"

Jenn's dad blew off everything having to do with why Nera was black. To him, the seal was black because the seal was black and who cared anyway when there were mouths to feed. "And giving her herring'll get you her DNA?" he asked Annie Taylor.

"In a manner of speaking, I think it will."

Bruce crossed his arms and gazed at Annie, as if studying her face for truth or lie. He finally said, "Well, selling bait's my business, so I'll sell you bait. But I hope you're not thinking of trying this experiment of yours—or whatever it is—alone. That seal's one hell of a lot stronger than you are and if you get in the water with a wild animal in a panic—"

"I'm a scientist, Mr. McDaniels," Annie assured him. "I know what I'm doing. And *what* I'm doing, I'm not doing alone."

JENN FOLLOWED ANNIE back to the trailer. Something new had been added to the overall clutter of Annie's possessions. On the table a map of the island was spread out. Next to it was a chart of the kind that boaters used. Both of them bore a large red *X*.

Annie came to Jenn's side and joined her in looking at the map and the chart. She said, "Chad found Eddie's boat."

"You guys are going after Nera," Jenn said.

"We're going after the boat first. I want my rent money back from Eddie Beddoe."

"What're you planning to do? Bring the boat up? How?"

"I'm not planning to do anything but take some pictures of it to prove it's there. Eddie Beddoe said find it, not bring it up. He better not change his part of the deal now."

"And then what? How're you getting Nera?"

Annie glanced at her. "Chad said he'd help."

Jenn said, "Oh," and she knew how she sounded. "Chad," she said. "Figures. With the way he looks at your butt and everything."

Annie said, "Are we back to that? Chad's just a friend, Jenn. I've got lots of friends. I've already said: He's yours if you want him."

"I don't want him."

"Whatever," Annie said. "Look. I have to move this project forward. There's a lot here on the line for me. I need the information that the seal can give me, Chad can help me get it, I can pay him for his help, and that's the end of the story. I wanted you to be the one, but—"

"The one what?"

"The one to help me underwater. The one to help me get the DNA from Nera. But after last time . . . I mean, it's pretty clear you hate the whole idea of diving, and I didn't want to press you about it."

"What if I want to?" Jenn asked.

"Want to what? To dive?" Annie shook her head. "You

weren't exactly taking to it like a duck to water, were you?"

"Hey, I just freaked. She came at me, I got surprised by her, and I freaked. It happened and it's over and I won't freak again."

Annie considered this. She ran a hand through her bright red hair. She said, "You'd have to do the final dive, the checkout dive."

"Okay. I'll do it. I want to help."

"Are you sure?"

"I'm positive."

Annie stood there for a moment. She stared at Jenn, as if studying her. Then she said "Okay, then," and she raised her hand and brushed her fingers along Jenn's cheek. It was the sort of fond gesture a mother makes to her child, and Jenn wasn't a child, so she jerked away. She said, "I'm not—"

Annie dropped her hand. She said, "Sorry. Sorry. My mistake, okay? It didn't mean . . ." Her voice drifted off.

"What? Mean what?"

"Anything. Nothing." Annie reached for the map and folded it. She did the same with the chart before she spoke again. She said, "I'll make the arrangements with Chad for the checkout dive, then. I'll tell him you're going to be helping me with Nera."

"Chad's not going to like it," Jenn said.

"I can handle Chad."

THIRTY-ONE

They sat in Chad's boat, bobbing on the water not far from Sandy Point. All four of them were wearing dry suits. Jenn and Becca would be going through the paces of their check-out dive with Chad Pederson while below them in the water at fifty-five feet, Annie Taylor would be taking the pictures to prove to Eddie Beddoe that she and Chad had found his boat.

"Everyone on the same page with this?" Chad asked them.

Silence among them was enough to imply agreement. Jenn took note of the fact that the FatBroad was watching Chad more closely than normal and doing the same to Annie Taylor. Her eyebrows were drawn together tightly, and Jenn figured she was hot for Chad and trying to work out whether he and Annie were doing the deed. As if, she thought. Like Chad Pederson would choose Fattie while Annie Taylor was breathing nearby?

Becca glanced in her direction, and Jenn could see she'd become red in the face. Who knew why but *whatever* had caused it, the FatBroad was quick enough to dismiss it. She started to get the rest of her equipment ready. She did the spit thing into her mask and rubbed it around. She looked perfectly calm. Of *course*, Jenn thought. Aside from hooking herself up to that pathetic Tod Schuman in Western Civ, there wasn't anything on earth that Fattie didn't seem to do well. Except holding on to Derric Mathieson.

Jenn's own nerves were strung out. If diving hadn't been the only way she could get close to Nera, she would have said forget it. Scuba was definitely not her thing.

"Ready, Jenn?" was an interruption to her thoughts. She roused herself and went through the same routine with the mask as the FatBroad had done. Annie was already in the water. Chad was still in the boat so he could assess their entry.

Jenn had mastered that, at least. Soon enough they were all swimming in Saratoga Passage's frigid water where, below her, she could see the flashes coming from Annie's camera. She was already near Eddie's boat. Jenn thought she could see its ghostly remains beneath them.

The check-out dive took less time than she'd expected. Chad took her through her paces in the water, did the same for Fattie, and a smile around his regulator told her that both of them were getting everything right. After fifteen minutes of equipment loss, equipment regain, equipment malfunction, equipment sharing, and everything else, Chad gave them the A-OK sign.

Then he pointed below where Annie's camera was still going off. He pointed to them and then to himself. He cocked his head. The implication was easy to figure out. Since they were in the water with their instructor, they could go deeper. Did they want to see what Annie had found?

Jenn didn't, since who the hell cared about Eddie Beddoe's dumb boat. But Becca nodded energetically, as if Eddie Beddoe's boat had just turned into the *Titanic*. So Jenn thought, Whatever. It wouldn't take long and the water was calm.

They headed toward it. As they approached, the boat began to take shape. Mostly what remained was the hull, dragged to this place by the strong currents that moved the tides of Saratoga Passage. As they got closer, Jenn could see an enormous hole in the hull. It looked like something made by a torpedo, blasting through fiberglass and flooding everything below deck. The boat must have sunk in minutes. Eddie Beddoe was lucky that he hadn't drowned.

Jenn saw Annie fin to what remained of the bridge, the flashing from her camera reflecting off something on the bottom of the passage. It seemed odd to her that something at this depth would reflect light that way. She headed toward it . . . which was when a dark shadow passed over her.

Jenn whirled to tell the FatBroad to back *off*, for God's sake. She didn't want her hovering so close, like someone expecting to be needed because she was such an *expert* at diving. But then she saw that Fattie was some distance from her and swimming at the exact same depth. Whatever had been swimming above her, then, had been something else.

Suddenly below her Annie's flash went crazy as she began shooting rapid-fire pictures. They were all out of synch with what they'd swum to on the bottom of the passage. Taking dozens of pictures of the old boat? Why?

Less than thirty seconds later she knew. Something brushed against her and just for an instant she thought of the FatBroad. Then light flashed from Annie's camera below, and in that light, Jenn saw the seal.

For an instant Nera hung above her in the water, suspended in the passage like a buoy. But then everything happened at once. And everything began with Nera shooting toward her.

One whip of her body and she was hurtling toward Jenn like a bullet, heading directly for Jenn's face. Jenn thought, *Don't panic, don't panic, don't panic, it's a seal,* but then the seal reached her, and things got worse.

Her mask was ripped off. Her regulator was torn from her mouth. She felt it yanked away from her so viciously that she thought she was going to lose teeth. Bubbles rose around her, rendering her blind. She broke for the surface, swimming for her life. Her lungs seemed about to burst. She pedaled frantically to get to air.

Something grabbed onto her ankle. Nera! She tried to shake the seal off. She kicked as hard as she could and lost a fin. Her brain was focused only on air. She tried desperately to get away, but she was unable to do it. She knew she would drown.

But then she felt the change. Two hands were encircling her ankle and jerking on it. She looked down and saw Fattie holding on to her and what she thought was, Damn SmartAss is trying to *kill* me! So she kicked harder, at Becca's face. She made contact with the other girl's mask and she knocked it off to float away.

Still, the FatBroad held on. God, Jenn thought, she was as strong as a wrestler. The harder she fought to get away, the harder the other girl's grip became. Then she removed her regulator from her mouth and waved it at Jenn. Jenn grabbed it, blew the water out, and began to breathe. Her panic waned and that was when she saw it.

Blood was flowing from the other girl's face.

WHEN THEY SURFACED, Chad and Annie were right behind them, Chad with their masks and Annie with the fin Jenn had lost. Becca was bleeding from a cut beneath her eye, and the blood rendered her face a mass of salt water tinted the color of beets.

Chad took one look at her, swore, and hoisted himself into his boat. He grabbed her by the armpits and hoisted her on board as well. Jenn and Annie clambered after them.

No one said anything at first, just terse words about how to take care of Becca. It wasn't until the first aid kit had been brought up from below and the butterfly bandages had been applied that Chad said, "What the hell happened down there? Did that seal attack you? Are you okay? What happened?"

All Jenn said was, "We better be certified."

"You're certified, all right. You did really good. Fast thinking on Becca's part. Good response with the buddy breathing on Jenn's. Nice slow ascent *despite* what happened. Good going. Every move was right on target."

Jenn glanced at Becca. One word from her and she would be cooked. Chad's declarations told her he didn't have a single clue about what had happened because he hadn't seen a thing. He was supposed to be responsible for them at depth, but he'd completely blown it. As for Annie, she hadn't seen anything either, and even now, she was huddled over her camera, going through the pictures she'd taken below.

Jenn said to Becca, "Thanks for the help. Sorry about . . ." She raised her eyebrows and inclined her head a bit to where their two masks lay on the deck.

"No problem," the FatBroad said in reply. "You were great. Weird about the masks, though, huh? What d'you think happened?"

She was covering for Jenn and with absolutely no reason except that they'd been partners underwater. Jenn said, "I owe you. You came through great," and both of them knew that Jenn meant more than she was saying and that Becca would keep her mouth closed about Jenn's being spooked once again by Nera.

WORD GOT OUT. Chad assumed the seal had been involved in a bizarre attack on the girls. When they arrived back at Langley Marina, one of the many seal spotters was just docking his boat. He saw them all. He saw Becca's bandages. A conversation occurred. And the seal spotters hotline became hot enough to burn.

The result was yet another meeting. The crowd was so great that it had to be moved: from the gallery at South Whidbey Commons to the Methodist church on the corner of Third Street. The seal spotters had managed to rouse the passions of people on every side of any debate about the black seal. When Jenn and Annie arrived, most of those people were arguing.

There were too many of them for the church's sanctuary, so they'd moved to a meeting hall in the same building and rapidly set up chairs in a helter-skelter fashion. At the front of these chairs and behind the pulpit dragged in from the sanctuary for this precise purpose, Ivar Thorndyke was trying to settle everyone down while next to him Becca sat miserably on a chair as Exhibit A in the case Ivar was presenting against *anyone* going near that seal.

She was completely hunched over, with a baseball cap on her head. She was wearing so much makeup that she looked like someone in disguise. Jenn gave her a glance and thought the obvious. Becca might have saved her from a watery grave, but someone needed to advise the ol' FatBroad about all the goop she put on her face. Except, Jenn thought with an inward start, it wasn't really quite fair to think of her as the FatBroad after what she'd done, was it? How bizarre, she concluded. All this time, she'd figured the other girl would be SmartAss FatBroad till the day she kicked off.

Becca raised a hand in a hello. She gave a grimace at the display Ivar was making of her. Jenn gestured to her to come over and join herself and Annie as they scored two chairs. Becca mouthed, "I can't," and indicated Ivar. He apparently wanted her as a living illustration of the points he was making.

He was at that moment saying, "Now how many times do I got to stress this, people? This is a wild animal we've been talking about, and the accent's on wild. If people approach it, someone is going to get hurt. More hurt'n this girl got. You get it now? So topic one is how to keep people away. Newspaper articles aren't doing it, obviously. We might have to go with signs on every public beach."

A woman cried out, "You ask me, that animal needs to be shot. It could be rabid."

To which someone else shouted, "Fish don't get rabid."

Which encouraged a guffaw and the retort, "A seal's not a fish, you fool."

Annie said to Jenn, "I *have* to explain. . . ." And she rose and called out over the din of voices, "Listen to me! It was just an accident. No one was hurt."

"Lookit that girl's eye!"

"Another inch and she woulda been blinded!"

"The seal was just curious," Annie insisted. "That's the nature of seals. They're playful and when—"

"No way was this playful!"

"You should've kept *away*," Ivar said.

"No one went near her deliberately, Mr. Thorndyke. We were below at a boat I'd been asked to find. Chad Pederson can confirm it. We were photographing it for the owner when the seal just appeared."

At this Eddie Beddoe surged to his feet. He'd been sitting by himself at the far side of the room. He shouted, "You're trespassing! All of you! You keep away from that boat."

Jenn frowned at this one. What the heck . . . ? She'd been

right there in his mechanic shop along with Annie when he'd challenged her to find the darn thing. And there was practically nothing of it left. What was he going on about?

Chad shouted back that Eddie himself had *wanted* Annie Taylor to find the boat, so what was the problem? How was she supposed to do it if she didn't find someone with a boat to help her?

"I didn't ask four goddamn people to find that boat," Eddie countered, swinging around to find Chad in the crowd. "So you tell me just what the hell's going on."

"That's beside the point," Annie insisted. "We found the boat together, we went down to get some pictures, the seal happened to be there, end of story." She moved toward the front of the room, where Ivar had set up his PowerPoint presentation with the oft-seen pictures of the black seal a shifting image on the screen. She handed him her digital camera and said, "Will you . . . ? Please?" and he grumpily cooperated. Annie went through the pictures that soon appeared on the screen till she found the one that she was looking for. It was a close-up picture in which Nera stared into the camera, black as the night. Annie spoke to them all about how close Nera had been to her when she'd got this shot, how the seal hadn't even seemed frightened by the camera, how whatever had happened under the water to Becca and Jenn was just a fluke and completely unlikely to happen again.

Discussion followed. Arguing followed. But Jenn studied the picture of Nera. She felt a shiver, and the hair on her arms rose. There was *something* behind the eyes of that seal. She didn't know what it was, but she could have sworn it was there.

She looked over at Becca who was, at that instant, turning toward her. Their gazes met and Becca nodded. She'd seen something too.

Ivar was saying, "You're telling us it's not dangerous, Miss Taylor, but Becca here was in the water with Nera, and so was Jenn over there. So maybe we should hear from them before we make any decisions about anything."

"What we should be deciding—what *you* should be deciding—is just to leave her alone," Annie said. "You wouldn't be deciding something about an orca, would you? Why're you deciding something about her?"

"If we're deciding anything," Eddie Beddoe declared, "then we should decide to shoot the damn animal like she should've been shot years ago when she started hanging around."

"Would that be when she sank your boat, Eddie?" someone called out.

General laughter ensued. Eddie turned crimson. He hiked up his jeans. It was a movement that prefaced his attack on someone, and Ivar Thorndyke interrupted him.

He said, "Let's hear from Becca and Jenn. They're the ones who tangled most with the seal. Jenn? Come on up here. Tell us what happened."

Jenn was reluctant, but she moved to the front of the room. Becca, she saw, had that earphone of hers plugged into her ear. Whatever music she was listening to, Jenn thought, she wouldn't have minded hearing it herself just now.

Becca rose when Jenn joined her. She murmured, "Same story, right?" and Jenn murmured back, "Sounds good to me." Since Chad and Annie were there, they could hardly tell another tale. She let Becca explain that they'd merely been spooked.

Becca said, "We didn't see her at first. She was down at the boat with Annie and—"

"That boat is mine!" Eddie Beddoe's words came out like a screech. "Everything *on* that boat is mine!"

"What d'you got down there?" an old fisherman called out. "Pirate's treasure?"

"Old booze, more like it," someone replied.

At this, Eddie Beddoe stormed for the exit. At the door he paused for a final swipe at the crowd. "You don't want to do something about that animal? Okay. Not a problem. Because I'm telling you, someone will."

THIRTY-TWO

Everything having to do with Eddie Beddoe felt wrong to Becca. First, you didn't tell people a seal sank your boat because seals *didn't* sink boats when boats were under power. How the heck could they? Second, you didn't ask someone to find your boat and then threaten them when they actually found it. Third, you didn't fixate on eliminating a seal that wasn't doing you any harm unless, of course, you thought it *could* do you harm. And fourth, if you did any of those things, you had a good reason for doing them. In this case, a reason seemed to equate to a secret, and a secret seemed to equate to that sunken boat. When she and Jenn had been on their check-out dive, Nera had been at that boat, she'd been above that boat, she'd been swimming around that boat. So . . . how outrageous was it, then, to conclude that Nera and the boat had something important to do with each other? And if Nera and the boat had something to do with each other, and if Nera was hanging around that boat, and if Nera returned to Langley year after year because of that boat, didn't it also stand to reason that she wasn't just making some strange pilgrimage to it? Something had to have been on that boat when it sank in Saratoga Passage. That seemed to Becca the only reasonable conclusion to reach when the facts were laid out.

Of course, she'd reached completely rotten conclusions in the past, so she needed to be careful with where her thoughts were taking her. But this time, at least, her thoughts *seemed* to have followed a logical progression. And this time, she decided, she would allow someone else *into* those thoughts to make sure she wasn't heading off in another wrong—and a disastrous—direction.

She couldn't talk things out with Ivar. One mention of the seal in connection with Eddie Beddoe and more trouble would ensue. Sharla, she thought, had way too many secrets to guard, starting with those little OshKosh overalls, and Annie Taylor was way too focused on getting to Nera's DNA to be at all helpful in any other matter. Seth thought the entire subject was nuts. Chad Pederson was too caught up with thinking about Annie Taylor. Diana Kinsale would probably advise her maddeningly to wait for more to be revealed. And so, much as Becca absolutely hated the whole idea, that seemed to bring her to Jenn.

She wanted a private conversation with the other girl, but that couldn't happen at school. So she followed her onto the bus the next afternoon, and when Jenn flopped onto a seat near the back, Becca removed the AUD box earphone from her ear and flopped down next to her, saying, "Hey."

What the . . . began Jenn's whisper. Becca was encouraged when the following part of the whisper was less obscene than usual and didn't have anything to do with her weight. She interrupted the flow of Jenn's swear words, since most of them seemed triggered by her surprise. She said, "I need to talk to you."

Jenn gave her a look. *God is she queer or something* came out so clearly that Becca nearly said, "No, I'm *not*, as if it's any of your freaking business." But instead she said, "Just listen, okay? Five minutes and I'll get off at the next stop that comes up."

Jenn rolled her eyes in a classic Jenn way. "Whatever," she said.

"Will you listen?"

"Do I have a choice? You're practically sitting on my earlobe. C'n you at least move over an inch?"

Becca had to smile. "Okay. Sorry." She gave Jenn more space, heard her whisper of *Kissing . . . cute enough . . . whoa . . .* and looked at her, confused. Jenn's face, however, was a blank.

"*What?*" she said. "What, what, what?"

Becca said, "Nothing. You seemed like . . . Never mind. Here's the deal."

"Thank God. You're going to have a long hike back to town if you don't get to the point."

"Right. Got it. I think something's on the boat."

"What boat?"

"Jenn . . . There's only one boat. You know what boat."

"Oh crap. *That* boat."

"Yeah, that boat. I think there's something down there with that boat. It's the only answer to what's going on. Obviously, Eddie Beddoe's flipped out about someone finding whatever's there. But Nera knows what it is, and she probably knew it was there the night that boat sank."

Jenn blinked. "D'you know how totally flipped out you sound?

Next you'll be telling me she sank that boat just like Eddie Beddoe's been saying. She sank it to get what she wanted off it."

"I know it sounds completely bizarre, but listen for a second. There was something about the way stuff happened during the dive. First, she was hanging around Annie and Annie was taking her picture along with the boat's picture, right?"

"Guess so."

"And she was all . . . cooperating with Annie. But when she came toward us, it was like she was tired of *trying* with Annie. It was like she'd been trying to tell her something, to say something to her only she couldn't 'cause, of course, she's a seal. But she needed something. She wanted something."

"Off the boat," Jenn said. "That's what you're saying?"

"It's crazy. I know. But you know how Annie has that one picture of Nera, the one where she's looking right at the camera? The one where there's something in her eyes? Well what I think is that she was trying to tell Annie about the boat, but all Annie wanted was her picture. So she came to us, to you, really."

"Oh great. And what am I, the Seal Whisperer? And d'you know how stupid this is? There can't be anything on the boat because there is no boat. It was just the hull and part of the bridge and hardly anything else."

"So it's in the sand or the mud or whatever the bottom of the passage is made of. But it's there."

"Okay, why doesn't she get it? Why's she *never* gotten it? The boat's just sitting there, a wreck on the bottom. She's swimming around it. Why doesn't she—"

Becca waggled her fingers in front of Jenn's face. "Because she doesn't have these? Because she's a seal? How's she supposed to pick something up?"

"With her mouth. I don't know. With her flippers. Whatever. How about with her nose? Who *cares*?"

"Eddie Beddoe does. He cares enough to try to shoot her. Jenn, what if the reason she comes back to Langley every single year has to do with that boat?"

"Then considering that Langley's built an entire festival around her, we'd better make sure that *whatever* it is, it stays there."

"But she's desperate," Becca said. "You felt that from her and you saw it in her and so did I. Don't pretend that you didn't. No one's gotten as close to that seal as you and I have, and we *both* know how it feels to be desperate."

"Oh we do, do we?" Jenn asked tartly. "What d'*you* have to be so desperate about? What do *I* have since you know so much?" *Off this island . . . scholarship is the only way . . . God God God I have to get back to soccer or I'm . . . loser for good and that can't . . .* said it all, Jenn's whispers becoming clearer and clearer.

"What I mean is," Becca said, seeing how close she'd come to the core of Jenn McDaniels, "we both know how it feels when you want something bad. Everyone knows how that feels, don't you think?"

Jenn shrugged. "Guess so."

"So why don't we help her? Because *if* we do, maybe Eddie Beddoe will leave her alone. Maybe Annie Taylor will, too. 'Cause between you and me . . . I don't think Annie's intentions toward her are all that noble."

Jenn considered this. *All those pictures and she didn't even notice . . . Someone taking bait from the pools and if she did that to my dad . . . But she says it's okay and for science and it can make her name . . .*

So clear, Becca thought. Why were this one girl's whispers becoming so clear? She said to Jenn, "Eddie Beddoe's trying to keep her from what's on that boat. I think we need to get it for her."

"That frigging boat." Jenn looked out the window. "That boat started everything. I don't even know how he bought it."

"What d'you mean?"

"You need to see where he lives. Or where he used to live. It's a dump. Boats cost big money. I sure as hell don't know where he came up with the bucks to buy it."

"Was it insured when it went down?"

"Probably not. He's one dumb bunny, that's for sure."

"D'you know exactly when it happened?"

"The boat? When it sank?" She shook her head. "Before I was born. I could try to find out from my dad. But why? Is that important or something?"

"Might be. So. Are you in?"

"For what?"

"For finding out what's on that boat, or near that boat, or wherever it is."

"I guess. But he's not going to tell us."

"I got that," Becca told her. "We're certified now. We're going to dive."

Jenn said immediately, "No way. It's not for me, Becca. I—" She stopped. *Becca . . . did I just call the FatBroad Becca?*

Becca smiled inwardly. She thought about saying, Yeah, you did. Very first time. What d'you think that means? But instead she ignored the use of her name and said, "I need a dive buddy, Jenn, and you're my dive buddy. I can't go down there alone. It won't take long. But we've got to do it and we've got to do it before Eddie Beddoe gets to her. Or anyone else, for that matter."

"You mean Annie."

"Well . . . yeah, Annie."

Jenn rubbed her forehead. She looked out the window at the forest they were entering. She finally said, "All right, all right."

When Becca threw her arms around her, she didn't pull away.

THIRTY-THREE

When Becca waved to her from the side of the road as the bus pulled off, Jenn automatically waved back. Then she knocked herself upside of her head. She said, "What the *hell*?" and wondered when things had shifted. She didn't even *like* Becca King. What the heck was she doing waving bye-byes at her?

As far as Jenn was concerned, Becca was turning out to be like everyone else when it came to that stupid black seal. It was as if the seal put a spell on people the moment they saw her, and Jenn absolutely could not work out why. She got the whole Nera Festival thing. Nera's miraculous yearly appearance in the waters around Langley meant money to everyone. She understood that. What she didn't understand was the degree of passion inside everyone *else* besides merchants and B&B owners when it came to the seal.

Even Squat, who was the very personification of reason, was starting to get behind the Nera equation. He'd said to her this very morning before Western Civ, "We *need* those numbers on that transmitter, Jenn. We get them, we get information. Didn't you tell me Annie Taylor was taking pictures of her? Well, you got to put your hands on those pictures. 'Cause if there's a close-up, we might be able to get the numbers from it."

Argh, she thought. *More* on that damn seal. And how was she supposed to put her hands on those pictures? Accessing what Annie had on her laptop was the only way, but Jenn didn't see how she could do that without Annie knowing what she was up to. She'd have to try for it when Annie wasn't there, but when she wasn't there, the trailer was locked. Course, she could break the lock or shove in the door because the thing was so rusty and flimsy it barely held anyway. But that would be something of a giveaway . . . unless she could sneak in when Annie was on the property: down at the beach, talking to her dad, doing *something* that took her outside. An emergency would be nice. Four flat tires on her car? A broken windshield? A fire near the trailer? A boat in trouble out in Possession Sound? What else was there? Someone conveniently thrashing around in the water would be nice, but considering its temperature, they'd probably be dead before Annie Taylor got to them. Jenn couldn't think of anything else that might work. It would, she decided, be way convenient if there was simply an extra key.

Her dad might actually have one, Jenn realized, since Eddie Beddoe had put him in charge of the wreck of a trailer in the first place. So when she finally reached home after the hike down Possession Point Road from where the school bus had dropped her, she went in search of him.

Bruce was in his brew shed, checking on six huge glass jugs of newly made beer. He was taking down information from a gizmo at the top of each of the enormous containers, and he was murmuring to himself. "Papa's best yet" he was telling one jug. "And you, fair friend, are a gold medal winner," he said to another.

When Jenn first spoke, he didn't hear her. She had to say, "Dad? *Dad!*" to draw his attention away from the row of his "little beauties," as he called them. He roused, turned, and gave her a lopsided salute. She sighed and figured he'd been doing some serious sampling of beers that were further along in their brewing cycle. Her mom wouldn't be pleased to discover this when she got home. Jenn knew she had to be quick, then, for her mom usually showed up in the island taxi just before dinnertime.

She said to him, "I got to leave Annie a note, Dad. Is there an extra key to the trailer?"

"She i'n't home?" Bruce McDaniels said and without waiting for an answer, went on with, "Whyn't you leave a note on the door? She's got a cell, doesn't she? How 'bout you call her?"

"How 'bout you tell me if there's a key?" Jenn said.

"Mouth," he told her.

"Sorry," she said. "It's just sort of important. It's about the seal."

Bruce raised his eyes heavenward. "Someone needs to curse the day that animal first showed up. I'm not a cursing man, however, 'cause you know how your mom feels about cursing, so it i'n't going to be me." He shook his head and added, "First the oil spill, then the seal, then everything went straight to hell and it's stayed that way."

"You mean like Eddie losing his boat?"

"Oh yeah. And Sharla wandering up and down the beach day and night like a widow woman waiting for her man to return from the sea."

"When'd that happen?"

"After the damn oil. *Everything* happened after the oil. Pollution on the beach, people walking around in hazmat suits, fishermen going elsewhere for bait, and who c'n blame 'em, the seal showing up like a yearly curse, and everything falling apart around here."

"Eddie's boat, too?"

"What say?"

"Did he lose his boat because of the oil spill, too?"

"He *bought* the damn thing after the oil spill and God knows how 'less someone was paying him a fortune 'cause of polluting our beach. Doubt that 'cause I sure as hell didn't see a dime."

Interesting, Jenn thought. What the hell it all meant was a mystery to her. It also wasn't getting her any closer to the key to the trailer, if there was one. She said, "So. . . .the key, Dad? Is there one? So I could leave her a note?"

He said, "Nope. Not s' far as I know. But that's her car, i'n't it? Doesn't sound like your mom's."

Jenn listened and heard the car. She popped her head outside the brew shed and saw that her dad was right. Annie Taylor was just arriving home in the late afternoon light. She had her camera in one hand, and her laptop tucked beneath her arm. She entered the trailer without noticing Jenn. Just like yesterday in the water, Jenn thought. There was only one thing on Annie's mind.

JENN KNOCKED ON the trailer's door about ten minutes after Annie's arrival. There was no answer. Jenn tried the door and found it unlocked. She opened it and went inside.

Oddly enough, considering the time of day, Annie was taking a shower. Jenn heard the water running from the bathroom and somewhere in the back of the trailer, music was playing. Jenn thought about calling out a hello, but then she realized this was her opportunity. She slinked over to where Annie had left her laptop on the table. She sat on the banquette. Luck was with her. Annie had logged on.

Jenn stared at the screen. The laptop's screen saver was a picture of Nera, in keeping with Annie's one-track mind. Life would have been perfect if the picture was a close-up of the transmitter Nera wore, but that wasn't the case. It was the seal head-on, face-to-face with Annie, the same picture Annie had showed at the meeting. There was that look in Nera's eyes, the chill-giving look. Perhaps, Jenn reasoned, Becca was right after all.

The shower switched off. Annie *would* be someone who conserved water, Jenn thought. She gazed at the screen and read its files. *Pictures* indicated where she ought to look. She clicked on this. There were dozens of folders, dates beneath them. She began to scroll down.

Annie began humming. A drawer slid open. A hairdryer went on.

Jenn got to the last file and clicked on it. It would be the most recent. If there was a picture of Nera's transmitter, it would be here.

But it wasn't Nera. It was, instead, Chad. He was completely naked, completely aroused, and completely grinning at the camera. The berth inside his boat was in the background, its covers tousled, its pillows out of place. On the floor around him was a pile of clothes. Jenn recognized Annie's olive turtleneck among them.

She stared. She felt sick. There were other pictures. She couldn't stop herself. She began to click through them. Chad and Annie. Annie and Chad. Chad alone. Annie alone. Posing and laughing, half clothed and naked. *I have a partner, her name is Beth.*

What else had Annie lied about? What else *did* she lie about? And why the heck was it so important?

"Jenn?"

Jenn jumped. She hadn't heard a sound. She hadn't noticed when the hairdryer was shut off. Naked Annie from the pictures was naked Annie standing in the short hallway that led to the bedroom.

"What are you looking at?" She moved toward her.

Jenn was frozen. She couldn't even remember how to get herself out of the file she was in. Annie stood next to her and looked down.

"Oh," Annie said. "Whoops. I see you found out. Is that what you were looking for? You could've just asked me. I would've told you the truth."

The only words that Jenn could come up with were, "What about Beth?"

Annie observed her, not making a move to cover herself up. "What about her?"

"You *said* you had a partner. You said she was Beth. You made me think—"

"I *do* have a partner. Her name is Beth."

"You're cheating on her."

"I guess it looks that way, huh?"

Annie finally left her side and went to her bedroom at the trailer's far end. She returned in a sweatshirt and sweatpants, a pair of socks on her feet. For once, Jenn thought, she didn't look stylish. But she also didn't look the least ashamed or even embarrassed. And she should be *something*, shouldn't she? Ashamed, embarrassed, regretful, sheepish. What she *shouldn't* be was casual, comfortable, and completely easy. And yet she was.

"Beth and I aren't celibate when we're away from each other," Annie said. "We don't have rules. If I know Beth—and I do know Beth—she's probably doing it right now with some baby-faced intern at the hospital where she's got privileges. It doesn't *mean* anything, you know. It's just . . . well, it's just sex."

Unaccountably, Jenn felt tears come to her eyes. She didn't understand in the least why she was on the verge of crying, and this infuriated her.

Annie said, "You're upset. I'm sorry. But you shouldn't have looked at my personal pictures."

"Why'd you take them?" Jenn demanded. "Everything they show and . . . it's *disgusting*."

Annie smiled. "Well it isn't, really, but I wouldn't expect you to understand that yet. Unless you've had sex yourself. With someone who knows what he—or she—is doing."

"I'm not a lesbo!"

"I didn't say you were. But I've seen how you look at me and, let's face it, at my age my gaydar is pretty good."

"Stop it! I told you to stop it, didn't I?"

"There's a way to find out," Annie told her. "If you're interested. Are you?" Annie touched her hair.

It was like a shock to her system. Jenn surged from the banquette. She shouted, "You stay *away* from me, you freak!"

She shoved her way past the marine biologist and stormed out of the trailer.

The rain had started to fall.

OUTSIDE, SHE TRIED to catch her breath. She tried to stop herself from crying. She tried to make her brain capable of coming up with some kind of plan.

The rain fell on her face and her hair and down her back, and she barely felt it. She knew she needed to get out of it, but she couldn't bear the thought of walking into her parents' house. The island taxi was parked to one side of it, which meant her mom was home. If Jenn walked over there and went in the door, one look at her face, and her mom would know something big had happened. And she'd want to know what.

No way did Jenn want to talk about any of it. Not about Annie. Not about Chad. Not about the pictures she shouldn't have seen.

Not about the offer that Annie had made. *That* made her sick, that offer of Annie's. *She* didn't know Jenn. No one did.

Jenn realized that she'd blown things in every possible way with her little sojourn in Annie's trailer. She'd failed even to *find* the pictures of Nera, let alone to scroll through them. So she was not an inch closer to seeing if there was a picture of that transmitter clear enough to read the numbers upon it. In that, she'd let Squat down.

She'd also failed to make any mention of using Annie's scuba equipment, and she'd needed to do that because of Becca and Becca's plan of getting down to that stupid boat without anyone being the wiser of what they were up to. So she'd let Becca down as well.

The only way to feel worse at that point was to consider soccer, the upcoming tryouts for the All Island team, and all the ways in which she had failed herself by not preparing for those tryouts daily. Even now, even here in the rain, she should have been practicing. But she wasn't doing that, she wasn't doing anything. She was the ultimate loser and in a few short weeks when she didn't make the team because she hadn't practiced enough, everyone was going to know that about her.

Who cared? Jenn thought. Who cared, who cared, who cared about anything? She'd never get off this stupid island and she was an idiot to think she ever would. She wasn't going to get a scholarship—athletic or otherwise—and even if she managed to get one, it would be to the worst college in the country in the worst possible location and when she was finished with whatever degree she decided to go for, she wouldn't be able to find a job and she'd end up back on the island anyway. She was trapped like a rat on a sinking ship, and the only thing that made *anything* better was—

She heard a moan. She was still on the step leading to the trailer's door, but the moan wasn't coming from inside the trailer. It was coming from . . . Jenn concentrated hard. The rain hit the trailer and pinged on its roof, but there was no wind to add to that sound. Faintly, Annie's music played and Annie's cell phone began to ring. But that was it. And then . . . the moan again. It sounded near, like from under the trailer.

Jenn jumped off the step. Part of her said to get away because she sure as heck didn't want to know what was under there. Part of her said that it was a wounded animal and wounded animals could be dangerous, so she needed to get her dad. Another part said ignore it altogether and by tomorrow it would be gone. But then the groan turned into a cry, and the cry spurred Jenn into action.

She went around the side of the trailer, dodging dropped logs from the woodpile, some nets of her dad's, four bait buckets, and a pile of floats. At the back of the trailer where the propane tank was, she heard the moan again and then the cry. It was quite close.

The trailer's skirt was partly removed, something Jenn herself had done when she first began to help Annie make the place livable. She should have put it back, but she hadn't thought to do so. Now she crawled beneath it as the moan sounded once again.

She followed it. Whimpering began. Then a cry. Then a deep and chesty cough. A *human* cough, Jenn thought. This was no animal. Some person was hiding under the trailer.

She nearly backed away at that point. The shadows were deep beneath the trailer, and since darkness was rapidly falling outside, it wasn't going to be long before nothing at all would be visible to her. She moved cautiously, calling out, "Where are you? I can't see you. Who are you? You okay?"

Nothing but the moan answered her. And then . . . ahead of her a shadow deeper than the rest of the shadows beneath the trailer. She advanced on it, her heart beating wildly. She said, "You okay? You need help?"

Nothing at first in reply to this. Jenn eased her way forward. And then she saw it.

A narrow band of light seeped from a worn spot somewhere within the trailer itself. Into the band of light an arm extended, its hand out and its fingers bent in supplication. The arm was attached to a filthy girl with matted hair so long it seemed to grow to her knees. She had grime on her face and streaks of mud on her clothes. She wore only a jacket, jeans, a pullover sweater, and socks. She wore only one shoe, a mud-clogged Nike. Her other foot looked injured. She herself looked half dead.

Her eyes met Jenn's and she shrank away. Jenn said, "You wait here," as if it were possible for the girl to run off in the state she was in. She added, "I'm going to get my dad."

She went to do so.

THIRTY-FOUR

"Better go faster," Jenn said to her mother. They were tearing along the southern part of Cultus Bay Road. Jenn's dad had phoned ahead to the Langley Clinic to make sure Rhonda Mathieson didn't leave for the day, so there was no fear in her that the clinic would be closed. There was a lot of fear, on the other hand, that the strange girl in the backseat would die before they got there.

"We still need to be careful, Jenny," Kate McDaniels said. "Deer jumps out of the trees and we're in trouble, sweetheart."

"She looks bad."

"Then we need to pray." Which was what she did, and since Kate McDaniels was evangelical with all the trimmings, she knew a lot of ways to talk to God. Some involved tongues, but she didn't go there now, for which Jenn was grateful. Instead she just asked the Lord to stay with them all and to guide them in knowledge of His Father's ways.

Jenn watched the girl. Her eyes were closed and her breathing was shallow. They'd hustled her into the car and covered her with a blanket, but her injured foot stuck out and it smelled like bad meat. Jenn could see the pus oozing out of her sock. It made her queasy. She turned away.

"D'you know her, Jenny?" her mother asked.

"Nope."

"Odd."

Indeed it was. The far south end of the island was sparsely populated. Possession Point was less populated still. Everyone in the place became known quickly. But not this girl. Jenn had never seen her.

When they pulled into the parking lot of the Langley Clinic, Rhonda Mathieson came outside immediately, zipping her fleece against the brisk April wind. She looked into the back-seat as Jenn and her mother got out of the car. She said, "Let's get her inside," and the three of them together muscled the girl into a sitting position first and, once out of the car, into a carrying position second.

They went into one of the examining rooms, which the girl filled quickly with the terrible stench of her unwashed body, her unwashed hair, her unwashed clothes, and her infected foot. Without a comment, Rhonda handed out medical masks. She said, "Bruce told me you *found* her?"

"Under Eddie Beddoe's old trailer," Jenn said. "I heard a noise. I went to look."

"Good on you, Jenn." Rhonda put on surgical gloves and grabbed her stethoscope. The girl's head lolled on her chest. She was sitting on the examining table, but she seemed only half-conscious. Her eyes were closed and she swayed to one side. Kate McDaniels grabbed her and lowered her to the table.

Rhonda began to examine the girl, listening first to her chest. She murmured, "Airway is clear but her lungs are congested pretty bad."

"Pneumonia," Kate murmured.

"Bronchitis more likely."

"Is she dying?" Jenn asked.

"No. But she needs some serious care."

"What about her foot?" Kate asked.

"Let's have a look." Rhonda picked the girl's foot up and manipulated it gently. It wasn't broken, she told them, but it was in bad shape. They would have to see about it. And she would have to stay off it.

"Seeing about it" involved first removing the disgusting sock and then exposing the foul and infected skin. There was pus everywhere, as well as debris, and when Rhonda began to clean the foot, Jenn felt her gorge rising at the sight, the smell, and the *clink* of something taken from a wound and deposited into a stainless steel basin. She moved away from the table and stepped back against the wall. The girl moaned and her eyelids fluttered.

"Looks like she's walked miles and miles," Rhonda murmured. "I can't imagine how she did it with her foot like this." She looked closely at the girl, who remained supine and close-eyed on the table. "Who are you, honey?" she asked her. "Where are you from?"

THEY HAD ONE answer before they left the clinic when Jenn's dad called with some information. He and Jenn's brothers Andy and Petey had gone outside to scout around once Kate and her mom had left for the clinic. They'd discovered an old wheeled suitcase behind the woodpile. There were clothes inside. There was a collection of rotten fruit. There was a whole layer of nutrition bars. And there was a note.

He read it to them when Rhonda put the phone on speaker:

My name is Cilla. I'm eighteen years old. I'm a good girl. I can't talk. I can hear but I don't always understand what you mean. It's time for me to be out on my own. I can work if you show me what to do. I want to work in exchange for food and a place to sleep.

Kate's eyes filled with tears when she heard this.

Jenn said, "How c'n she hear but not talk?"

Kate said, "Autism, Rhonda?"

Rhonda said, "If that's the case, the parents need to be shot for . . . for whatever they did. Did they just dump her at Possession Point?" Into the phone she spoke to Bruce McDaniels. "You hang on to that, Bruce. You hear me? You hold on to that note."

"Sure. But why?"

"Because Dave's going to want to deal with this. Someone abandoned this poor girl somewhere and, eighteen or not, abandoning a teenager who can't even talk . . . Don't get me started. You'll be hearing from Dave."

RHONDA CONCLUDED HER dealings with them by scouting out a pair of crutches, telling them Cilla needed to stay off her bad foot, and packing up clean bandaging as well as three kinds of antibiotics. One set was for her lungs, she said, and the other two were for the infection in her foot. "Make sure she takes them all," she instructed them. And to the girl, "Cilla? You've got to take every one of these pills. No cheating, okay? Cilla? You hear me, honey?"

Cilla's eyes opened at that for the very first time. Rhonda smiled and said, "Good. You know your name, don't you? Well, I've got some crutches here for you and you're a pretty sick young lady, but you're going to be okay if you do like I say. I bet that foot of yours hurts like hell. So you use these, okay?" She held up the crutches.

Cilla shrank back like a puppy expecting to be hit. Rhonda reached out and gently petted her filthy head. "Don't be scared," she told the girl. "You're safe with us."

"I can drive her up to Whidbey General if you think she can tolerate the trip," Kate said. "Jenny can sit with her"—which was the last thing Jenn wanted, as the girl's speechlessness gave her the shivers, and her smell was so bad Jenn had a good idea it would rub off on her without any trouble—"in the backseat, and if you phone ahead for us—"

"Kate, this girl with her troubles . . . ? Whidbey General is going to scare the hell out of her. I'd take her home myself, but she's got to be supervised twenty-four/seven. She's got to take that medicine. D'you think . . . ? I hate to ask it, but I know that Bruce is usually at home."

Kate didn't hesitate. Nor was Jenn surprised. Her mom could recite scripture by heart, and taking care of the sick was going to be somewhere in one of the Testaments. "Help us get her to the car," Kate said. "She can share Jenny's room till Dave finds her people."

Oh, great, Jenn thought.

EVERYONE CAME OUTSIDE when Kate and Jenn returned to Possession Point. Even Annie emerged from her trailer, alerted by the boys that a half-dead girl had been hiding right beneath her and she could've been murdered at night in her bed. Jenn found her and she was all bloody and foaming at the mouth like she had rabies, was Petey's contribution. His father cuffed him and told him not to be mouthy, but what he'd said was enough to get Annie away from whatever she was doing once she heard the car.

One thing everyone noticed was the girl's smell. The boys shouted "Peee-you!" and shoved to get a better look at her. "Dad says she's Cilla," Petey cried. "Hey Cilla! Hey Cilla!" Andy shouted.

Bruce grabbed each boy by the shoulder and gave him a good shake. The girl shrank back and looked around fearfully. Then she stretched out her hand at Annie's trailer.

"Well, looks like she recognizes where she is," Bruce noted.

They began together to get her from the car and into the

McDaniels house, but it soon became apparent that the girl was going to have nothing to do with this. She started to fight them. She made inarticulate cries that tried to communicate *something* and she flung her entire arm toward the trailer, her fingers spread wide.

"Good Lord. She *can't* want to stay in there," Kate said. And then quickly, "Sorry, Annie, but . . ."

Annie held up her hand. "No offense taken. And there's not enough room anyway."

But nothing else was going to do because every attempt they made to get Cilla into the gray clapboard house was thwarted by her arms, her legs, her shrieks, her arched back, her flung head. Bruce said he didn't think they had a choice in the matter, and Kate agreed. The boys said, "Phooey! No fair! We wanted her!" and stomped up the steps to their rickety porch before their dad could discipline them once again. Kate said, "Annie?" and Jenn waited to see what Annie would do. This would put a real cramp in her style, she thought. It would also slow down her attempts to get to Nera.

Annie didn't have much choice in the matter, considering the girl's condition and the fact that Bruce and Kate promised to help care for Cilla. She said reluctantly, "I guess she could sleep on the couch."

"Bruce, get the extra blankets and sheets and pillows," Kate said quickly, as if afraid that Annie Taylor would change her mind. This was pretty reasonable, Jenn thought. Annie didn't look like someone who was throwing out the red carpet.

ONCE THEY GOT Cilla into the trailer, within five seconds it became clear what Job One was. The stench of the girl filled the whole place. Someone was going to have to wash her.

Kate McDaniels said, "We could . . . Could we start with her hair? We could do that in the kitchen, since she needs to keep that foot of hers dry."

But they soon found out that anything having to do with cleaning the girl was going to be easier said than done. She seemed terrified of water. When they eased her to the sink and turned on the faucet to let the water warm, she reared back, lost her balance, and nearly fell as she tried to retreat. "We only want to wash your hair, hon," got them only a response of inarticulate cries and yowling. This grew louder when they made a try at bending her over the sink. Jenn figured that the noise the girl made was loud enough to be heard all the way down to the cottages at Possession Shores.

Still, it was obvious the girl had to be cleaned. She needed to be washed and scrubbed and the clothes she was wearing had to be burned. And all of this needed to happen soon, Jenn figured, before the rest of them passed out from the smell.

She said, "She thinks you're going to hurt her, I bet."

"Jenn's right," Kate said. "This isn't going to work."

"We can hardly take her outside and hose her off, can we?" Annie sounded impatient. This unexpected visitor was putting a real crimp in her plans.

Kate frowned at Annie's tone. She seemed to assess Annie for a moment before she turned back to Cilla and spoke to her gently, the way Rhonda had spoken to her at the clinic. She used her name a lot. She told her the plan: Just trust us enough to bend over the sink and let us wash your hair. We won't hurt you, hon.

"We want to wash your hair, Cilla. Will you let us do that? Just your hair, hon. It won't hurt. I promise."

As Kate talked, she rubbed Cilla's back, and perhaps it was the gentle tone of her voice or the softness and the warmth of her touch, but the girl grew calmer. She allowed herself finally to be led to the sink. Kate kept up the calm talking and the gentle rubbing—almost like petting an animal, Jenn thought—as Annie washed the girl's hair.

Next came bathing, but there was only a shower and it was pretty clear that Cilla wouldn't be able to stand under a shower-head and wash herself. That left someone to volunteer to go into the shower with her once they had her foot encased in a plastic bag. When Annie sighed and said, "I guess I'll do it," what Jenn thought of at once was what could happen. She thought of Annie coming on to her. She thought of Annie with this poor girl who couldn't even talk. She said, "No!" without a pause.

Annie looked at her long. "Oh please. As if. It's not what you think."

Kate McDaniels looked from Jenn to Annie. Again her eye-brows drew together. Jenn knew she wondered, and who could blame her? But there was no way she was going to explain to her mom what her outburst had meant. She said, "I was just thinking . . ." and could come up with nothing except, "How can you get her into the shower without Mom?"

Annie said, "Well I'm going to have to, aren't I? There's barely room for two people in that bathroom and no way can three fit. So unless you want to be the one to wash her . . ." She said this last pointedly.

Jenn felt her face take fire. But she shrugged and said nothing. When Annie had gotten Cilla to the bathroom, Kate McDaniels said quietly, "Jenn. Is there something . . . ?"

To avoid an answer which she didn't want to give, Jenn went outside where her dad and the boys had left the girl's suitcase on the front porch of the house. The rotten fruit had pretty much done a job on the clothes. There was nothing inside that wasn't creeped out by the smell of the food gone bad or by the food itself. She went in the house and rooted around. Her own clothes would be way too small for the girl, and so would her mom's. But she found a thrift store flannel shirt and a threadbare pair of jeans among her dad's belongings, and she took them back to the trailer, with her father and the boys following behind her to witness the next development.

Bruce brought the sheets, pillows, and blankets. Petey and Andy each held a can of Campbell's tomato and rice soup. They trooped across the property and into the trailer. The moment all of them had assembled expectantly just inside the door, Annie and Cilla came out of the bathroom. A collective gasp ensued. Then there was silence.

The clothes Jenn had scouted for hadn't been needed, for

Annie Taylor had dressed the girl in some yoga clothes. But it wasn't the clothes that garnered the gasp and the silence. It was Cilla herself.

She was beautiful. She had the palest skin Jenn had ever seen, like someone who'd never spent even five minutes in the sun. She also had the darkest eyes, and her hair was so black it was almost blue. Annie's clothes were actually too big for Cilla because she looked like someone who hadn't had a square meal in weeks. But even with clothes hanging on her like a refugee, she would have stopped traffic if she'd walked down the street.

"Well," Bruce McDaniels said.

"Glory be to God," Kate McDaniels agreed.

No one had anything to add to this, but it didn't matter, because someone knocked on the trailer's door at that point, and Annie opened it to Dave Mathieson. The under sheriff of Island County had a clipboard in his hand and a digital camera in his pocket.

"Rhonda tells me you've had some excitement over here," he said by way of introduction. "I take it this is the young lady in question."

PART SEVEN

Heart's Desire

THIRTY-FIVE

Derric sat in his bedroom in the new leather chair his mom had bought him, the one to replace the ancient beanbag. He threw balled-up pieces of paper into the new wastebasket beneath his new desk, and he tried to feel grateful. His mom had done every single thing right: from making every possible effort to prepare him for adulthood to changing his room from boy's to man's when his spirits were low.

Yet he'd been treating her badly since she'd gotten rid of that chair. He'd been sullen and uncommunicative. Once those letters to Rejoice had been tossed out, it was like he'd become a different person. He didn't want to be the way he was toward her now, but he didn't know how to get back to the other Derric he had been.

He stirred in the chair. He reached for one of his notebooks and he opened it to a blank piece of paper. He wrote *Dear Rejoice* at the top of this, as he'd done so many times for the last eight years. Then he just stared at his sister's name and asked himself what the heck he was doing.

Who did he think he was kidding? Who had he ever thought he was kidding? His sister had never read a single one of his letters and she never would. And *if* he'd ever mailed them off to her, would she have been *able* to read them then? *Could* she read? Had she been taught? He didn't even know where she was, for God's sake. She could have been adopted like him, and he would have no way of knowing. For all he knew, she could even be dead.

He tore the paper from the notebook. He balled it up and threw it to join the other papers he'd been tossing in the wastebasket.

Someone knocked on his bedroom door. His dad's voice said, "Derric? C'n I come in?"

Derric said sure, and his father entered. He was still in his uniform from the sheriff's department. He had his hat in one hand and a plastic shopping bag dangling from the other. He must have just got home from work, Derric thought. He looked at the clock on his bedside table. It was nearly time for dinner.

Dave Mathieson said, "I think these are yours," and he opened the plastic bag he was carrying. He brought out two rubber-banded stacks.

Derric saw what they were. From head to toe he felt encased in ice. *Rejoice* was written at the top of the stack, as it would be written on all of the envelopes that were held by each of the rubber bands.

Derric waited for the worst to come next. For what does a father say to the adopted son who'd abandoned his only sister in Uganda and then spent eight years writing phony letters to her?

"I didn't read them," Dave Mathieson said. He placed the letters into Derric's lap and sat on the edge of the brand-new bed. "But they *are* yours, aren't they?"

"How'd you get them?" Derric managed to say.

"An artist in Coupeville brought them by the office this morning. He scored that old beanbag chair the minute it showed up in the trash. Turns out he's a regular at the holding spot where things get dumped. He makes his art with found objects."

"A beanbag chair?" It hardly seemed credible.

Dave Mathieson smiled. "That's what I thought. But he wanted the chair for its stuffing. Took him a while to open it up because he didn't need it till he was ready to ship something. He found the letters inside, read a couple, saw Uganda mentioned, and saw your name. He put it together."

"Just from *Uganda* and *Derric*?"

Dave shook his head. "He saw the story in the *Record* when you fell last autumn, so he knew who you were." Dave slapped his thighs and began to get up. "He brought them by the station for you. How about that, huh? Pretty nice of him, you ask me, when you think he could've just as easily tossed 'em. I got his name and address if you want to say thanks." He looked at Derric more earnestly, it seemed. "Do you?" he asked him. "Want to say thanks, I mean."

Derric nodded. He picked up the letters that his father had placed in his lap. He wanted to press them to his chest, but he knew exactly how odd that would look. Just about as odd as hiding a bunch of letters inside a beanbag chair. Explanations were hanging there in the air, waiting to be snatched at and spoken by him. But he didn't know how to grab them or how to speak them or what would happen if he ever did.

Dave headed for the door. But there he paused. He hit the jamb lightly with his fist. He said, "Son, I'm not about to pry. I know something's going on with you. This breakup with Becca. Then Courtney. And now this Rejoice . . ." He nodded at the letters when he said her name.

"Dad," Derric said, his voice low and a warning.

"I know, I know. Your business is your business. But I remember sixteen. How it was, I mean. The kinds of things I did and the feelings I had. I c'n see you've spent a hell of a lot of time writing to someone back in Uganda and I'm wondering . . . I know that life was tough for you there. Before the orphanage and in the orphanage. But you know you can talk to me, don't you? Is there anything at all you want to tell me?"

Derric thought about *want* because want was exactly the word. He did want to tell his father. He wanted to tell him the story from start to finish. But *can't* stood in the way of *want*. He looked at his dad and saw the worry on his face. He also saw the love in his eyes. But worry and love were not enough.

He said, "I'm okay, Dad," and he offered a wry and specious smile. He hoisted the letters and said, "Girls, you know," in one of those just-us-boys kind of ways.

Dave looked at him and said, "Okay, then," but he didn't sound convinced at all by Derric's act of good cheer.

THIRTY-SIX

Becca waited for Jenn to give her the sign that she'd arranged to borrow Annie Taylor's scuba equipment. She figured there was no point in asking Ivar to help them out with his boat until Jenn was ready, and considering how little enthusiasm the other girl had for diving, she knew she might have to put some effort into convincing Jenn all over again that a dive down to Eddie Beddoe's boat was the only way to go. But when she said to her, "So? D'you get the equipment?" before class the next day, her response was, "Crap. Damn. I forgot."

Jenn's whisper of *once we found Cilla I totally* suggested that she was neither lying nor stalling. But Becca could hardly say, "Who the heck is Cilla?" in reply to a whisper so instead she said, "Gosh, you for*got*? What happened?" and hoped for more information.

It came in the form of "Someone's staying with Annie. She's sick. We all got roped into helping take care of her, and Mom and I took her to Langley Clinic. Then everything got all . . . all involved with my family and Annie and . . . I forgot." She made a face and slapped the heel of her hand on her forehead, saying,

"Squat wanted me to find out something, too. I didn't do that, either. I blew it."

"Squat?"

"Yeah." But she was cagey about what it was that she was supposed to do, just that it was information and it was probably nothing but she'd told him she'd try and now he was going to be pissed because if she didn't, then he couldn't and *maybe that's why I didn't like his tongue but maybe . . . hers no way.*

Becca blinked. His tongue? Hers? No way? What the heck? She said, "Okay, but we can't . . . Jenn, this is important. You know that, don't you?"

Jenn bristled and said she most certainly did but Becca needed to chill for God's sake because she had a lot going on at the moment *and* she had to get back to soccer since the tryouts were . . . God they were in a week and she was majorly blowing it and—

"Okay, okay," Becca said. But she felt confused.

After school, Becca went into town. While things weren't moving forward on the diving-to-Eddie's-boat front, there were other things hanging in the air for her and one of them was where the heck she was going to live. The charms of the tree house had long ago faded, after only a month of having to use the showers in the girls' locker room at school, and with the weather improving, how long could she reasonably expect Seth's grandfather *not* to be taking walks in his own forest? If nothing else, he'd come out to maintain his trails. He'd also want to see how the tree house had held up over the winter, wouldn't he? And if he did that, he was sure to find her. So she took the bus into Langley and got out near the Cliff Motel.

She didn't go into the office at first. Instead she walked across the street where from beneath a newly leafing tree at the performing arts center, she could gaze at the place and its ten rooms, and she could think of what ten rooms meant to Debbie Grieder and her grandkids.

She *hated* to ask Debbie Grieder if she could have one of her rooms because she knew that Debbie would give her one at once. That was who she was. And while Becca badly wanted to take advantage of this, she hated to take advantage of Debbie. Sure, she would be working in exchange for the room: she could help clean the place and she could babysit Chloe and Josh when Debbie went to her AA meetings. But having someone help out at the motel in this way didn't put money into Debbie's pockets, and that was a sticking point for Becca. Everything, she thought morosely, always came down to money. And even if that hadn't been the case, the one time Jeff Corrie had shown up in town, he'd chosen the Cliff Motel as a place to stay. If he showed up again . . . Becca couldn't risk it.

She heard Josh's shout, and she saw that he and Derric had come out from Debbie's office/apartment and were setting up an archery target against one of the trees in the vacant lot next door. Josh was yelling, "Betcha I make the first bull's-eye. Betcha betcha betcha," while Derric called out, "No way, dude."

Becca watched them for a moment, unseen. Her heart was heavy at the thought of Derric. She watched the two boys take up position and shoot rubber-tipped arrows at the target. It was a child's play set of bows and arrows, and she could tell that Derric was taking care not to break his. His arrow went wildly wrong. Josh's hit the target although not the bull's-eye. Josh gave a war whoop and did a war dance. Derric laughed and rubbed the boy's head. Then Josh saw Becca.

"Hi, Becca!" he cried. "We're playing arrows! You want to play?"

She grimaced inwardly. She felt like an idiot spy. She called back, "Hi, Josh. Looks like fun," and she started moving in the direction of town. But that was when Chloe bounded outside. She, too, saw Becca and she called out, "Becca! Becca! Grammer made oatmeal raisin cookies! They're her special . . . her special . . . her specialness. I'm taking one to Josh 'n' one to Derric." She held up her hands, a wrapped cookie in each.

Becca didn't have the heart to walk away from Chloe. She crossed the street and fondly cupped her head. She said, "Oatmeal raisin? Those're definitely the best."

"Then you better have one now 'cause me and Josh're eating them all tonight!"

"I bet your grammer won't like that," Becca said.

"Shhh! Don't tell her!" And Chloe skipped off.

Becca watched her go. Well, she thought, it seemed more or less meant. She went into the office and through the living room with its comfortable old maple furniture and its general Chloe-and-Josh clutter. She found Debbie Grieder in the kitchen, spooning batter onto a cookie sheet. A rack held at least two dozen cookies already baked. Becca's mouth watered at the smell of them.

Debbie smiled at her. She had her graying hair pulled back from her face in a lopsided ponytail, and her scarred forehead had a Chloe-sized flour handprint on it. She wore an apron that was thoroughly messed up with cookie makings, and when she saw Becca glance at it, she whispered *face on that girl . . . look a sight I know . . .* and she laughed and said, "Cooking ain't my thing, darlin. As you well know. But cookies, on the other hand . . . ? You better have a few. Milk's in the fridge. Pour us both a glass."

Becca went for the glasses, comfortable in the knowledge of where things were. She caught another whisper of *lost so much . . . pretty with the hair . . . but he said and I guess kids know when something's right,* which Becca assumed had to do with Derric. She sighed. *Another* reason she couldn't possibly return to this place. Derric would be here. And how would that seem? Like she was stalking him or something? Oh probably, she thought. Because the one thing she was definitely learning was no matter how bad things were, they could always get worse.

When Debbie had the next cookie sheet in the oven, she scored a cookie for herself and dropped onto a chair at the kitchen table. She pulled a copy of the local paper off the seat next to her and, biting into a cookie, said to Becca, "You see this, darlin? There's another mysterious girl come to the island, just like you," and she turned the paper in Becca's direction.

On the front page a large picture of a girl was featured. Beneath it was the name CILLA. The headline asked DO YOU RECOGNIZE THIS GIRL? and the story that went with it gave the details.

Becca skimmed this story. The relevant bits fairly leaped out at her: Possession Point, Jenn McDaniels, a trailer, a suitcase with a note inside, a girl who couldn't or wouldn't talk, the Langley Clinic, and a thousand questions.

DEBBIE GRIEDER KNEW nothing more than what was in the story. If Becca was curious, she pointed out, Rhonda Mathieson would know the details, since the girl had been taken to the Langley clinic and Rhonda would have seen to her. Fact was, Derric could probably fill her in on more information. He was just outside with Josh and if Becca asked him—

"Oh, it's okay," Becca said. The last thing she wanted was to have to ask Derric.

Debbie eyed her and said, "Sorta went south? You 'n' Derric?"

Becca shrugged. "Guess so. I blew it. Maybe we both did. I dunno. Whatever."

Kids was Debbie Grieder's whispered response to this. Becca couldn't blame her for that inner tone of amusement and resignation. It was all pretty dumb and it would sound dumber if she told Debbie how lame she'd been. Debbie said, "True love never goes smooth, girl," but Becca found that she couldn't agree. If love was true, it was natural, she thought. Wasn't that how it was supposed to be?

In any case, she couldn't stay at the motel with Debbie, not even sleeping on her couch. It was bad enough seeing Derric at school. Seeing him out of school would be excruciating.

There was nothing for it but to go to work. At least she could earn a little money so when she found a place she would be able to pay her way. Soon after she'd consumed her oatmeal cookie, she took off for Heart's Desire. Two bus rides deposited her where she'd left her bike hidden among some trees. Then a fast pedal along Double Bluff Road and a right at the stop sign put her on the final climb up the bluff to where the farm stood.

When she arrived, it was to the sound of dogs' rapturous barking and to the sight of Diana Kinsale's pickup truck. She saw four of Diana's dogs bounding around the yard that surrounded the house while Oscar watched from the porch where he'd positioned himself near the mudroom door.

Becca went through the kitchen, where a pot of spaghetti sauce on the stove was filling the air with a heady fragrance. She lifted the pot's lid for a better smell of it, and her mind went to thoughts of coming home after school to the scent of her mom's baked beans. Her throat got tight for a second, and she cleared it mightily.

Nope, nope, *nope*, she told herself. She wouldn't go there. Things were already tough enough.

She went into the mudroom for a quick hello and found Diana in the haircutting chair. Diana's hair was wet and her shoulders were covered by a plastic cape. Sharla was standing behind her. They both were looking into the mirror, and they seemed to be considering what sort of haircut Diana needed. When Becca entered, Diana gazed long and hard at her face then held out her hand. Becca took it, and Diana's careworn hand was warm to the touch. It moved quickly to grasp Becca's arm, and the feeling was what it always had been: a soft heat and the sensation of being unburdened. She said to Becca, "You stay right where you are and supervise what Sharla's intending to do to me. I think I need you here for courage. Okay with you, Sharla?"

"No problem," Sharla said. "She's next anyway, and don't you protest, Miss Becca, 'cause I see you winding up to do so. You're getting too shaggy, and there's no way I intend to let a haircut by Sharla Mann end up looking like a dog groomer did it."

Sharla set her hands on Diana's shoulders and positioned the chair to its best height. When she did this, however, things altered in the mudroom. Becca felt a slight jolt from Diana's hand, which was still on her arm, and her vision altered to gray and to black and for an instant she thought she was fainting.

Before she could exclaim in some way, though, a picture distinctly flashed into her mind. It was clear like a photograph, and then it altered to become like a film. But it was jerky, the way a film is when the moviemaker wants the finished product to seem like something seen through a person's eyes.

Flowered curtains covering a window through which daylight showed. A couch with sagging cushions. A kitchen in which a chair bore a tall stack of blankets and a scarf tossed atop them. And then, just like someone's family videos, the jerky image of a toddler unsteady on its feet but walking forward.

Becca took a breath that rasped loudly. Diana removed her hand from Becca's arm, saying, "You all right, my dear?" and at her words Becca's vision altered again and she was back in the mudroom. Diana was watching her closely, and Sharla was fingering Diana's hair the way a stylist does just before using the scissors. Around them all, the mudroom was the mudroom, but Diana's face told Becca that Diana *knew*.

Somehow she'd taken another step. She didn't understand the journey, and she had no clue about the destination. But she was growing closer to it, whatever it was and whyever it existed.

THIRTY-SEVEN

Get the gear yet? comprised the note that Becca passed to Jenn during Western Civ class the next day. Jenn made a face that indicated she still hadn't done so, and Becca figured the mysterious girl at Possession Point might be why. So her next note to Jenn was *What's with this Cilla chick? I saw it in the paper*, to which Jenn mouthed *Tell you later*.

Later happened after school, since immediately at the end of Western Civ, Jenn got accosted by Squat Cooper who wanted to know "Look, d'you want my help or not 'cause if you do, you got to do your part," to which Jenn said, "Hey. Chill, dude. It's not like I'm not trying." And *later* only happened at all because Becca followed Jenn onto the school bus.

She plopped down on the seat next to Jenn and said, "Well?"

Jenn said, "Geez, you're the persistent one, aren't you?" But then she told the story of the girl she'd found hiding beneath Annie's trailer: how they'd taken her to the clinic, how they'd tried to get her inside the McDaniels house, how she'd acted like someone being dragged to the guillotine and only settled down when they deposited her in Annie's trailer. She'd been really sick and she'd stayed really sick and the only good thing about the entire enterprise of having her on the property was that Annie hadn't been able to get away long enough to try to trap Nera.

Bet ol' Chad is hurting for her what a joke came with this story, and along with the tale of Annie being trapped on the property, Becca figured out that the longing looks Chad had been casting on Annie Taylor's body had led to something. But before she could ask Jenn about this, *antibiotics should have helped* slipped out among the whispers, and Becca wasn't surprised when Jenn went on to say that the antibiotics given to the girl didn't seem to be making a dent in her illness.

"She had this old roller suitcase with her," Jenn said, "and it looked like it had been dragged from Canada, I swear. There were clothes inside and a bunch of old rotting fruit and some Clif bars and a note. That's how we knew she could hear but not talk. All she does is make noises."

"What kind?"

"Like . . . I dunno, Becca. You have to see for yourself. If she's awake. She might not be 'cause, like I say, she's sick."

Noises, Becca thought. She frowned and wondered and looked out the window as the farmland on either side of the road they were on morphed to deep forest where shadows lay thickly on the ground. Not being able to talk didn't equate to not being able to think, Becca figured. Chances were good that the girl would have whispers.

———

THE AFTERNOON WAS gray upon gray. The sky and the water were the color of stainless steel, with a cloud cover high above that spoke of rain and choppy waves below that slapped against the piles of driftwood on the shore.

Annie opened the trailer door at Jenn's knock. She said, "Thank *God*. I've been in jail all day. I need a freaking break. Your mom's been gone for hours with the taxi, and your dad's . . . I have no idea what happened to him. Testing beer probably. Under the table. Passed out. Whatever."

"Hey," Jenn said sharply.

"Sorry," Annie said. "Like I said, I need a break. You good to stay?" She said hi to Becca and ushered them inside. She said, "She's not any better and I keep telling your mom she needs to go to the hospital. I told your dad, too. But nothing's happened." *Chad could but . . . not enough time and I need to* made a background to this.

The trailer, Becca saw, was cluttered with Annie's belongings, and it looked as if she'd been trying to work. There were documents on the table, filing folders on the floor, her laptop was running, and papers with diagrams and scribbles on them were scattered on the banquette.

Jenn looked around and said to Annie, "So, where is she? I thought she was sleeping on the couch."

"In the bedroom. Since she wasn't getting better, I thought if I put her in the bedroom . . . It's warmer there, and when she's out here, she just stares. It's unnerving. I've called Rhonda Mathieson and she's been here twice but all she says is, 'These things take time.' Like I've *got* time to waste?"

She strode to the couch and picked up her jacket, which lay upon it. "So you're on duty now. I'm out of here for a while," she told Jenn. "Nice to see you, Becca," she added.

Becca nodded and offered a wry smile. But the smile was more to cover her astonishment at what she saw. The limp curtains hanging over the window above the couch were the curtains she had seen in her vision. So was the couch. So was the route along which the toddler had walked.

BECCA THOUGHT THAT Jenn would lead the way to the girl Cilla once Annie left them alone in the trailer. But instead she made a dive for the marine biologist's laptop. She said, "Oh yeah, oh yeah, oh yeah," and she began typing frantically on its keyboard. *Transmitter picture and those numbers* explained what she was doing, but Becca asked her all the same.

"Squat says that the transmitter on Nera'll have numbers on it and if we c'n get them, we c'n find out more about her. Like maybe where she's from and why she never shed it or something."

Becca wasn't sure how this got them anywhere—like close to Eddie Beddoe's boat—so she went in the direction of the bedroom, where she could see the form of someone lying beneath the covers, her face toward the wall. Becca murmured, "Hey. Hi. You awake, Cilla?" and the figure turned. She fixed great dark eyes on Becca's face. She gave a start of fear. Becca said, "S'okay.

I'm a friend of Jenn's," which didn't seem to reassure the girl, so she added, "She lives in the big gray house? Her family's helping take care of you?"

The girl whined, a long low sound akin to a dog waiting to be fed. She scrabbled her fingers on the pillowcase beneath her head. She showed her teeth briefly. She backed away.

Becca listened hard. In the otherwise silent room, she heard the sound of Jenn's typing on the laptop's keyboard and she heard Cilla's breathing, which was strained and uneven. But that was all. Not a single whisper was coming from the girl. She was wide awake, but there was nothing recognizable escaping from her head.

She should have been dead for this to be the case, Becca thought. Everyone on the planet had whispers. Unless . . . There was one person on Whidbey Island who had absolute control over her own whispers.

They needed Diana Kinsale to look at Cilla. If anyone could read her, it would be Diana.

THIRTY-EIGHT

Jenn didn't get why Becca wanted Diana Kinsale to visit Cilla. But on the other hand, she didn't much care about it. She'd gotten what she needed from the pictures stored on Annie's laptop, and once she had them she was willing to agree to just about anything so that she could get back across the property to her own house where there was a phone. She had to call Squat with the information. She'd found a perfect shot of the transmitter and she'd scored the numbers on it. But she'd also found among the papers scattered on the banquette notes in Annie's writing telling her that the marine biologist was one step ahead of them. The transmitter's numbers were there. So was a phone number. So was *Monterey Bay* with two exclamation points. Obviously, they had to find out what it all meant.

So when Becca mentioned Diana Kinsale and could they come back so Diana could try to talk to Cilla, Jenn said, "Whatever. S'okay with me. We finished here or what?" and she tried not to shove Becca out of the trailer ahead of her. She did point out that Becca was one hell of a long way from town and how did she intend to get home now that she'd come all the distance to

Possession Point. Becca's answer was, "C'n I use your phone?" which was fine by Jenn, since that got them out of the trailer and one step closer to where she herself wanted to be. She would have vastly preferred Becca never to see the inside of her house, but she didn't see any option but to allow her the use of their phone.

Becca used it to call Seth Darrow. She explained where she was. She struck a deal. If she started walking, would he be willing . . . ? Thanks, Seth. I owe you. He said something. Becca laughed.

Jenn felt a little stab at all this. Jealousy? she asked herself. Of *what*? No way.

Becca was heading out to start hiking up Possession Point Road when Jenn's dad tromped up onto the porch. His "Hey, hey, hey," at the sight of Becca told Jenn he was tipsy from home brew testing. But he wasn't actually drunk, and what Jenn thought was maybe he'd be tagged by Becca as just the oddball friendly type. He sure as hell looked the part. His hair was Ben Franklin to the max today, and for some reason he'd decided on running shorts for his garb. His legs stuck out like a rooster's from them, his feet and legs encased in sandals and striped knee socks.

She introduced them. Before she paused to consider what it meant, she said, "This is my friend Becca King. From school and from diving," and then she felt flustered that she'd used the word *friend* without even thinking.

Becca shot her a smile. For his part, Bruce was thoroughly delighted. Jenn could see this one all over his face. Had her mom been home, her parents probably would have built an altar and sacrificed something in thanksgiving. Up to this point, her friends had been boys, her acquaintances had been her fellow soccer players, and that was it. That she would actually *have* a girlfriend, that she would—as far as her dad knew—bring this friend home from school to hang out, that this could possibly mean their kid was somewhat of a normal teenager after all . . . It was major hallelujah time, Jenn thought with resignation.

Bruce said expansively, "Welcome, welcome, wel*come.* Be it ever so humble—and it sure as heck is, eh?—you're welcome to our palatial abode. What brings you here?" And to Jenn, "I hope you've offered worthy refreshments."

Jenn didn't say that they had worthy refreshments exactly like they had gold bars under the house. Becca hurriedly said, "Oh, I was just leaving. I just came over to . . ." and she looked at Jenn.

"She wanted to see Cilla," Jenn said.

"There was a story in the paper," Becca explained.

Bruce looked from Becca to Jenn to Becca again. He seemed thoroughly unconvinced by this tale. "Bit of a curiosity, eh?"

"When the paper said she could hear but she couldn't talk," Becca offered.

"Thought you might be able to I.D. her?"

"You never know," Becca agreed.

And then as far as Jenn was concerned, Becca asked the strangest question of her dad. She said, "Did a little kid ever live over there, Mr. McDaniels?"

"Over where?"

"Inside that trailer."

"Not hardly," Bruce said. He shot Jenn a look and then went back to Becca. "Why d'you ask?"

Becca said, "Just wondering, is all. I guess I thought maybe Cilla showed up 'cause she used to have a friend here or something."

"That wouldn't be the case," Bruce said. "No how and no way." And to Jenn, "Did your mom leave a note about starting dinner?"

Jenn could tell her dad was very deliberately dismissing the subject and she could see from Becca's expression that she was thinking the very same thing. But Becca said nothing else except, "I better get going," and left Jenn alone with her father.

Bruce didn't waste time after Becca left. He said to Jenn, "Should I or should I not be thinking something's going on?"

"Going on where?" Jenn asked him innocently.

"I b'lieve you know what I'm talking about."

Jenn went to the kitchen to inspect the dinner possibilities. There were two lone pork chops in the refrigerator. Five potatoes, a bunch of limp carrots, and four onions sat on the counter. A pork stew? she thought. Light on the pork and extremely heavy on the stew? Looked like it to her. She got out a pot.

"Jenn," her dad said, "you want to answer me?"

"You know what I know," she told him.

He said, "Don't be smart."

"I'm not being smart. All's I know is she wanted to see Cilla so she came with me on the bus. Annie took off and left us with her and we stayed for a while and now she's asleep and that's all there is to know. Becca works afternoons sometimes for Ivar Thorndyke, though. An' he lives with Sharla and Sharla lived in the trailer and maybe Sharla said something about a kid who used to live there before her or maybe a kid who used to live in Possession Shores and maybe . . . I dunno."

She rustled around for the potato peeler. She found the vegetable brush in a drawer. She went for peeling the potatoes first. She waited for her dad to depart.

He didn't. He said, "No one lived there before Eddie and Sharla, okay? And that place did a job on them. Ended up with Eddie thinking he was a charter fisherman and Sharla wandering the beach, crooning to a stuffed seal, saying it was her baby, and getting herself put away in the loony bin. *That's* what that trailer does to people when they spend too much time in it. Annie Taylor'd be wise to get herself away."

"A *trailer* doesn't make people crazy," Jenn scoffed. "Like . . . what's it supposed to do? Pollute someone's brain? This isn't a Stephen King novel, Dad."

"Stephen King, Stephen Schming, I do not care. All's I know is Eddie Beddoe didn't wear a hazmat suit when they were cleaning the beach from that oil spill all those years back, and he carried that oil right inside that trailer, and he and Sharla were cooped up with it, and from that moment on, neither one 'f them was the same person they'd been. Come to think, you're spending way too much time over there. Let's call a halt to that."

"Come on. That trailer's not hurting me."

"No? When'd you last attend to your soccer, Jenn? You want to tell me that?"

"I been practicing."

"Like hell you have. Your mind's taken up with other things and that's what happens. You start thinking wrong. It happened to Eddie, it happened to Sharla, and I will not have it happening to you."

Jenn rolled her eyes. "As if," she said.

"You prove to me otherwise, or you stay away," he warned her.

WHEN JENN HANDED over to Squat the information on the transmitter that she'd scored from Annie's laptop along with the phone number and the location Monterey Bay, he told her that there was one hell of a *very* serious aquarium in Monterey Bay and a serious aquarium meant serious scientists associated with it, which may or may not mean serious information available on seriously different seals. *Scientists* and *seals* triggered thoughts of Annie being ahead of them in her quest for information about Nera. It also equated to Annie being way ahead of them when it came to plans.

They went to Squat's house. They used Squat's laptop and the phone. Their first hope was that the phone number Jenn had found was associated with the aquarium, but that wasn't the case. It took a while for them to follow the leads and work out who had received Annie Taylor's call. For when they called the number, they ended up with the school of life sciences at California State University. That CSU was in a place called Fort Ord wasn't particularly helpful. That Fort Ord turned out to be up the road from the town of Monterey and practically sitting on

Monterey Bay . . . That was something else altogether.

Jenn watched and listened as Squat navigated his way through various phone calls to various people. Depending on the person he was talking to, he morphed himself from a graduate student to a police official to a research assistant to a volunteer for a wild life rescue operation. She marveled at his ability to converse amicably with all these telephonic strangers.

He finally narrowed things down. She'd watched over his shoulder as he'd written *evolutionary, ecological, micro, human,* and then *marine!* on a notepad. Finally, he actually found the person Annie Taylor had called. He didn't mention her name, but he didn't have to. All he referred to was Whidbey Island and he'd used the terms "old transmitter on a seal up here," and then he was listening and giving Jenn a thumb's-up and taking notes as fast as he could.

She threw her arm around his shoulder and planted a kiss on his cheek and then stuck her tongue in his free ear. He waved her off, held up a finger to say "wait a second," and ended the call with a formal, "That's going to be helpful to our efforts up here, Dr. Parker . . . Yes, that's right. *F-e-r-g-u-s.* Fergus Cooper . . . In the acknowledgments? Absolutely . . . No question about it. You've been really helpful."

And then it was over and Jenn was saying, "What, what, *what?*"

Squat said, "I got to say it. Sometimes I amaze myself."

"*Tell* me."

"You putting out if I do?"

She punched his arm.

"Ow! Okay, okay. I got the goods. Annie Taylor got there first, by the way. Once I said Whidbey Island—"

"Yeah, I figured that."

"—the guy, Dr. Michael Parker's his name, gave me the story. *And* he said he'd already told it to Annie. Anyway, first of all, that transmitter's way old. Over twenty years, and this guy Parker said he was surprised Nera's still got it on."

"It's older than the oil spill, then," Jenn pointed out. "Which says Nera's not some mutant who was *born* a mutant because of the spill."

"Yeah. She got it put on as part of a study in Monterey Bay and here's what's cool. As soon as I said coal black seal, this dude Parker knew exactly who I meant. Or what I meant, since I guess Nera's a what and not a who, huh? Anyway, Parker says they were tagging all the seals and sea lions from a whole section of the coastline in California. Part of a study of feeding patterns and breeding problems and stuff like that. It was for the EPA and they were doing a study that went from Cambria to Santa Cruz . . . something like two hundred fifty or three hundred miles. But the black seal? She moved out of range within a week, he says."

Jenn frowned. Squat was acting like someone who expected fireworks to go off at the conclusion of his story. She said, "So?"

"So that's not how seals behave, this guy Parker said. He was totally amazed that she was up here at all, he said. And he was totally flipped out when Annie told him that she showed up around Langley every year, practically on the exact same date.

And he said that when she was down there and they tagged her with the transmitter, it was like she knew they wanted to study her down there 'cause she totally disappeared. I mean, she moved out of range. And when Annie told him Nera still had the transmitter on, he said 'That's one hell of an interesting seal,' *and* he said Annie's gonna make her name in marine science if she can identify Nera, especially if it turns out she's some new species or something like that. See, he said that everyone down there thought she just had that skin thing . . . What's it called? Opposite of being albino?"

"Melanism," Jenn told him. "That's what Annie called it."

"Yeah. That was it. He said Annie said she doesn't think it's melanism at all because Nera doesn't look like any kind of seal that belongs around here anyway. So *if* she's never shed that transmitter and if she doesn't have melanism but is coal black because of the *kind* of seal she is, *that* means she's some sort of new seal that no one in marine science knows about."

"Except Annie Taylor," Jenn noted grimly. "And she's going to want to identify her, huh?"

"She's going to want to figure out what she is, that's for sure. I mean, what kind of marine biologist wouldn't? You ask me, this guy Parker is probably buying a plane ticket right now so he can beat Annie Taylor to it."

Jenn felt uneasy with all of the implications that were becoming apparent, most of which had to do with the safety of the seal. She didn't know a thing about the process for declaring something a new species, but she was pretty certain a few photographs of Nera were not going to be sufficient proof to the scientific community. They would need a lot more than that to declare Annie the discoverer of an entirely new species of mammal. They were going to need the animal herself. Failing that, they were going to need a heck of a lot of DNA and whatever else they could get their hands on.

Squat said in a meditative voice, "There's this one odd thing about all this stuff, though."

She glanced at him. He was resting back against the sofa, looking thoughtfully up at the ceiling. He had his arms behind his head, and his T-shirt rode up to show a band of white stomach and a rust-colored tuft of hair crawling down into his jeans that made Jenn get hot-faced and look away. She said, "What?"

"Well, all the whacked-out seal spotters on the island know about her, right? She's got her own website or whatever and they call each other the minute she shows up. They have meetings about her and . . . look at Ivar Thorndyke making sure everyone keeps away from her. You'd think *someone* around would've noticed she's different besides just being black, wouldn't you? I mean someone a hell of a long time before now."

"Before Annie showed up."

"Yeah. So the question is, why *didn't* anyone? And if someone did . . ." He glanced at her.

"I guess we know who it is, huh?"

"Ivar."

They looked at each other. "What d'you think he knows?" Jenn asked.

"I don't think that's the question," Squat replied.

"No? Then what?"

"Why doesn't he want anyone *else* to know?" He yawned then and scratched his stomach. He saw her eyes follow the route his hand had taken. He said, "So . . . ready to pay up?"

"Tongues or what?"

"Or what," he said. He pulled off his T-shirt.

She had a moment.

Lesbo freak.

No way, she told herself. She pulled her T-shirt off as well.

THIRTY-NINE

Diana Kinsale had learned about the girl at Possession Point the way most everyone else had: through the local newspaper. So she knew whom Becca was talking about the moment Becca brought up the topic. She agreed that something wasn't right about the whole situation, and when Becca told her that Cilla had no whispers, Diana walked to the window of her sunroom, where she spent a few minutes looking out at Saratoga Passage.

It was one of those moments when Becca wished that Diana herself had whispers. There was something about how gravely she looked upon the water that told Becca once again that more was going on than met the eye when it came to some of the adults in town.

Finally Diana turned from the window. She said, "I'm not sure how useful I can be in a situation of physical illness."

"I know you can't make her better," Becca replied. "But I thought . . . well, maybe between you and me, we could figure out who she is. We could maybe find her parents or something because it seems like they'd want to know she's sick."

Even as she said these words, Becca felt the small stone of

sorrow that she always carried grow a bit heavier in her chest. Parents. A mom. Her own mom. She coughed, swallowed hard, and pressed her lips together.

Diana watched her, her face concerned. She said quietly, "Let's go, then. I don't know what we can do, but trying is better than doing nothing, isn't it?"

When they arrived at Possession Point, it was to find Chad Pederson's truck parked next to Annie's Honda. No one was around the McDaniels house, but Chad and Annie stood out on the dock, and they looked like people having an intense conversation. Becca watched them for a moment, her eyes narrowed. Annie was pointing northeast into the water and then gesturing to the right of the dock where boats pulled up so that Jenn's dad could sell bait to the fishermen who piloted them. So intent were they upon what they were saying that they didn't notice Becca and Diana. Becca figured this was all to the good. It would be easier for them if they could see Cilla and try to read from her without Annie Taylor clouding the air with whispers.

They went inside the trailer. Cilla was lying on the couch, a comforter pulled up to her neck. Her breathing was loud and her eyes were half-opened although she appeared to be asleep. Her long dark hair was a tangled cloud around her shoulders. It descended all the way to the floor, and Diana picked up a lock of it and held it gently in her hands.

She said, "Hello, Cilla," as she sat on a chair that Becca brought to her. "How are you, my dear?" But on the couch, Cilla didn't respond.

Becca stood behind Diana's chair. As before, she tried to hear something coming from Cilla. But just like Diana, there was nothing to hear.

With a soft touch, Diana put the back of her fingers on Cilla's temple in a simple touch. She murmured, "You're safe. You've had a long journey to get here, Cilla. I expect what you'd like most is to go home."

Becca watched as Diana moved her hand from Cilla's temple to her forehead, which she massaged tenderly. "It would be lovely, wouldn't it," Diana said, "to be in a place where safety is all that someone knows."

Becca's throat closed. Like Cilla, she found it hard to breathe. It was the thought of safety, which she had not known in these many months since she'd come to Whidbey. It was the thought of a gentle touch on a feverish forehead. It was missing everything that she had lost.

Diana looked at her. She seemed to read it all. She said, "I would make your journey easier if I could, but there are limits to what's possible for me. And for you, too." And saying this, she drew Becca around to her side while still she caressed Cilla's forehead. Becca felt Diana's arm encircle her waist and a warmth took the place of the desolation she was feeling.

Then it changed. Instead of Cilla lying on the couch in front of her, Becca saw water. It was calm and dark as the night and she was moving through it. She was under it. She was on top of it. She heard the *thrub* of an engine flowing through it. Then the water was heavy, like a canvas weighed down by a thousand stones. She rose to the surface but it was black night and there were no stars. She could no longer breathe. She twisted and turned and looked for someone, for something, for a way to go until she felt hands, gentle as a sigh, and they smoothed and smoothed the length of her body. She was a butterfly emerging from a cocoon and outside the cocoon there was air, *air*. And then there was nothing but stumbling on unsteady feet and falling onto sand in the moonlight. Then the sound of footsteps. A gasp. And then in water nearby a smooth head rose. Then bright lights struck and they were everywhere and whatever it was in the water was gone.

Becca's vision cleared. Her heart was slamming in her chest, and she saw that Cilla's eyes were open and that Cilla was watching her. Diana's arm was no longer around her waist. She, too, was watching Becca.

She said to Becca, "Something's happened, hasn't it? And it happened once before, with Sharla."

Becca didn't know how to tell her or even what to tell her. She had no possible way to explain. It was being there with her and with Cilla but not being there with her and with Cilla; it was being there with her and with Sharla and not being there with her and with Sharla. It was like the whispers but it was more than the whispers. She didn't know what to call it.

She said, "This's about water. But I don't know why."

Diana said thoughtfully, "Yet things generally end the way they begin, in my experience."

Becca said, "Eddie Beddoe. He's where it started. That day on Sandy Point when he was shooting at the water."

"You're probably right," Diana told her.

THEY WENT TO Eddie Beddoe's car repair shop, across the street from a line of renovated old mercantile buildings that comprised the shops of Bayview Corner. As they approached the ancient gas station that housed Eddie's establishment, Diana pulled to one side of the road. She said to Becca, "A reason for showing up would be good," and she got out of the pickup and fiddled underneath its hood. When she got back in and turned on the engine, the truck misfired badly. Diana pulled into the forecourt where once the gas pumps had stood. Eddie came out of the shop, frowning at the noise from her truck and wiping his hands on a stained red rag.

Diana glanced at Becca before she climbed out of the pickup. "Ready, then?" she asked.

"Guess so," Becca told her. She wasn't sure how they were going to get anything out of the unpleasant man, but she would wait for a moment when it looked as if she could make a connection that he wouldn't be wise to.

Diana said to Eddie, "It's misfiring badly. Do you have time . . . ? To tell you the truth, I dread knowing. If it's a head gasket, I'm in big trouble."

Eddie glanced at Becca briefly. He said to Diana pleasantly enough, "Didn't sound like a head gasket to me when you pulled in," but his whispers told another tale about how he was feeling about their presence. *Little bitches two of them . . . all the trouble . . . no way are they . . . with that hot pants scientist . . .* came to Becca broken in parts as always, but it was a simple matter to interpret them. "Lemme take a look at her," he said.

He lifted the hood. After a moment, he said, "Yeah, that ain't no head gasket. Shut her down, will you?" and when Diana did so, he messed around under the hood. He emerged with two spark plugs, saying, "This here's your problem. One of them's wasted and the other's about to be. Wait a second," and off he went into his shop.

"Anything?" Diana murmured to Becca.

"Just that he's mad at me and Jenn. Or you and me. It was hard to tell. And . . . he's not a very nice man."

As Eddie approached again, Diana smiled at him. He disappeared beneath the hood, replaced the spark plugs, and told Diana to start the truck up again. It purred. Diana thanked him and said, "What do I owe you?" to which he answered, "Come on inside."

Becca followed them into the office, which was redolent of motor oil and grease. It was also so filthy that she took care not to touch anything, since it looked as if flesh-eating bacteria was the most likely resident of the place, and she waited for the moment to present itself.

Eddie wrote up the bill for the spark plugs. As she waited, Diana said to him in a friendly way, "I heard the good news about your boat being found, Eddie," and in that way she had of connecting with people, she put a hand on his arm. "Becca here was the one to tell me. Have you two met? She was with me that day on the beach at Sandy Point, but I don't think I introduced you two then." She extended her hand to Becca, and Becca took it, seeing the direction in which they were heading. She said to

Eddie Beddoe, "Oh yeah, hi," and she heard Diana add, "Becca and I met in the most unusual—" before silence hit her.

She was in open water. But this time, she was on a boat. She saw its stern along with the waves that hurled themselves onto its deck. And then beyond the boat . . . the sleek black head of Nera in the water. She was a bare ten yards away, but she didn't come closer. She rode the waves with ease. The boat's motor gunned. Then things went awry as the boat came about. The boat aimed for the seal. Nera dove. Water washed the deck.

Becca struggled to escape Diana's hand on hers. She knew where the vision was heading.

Eddie was saying, "Piece 'f crap and I should've knowed better but I didn't. Thing is, people got to stay away from that wreck. Wreck's dangerous and them two girls should've knowed it."

He didn't look at Becca as he spoke, but this was just as well because she was feeling light-headed and a bit sick to her stomach. It wasn't all due to the sudden sensation of being out on the water, though. It was also due to understanding what Eddie Beddoe had tried and failed to do to the seal.

FORTY

There was only one way to get out to the place where Eddie Beddoe's boat had gone down. The problem with this was that there were only two people who could help her get out there: Chad Pederson or Ivar Thorndyke. One word to Chad, and Annie Taylor was going to know they were up to something and she was also going to want to know exactly what that something was. That left Ivar, who might agree to ferry Jenn and her out to Eddie's boat, but only if he was certain that the coal black seal wasn't anyway near it.

"No big deal," was how Jenn put it when Becca laid the facts out for her. "The seal spotters' website tracks every move she makes. If she's anywhere near that boat it'll be on the Web."

The best idea seemed to be to make Ivar part of the expedition's planning. So when Becca found him in the kitchen of the farmhouse cooking up a batch of Thorndyke's Famous Fire-on-the-Tongue Chili, she began cleaning up the mess he was making, and she waited for a chance to bring up the subject of another scuba dive to that boat.

She used the idea of getting back on the horse that has bucked one from the saddle. She'd been spooked and so had Jenn, but she thought it might be a good idea for them to try another dive to Eddie Beddoe's boat together. They were certified now, so they didn't need Chad Pederson to accompany them. Would Ivar be willing . . . like maybe on a day he was fishing or something? She let the rest of her request hang in the open air.

At first Ivar said no how, no way. That seal was hanging around the boat, hanging around Langley village, hanging around Sandy Point. She'd even swum as far as Bell's Beach one day—way up along Saratoga Passage—and no one knew where she'd turn up next. Becca was pleased at this turn of topic, since it allowed her to bring up the seal spotters' website, which she did.

They continued their conversation over dinner, an invitation to taste the Fire-on-the-Tongue chili. The evening was fine, so they took their bowls out onto the farmhouse's wide wraparound porch and they sat there with Sharla, sharing a pitcher of lemonade, a box of saltines, and a tossed green salad. Sharla was quiet, but she was listening. At the first mention of Eddie Beddoe's boat, her whispers shot straight into the air.

Where it sank . . . that's where he . . . I swear I swear . . . it's all over unless he can . . . if he does then I will go . . . we both said that Sharla's calm presence hid a troubled mind. But she said nothing, and Ivar's whispers of *try something I know they will and then when she comes to the shore . . . damn . . . if I'd never seen the blasted woman . . .* confirmed that Annie Taylor and her intentions remained large on his mind. So Becca played that angle with a by-the-way. She told Ivar she'd seen Annie Taylor and

Chad Pederson on the dock at Possession Point. They were up to something, and since Annie's pictures of Nera had been taken at Eddie Beddoe's boat . . . Didn't it all seem to tie together? If she and Jenn did their get-back-on-the-horse dive down to Eddie Beddoe's boat, maybe they could find out why the seal had been hanging around it.

Sharla whispers went loony with *no no no . . . stop . . . don't you dare . . . if you take her* while Ivar's grew furious with *stop her* and *because if she knows then God help us all.* Everything combined to tell an even stronger tale about the need to get down to that boat. Becca wanted to yell, If I know *what*, Ivar?, but instead she made a dive with Jenn, and Eddie Beddoe's boat, and Annie Taylor's intentions all seem part of a reasonable whole.

So ultimately, Ivar agreed. Plans were laid. She only needed Jenn to snag Annie Taylor's equipment, and they'd be ready to roll.

JENN GOT HER hands on the scuba equipment without any trouble. Annie and Chad, she reported to Becca, were gathering what they needed to entrap the seal: nets and floats and her dad's guarantee of excellent bait. When they weren't doing that, Annie was tending to Cilla or—with a scoff—she was "tending to Chad, if you know what I mean." Scoring the scuba equipment? No problemmo. Annie didn't even know it was missing.

Becca and Jenn donned their dry suits as Ivar chugged clear of the marina. Becca had a plan to find the boat a second time, and Ivar agreed that it might well work. She'd remembered from their previous dive that the boat was lying offshore not too far east from Sandy Point, where a funicular railway gave a house on the bluff access to the beach below. All they needed to do was to find that same funicular railway once again, motor out from that point to where Ivar's depth gauge told them the bottom was at fifty feet, and swim down to the wreck of Eddie's boat, which should be right there. Just as it had been lying there when they made their dive with Annie and Chad.

Ivar agreed to this. Once out of the marina and the environs of the harbor, he opened the throttle. Sandy Point was no great distance away, and the funicular was even closer. Within ten minutes they were bobbing in the water, where it was deep enough for the boat to rest and where they could see the same funicular carving its mechanical pathway straight down the side of the bluff. From there it was all about the depth finder. They slowly headed out into the passage, whose water on this fine spring day was glassy and clear. At fifty feet, Ivar tossed the anchor over the side. He said to Becca, "You be careful," and to Jenn, "You, too. I want you back up here in less than fifteen minutes or I'm coming after you, dry suit, wet suit, or no suit. Understand?"

They nodded and donned the rest of their equipment. Becca said to Jenn, "Ready?" and when she heard the whisper of *no Chad in case anything happens down there*, she added, "Don't worry. We're dive buddies, right?"

Jenn didn't look reassured but she nodded gamely. Becca took the lead once they were in the water. The seal spotters were claiming on this day that Nera was in the Glendale area heading toward Columbia Beach, both of which were north of Possession Point. That put the Mukilteo ferry between where they themselves were and the seal. She might return, but probably not this day. At least that was what Becca told herself and what she told Ivar once he showed her where Columbia Beach actually was on a map of Whidbey Island.

Down they went. Slowly, the shape of the sunken wreck emerged below them as it had before. Becca kept her eyes open for a sighting of the seal, but she didn't see her. Just lots of fish that she couldn't name, Dungeness crabs scuttling on the bottom, and the torpedo-shaped hollows that were left by gray whales in their search for ghost shrimp.

Because of the depth, they didn't have much time to see if the boat sheltered something that Nera had wanted. In the years since the craft had sunk, salt water and the tide and rough weather had done a lot of their searching job for them. There was little enough around the boat, so when Becca saw the box half-wedged into the sandy bottom, she was sure that was what they were looking for.

She turned to Jenn and pointed to it. Jenn nodded, glanced around fearfully, as if expecting Neptune to arrive and go after her butt with his trident, and she indicated that she would follow. Becca felt her close behind, so close that her fins were scraping Jenn's face.

The box was metal, in part corroded and in part hosting tiny crustaceans. It was tipped drunkenly to one side, and while it looked heavy, this did not turn out to be the case. It was, in fact, disappointingly light. When she and Jenn jiggled it to release it from the sand, it came quite easily, as if it had merely been waiting for them to show up and take it out of the water.

This, too, proved easy. One of them could carry it under her arm. Clearly, if they were venturing into the area of finders/keepers, whatever was inside the box, it wasn't going to be pirate's gold.

Slowly they surfaced, watching their depth and taking their time. When they made it to the top, Ivar was waiting for them on the platform on the stern, by the boat's engine. Becca shoved the box onto this platform and took the hand that Ivar extended to her. Jenn did the same. In short order, they were back on the deck of the boat and along with Ivar they inspected the box.

Ivar picked it up and shook it, saying, "What've you got here?"

"Don't know for sure," Becca told him. "But it could be what Nera's been after."

They inspected the box and found it locked. The lock was crusty, and even if they'd had its key, no key was going to open the thing.

"C'n we break it?" Jenn asked.

"Back at the farm," Ivar said. "I've got the proper tools there, if you think it's worth it."

"Oh, I definitely think it's worth it," Becca said.

FORTY-ONE

Everything should have been easy from there. But that was not how things played out. They motored back to Langley's marina, and Ivar cut his speed as soon as they were in the harbor area. Jenn could tell that Becca was raring to go to town on the metal box. She kept looking at it and then looking at Ivar. She seemed to be trying to read him like a book.

By the time they were approaching the slips, both Jenn and Becca had their equipment and their dry suits off. When Ivar cut the boat's engine, Becca jumped out and dealt with the boat's lines. Jenn shot the hull fenders over the side while Ivar picked up the girls' equipment. They'd used an old heavy plastic wheelbarrow to get it from his truck down to the dock in only one trip, and Ivar started to hand it to Jenn one piece at a time to stow it inside. When this was done, Ivar handed the box over to Becca. She tucked it beneath her arm. That was when Eddie Beddoe stepped out from behind a cabin cruiser in the very next slip.

He had his rifle. Everyone froze. He said, "I'll take that, little lady. Thanks very much for bringing it up."

Jenn grabbed the box from Becca and held it fast. She said, "It's salvage and you know the rules."

"What I know is that you have something there that's mine and if you know anything—like what's good for you—you'll hand it over before someone gets hurt." He raised the rifle to his waist.

Ivar jumped out of the boat. He said, "You going to shoot one of us, Eddie? You advanced from just breaking people's arms, huh?"

Becca said for some reason, "It was *him*? Not the seal?"

"That's the size of things," Ivar said. And to Eddie, "Put that damn rifle down before someone gets hurt."

"Once little missy over there hands me that box," Eddie said, and he strolled quite casually over to the slip where Ivar's boat was moored.

Jenn looked around. There had to be help somewhere. But the marina was completely empty of people. The lights in the chandlery were off as well, and Chad's truck was gone from the parking lot, too.

Eddie said to her, "Time you handed that over, Jenn. Someone's going to get hurt if—"

"You're way too scared to shoot at anyone," Becca cut in. She sounded and looked so sure of herself that Jenn felt her eyes get wide. "What're you so scared of? What's in that box?"

"Doesn't concern you."

"Who does it concern?"

"Give me that damn box!" To make his point and, perhaps, to indicate that being scared was the least of what was going on with him, Eddie raised the rifle and set its sight on Becca.

"Hey," Ivar shouted.

"He's not going to shoot me," Becca said.

"You're crazy," Jenn told her. "Here. Take it." She thrust the box in Eddie's direction. He snatched it from her as Becca cried, "No! Don't!" He retreated at a jog down the dock.

Ivar called after him, "There's things you can't keep private, Eddie. No matter how you want to."

"We'll see about that," was Eddie's reply.

"SHE TOLD HIM," was all that Ivar would say. "Had to have called him. He wouldn't've known otherwise." He sounded grim. They were tearing north on the island's main highway. Becca seemed to know what Ivar meant, but Jenn was completely in the dark.

All of their equipment was in the back of Ivar's truck, and Ivar sat hunched over the steering wheel. His gaze was glued to the road, and Becca's gaze was glued onto him. She was wincing, as if something was hurting her eyes. It was all too wacky for Jenn to understand. *Something* was going on. She just didn't know what.

Since they were roaring north, she figured they were on their way to Ivar's farm. That meant that the *she* Ivar was talking about had to be Sharla Mann. *That* seemed to mean that whatever was in the box that Eddie had taken from them was something that Sharla knew about because if *she* was Sharla and if *she* had told Eddie Beddoe they were heading out to his boat, there had to be only one reason why, and the box was that reason.

At Heart's Desire, Ivar pulled to a stop right in front of the steps leading onto the porch. They went in through the kitchen and Ivar told the girls to wait in the living room. For some reason, Becca asked Ivar if he was sure. His response was a grim, "I've never been so sure of anything, Becks," and he strode to the mudroom door.

"It's time for some talking," Jenn heard him say to Sharla. "Eddie and his rifle made our acquaintance about twenty minutes ago in the Langley marina."

"*Eddie?* Oh my God!" Sharla cried.

"Yeah. That's about it. 'Oh my God.' I got two terrified schoolgirls in the living room, Shar. Now me alone, I don't give two damns about Eddie Beddoe. He c'n break my other arm and both my legs and—"

"It was Eddie? *Eddie* did it? You always said the seal."

"Oh hell yes it was Eddie who did it and me the fool trying to protect you from knowing the worst about the man when alls along I expect you've known the worst real good. Now I don't care what that fool man does or what he doesn't do, but he pulls a rifle and points it at a couple of girls and you and me have some talking to do because we both know there's only one way Eddie knew where we'd be today and I'm looking at her."

"I only thought—"

"Sharla, I do not want to know what you only thought. It's time to talk and I'll be in the living room waiting."

Then he left her, and Jenn heard him striding across the kitchen. He came into the living room with a face that looked like stone. After a few very tense minutes of silence, Sharla joined them. She was wearing her work smock with color stains on it, and her gaze shot around the room like a finch's when the bird's seeking food. It settled first on Jenn and then on Becca. She said, "I'm sorry," and wiped her hands down the front of her smock. "He's not a bad man. It's just that he's not right in the head. He used to be. But then . . . he wasn't."

Jenn saw Becca's eyes get narrow and her look get sharp, as if she was making more from this than what was said. Becca glanced quickly at Ivar and then back at Sharla, and she seemed to be reading the air between them. Everyone was shooting looks at everyone else. Jenn wondered what the heck this was all about. She wondered about Sharla and she wondered about Eddie. But she also remembered that what connected them was their life in that trailer on the edge of the water at Possession Point.

Then she suddenly knew. She said, "Holy crap. It was that oil spill, huh? 'Cause you and Eddie were locked up in that trailer after the oil spill and Eddie hadn't worn a hazmat suit and there were fumes and oil all over the place and after that, he was totally different."

"That damn oil slick," Ivar said. "It changed everything for everyone in Possession Point."

Sharla took a deep breath. "Not everyone," she said. "Just me and Eddie. We were the ones got changed." She lowered herself to the very edge of the sofa, like a woman ready to spring to her feet and run for the hills. Only there were no hills. There was only the bluff and, beyond the bluff, the drop to Useless Bay.

"It's time," Ivar said to her. "I don't know what it is but

whatever it is, it keeps us apart, you and me. It's time, Sharla."

"I found the overalls," Becca told her. "They were in that trunk in the chicken coop."

"Oh God," Sharla said. "They were the only things . . . He said everything and he checked it all to make sure, but he didn't notice. They were all I had left."

"Of what?" Jenn asked, just above a whisper, although she wasn't sure she wanted to hear the answer. "All you had left of what?"

"There was oil on the beach," Sharla said.

"But there was more than oil," Becca murmured.

Sharla lowered her head. Her voice sounded as if she was forcing the words out. "There was a child. Little. Barely a toddler. She was sitting there on the beach in the cold. She was naked. Eddie found her, just sitting. With no one around and her naked and shivering in the night. Not making a sound. It was like she was . . . like she was waiting for him to find her. He brought her to the trailer that way. With no one to take care of her. Just me and Eddie."

No one said a word. Jenn looked at Ivar, whose face was grave. She looked at Becca and saw her eyes were closed and her hands were clenched into fists on her knees. Jenn waited for more although she was beginning to feel she knew where the story was heading: to days that were spent inside that trailer without coming out, but now with a reason for staying out of sight.

Sharla said, "I saw that baby and I knew she was our chance. I said *how* could a baby be all alone and naked on a beach and not a scratch on her, not a mark, with oil coming up onto the sand from the water and getting on everything and yet here was this baby with *nothing* on her, not a single thing. I said to Eddie that she had to be sent to us by God and Eddie didn't disagree."

Ivar surged to his feet. Sharla shrank back. For a second it seemed as if he would charge across the room at her, but instead he walked to the window and looked outside at Useless Bay. His fist hit the pane gently but he didn't speak. Becca looked at him, her mouth forming an O that seemed surprised.

"I thought we'd hear something," Sharla said to Ivar's back. "I thought we'd read something. About a boat that had been wrecked somewhere, about someone drowned, about anything that we could connect to that baby, but there was never a thing. I said to Eddie, 'Can't we keep her till there's a story in the paper about a missing baby?' And he didn't say no and we waited and waited. For a month. Six weeks. I don't remember. But there was nothing. So I said to Eddie, 'Who would abandon a baby on the beach in the middle of the night? Whoever did a thing like that doesn't want the baby and will only abuse her if they get her back.' See, I wanted her and I knew I could take care of her and I told Eddie that."

"Lord my God," was a murmur from Ivar. He pressed his forehead to the window.

"Eddie went along at first because I was . . . See, I was so crazy for that child. No one was ever going to give us a baby to live with us in that trailer, see. But here God had given us one. Only Eddie decided it wasn't good for her, wasn't a good place to have a small child, so he took her away. I waited then for the sheriff to come and ask me why I hadn't reported her earlier, but he never came. And then I waited for a story in the paper about that baby being handed over to the authorities or found somewhere else that Eddie might've put her, but there wasn't a story. And then . . . then . . . I didn't ask him where he'd taken her. I was too afraid to know what he had done."

Jenn felt every drop of blood drain from her face as she put the pieces together. The baby and that box on Eddie Beddoe's boat. That box that weighed so very little that *whatever* it contained, it wasn't a fanciful treasure of gold and jewels. It was something terrible and something frightening, and Eddie Beddoe had been desperate to get to it and was equally desperate to get rid of it now.

"Oh, Sharla girl," Jenn heard Ivar say.

Sharla began to weep. "I'm so sorry," she said.

FORTY-TWO

In the truck again, Becca had rummaged through her belongings. She'd found the AUD box. It wasn't so much that she wanted to avoid the possibility of hearing any more whispers, though. It was rather that she'd been bombarded with whispers since the moment Eddie Beddoe had confronted them at Langley's marina. Then, at Heart's Desire, so much had been coming at her from both Ivar and Sharla—not to mention from Jenn—that she had reached the point where her head was aching. What was worse was that the barrage of whispers was making it difficult for her to think. The past and present of the whispers were overlapping each other, too. She had to do something to wall them out.

She had the earphone in her ear when Jenn whispered tersely, "What the crap? I can't *believe* you're listening to music!"

This required, at long last, a quick explanation about the AUD box's function in relieving Becca's "auditory processing problem." Jenn accepted this with the words, "I always wondered why you never got busted for wearing that damn thing," and the matter was settled. At that point, Ivar said, "I'm taking you girls home.

There's things needing to be done right now and neither of you needs to be a part of them."

Jenn said, "Uh . . . Isn't calling the sheriff what needs to be done? We got a pretty good idea why Eddie wanted that box, don't we? You ask me, the sheriff's gonna want to know what's in it and Eddie's gonna want to make sure he never finds it."

Ivar glanced at her and then at Becca. He said, "Maybe so, but I want to give that man a chance to do the right thing, just once in his miserable excuse of a life."

"Which is what?"

"Turning that box over to the sheriff on his own and telling the damn truth."

"Isn't that gonna land him in jail?" Jenn asked. "I mean, he took a baby, according to Sharla. Then he got rid of the baby. How's he gonna want to talk about that?"

"He's not. Which is why I need to take you girls home, so's I can convince him."

Becca said, "No way. You go to see him alone and there's no one there to keep him from doing something crazy, Ivar. All three of us go, and what's he going to do? Shoot everyone at once? Shoot anyone at all and have two witnesses to it? Anyway, he didn't have bullets in the rifle."

Ivar shot her a look and so did Jenn. Jenn was the one to say, "And you know this how?"

"I just know," she said, for what else could she tell them that would not betray how she'd heard Eddie's thoughts?

"Oh, that makes me feel a hell of a lot better," Jenn remarked.

"Really," Becca said, and to Ivar, "we'll be okay. Where d'you think he is? He's gonna want to get rid of that box. Where's the best place?"

Ivar thought about this. He finally said, "Glendale. There's woods above it. Eddie's got a place there. Take that box into the woods behind his cabin and it's gone till he decides it's not."

He proceeded to drive them to Glendale at a good clip, choosing the route that offered the most speed, which was coursing down the highway and then along the fields and woods on either side of Cultus Bay Road. Then they were in woods that were thicker than ever, winding above a deep cut in the land through which the Glendale Creek flowed out to Possession Sound.

They came out into a tiny community comprising an ancient long-abandoned hotel, the skeletal remains of a pier jutting into the water, and a scattering of wind- and rain-blown houses. This was no idyllic vacation spot but a hard-bitten kind of place that was off the beaten path and mostly forgotten.

Ivar took a dirt road of the sort that anyone could easily overlook. It carved a narrow, dark passage back into the forest, marked only by a blue reflector and three tumbledown mailboxes leaning precariously on two-by-fours planted into the ground.

They passed a single-wide trailer overgrown with every possible kind of forest creeper. They passed a cabin fronted by an ancient VW van on blocks. Finally they came to Eddie Beddoe's property, identified only by a chain that passed across its ingress along with a pockmarked NO TRESPASSING sign hanging from the chain.

The chain had no lock. Jenn hopped from the truck and dealt with its removal from the route. Ivar drove forward, and she jumped back aboard. He drove some three hundred yards into the distance, to the point at which a red metal roof just became visible through a break in the trees.

Ivar parked at the point where the rooftop was visible. He told the girls to stay well behind him. Becca decided this was the moment to remove the AUD box's earphone from her ear in order to take the best reading she could off the area. But there was nothing but Ivar's broken whispers about the baby Sharla had spoken of, along with his thought of caution and of his concern for them. Mixed in with these whispers were Jenn's, which signaled her determination to be cool.

Eddie wasn't far. His truck was parked next to a small cabin that they came to. One glance inside and Ivar brought out the man's rifle, which had been on the floor. He checked it for bullets and then glanced sharply at Becca. *How'd the girl know* was written on his face, as easily recognizable as the whisper that accompanied it. She nodded at him. Eddie had either spent all his ammunition firing uselessly into the water with the hope that he might somehow hit Nera, or he'd shown up at the marina with the intention of frightening them but that was all. In either case, they were safe unless he had another weapon on him.

"Listen," Jenn said in a low voice.

For a moment, though, it was only the call of Steller's jays that they heard, as well as the high-pitched cry of an eagle. Then, though, the sound of metal hitting metal echoed. It was coming from behind the paint-flecked cabin.

Ivar turned to the girls. He said, "Don't you make me sorry I brought you. You stay behind me. This man's not dangerous by nature, but his mind's gone bad and you've seen that already. Got it?"

They nodded. Becca said, "We don't want you to get hurt either."

"I don't intend to get hurt," Ivar replied.

Together, then, they headed around the side of the cabin, toward the back. They found Eddie Beddoe using the nonbusiness end of an ax against the lock that held the metal box tightly closed. He was in a clearing but all around him was forest, thick with both trees and an undergrowth of ferns, salal, huckleberry, a snarling mass of vines and creepers. Becca saw this and knew Ivar had been right. If Eddie's intention was to hide the contents of that box in the woods, there would be no way of finding it.

What remained was the question of why he was opening the box at all instead of just dashing into the forest with a shovel to bury it. Becca looked around for the answer to this question, and she saw it in fairly short order. In an oblong pit of stone, Eddie had constructed what was going to be a roaring blaze the moment he set a match to it. The smell of lighter fluid was thick in the air, just in case there remained any doubt in this matter.

Becca felt Jenn's hand clutch her arm. "He's gonna burn that baby!" she whispered fiercely. "He's gone burn her bones!"

"He's sure as hell gonna burn something," was Ivar's take on the situation. He stepped forward with Eddie's rifle dangling from his fingers and he said, "You're gonna need a fire hotter'n hell, Eddie. What'd you do to that baby? How'd that baby die?"

When Eddie swung around, *what the hell . . . that bitch told . . . should've hidden it . . . got rid of . . . but it wasn't enough* swung around with him. Becca heard the whispers as if they were objects slapping the air. But his words were, "What the hell're you talking about, Thorndyke?"

"You drown that baby? You hit that baby on the head? You give that baby something to make it sleep and then you weigh down that thing there and toss it overboard?"

Ivar's words were harsh, but his whispers were not. They were *should have known . . . should have seen . . . no point to an act of loving when it ends like this,* which Becca did not entirely understand. Yet she felt desperate to know the entirety of what was happening between the two men, and she wondered if there was any possibility. . . . She'd needed Diana before, Diana had been the conduit of the visions, but perhaps . . . if she—Becca— touched this man as Diana had touched him . . . in this most desperate of situations . . .

"This ain't no baby," Eddie snapped. "That what you think, Thorndyke? That what she told you?"

"Maybe you dropped that baby on its head," Ivar said. "An accident, like, and you never could say. So you stuffed that child into a box and then you threw that box overboard."

"I tol' you this ain't no baby, you fool. You think otherwise, you call the cops and have 'em bring their handcuffs along."

"I'm giving you the chance to do what's right. You speak the truth about that child so I c'n give Sharla some peace of mind."

"Sharla, Sharla," Eddie scoffed. He said her name like a nasty word. "You wanted her from the first, didn't you? Well, now you got her and you're welcome to her and I got *this* and if anyone's making anything right, this is gonna do it. Right here and right now."

"You intend to answer me straight?" Ivar asked him. "You keep that baby hidden somewheres till you could kill it? That what happened when you took the child away? You cram its poor broke body into that box and—"

Eddie laughed so wildly that for a moment Becca thought he was drunk. Except his whispers weren't drunk and neither were Ivar's. Along with Jenn's whispers, the air was swarming.

What he thinks . . . damn fool . . . should've gone home 'cause something bad's gonna . . . somebody needs to call . . . let it happen and it doesn't matter . . . Sharla, Sharla . . . wish I'd left it where I found it . . . the seal comes because . . . there she was naked and beautiful and . . . It all confused her. She could get no clarity on anything that was going on. She felt so strongly that she needed to touch Eddie Beddoe as Diana had touched him because that seemed the only route to clarity.

She took a hesitant step forward. Ivar grabbed her arm. He said, "I told you to stay—"

"You gotta let me. Please."

Losing no . . . can't live with . . . nuts, that what were the reactions of both Ivar and Jenn to this idea. But she gently removed

Ivar's hand from her arm and took another step in Eddie's direction.

Eddie said, "You best call the sheriff now. Use the phone inside. He's gonna be real happy to come all the way out here and see what I'm getting ready to burn. Go on. Go on. Use the damn phone 'cause I c'n see you ain't gonna believe me over a woman who's been a nutter since the day she's born."

He lifted the ax again. He used its blade this time, against the box and against the lock. The lock fell off and Eddie opened the box. "Come 'ere," he told them. "You all's so hot to see what I got. You want your salvage or whatever you think. Here it is."

He upended the box. What tumbled out of it was the furry skin of a very small seal: a head-to-toe skin that looked almost like a costume, so perfect was it and so perfectly had it been preserved.

"What the heck . . . ?" Jenn was the one who spoke.

Ivar said nothing but his face was a ghost's.

"This is what was on the beach that night, you fools," Eddie said. "This is the baby Sharla's been going on about. You got that, all of you? This is the damn baby, which she stuffed like the maniac she is and which she carried round like an idiot till I took it off her."

"What're you saying?" Jenn demanded. "Are you saying Sharla skinned some seal like . . . like a seal clubbed in Newfoundland or something?"

"Course not because there *was* no damn seal. There was no damn nothing. There was only this and it was covered in oil and damn fool I was, I thought I could clean it and maybe sell it for something but what does Sharla do? She carries it around like it was some pet, like it was some *kid*, for God's sake, like a baby in a blanket till I finally get it away from her and toss it from the boat."

But there was so much more, and Becca heard it all. *Sharla she said . . . weirder and weirder . . . someone's out there and we're gonna find . . . shot her when I could have . . . Dad told me and I remember . . . my woman and not yours never yours . . . I did this to her . . . to them both and now . . .* All of it battled in the air around her, telling Becca the truth was close, but they hadn't reached it and no one believed what anyone else was saying at that point. But all of them had moved close to Eddie. She could risk touching him if he became calmer.

She said, "C'n I see it? Why d'you want to burn it?"

"'Cause it's been the curse of my whole damn life." Danger emanated from the man, but Becca took a step closer and put herself next to him as Ivar and Jenn looked at the sealskin on the ground.

She put her hand on Eddie's arm. She felt his muscles, as tense as telephone wires. She felt from him the desperate madness that guilt causes a person to feel, and this seeped from him even as she saw in a blink only the sight of a small child on the beach and in that child's hands, this very sealskin which the child rubbed and rubbed as if it were the only comfort available.

She said, "No. That baby was there. Sharla didn't lie."

Eddie pulled away from her furiously. "You're as whacked out as she is."

"That night on the beach. The oil slick night. There was a baby on the beach."

"Oh you don't know—"

Jenn made a sound, half the mewling of a kitten, half a gasp of fright. "The timeline," she said as they looked at her. "The timeline is wrong."

"What timeline?" Ivar asked her.

"My dad said . . . It's the boat, Becca. It's the boat on the bottom."

"Like *you're* making sense, girl," Eddie sneered.

"Where'd you get that boat?" Jenn demanded. "How'd you get that boat? My dad said you just . . . just had it one day for a fishing business. But he never said how you got it 'cause he didn't know. But boats cost thousands and you never had a boat before that oil slick. You never had the money for a boat or else why would you have lived in that trailer and where'd that boat come from? Where'd you get that boat?"

"Nera," Becca said. For it all fit together, of a piece, and nicely. "Nera knows, doesn't she? And that's why Nera has to die."

"That damn seal," was Eddie's answer. He threw the ax aside. He kicked the metal box away. The sealskin was something he did not touch.

FORTY-THREE

"That's what she's wanted all this time. She's wanted that skin. That's why she was at the boat. And that's why she comes back to Whidbey Island every year."

Jenn heard this and cocked her head at Becca. They were in Ivar's truck, heading away from Glendale, with Eddie Beddoe following them. Ivar had given him no choice in the matter. It was come with them or talk to the sheriff about how he ended up with a boat without the means to pay for it.

To this idea, Eddie had scoffed, "You think the sheriff cares how I got a boat that's been underwater for near twenty years?"

Ivar had replied, "I think he'll be in'erested once he talks to Sharla. And the only way you're going to avoid that happening is by seeing things to the finish."

"What finish you got in mind?"

"The one you've been scared of for years." Ivar had looked long and hard at Eddie Beddoe when he said this, as if he was communicating in a secret language. Jenn had glanced at Becca to see if she had the same idea. Becca's gaze kept jumping from one man to the other.

The finish Ivar was talking about turned out to be in Possession Point. When they got there, it was late afternoon. The shadows from the forest above the point were deep, the trees throwing long caverns of darkness upon the road. A slight breeze was stirring the new spring leaves on the alders and the cottonwoods, presaging a stiffer wind as the night came on.

Jenn had been trying all along to keep up with what was going on. Becca seemed to be making huge leaps of understanding everywhere, this whole business of Nera wanting that sealskin being one of them. Why a seal might want another seal's skin didn't make sense to her. She kept tossing this around in her head. Finally, Becca turned to her.

She said, as if reading Jenn's confusion, "It's about that oil slick. When was it, Jenn? What time of year? I bet *anything* it was the exact same time of year that Nera always shows up."

Ivar glanced at Becca. He looked from her to Jenn. His expression said that Becca was right.

"She must have seen everything from the water that night," Becca murmured. "She must have been watching."

"But Eddie said he didn't get rid of that skin right away. So what'd she do? Wait to see him lock that skin in a box? Why? It doesn't even make sense. And I don't get why you think there was really a baby, too."

"I think we're close to finding out everything," Becca told her.

Ivar looked at her and frowned. He seemed worried about how things were going to play out.

He had good reason, as it happened. When they rumbled down the lane that led to her family's house, Jenn saw a couple of things at once. Her mom's island taxi was gone; the family heap was also gone, indicating her dad had taken the boys somewhere; and Chad Pederson's truck was parked alongside Annie Taylor's Honda. Once Ivar pulled past these two vehicles, all of them saw at once that Chad and Annie were up on the dock where the boats tied up in order to buy bait.

Bait was what Annie and Chad had with them, two big buckets of it. They were tossing live herring into the water. And in that water, the sleek black head of Nera moved. Back and forth she swam, as if trying to decide whether she could trust them enough to get to the food. When either Chad or Annie managed to toss a herring close enough to her, she snapped it up. But she seemed wary of them, as well she needed to be. For on the shore at the end of the dock and just a few feet from the water lay a large fishing net. Next to this was a chair that Annie had brought from the trailer. On this was her laptop along with an array of supplies that Jenn couldn't make out. But she figured that they probably were what she needed to get her samples from the seal. Containers, tubes, and slides for blood, tissue, and whatever else, as long as the seal lived through the terror of being netted and dragged to shore.

Ivar jerked his truck to a stop and was out of it in an instant, yelling, even before Eddie Beddoe pulled in behind them. "You hold it right there!" he shouted. Out in the water, Nera backed off.

Annie swung around, crying, "Ivar, stay where you are. We're not going to hurt her. You're scaring her!"

Ivar charged toward the dock. He shouted, "You don't know

what the hell you're doing. That seal's dangerous. She's *always* been dangerous. She's capable of anything. She's attacked before and she'll attack again."

"He knows, he knows," Becca murmured. "He's known from the first. He's *always* known."

Jenn said, "Huh?" and turned to her. She saw her fingering the earphone of her hearing device, but she didn't use it.

"Ivar," Becca said to her. "He's always known about the seal."

"Well, duh. He's been going on about her ever since I was born. So has everyone else."

"But not with his reason."

Jenn saw that her friend was totally focused on Ivar and she turned to see what was going on. Ivar was on the dock, shouting and waving his arms. Nera had backed off some distance. Annie was crying, "Make him stop, for God's sake. We almost had her."

This turned out to be Chad's cue, apparently. He charged toward Ivar as Ivar shouted, "Get back! Go on! Scat!" at the seal.

In response, Nera began to bark. The sound was loud, and it echoed as it hit the bluff. As if in answer, gulls started to caw. And then suddenly Eddie Beddoe was among them as Chad reached Ivar and blocked his route to Annie.

"You keep that damn animal away from me!" Eddie yelled. "I'll do what needs to be done, Thorndyke, but you damn well better keep her away."

"What's he gonna—" But Jenn stopped her own words when she saw what he had in his hands. It was the metal box from his boat. Its top was open. She could see the sealskin lying within it.

But unlike the others, he didn't approach the dock. Instead he walked to a large driftwood log, one of hundreds that lined the shore. It lay to the far side of the beach at a distance from everyone. As he made his way toward it, Nera began to follow him in the water.

"Stop him! Chad, stop him!" Annie cried.

"Don't you touch that seal!" Ivar yelled at Eddie Beddoe.

"I look like I want to come anywheres near that thing?" Eddie shouted back.

"Chad! Please!"

And Nera barked wildly.

Chad jumped from the dock and went after Eddie. Jenn and Becca looked at each other, nodded as one, and went after Chad. Ivar came off the dock, crying, "You damn well know what she wants, Eddie. Give her that skin and do it now."

As Chad stormed the beach, Annie thundered down the dock. She was shouting, "Take the net, the net!" and Chad turned to grab it.

This gave everyone the chance they needed. Ivar grabbed Annie as she tried to get past him. Becca and Jenn tackled Chad. Eddie made his way to the driftwood log. He lay the small skin across the top of it.

Out in the water, Nera watched him do it. She swam back and forth and barked and barked. She looked from the seal skin to Eddie to the people on the beach. And she continued to bark.

"Let me go!" Annie screamed. "It'll just take a moment. I won't hurt her. I swear it."

"You never known a thing 'bout what you're doing," Ivar growled. "I been trying to tell you, but you got only one thing on your mind."

"Baby." It was a murmur from Becca, which Jenn heard. Between herself and the other girl, Chad had ceased to struggle, but they held him firmly nonetheless. Becca's face, though, said she was in another place altogether. She murmured again. "There was baby only it was a seal it was always a seal and I don't know how. Because he's saying the seal the seal baby out of the seal and what does that mean?"

"*Who's* saying?" Jenn demanded.

Annie had begun fighting Ivar, shrieking, "This is my career! Let me go! I have the right to—"

"You got the right to nothing," Ivar told her. He held her fast. He began to move her away from the water. He shouted to Jenn and Becca, "We got to get them both to the trailer. You hear me, Becks? We got to get inside and close the curtains and we got to stay there."

"No!" Annie's scream was shrill.

It was so high pitched that it startled Jenn. She lost her grip on Chad. He stormed toward Ivar. Eddie began to run toward Ivar as well. Out in the water the seal barked and barked. Becca murmured, "Eddie. He knows it all, too."

To Jenn, the world was going mad.

And the trailer door opened.

Cilla came out.

Cilla's World

I have lived for this moment. I did not know this, for until this moment the world has been a frightening place.

Even now I am sure of nothing, for people are shouting, the water from the passage is slapping at the pebbles upon the shore, and out in the water a seal is barking. This, finally, is what I recognize. It is, finally, something I am sure of. But I don't know why.

I am asleep when the chaos begins outside of the trailer. My strength is all but gone because of my illness, but I know, listening from inside the trailer, that I am intended to see what is happening beyond its insubstantial walls. From seeing, I know that I am meant to understand. And now I realize that, from the instant I found myself alone with the mommy and the daddy gone, every moment has led to this.

I am Cilla. I am eighteen years old. I am a girl who cannot talk but who can hear. I will do what I am told if people are good to me. This is how it has always been.

Beyond the walls of the trailer, I see the woman who has cared for me. I see the girl who found me. Not far away, I see a man backing off from a driftwood log as big as an orca, and he possesses a face that I never thought to see again in my life. It's a face that was buried within my memories, but seeing it now, I begin to recall. I remember his arms as they lifted me. I remember seeing, over his shoulder, the night and the water deep and black.

And there he is, backing away from the orca driftwood. On that wood he has placed something. It is lumpy and misshapen but it draws me, and so I step out of the trailer and into the evening air.

The people before me fall back. The woman who has cared for me cries out something, but I hear her only dimly now. An old man with her cries out as well. I look toward them both and then away.

I walk past them all. I approach the driftwood and what lies upon it.

FORTY-FOUR

The black seal in the water swam cautiously in Cilla's direction. On the beach, no one said a word, although their whispers crashed into the air so loudly that Becca could not distinguish among them. Instead she watched as Cilla reached the driftwood log where Eddie Beddoe had placed the small sealskin. She climbed upon the huge log and lifted the sealskin to her face. A few yards from shore, Nera swam back and forth.

"She wants to come onto the sand," Becca said.

"She damn well *can't*," Ivar replied fiercely. In the surprise of Cilla's emergence from the trailer, he'd loosened his hold on Annie Taylor. She ran to the dock for the bucket of bait, as if intending once more to lure the black seal to the shore. She flung a few herring toward her, but Nera ignored them. She ignored Chad, too, released from Jenn and Becca's grip. He was looking from the seal to the girl on the driftwood, even as Nera swam back and forth and watched the girl.

Cilla buried her face in the sealskin. The skin was as black as the coming night but not, Becca saw, with the long-ago oil that had spilled into Possession Sound. It was black like Nera, and it told the true tale of Nera's yearly return to Whidbey Island.

"It was hers," Becca murmured. "That's why she kept coming back. It was hers."

"The skin? Nera's?" Jenn asked. "But me and Squat found out . . . That seal doesn't shed her skin, Becca."

"Not hers. Not Nera's. The skin was the baby's."

"What the hell . . . ?"

Becca looked at Ivar and concentrated hard. What she caught among everything else was an answer to all the questions she'd had and had asked about Nera. It came as *not here not now keep out keep away because they'll see and when they know . . .* and she understood from this that she had been right. All along Ivar Thorndyke had known everything there was to know about the coal black seal.

Cilla rose. The black sealskin in her hand, she walked to the edge of the water. Nera swam closer. She was in the shallows, at the point where she could no longer submerge.

Annie began to ease down the beach toward her. *This is it . . . this is it.* She continued to throw the bait. She said, "Chad? Chad! Will you help?" but Chad didn't move his eyes off the seal.

Cilla walked toward the animal. The seal came toward her.

"No," Ivar said as the seal came closer. *If it happens here and now there'll be no protecting . . .* "No. No!" He took off for Annie while, in the water, the seal looked at Cilla, then at Chad nearby. And then at Annie, who was lightly tossing the herring her way, who had stooped and picked up the fishing net, who had grabbed up a scalpel that glittered in the fading light of the day.

"No!" Ivar said. . . . *no ending like this . . .*

Chad moved at last, blocking Ivar, holding him back. In the

water, the seal came closer, Possession Sound barely inches deep on her now.

Cilla walked toward the animal.

"Stop her," Ivar cried.

"Chad," Annie said, "hold him where he is." She set the bait bucket down. She took up the net in both of her hands. She approached the seal as the seal watched Cilla moving toward her.

"For God's sake, stop her," Ivar said. "Becca, Jenn, don't let her get near!"

"Let's go," Jenn murmured, and she took off for Annie as Becca did the same. But at that moment, Eddie Beddoe strode past them across the sand, from behind the trailer where he'd retreated. He had his rifle.

"You done enough meddling," he said to Annie. With his free hand, he grabbed the net, wrested it from her, and threw it to one side. She cried out. He shouldered the rifle and snarled, "You go near that animal, you deal with me. And it won't be nice for either of us."

"Praise God," Ivar said.

"God ain't got nothing to do with this, Ivar," Eddie said. "An' you know that 's well as me. Now back off, the lot of you. Get away. Scat. You first, Miss Scientific Genius. And Mr. America over there? Get your hands off Thorndyke. Anyone going to punch him out, it's gonna be me. Now you all back *away.*"

They had no choice. Four of them knew the rifle wasn't loaded. But Annie and Chad were not among the four. They moved a distance away from the water and they watched as Nera finally made her way onto the sand. It was twilight, and they saw what happened next as if in the middle of a dream.

The coal black seal walked out of her skin. It was as simple as that. She emerged as a woman, paler than pale, unclothed to her toes. She had long black hair that fell to her knees, and she carried the sealskin in her hand, as if it were a cape and not what it was, which was the sign of her identity.

"Oh. My. God," Jenn murmured. "What the hell is it? Where the hell are we?"

"A selkie," Ivar Thorndyke said. "And you're where you always were, on Whidbey Island."

"A *what*? She's a *what*?"

"A selkie," he said. "Human and seal at once. Land and sea at once, because of her skin."

"You always knew it," Becca said to him. "And Eddie always knew it, too."

CILLA AND NERA approached each other. Cilla gave the woman the baby sealskin she held. Nera looked at the skin and then at the girl, and she draped the skin around Cilla's shoulders. Nera touched Cilla's face. Cilla touched hers.

Jenn whispered, "Cilla was the baby! The one Eddie found on the beach that night. That's *her* skin, isn't it? *She's* what Nera's always come back for."

Becca heard this but looked at Ivar. *Too late sweet woman . . .* The words were so clear, and she caught a flash of vision as she heard them, although she didn't know if the vision came from Ivar or merely from her own imagination. In it, a woman emerged from the water at night, a beautiful woman with long black hair, a woman seen by Ivar from shore.

"It's too late," Ivar said aloud.

"For what?" Jenn asked.

"For what they both want."

Becca looked at Nera and Cilla in each other's arms and understood at last. "She's always just wanted to take care of her little girl," Becca murmured. It was, after all, what most mothers wanted.

As they watched, Nera handed Cilla the sealskin she had stepped out of when she'd left the water. For her part, Cilla stepped into the skin as easily as if it had been her own. For a moment on the beach, she was Cilla, the girl who could not speak. Then she became the image of her mother at the edge of the water, and as a seal she re-entered it. Then she was gone.

The dark-hired woman watched her go, the baby sealskin clasped to her bosom. Then she herself walked into the water. She dove quickly and deeply to where the water was coldest, where unprotected from its fierce and frigid touch, she would quickly die.

WHEN IT WAS over, those left on the beach were silent. Their thoughts were present and Becca caught them as fragments, but she tried to ignore them because she wanted to have her *own* whispers for once. She wanted to think about what she'd heard both in conversations and in whispers and about what she'd seen there on the beach.

What she understood from what had happened was that Eddie Beddoe had seen the transformation of woman-to-seal all those years ago, the night of the oil slick. It was, after all, the only possibility left. Nera and her pup had been caught in the oil, but the baby would not survive if her juvenile skin was not cleaned of the sludge that would poison her. So her mother had brought her to shore, where they'd both transformed. And Eddie had come upon them, a frantic mother trying to save her child the only way she'd known but without anything that she could use to clean the skin of the sludge upon it. He'd shone a light upon her in the darkness and she had fled instinctively from the danger that this light presented. But she'd left the child and he'd grabbed the child up, knowing in an instant that no one other than a fully grown seal would ever come looking for the baby he'd found. He'd seen an opportunity and he'd taken it. But then what? Becca wondered.

Ivar supplied the answer. He said to Eddie, "Sharla thinks you killed that baby. But you didn't, did you? You sold her or you traded her, didn't you? To get that damn boat."

"Oh what the hell's it matter now?" Eddie asked. "Everyone's got what he wants. 'Cept her, of course."

Her was Annie, who stood stunned next to her equipment. It was useless to her now because the only piece of equipment she hadn't thought to bring from the trailer was the camera that might have proved a story that no one other than the five other people on the beach would ever believe. The woman was gone now, the girl was gone now, and whatever Annie Taylor had wanted from them was gone as well.

"Sharla don't have what she needs from you," Ivar said. "But she's gonna get it, Eddie. Let's go."

"I'm not—"

"What you *are* is someone who's gonna tell his ex-wife the truth. Not the truth about Nera 'cause who the hell'd believe any of us if it comes to that. I'm talking about the truth of that baby. You're gonna set Sharla free by telling her exactly what you did. It's time to end this, man. And you sure as hell know it."

Eddie looked at Ivar long, then he looked at Becca, then at the rest of them. "What the hell," he said. "There's been enough trouble because of that damn oil slick and what it brought to shore."

"You just helped make it right," Ivar said. "I say it's time we all moved on."

He headed toward his truck. Becca followed him. She said to Jenn, "You okay?" before she left.

Jenn nodded. Her gaze was on Annie. "I don't think she is, though."

Becca followed her gaze. She heard *ruined* from someone, but she wasn't sure if it was coming from Annie or from Chad who approached her on the sand. Annie was kneeling by her useless equipment, looking stunned. Chad put his hand on her shoulder and said her name. She shook him off.

"Too late," she said.

"Yeah," he agreed.

For both of them, was what Becca thought. But maybe not for Sharla and Ivar. Perhaps some good could come out of this.

FORTY-FIVE

When Jenn blew the All Island Girls' Soccer team tryouts two days later, she knew she had only herself to blame. The coach told her, "Next year. Work harder on your school's team, on the local rec team, and you'll have a good chance. You've got the speed we need but not the dexterity in passing. That's your target. I want to see you here next year. Hey, don't look so glum. You're what . . . fifteen? All is not lost."

But it sure felt lost. Everything. Kaput. Straight down the drain. She sat on the porch steps at her parents' house and prepared to tell them she'd flushed the toilet on herself. She stared across the property at Annie's trailer, and she willed it to explode into bits and to take Annie Taylor with it.

Annie emerged. On the previous day, she'd starting packing her belongings for the trip back to Florida. She'd been sorting through things and throwing out things and hauling things out to the silver Honda. She looked about finished, and that was the case. She came across to Jenn and said, "So. I'm out of here today."

Jenn looked at her. She was definitely still Annie: trendy from her spiky red hair, to her cropped yellow pants, to her manicured toenails painted dusky orange. But she wasn't the same Annie that Jenn had so admired. A lot of water passing under the bridge had washed that Annie Taylor away.

"You look like I feel," Annie said. "Sometimes things don't work out, I guess."

"Yeah. Whatever," Jenn said. "Where're you going?"

"Home. To Beth."

"What about Chad?"

Annie shook her head in the way that said, "You still don't get it, do you, child?" The expression on her face made Jenn want to sock her, but she restrained herself and waited for Annie's reply. Annie said, "Jenn . . . Look, it was just for fun."

"I thought you were . . . you know."

"Lesbian? I am. More or less. Most of the time." Annie ran her hand back through her hair. It stayed just as it was, spiky and stylish. "Other times? It doesn't matter, don't you see? He's just a kid." She cocked her head. "You can have him, you know. If you want him. He's pretty easy that way. *If* you want him. Do you? Because I've had a feeling about you from the day I met you."

Jenn rose abruptly. "So long," she said, heading for the door. "I'll tell my parents you said good-bye."

"Sure. But, Jenn . . ."

Jenn turned back. Annie was squinting in the sun. Squinting, she didn't look quite the same. She looked shifty, somehow, she looked crafty, unwise.

Annie said, "If you ever want to call me . . . to talk about things you might not be ready to talk about now . . . ?"

"Right," Jenn told her. As if, she thought. She went into the house and didn't emerge until after Annie Taylor had driven away.

HER PARENTS DEALT with the soccer information just fine, as things happened. Her mom talked about God's will. Her dad talked about next year. But it sounded to Jenn as if their real feelings had to do with the relief of not having to worry about coming up with the money to pay for her soccer equipment and the extra coaching that went along with membership on the All Island team. She wanted to tell them that that had been the whole point of getting entangled with Annie Taylor in the first place. She knew her parents would never have the money she needed for that team, so working for Annie was supposed to be her way of collecting the funds required. But nothing had turned out the way it was supposed to turn out.

Becca didn't see things that way. She said, "Hey, you got me. A BFF."

"Yeah," Jenn said without enthusiasm. "Who woulda thunk it?" *Me and the FatBroad*, she added silently.

Becca's eyes narrowed. "I lost a bunch of weight," she said. And just when Jenn was about to accuse her of reading her mind or something, Becca added, "That's what I got out of it. A girl-friend plus losing weight. Pretty cool."

"Whatever," Jenn said. "What're you doing anyway?"

Becca was leaving the new commons in the middle of lunch,

having powered down a hard-boiled egg and a plastic bag of carrot sticks in record time. Becca told her she was heading to the library. To why, she said it was about the selkie, although she didn't use the word *selkie*. She just said in a low voice "that seal." She told Jenn to come with her if she wanted to. She added, "BFF, you know. We hate to be separated from each other."

Jenn rolled her eyes, but she followed Becca. She watched as her friend logged on to the Internet. She Googled *selkie* as Jenn drew up a chair. Jenn said, "What's the point? It's not like anyone would believe a word of it if we said what we saw."

"I know," Becca said. "But there's something . . . . I dunno, but don't you get the feeling there's part of the story missing somehow?"

"Like what? Like the part where we find out she's really some lady who's been swimming around in a seal costume for the last eighteen years? That makes a hell of a lot more sense than . . . than what we saw."

"Where did Cilla come from, Jenn? And how did she know what to do the second that lady handed over the skin?"

"Where the hell d'you think she came from? We already guessed she was a selkie baby."

"Yeah, I know. But . . ." Becca ran her finger along the screen as she read. Then she clicked to another site. Then a third and a fourth. Jenn couldn't keep up with her and didn't try. Instead she leaned with her back against the computer table, her legs stretched out in front of her, her elbows supporting her. She found that she was perfectly at ease with this girl she'd hated from the moment she'd first seen her. How crazy was that? Maybe anything was possible.

"Here it is," Becca said.

"Here what is?"

"How it happens."

"How what happens?"

"How selkies have babies."

"Uh . . . If you need to read about how animals have babies, Becca, you need to have a chat with Rhonda Mathieson. She'll give you the whole enchilada on that one, complete with rice and beans. *Plus* all the condoms you need just in case you want to try things out."

"I'm serious. Listen to the story. It says they come to shore and mate with a man. Not a seal, Jenn. Not another selkie. They mate with a man." She looked at Jenn, her eyebrows raised. "Do you see what that means?"

"It sure as hell can't mean she had a thing for Eddie Beddoe."

"Not Eddie Beddoe. Nope. Not him."

"Then . . . ?" And when Jenn thought back, she saw it all herself. "You mean Ivar? You mean Cilla was his . . . his . . . his what? His daughter? His selkoid offspring?"

Becca logged off the website and said, "I don't see how it could be anyone else."

"Sure explains why he was so determined to keep Nera away. I mean, you said he must've known what she was all along or why else would he care so much about people getting close to her?"

Becca nodded. "It's sad, though, don't you think? He probably never even knew the selkie had a baby and that baby was his."

"Bummer," Jenn said. Then she slapped her forehead. "What the hell's going to happen to Langley's Nera festival? It's next weekend and something serious is going to hit the fan when she doesn't show up."

"Want to check out what happens?" Becca asked her.

"Would not miss it," Jenn said, and it only came to her later that she'd accepted the invitation from Becca without a second thought.

FORTY-SIX

Derric hadn't felt particularly excited about going to the Welcome Back Nera festival in Langley, but he'd promised Josh. So they went. The day was brilliantly sunny, and he ended up moderately cheered by the general nonsense of a Langley celebration. Colorful arts and crafts booths lined First Street and Second Street, helium balloons created big arches over the entrances to the festival and over each walkway that existed between the old clapboard buildings, and a score of people were, as usual, walking around in totally insane undersea costumes.

All of this delighted Josh. His excitement brought a smile to Derric's face. After munching their way through a bag of kettle corn, they ended up inside the old Second Street firehouse, where a glass blower had established a business. There they engaged in blowing their own Neras. Josh's looked like a banana slug. Derric's looked like a snake attempting to digest a giant rat. They were laughing about these outside on the sidewalk when Derric saw Becca across the street.

She was just coming out of the chocolate shop, Sweet Mona's. She was with Jenn McDaniels and an older couple who were holding hands. The guy wore thick glasses, and a ponytail emerged from beneath his baseball cap. The woman with him wore jeans, boots, and a hoodie zipped to her chin despite the fine weather. All of them headed toward South Whidbey Commons where music was being played by a marimba band. They didn't get far when someone shouted Jenn's name, and Squat Cooper joined them. He began talking earnestly to Jenn.

She listened, arms akimbo. Becca spoke, first to Squat, then to Jenn. Squat and Jenn broke off from the others, and the older couple continued on their way to the commons. That left Becca alone and she looked around briefly, as if trying to find companionship.

Her gaze met Derric's. Josh saw her then and yelled, "Lookit! Me and Derric just made these! Which is better? You got to decide."

She walked across the street to them. She stood before them in a patch of sunlight and it fell on her hair and made it glow. She seemed to be glowing as well. Happy, Derric thought. She looks really happy.

"Okay, let me see," she said. She looked them over, sucking her lip thoughtfully. She said, "Well . . . Seems to me that yours looks more realistic, Josh, and Derric's looks more . . . artful, I guess. I mean, I've never really seen a yellow slug in person but—"

"It's Nera!" Josh shouted. "It's s'posed to be Nera!"

Her eyes got wide behind her thick-framed glasses. She said, "Whoops! Sorry! Well, in that case, it's *definitely* you. I got confused by the color, but now I can see what she's supposed to be."

"We didn't want her to be black."

"Yesssss. Good decision. Yellow's prettier, huh? Green is, too." She said this last to Derric, and then to Josh, "Is your grammer here? Is Chloe?"

"They're in Seawall Park. That's where we're going 'cause the Nera ceremony is happening in a couple of minutes. Every year she shows up and we want to see her."

Becca reached out to smooth his roughed-up hair. "Would it make you sad if she didn't come? She might not, you know."

"Oh, she'll come," he said confidently. "Want to come with us and see for yourself?"

Becca glanced at Derric. He felt a bit of a rush. He thought how he'd like to talk to her the way they once had talked. He wanted there to be an opportunity to say what he needed to say to her, to explain somehow, to offer her—

"I'd like to come," she said quickly, looking away from him to speak to Josh. "But you have to try not to feel too bad if she doesn't show up. Seals move on sometimes. Just like people. It happens all the time."

WHEN JOSH RAN on ahead of them, Derric and Becca fell into pace with each other. Derric felt his heart pounding a little harder than usual. He glanced at Becca, but she was looking around, taking note of all the different people who were there.

She said a little nervously, "I didn't think there'd be so many."

He said, "People? They come from all over the island. From over town, too. It's the first chance for people to get wacky after winter."

She smiled, displaying neat white teeth. "'Wacky after winter.' That's what they should call this. Not Welcome Back Nera."

"Yeah. Not bad." And then there didn't seem to be anything else to say. Only, there was, but he didn't know how to say it or where to begin.

Ahead of them, Josh was worming his way through the crowd and he yelled over his shoulder, "Come *on*, you guys," before he was lost to view.

Derric thought Becca would pick up her pace then, but she didn't do so. She continued to look around. Side to side and over her shoulder and beyond the shoulders of the crowd in front of them. It came to him that she was looking for someone. He pretty much figured who it was.

He said, "Down in Seawall Park," as the music began to drift up from that direction. It was gypsy jazz on guitar, accompanied by bass and mandolin. Seth Darrow's trio was entertaining the crowd as they waited for Nera.

Becca turned to Derric. She brushed an errant lock of sun-kissed hair from her face. She said, "I wasn't looking for Seth."

Then who . . . ? he wondered, because it had to be someone and it sure as heck wasn't him. She'd stopped looking for him in November. She'd more or less run from him. He still didn't know why.

She seemed to be gazing right into the heart of him. She said,

"Derric . . . Is that why? Is that what happened with us? I don't understand. I felt safe with you."

He looked away, driving his hands into the pockets of his jeans and hunching his shoulders. "Not safe enough," he said.

"Huh?"

"It's what happened, Becca." For when she'd needed someone, she'd gone to Seth Darrow and not to him. And it was Seth Darrow, not Derric, who held her secrets close to his heart.

Her eyes grew wide, as if she suddenly understood everything in an instant. She said, "Oh no. You've thought *Seth* was more important to me than you, didn't you? Because he helped me last November. Because he knew of a place that I could go when I had to leave the motel. Because I wouldn't tell you, when all along Seth knew and you thought that meant . . ." She put her hand on his arm. He felt the warmth of her as he'd felt it from the very first: that very odd-looking girl who'd come to the island and had spoken to him in a way that no one else ever could.

Around them, the crowd surged toward the water, and they were carried along with it although they were suddenly no longer a part of it. "You trusted him when you didn't trust me."

"I was trying to *protect* you."

He shook his head bleakly. He felt so small. He said, "Do I look like I need protection? I fell down a bluff, Becca. I broke my leg. I hit my head. Does that mean I couldn't take care of you if you needed taken care of?"

"No," she said, as bleakly as he felt. "*No.*"

"Then why wouldn't you—"

A shout went up from the crowd. The final notes of music played, and suddenly they were swept along. They moved past the old, abandoned Dog House Tavern, and descended to Seawall Park below it. Seth and his trio were taking their bows to appreciative applause as the mayor of Langley mounted a purpose-built stage. He was wearing a top hat with a stuffed black seal leaping dolphinlike across its brim.

He didn't have a chance to say a word into the microphone. Someone shouted, "Look!" and the black seal was there. She was not fifty yards from shore where a Zodiac floated and two seal spotters waited as they did every year, with fishy treats for their guest. But this time, Nera didn't stop for a treat. She lifted her black head and observed them but she didn't bark. Instead she circled the Zodiac five times. She lifted her head once more. Then she dove. And was gone.

"I think that was good-bye," Becca murmured.

Derric thought so, too. It struck him with sorrow for some reason. He said, "That's not something I want to do."

"What?" Becca turned from the water, and when her gaze met his, he saw a faint blush wash across her cheeks.

"Say good-bye. To you. I thought I did. I thought, I don't need this . . . this whatever it is between us because I seriously don't know what to call it. But without you, Becca . . ." He ran his hand over his hair and it came to him that he wanted to shave it off, that being the way he'd been before, being *of* Kampala and *from* Kampala was who he wished to be again. Only now he wanted to be the real Derric, not an imitation, but the boy who'd made one promise that he'd failed to keep. He said, "Someone gave the letters to my dad. He found them, some artist who needed the beanbag stuffing. He figured out the rest. I mean, he figured who they belonged to. Dad saw her name."

"Rejoice's?"

"He thinks she's someone in Kampala. I mean, a girlfriend. He doesn't know she's my sister."

Becca nodded, gazed at him deeply. "What're you going to do?"

His lips curved in a very brief smile. "Thank you for asking."

"Huh?"

"Instead of telling. You always used to *tell* me what I was supposed to."

"I'm sorry," she said. "I'm sort of working on that. On not doing it, I mean."

"Me, too. I'm sorry, too. The other stuff . . . Courtney and . . . and whatever . . ." He wondered if he could tell Becca about that, most especially about what he'd learned about himself in those feverish moments with Courtney hidden away in the trees. He'd spoken to her since. He'd said how messed up he'd been, how messed up he'd felt, how sorry sorry *sorry* he was that things had gone the direction they'd gone, which was way too far, but even then—

"It's okay, it's *okay*," Becca said, and she looked as if she wished to cover her ears. When he said nothing more, she seemed to relax. She said, "There's personal stuff, you know? Like you and Rejoice are personal stuff that you've got to take care of someday but it's not my business and I get that now. It's just that sometimes . . . It's hard, you know? Knowing where to fit everything in. It's hard, huh?"

"Part of it is. But there's other parts." He hesitated. He didn't know how he would manage to say it, but it was now or never, so he went on. "I want to fit you back into my life. Becca, I want to do that now."

She smiled, then. It was, he thought, a most radiant smile. She said, "I want that, too. Really. Just like you."

The relief was enormous. It felt to Derric like coming home. It felt like coming to a place he'd always belonged, and when he drew her to him and kissed her, he understood that the destination had been worth the journey he'd taken to get there.

FORTY-SEVEN

Jenn couldn't figure out what Squat Cooper wanted to talk about, but she went along with it. They walked to the end of Second Street, but on their way he didn't say a thing. It wasn't until they crossed over Cascade and they came to the bench from which they could gaze at the distant, perfect peak of Mount Pilchuk that he got around to saying anything at all.

By that time she was a little impatient. He'd worn a totally serious expression when he'd come upon her with Becca, Ivar, and Sharla. He looked like someone about to announce either the death of a parent or a sudden plan to move to another state. It turned out to be neither of those things. He wanted to talk about what he called "us."

He began with, "I don't get what's going on with you."

She began with the answer, "Huh?"

He said, "Come on, Jenn. You know what I'm talking about. I mean . . ." And then his face grew red. "I mean, that *was* you upstairs in my house, right? Minus the shirt and the bra and all the rest?"

She felt herself growing hot under his gaze. Okay, they'd been naked and they'd moved to his bedroom, but that was it. Things hadn't gone anywhere close to *anywhere* close. Below them, the banging sound of his scabby brother's entrance into the house had put an end to that. At the time, she'd been disappointed . . . or something. Afterward, the truth was she'd been relieved. They'd scrambled back into their clothes accompanied by the sound of Dylan rummaging for food in the kitchen cupboards. His "Oh *man*," along with companion swear words, had told the tale of his frustration.

Squat's frustration was of a different kind. He drew his Jockeys up over an impressive hard-on. Even with his jeans redonned, she could still see the bulge. They'd scooted out of his bedroom and back to the boys' study area. They were on the couch watching MTV on the flat-screen TV when the odious Dylan showed his acne-infested face.

"Whoa!" he said. "Didn't know you two were here. How's it going, little bro? You turn this lesbo yet?"

"Shut up," Squat said.

"Good idea," Jenn agreed. For good measure, she put her hand on Squat's thigh. Dylan saw the move and laughed.

"Like that would convince me?" he said to Jenn. "You ever get laid by the sexed-out redhead babe?"

Squat looked at her. She said, "He means Annie Taylor," she told him. "And no, Dylan, in spite of what you apparently want to keep thinking, I don't do women."

"Oh right," he said. And then to Squat, "I'm telling you, Squatster, you are wasting your time. How far'd you get anyways?

Bet she hasn't put out anything. Okay, maybe tongue, but *that's* going to be your limit, bro."

"Will you get out of here and leave us alone?" Squat said. "'Cause I'm telling you, Dylan, if you don't make tracks—"

"Yeah. Whatever," Dylan said. "But don't come whining to me when zippo happens, okay? Because that's what's in store for you, bro: zippo, nada, and zilch."

Squat stirred, as if to get up and go after his brother, but Dylan beat tracks to his room. His door slammed and music ensued. Top volume. There was hardly a point to watching MTV after that.

No other opportunities for alone time with Squat had presented themselves. Lots had happened—Cilla, Nera, the whole selkie business, her failure to make the All Island Soccer team— and the truth was she hadn't thought about Squat at all. At least not in the way he seemed to be thinking about her. Jenn felt bad about this, but that was just how it was.

She said, "Oh. Upstairs at your house. But . . . We're friends, aren't we? I thought we were friends."

"We're more than that," he said. "Or at least we were. You know what I mean. If Dylan hadn't shown up that day . . . We were *heading* somewhere." His face grew redder. He looked so appealing blushing that way that Jenn wanted to throw her arms around him, just because he was so nice, such a decent person, so good of heart, so completely Squat. But she also understood that throwing her arms around him was *all* she wanted. Everything else . . . That had been joking around. It had been trying to convince herself. It had been exploring, wanting to see, needing to understand if Annie Taylor and even the revolting Dylan had been right about her. She *didn't* know yet. But she was close to knowing. When she was ready, she would accept the truth.

She said, "I guess . . . I don't think I really wanted to go there, where we were heading. I mean, I *thought* I did. And maybe I would've although it would also have been a totally dumb move."

"Thanks," he said sourly.

"Come on, think about it," she told him. "We're fifteen years old."

"So? Other kids—"

"Got it. They have sex at twelve. Dylan probably had sex at nine if he could get it up then. But you and me? We're not like them, Squat. And even if we were . . . it's just that . . . I'm not sure."

Squat cast a look over his shoulder at her. He was hunched forward on the bench, his arms on his thighs. He looked, momentarily, disgusted. He said, "So he was right, huh?"

"Who?"

"You *know*. He was right all along and everything was . . . It was you trying to prove something to yourself, at my expense."

"It was not!" she protested. She jumped to her feet and stood in front of him. "Hey, me and you have been friends since we were *five*. What d'you think? That means nothing?"

"You were using me."

"Like you *weren't* using me? If I was using you, it goes both ways and you know it. You wanted a first and it wasn't me. I wanted to . . . I don't know. I wanted to . . . to understand some things, and you were there. We *always* joked with each other and talked about sex and love and marriage and all sorts of junk but you *knew* it was a joke and you can't say you didn't. You just used it as a key of some kind. To unlock a door and the door was me. And when it was open, I figured here was the chance to . . . to see in some kind of mirror and the mirror was you."

He looked up at that. He leaned back against the bench and observed her. He said, "I don't think I ever heard you say so much."

"Yeah? Well get used to it. I got lots to say."

He blew a chuckle out of his nose, more or less. "Whatever," he said.

"What's that s'posed to mean? I hate it when people say 'whatever.'"

"You say it yourself."

"Not anymore." She waited, one hand on her hip, one foot tapping against the gravel on which sat the bench. "Well, whatever *what*?" she demanded.

He rose and sighed. "Whatever you want," he said. "It's been since kindergarten we been friends. I guess it's sort of dumb to dump you now."

"Yeah but friends like *what*, 'cause we got to be straight with each other," she said.

"Friends like . . . like friends," he told her.

"And you're okay with that?"

He thought about the question. He looked out at the water and then back at her. "Long as you keep your T-shirt on, I guess."

FORTY-EIGHT

They had all agreed that the secret of Nera was one they needed to keep. As for what had happened to Cilla . . . She'd disappeared from Annie's trailer one day. It would be easy enough to manage all parts of the story, they'd reasoned. Nothing existed to prove something sinister might have happened to Cilla, and no one had documented Nera's transformation. Beyond that, not a soul would believe such a thing as a selkie was possible. Whidbey Island was a place of art and music and magic and mystery, to be sure. But some things asked for a leap of faith that most people couldn't make.

Becca, though, knew differently. There was one person on Whidbey Island who would understand exactly what had occurred.

So a few days after the Welcome Back Nera festival, she sat with Diana Kinsale on her deck overlooking Sandy Point. There, she told Diana the story. She told her all the ins and outs of it, ending with what she'd seen that evening on Possession Point.

Diana didn't seem at all surprised. But then, she was a woman who'd learned acceptance of the incomprehensible a long time ago. She merely lowered her hand to Oscar's head and caressed it as she watched the rest of her dogs gamboling and sniffing on the slope beneath them. She said, "A selkie. I always did wonder why Ivar was so intent upon keeping everyone away from that seal."

"He didn't want anyone to know. If people got too close, she might've come out of the water and stepped out of her skin in front of them. And then . . . Who knows what would've happened to her?"

"One can imagine the uproar." Diana laughed quietly. "Lord, the Langley city fathers would have gone . . . what's the term I need?"

"Gone bananas," Becca said. "CNN, MSNBC, CBS, Fox, you name it." They were quiet for a moment considering this: what would have been made out of Nera had anyone known what she was capable of doing once her body hit the sand. More than a Welcome Back Nera festival, that was certain. The village would have been put on the map, but the reason for this would have led to disaster.

"He's a good man, Ivar Thorndyke," Diana said. "It takes a lot for a person to risk being mocked in order to protect something that he couldn't have explained to people if he tried."

"They would've thought he was crazy. I bet most of them think he's crazy anyway."

"We're all a little of that," Diana said. She'd been gazing at the water, but now she turned to Becca. "What else?" she asked.

Becca blushed. "Me and Derric."

Diana smiled. "Ah. That's resolved? Good. You and Derric have something special."

"He was . . . It was about Seth, why he was upset." Becca told that story as well. Diana listened, her expression thoughtful. At the end, Becca said, "It would be so nice to have a place to live, Mrs. Kinsale. I mean . . . a real place. Like . . . well, like here."

"Are things not working out at Debbie's?"

Becca quirked her mouth. All these months of lies. Yet if she didn't tell Diana the truth at last, they couldn't move forward. She had to risk it. She said, "I haven't exactly been there. At the Cliff Motel, I mean."

Diana's face went very still. She said, "Where have you been, then?"

And Becca allowed the tale to come tumbling out: the tree house, the woods, Ralph Darrow's property, her flight from Langley the previous November.

"In a *tree house*?" Diana said. "All through the winter? Debbie didn't know this, did she?"

Becca grimaced but she still went forward. "She thought I was here, with you."

Diana did not look pleased. She said, "Badly done, Becca. Very badly done. Lying to me. Lying to Debbie. Living in a tree house. Was this Seth's doing?"

"Don't blame Seth. It's just that . . . I needed to get out of Langley. Last November, something happened and . . ." She was at the point she always reached with people, the Jeff Corrie point, the what-to-tell-in-place-of-telling-everything point. Still she couldn't reveal it all. The anguish of not being able to say every-thing felt like something clawing at her insides.

Diana put her hand on Becca's shoulder. And there it was: that warmth and lifting. Becca said to her, "If I could only live here with you . . ."

Diana looked at Becca for such a long time that Becca turned her own gaze away. Diana said her name and nothing more until Becca returned her gaze once again. "The time isn't right," Diana told her. "At some point it will be. You'll be here eventually. But not yet."

"You always say that."

"Because it's the truth. If you were here with me, you'd miss the lessons you're meant to learn. I don't want that to happen to you."

"What am I going to do then? Hide out in a tree house for-ever? Where am I supposed to go?"

"You'll know where to go because it will be revealed. I suspect you've always known anyway. It's only your impatience that gets in your way."

"You say I'll always be safe on the island, but I don't feel safe," Becca said bitterly. "You say the time of danger has passed, but it doesn't *feel* passed."

Diana reached for her hand. Becca had clenched it on the arm of her chair, and Diana folded her own hand over the fist she'd made. She held it there as she spoke, saying, "Your place is here on the island as it has been from the first. Nothing and no one will be able to take you from it."

"How do you know that?" Becca demanded.

"It's what I see."

"How do you see that?"

"Because I'm patient."

BUT BECCA WAS not. How could she be with so much about her life at stake? She sought a form of reassurance that went beyond the kind words of a woman whose touch lifted her fears and soothed her spirit. She went from Diana's to the library in Langley. Inside the library, she sought the computers and typed Jeff Corrie's name into a search engine.

As before the Internet gave her a number of choices when it came to Jeff. The first dealt with his "investment" firm, an old interview with Jeff and his partner Connor and what they were supposedly doing to enhance the financial lives of San Diego retirees. Then there were the articles about the good works Jeff and Connor had done in the San Diego area in order to drum up business, raise their profile, and encourage people's trust in them. Then there were the first rumblings of suspicions. Then there were the disappearances.

There were three disappearances that Jeff was now being questioned about, according to the San Diego newspaper. Jeff Corrie's wife and stepdaughter were missing as well as his business partner Connor. As was logical in this kind of situation, the last man standing was the first man under suspicion. Jeff was the common denominator in the lives of the people who'd disappeared. The police found this intriguing. So, it seemed, had the FBI and the IRS.

Jeff had done the wise thing. He'd talked to no one but his lawyer. Still, things were looking bad. His investment firm's doors were closed and its books were under scrutiny. As for Jeff himself? He hadn't been arrested for anything yet. But the fact that he wouldn't talk about a thing was making him look suspicious.

Arrest him, arrest him was what Becca thought. But for what? Unless she went back to San Diego and spoke to the police, there was not yet a thing for them to arrest him for. And even if she went back, what was she supposed to tell them? "I hear people's thoughts," she would say. "And I heard his and he killed Connor and that's why we left."

"So where's your mom?" they would ask her, looking at each other the way people do when they're ready to call the guys with the straitjackets to take someone away.

"She left me on Whidbey Island and she hasn't got back yet."

"When did she leave you there?"

"Last September."

"What? To fend for yourself? A kid? What was she so desperate about and what the hell was she doing abandoning you? D'you know just *how* against the law that is? Where is this woman? We'll need to find her."

"It's not like it looks. See, we knew what Jeff had done. We knew."

"Yet you didn't report him. Why?"

And then they'd be back to hearing thoughts.

What Becca concluded from her Internet search was that, despite Diana's words, Jeff Corrie was still out there. He was looking and he was waiting. Until things changed for him, he would be intent on finding her any way that he could.

AT LEAST, BECCA thought with resignation, the weather had improved . . . a bit. Middle of May and she'd thought the Pacific Northwest rain *might* have let up by now. It hadn't done that, but at least the temperatures were rising. So, she told herself, if she had to stay in the tree house for a few more months, she could let go of worrying about how to keep the woodstove going day and night.

Finding a place to shower would be rough once school was out, however. But if she kept working for Ivar there was always a chance that she could shower at Heart's Desire in exchange for taking on the bathroom cleaning duties. Or perhaps at Derric's? No. That would always be a problem because of his dad. While she'd finally told Derric where she was staying, he'd sworn not to tell either one of his parents, and they were sure to ask him what was going on with Becca King if she started using their shower on a regular basis.

She would need to get creative, she thought. It was turning out that being creative was what being on her own was all about.

She was thinking of all this on her way through the woods. She'd gone from Diana's to Heart's Desire for her afternoon work, and now at day's end, she was ready to rest. She'd stowed her bike in its hiding spot beneath the trees, and as she hiked along the trail from Newman Road to the tree house, she could see the new spring growth around her everywhere. She could see, especially, how it was beginning to encroach on the path from Newman Road. She would have to borrow some clippers from Ivar in order to cut back the salal, the blackberry, and the huckleberry bushes that were stretching out to obscure the trail. Ralph Darrow would soon be doing the same thing on his other forest trails, she decided. She was going to have to be extremely careful with her comings and goings now.

As always, she paused when she got to the clearing with its twined hemlocks and the tree house in their embrace. She listened but heard no sound other than the usual birds and the angry chattering of squirrels warning each other of her approach. She made for the stairs, then, and climbed quickly to the trapdoor in the deck. It felt oddly good to be home, and how additionally odd it was to think of this little shelter as home at all.

She opened the door. She was surprised to see that Seth was inside. He was sitting on the camping stool next to the stove, not doing a thing, which was completely unlike him. Usually he'd be playing his guitar or he'd be struggling with his battered copy of *Siddartha* or he'd be messing with the woodstove. Something more than just sitting, though.

She said, "Hey! I didn't see your car on the road. Did you come from your grandpa's?"

Seth didn't have a chance to reply. A gravelly voice said, "He did indeed. Come in and join us."

Becca gulped. She stepped inside and shut the door. Doing this, she saw Ralph Darrow sitting on her camping cot. He wore a suede jacket and a wide-brimmed hat that made him look a little like Wild Bill Hickock, since his sandy gray hair was long and flowing and his mustache was impressive. Becca looked from him to Seth to him again. She didn't know what to say.

This turned out to be no problem, since Ralph was the one to do the talking. He said, "You must be my grandson's 'tutor,' she of the jealous boyfriend and the applied math."

Becca said nothing. She was straining for whispers and it didn't take long to hear them. *When will he ever . . . in it deep so she might as well . . . age of this child . . . has no idea how much trouble it can . . .* didn't give her much to go on as to how she was supposed to answer. She went for part of the truth and hoped for the best.

"We've figured it out, me and Derric," she said eagerly. "That's my boyfriend. See, he didn't get why there were things I wouldn't tell him. Not about Seth but other things. And he was upset about me tutoring Seth and *I* got upset and it went from there." She cast a glance at Seth. His face gave her nothing.

"I expect that's true as far as it goes," Ralph Darrow said, "but the way I see things"—he looked around the tree house's single room—"explaining the finer points of applied math doesn't require a sleeping bag, a Coleman stove, a lantern, flashlights, and a pile of groceries. All of which, aside from the groceries, happen to belong to me."

She said, dumbly as she was to think later, "It gets dark early in the winter here. So we needed the lantern—"

"Beck," this from Seth. "He knows. He came out here 'cause that's what he does when the weather gets better. Just to check and make sure everything's okay."

"Care of one's property," Ralph Darrow told her. "It's part of the responsibility of ownership. Now this little place I consider my property. What do you consider it?"

She swallowed. "I know it's yours."

He said to Seth, "And you, favorite male grandson?"

"Yeah," Seth said. "I know it's yours."

"About how many ways have you lied to me, you think, Seth?"

"Grand . . ."

Why won't he see . . . and now he thinks . . . just tell me the truth and when I . . . the law is the law . . .

"No 'Grand' now. How many ways have you lied? Lies of omission, lies of commission, and outright falsehoods. You've been packing those into our conversations and our interactions for months. Every time you stepped onto this property and didn't mention you'd stowed a young girl here. How old are you?" This last he asked Becca.

"Fifteen, sir."

"Good God in heaven, Seth. Truly, I thought you had more sense." *Is he actually . . . what's he thinking . . . he'll end up in jail and that'll put his dad in the grave . . . fifteen years old fifteen years old fifteen years old . . . can't be because no way . . . no way no way . . . I c'n see his face tells me . . .*

"There's nothing going *on*, Mr. Darrow," Becca said. "I mean, between me and Seth . . . I mean, we're just friends and we're not using this . . . I mean, it's not what it looks like. I'm staying here, is only what it is."

"Who are your people? Where's your family?"

Becca looked desperately to Seth for help. She didn't know Ralph Darrow other than to have seen him at a distance. She knew Seth was close to the old man. He was as close as she'd been to her own grandparent. But that was all she knew. "Grand's cool" didn't cut it when it came to trespassing, to using someone's property as one's own, and to being someone who looked like a runaway because what the heck else was he supposed to think?

"I don't . . ." How to tell him, Becca thought. What to tell him that he might believe. How to walk a line between truth and falsehood. How to stay safe in a complicated world. "I don't have any family here," she settled on saying.

"And that means what?" Ralph Darrow asked her.

Seth said, "Grand, she's got no one on the island. She was supposed to stay with Carol Quinn. Her mom brought her here to stay with Carol. But when she got to the house and found out that Carol'd died—"

"Way I remember things," Ralph cut in, "Carol Quinn died last September, Seth. And are you telling me this girl's mother dropped her off on Carol Quinn's front porch and left her there without stopping to see she got inside the house? Without a halloooo to Ms. Quinn and a here's my daughter, ma'am, and she's going to be staying with you for God only knows how long and God only knows why? Is that what you want me to believe?"

Lying again and how much longer: ... *what I know and it isn't everything*...

Becca said in a rush, "My mom and I were trying to get away from my stepdad. But we knew he'd follow us when he could, so she wanted to leave me with Carol Quinn while she got us a place where we'd be safe. That's where she is now but I don't know exactly where ... I mean her address or anything ... because I had a cell phone and then I lost it and I was staying with Debbie Grieder at the Cliff Motel but I had to leave because the sheriff came, only he wasn't looking for me only I thought he *was* looking for me, so I left."

"She was in the Dog House," Seth added. "That's where I took your camping gear at first. You know the Dog House. The old tavern in Langley?"

Ralph shot him a look. "I've lived here for seventy-two years, Seth."

"Sorry. I was just trying—"

"Stop trying," Ralph said sharply. "Your trying is what gets you into trouble."

Becca saw the hurt on Seth's face even as she heard *not fair ... no excuse this time . . . people need you and you always said . . . right thing wasn't it ... not a stupid boy but when will he ever* . . . And she knew she'd caused the division between Seth and his granddad.

"That's not fair," Seth said and he sounded numb. "She needed help and you would've helped her. You know you would have helped her, Grand."

"I do not know that, and neither do you," Ralph said. "And

one of the reasons we'll remain in ignorance on that subject is that you didn't tell me what was going on. You didn't give me the opportunity to act. And that, Grandson, is only one of the mistakes you've made. Do you understand that?"

"I was trying to—"

"Seth, you've made a lot of mistakes through the years, and that's part of growing up and I understand that. But this mistake here . . . It's an important one. I c'n see that you meant well by this girl. But meaning well and doing the right thing are different, and you've got to learn that because I can't be responsible for what your heart tells you to do if you don't involve your head in the process."

Stupid stupid loser loser loser told Becca how Seth was taking this, and that didn't seem right at all. She said, "Mr. Darrow, I put him in this position. See, my stepdad showed up one night at the Cliff Motel. I couldn't let him find me. Seth was with me and I asked him . . . I begged him Mr. Darrow . . . to get me out of there. This is where he brought me. And it's kept me safe. *He's* kept me safe."

"That may well be," Ralph Darrow told her, "but he's walking on the wrong side of the law in this, and there's not a Darrow on the island who's ever done that. Seth knows it. He knows both parts of it. Now collect your things."

"Grand!"

"I'm not hearing more, Seth. I've heard enough. You c'n pack up all this camping gear. I'll see to the groceries. The subject is closed."

Hard as nails . . . when she needed help and you always say . . .

proud of me but . . . can't see things clearly and when he needs
to . . . parents involved . . . no progress at all . . .

It was too painful for Becca to listen to more. She found the
AUD box and plugged in its earphone and settled the earphone
in her ear. The static was loud and it was soothing. Dully, she
began to gather her things. They were few enough and most of
them were in bags already. Clothes and school books made up
the lot of it. It wasn't going to take more than one trip to vacate
the tree house. That was for sure.

THEY MADE A solemn procession through the woods. Ralph
led the way, and he took them in the direction of his house,
not Newman Road. For this Becca was moderately grateful. At
least she could stow her belongings on Ralph's porch while she
scouted out a new place to live.

Behind her, she heard Seth say, "Sorry, Beck," and she glanced
back at him. He looked more miserable than she'd ever seen him.

She said, "'S okay. It's not your fault. I'll work it out."

"Not if he calls the cops," Seth said.

"Maybe even then," was what she told him. She had trouble
believing this, however. Calling the cops meant calling Dave
Mathieson. She couldn't see how that was going to lead to anywhere good at all.

They were silent the rest of the way, the only noise coming
from their footfalls on the damp forest floor. It began to rain just
as they hit the outer reaches of Ralph Darrow's great rhododen-
dron garden. The huge shrubs there were beginning to bloom.

They were spotted with red and pink and white and yellow. In a week or so, they'd be a mass of color backed by the fresh cool green of the trees.

They crossed the grass and climbed onto the wide front porch. There were four rocking chairs on it along with a picnic table and benches for outdoor meals during summer. Becca dumped her belongings on this table. She pulled out a bench and waited for what was coming next. If worse came to worse, she could make a run for it, she figured. Ralph Darrow wasn't about to tie her up till the sheriff got there. He didn't seem the type.

He did look at her though as she dropped onto the wooden bench with a thud. He frowned and said, "What do you happen to be doing now?"

She said, "I figure I'll wait out here if it's okay. Or maybe . . . Seth's car's here, right? He c'n drive me to . . ." She didn't know where. Diana's? Debbie's? Heart's Desire? Back to the Dog House for another sojourn in that creepy place? She didn't know. She wanted not to care, but that wasn't happening. She said, "I'm just sort of hoping you won't call the sheriff or anything."

"I have no plan to call the sheriff," he told her.

She looked at Seth for guidance. He was watching his grandfather. He'd set the camping equipment on the porch and, like Becca, he was merely waiting.

He said, "Grand . . ." And his voice was cautious.

Ralph said to Becca, "Get yourself and your belongings inside."

She didn't move. She didn't know what to think. She said, "I don't get . . . 'Cause you said . . ."

"What?"

"About the law and the Darrows and being on the wrong side of things," Seth clarified.

Ralph nodded at this. Thoughtfully he groomed his Fu Manchu mustache. "Darrows don't operate on the wrong side of the law," he agreed. "But they also don't leave teenagers living in the woods. Between those two things, a Darrow decides."

"You mean . . ." Seth said.

"You talk to me next time you think you know the way of my world," Ralph Darrow told him. "Now are we standing outside and discussing this further or can we go in and get this girl set up in a proper accommodation?"

"I guess we can go inside," Seth said. "You okay with that, Beck?"

She was more than okay. "Mr. Darrow," she began.

"Not a word," he told her. Then he nodded sharply and opened the door.

TURN THE PAGE FOR A LOOK AT THE
NEXT BOOK IN THE SERIES . . .

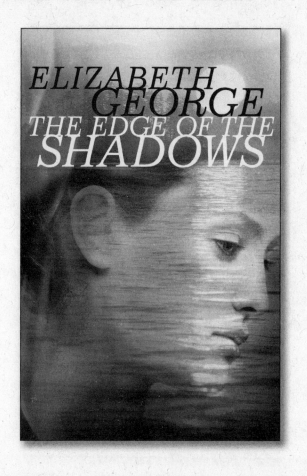

ONE

The third fire happened at Island County Fairgrounds in August, and it was the first one to get serious attention. The other two weren't big enough. One was set in a trash container outside the convenience store at a forested place called Bailey's Corner, which was more or less in the middle of nowhere, so no one thought much about it. Some dumb practical joke with a sparkler after the Fourth of July, right? Then, when the second flamed up along the main highway, right at the edge of a struggling little farmers' market, pretty much everyone decided that *that* one took off because an idiot had thrown a lit cigarette from his car window right in the middle of the driest season of the year.

But the third fire was different. Not only because it happened at the fairgrounds which were just yards away from the middle school and less than a quarter mile from the village of Langley but also because the flames began during the county fair when hundreds of people were milling around a midway.

A girl called Becca King was among them, along with her boyfriend and her best girlfriend: Derric Mathieson and Jenn McDaniels. The three were a study in contrasts, with Becca light-haired, trim from months of bicycle riding, and wearing heavy-rimmed glasses and enough makeup to suggest she was auditioning for membership in the reincarnation of the rock band Kiss; Derric tall, well-built, shaven-headed, African, and gorgeous; and Jenn all sinew and attitude, hair cut like a boy's and tan from a summer of intense soccer practice. These three were sitting in the bleachers set back from an outdoor stage upon which a group called the Time Benders was about to begin performing.

It was Saturday night, the night that drew the most people to the fairgrounds because it was also the night when the entertainment was, as Jenn put it, "marginally less suicide-inducing than the other days." Those other days the entertainment consisted of tap dancers, yodelers, magicians, fiddlers, and a one-man band. On Saturday night an Elvis impersonator and the Time Benders comprised what went for the highlight of the fair.

For Becca King, with a lifetime spent in San Diego and just short of one year in the Puget Sound area, the fair was like everything else she'd discovered on Whidbey Island: something in miniature. The barn red buildings were standard stuff, but their size was minuscule compared to the vast buildings she was used to at the Del Mar racetrack where the San Diego County Fair took place. This held true for the stables for horses, sheep, cattle, alpacas, and goats. It was doubly true for the performance ring where the dogs were shown and the horses were ridden. The food, however, was the same as it was at county fairs everywhere, and as the Time Benders readied themselves to take the stage after Elvis's final bow during which he nearly lost his wig, Becca and

Derric and Jenn were chowing down on funnel cake and kettle corn.

The crowd, who turned up to watch the Time Benders every single year, was gearing up its excitement level for the performance. It didn't matter that the act would be the same as last August and the August before that and the one before that. The Time Benders were a real crowd pleaser in a place where the nearest mall was a ferry ride away and first-run movies were virtually unheard of. So a singing group who performed rock 'n' roll through the ages by altering their wigs and their costumes and re-enacting the greatest hits of the 1950s onwards was akin to a mystical appearance by Kurt Cobain, especially if you had any imagination.

Jenn was grousing. Watching the Time Benders was bad enough, she was saying. Watching the Time Benders at the same time as being a third wheel on "the Derric-and-Becca looove bike" was even worse.

Becca smiled and ignored her. Jenn loved to grouse. She said, "So who are these guys, anyway?" in reference to the Time Benders as she dipped into the kettle corn and leaned comfortably against Derric's arm.

"God. Who d'you *think*?" was Jenn's unhelpful reply. "Y'know how other county fairs have shows where has-been performers give their last gasp before they finally hang it up and retire? Well, what we got is *unknown* performers re-enacting the performances of has-been performers. Welcome to Whidbey. And would you *stop* feeling her up, Derric?" she said to their companion.

"Holding her hand isn't feeling her up," was the boy's easy reply. "Now if you want to see some serious feeling up. . . ?" He leered at Becca. She laughed and gave him a playful shove.

"I *hate* this, you know," Jenn told her friend. She was returning to the previous third-wheel-on-the-looove-bike topic. "I shoulda stayed home."

"Lots of things come in threes," Becca told.

"Like what?"

"Well . . . Tricycle wheels."

"Triplets," Derric said.

"Those three-wheel baby buggies for joggers who need to take their kids with them," Becca added.

"Birds have three toes," Derric pointed out. Then, "Don't they?" he said to Becca.

"Great." Jenn reached for more funnel cake and jammed it into her mouth. "I'm a bird toe. Lemme send that out on Twitter."

Which would, of course, be the last thing Jenn McDaniels could have done, since among them Derric was the only one who possessed anything remotely close to technological. Jenn had neither computer nor iPhone nor iPad nor laptop, because her family was too poor for anything more than a third-hand color television the size of a Jeep, practically given away by the thrift store in town. As for Becca . . . Well, there were a lot of reasons why Becca remained at a distance from technology and all of them had to do with keeping a profile so low that it was invisible.

The Time Benders came forth at this point, climbing onto the stage past amplifiers that looked like bank vaults. Their wigs, pegged pants, white socks, and poodle skirts indicated that—

just like last year—they'd be starting with the fifties. The Time Benders *never* worked in reverse.

The crowd cheered as the show began, lit by the rest of the midway with its games of chance and its creaking thrill rides. The best of the fifties blasted forth at maximum volume. Over the noise, Jenn shouted at Becca, "Hey, you probably won't need that thing."

That thing was a hearing device that looked like an iPod in possession of a single ear bud. It was called an AUD box and, despite what Jenn thought, Becca didn't use it to help with her hearing. At least not in the way Jenn thought she used it. Jenn and everyone else believed that the AUD box helped Becca understand what was being said to her by blocking out nearby noises that her brain wouldn't automatically block: like the noise from other tables that you might hear in a restaurant but normally be able to ignore when someone was talking to you. That was what Becca let people believe about the AUD box because it did, actually, block out *some* noise. Only, the noise it blocked was the noise inside the heads of the people who surrounded her. Without the AUD box she was bombarded by everyone's thoughts, and while hearing people's thoughts *could* have its benefits, most of the time Becca couldn't tell who was thinking what. So since childhood, the AUD box was what she wore to deal with her "auditory processing problem," as her mom had taught her to call it. Thankfully, no one questioned why the AUD box's loud static helped her in understanding who was speaking. More important, no one knew that without it, she was one step away from reading their minds.

Becca said, "Yeah, I'll turn it down," and she pretended to do so. Up on the stage, the Time Benders were rocking and rolling through "Rock Around the Clock" while on either side of the stage, some of the older audience members had begun to dance in keeping with the music's era.

That was when the first gust of smoke belched across the heads of the crowd. At first, it seemed logical that the smoke would be coming from the line of food booths, all doing brisk sales of everything from buffalo burgers to curly fries. Because of this, the Time Benders audience didn't take much note. But when there was a pause in the music and the Time Benders were getting ready for the sixties with a change of costumes and wigs, the sirens hooting from the road just beyond the fairground's perimeter indicated something serious was going on.

The smell of smoke got heavier. People started to move. A murmur became a cry and then a shout. Just at the moment that panic was about to set in, the regular MC for the show took the stage and announced that "a small fire" had broken out on the far side of the fairgrounds, but there was nothing to worry about as the fire department was there and "as far as we know, all animals are safe."

The last part was a serious mistake. "All animals" meant everything from ducks to the 4-H steer lovingly brought up by hand and worth a significant amount of money to the child who would sell it at the end of the fair. In between ducks and steers were fancy chickens, fiber-producing alpacas, award-winning cats, sheep worth their weight in wool, and an entire stable filled with horses. Among the audience for the Time Benders were the owners of these animals, and they began pushing their way in the direction of the buildings in which all the animals were housed.

In short order, a melee ensued. Derric grabbed Becca and Becca grabbed Jenn, and they clung to each other as the crowd surged out of the midway and past the barn where the crafts were displayed. They burst out behind it into an open area that looked onto the show ring and to the buildings beyond.

At the far side of the show ring, the stables were safe. The fire, everyone saw at once, was opposite them on the side of the show ring that was nearer the road into town. But this was where the dogs, cats, chickens, ducks, and rabbits had been snoozing in three ramshackle sheds that flaked old white paint onto very dry hay. The farthest of these sheds was up in flames. Fire licked up the walls and engulfed the roof.

The fact that the fire department was directly across the street from the fairgrounds had the effect of getting manpower to the flames in fairly short order. But the building was old, the weather had been bone dry for nine weeks—almost unheard of in the Pacific Northwest—and there were hay bales along the north side of the structure. So the best efforts of the fire department were directed toward keeping the fire away from the *other* buildings while letting the one that was burning burn to the ground.

This wasn't a popular move. There were chickens and rabbits inside. There were dozens of 4-Hers who wanted to save those animals, and the news that someone had apparently released them at some time during the fire only made the onlookers crazed to get to them before they all got trampled. Soon enough there were too many fire chiefs and too few onlookers and enough chaos to make Derric, Jenn, and Becca head for the safety of the stables some distance away.

"Someone's going to get hurt," Becca said.

"It ain't going to be one of us," Derric told her. "Come on, over here." He took her hand and Jenn's, and together they made their way beyond the stables to where a woods grew up the side of a hill to a neighborhood tucked back into the trees. From this spot they could watch the action and listen to the chaos and while they did this, Becca removed the ear bud from her ear and wiped her hot face.

As always, she heard the thoughts of her companions, Jenn's profane as usual, Derric's mild. But among Jenn's colorful cursing and Derric's wondering about the safety of the little kids whose parents were trying to keep them away from the fire, Becca heard quite clearly, *Come on, come on . . . get it why don't you?* as if it was spoken right next to her.

She swung around, but it was dark on all sides, with the great fir trees looming above them and the cedars leaning heavy branches down toward the ground. At her movement, Derric looked at her and said, "What?" and then shifted his gaze into the trees as well.

"Is someone there?" Jenn asked them both.

"Becca?" Derric said.

Out of here before those kids . . . was enough to give Becca the answer to those questions.

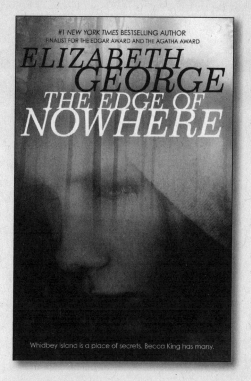